# THE MAN WHO KNEW
# TOO MUCH HITCHCOCK

**Sean McCloy**

# CONFIDENTIAL

NOT TO BE TAKEN OFF PREMISES

CASE NOTES NOT TO BE DESTROYED

These records should be retained

because of special significance

## ADDENDUM TO PSYCHIATRIC REPORT
### ON INMATE ████████

Enclosed within this file is the manuscript
recovered from inmate ████████'s cell.

The manuscript is autobiographical in nature.
It reveals a litany of character traits that I
have already explored in the inmate's
psychiatric report, so I will refrain from
repeating them here.

In interview, Mr. ████████ has repeatedly
asked that the manuscript be returned to him.
On further interrogation, he has admitted
harbouring a strong desire to submit it to
publishing houses.

I cannot pass judgement on the veracity of much
of the narrative chronicled within or, indeed,
if the manuscript is of any literary merit. My
professional view, however, is that **(i)** because
of his status as a Category A prisoner, and
**(ii)** because of the ongoing investigations into
Mr. ████████'s past, **THIS MANUSCRIPT SHOULD
NEVER SEE THE LIGHT OF DAY**.


Dr. A.N. Legatore

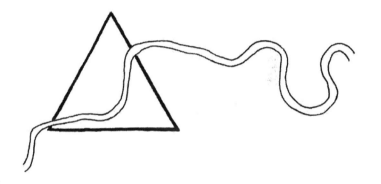

Last night, in my dreams, I returned to the house in Plouthorp Street...

At first, the structure appeared to me as if viewed through a fog, an inky silhouette set against the night sky. As I drew closer, however, the outline grew more distinct and I recognised the place. The three-storey property stands alone in a cobbled cul-de-sac, on a square of ground enclosed with wrought iron railings.

Standing before the house, I saw that at some point during my enforced period of absence, the gate had been padlocked by the authorities. Any sense of frustration at being unable to gain entry was but momentary, for suddenly I was granted the power to pass with ease through the gateway. However, my destination tonight was not meant to be the main house and I felt myself being spirited towards the left, towards the adjoining part of the property. In the past, if I found myself in a prosaic frame of mind I would refer to this section of the house as "the adjunct." In a more poetic mood, I would call it "The Temple." As I paused to regard the exterior - with its imposing oak-panelled doors flanked by ionic columns and ever-encroaching ivy, with its weathered entablature marked by mysterious carvings that I have strained to decipher - I was filled with the sense that I was about to re-enter a sacred space. A sacred space that may have been conjured from another era altogether. Referring to it as "The Temple" therefore feels entirely appropriate to me. Besides, that is how *he* referred to it.

I began to ascend the steps that led to the doorway and, magically, found that no key was required to gain entrance. As if sensing the owner's presence, the heavy oaken doors opened noiselessly and I once again found myself home.

Inside, the scene that greeted me was one I was already familiar with and one that I have seen recreated in the pages of newspapers I have managed to surreptitiously smuggle into my quarters. I cannot blame the media for their coverage of my alleged crimes and part of me is amused at the monikers they have bestowed upon me – The Monster, The Mindless Maniac, The Twisted Mastermind Behind The Occurrences In The Hitchcock House of Horror.

Perhaps you think you already know me. I myself have read the abridged case histories in the tabloid newsprint, promising to take the reader inside the mind of a warped individual. I too have studied the double page spreads, complete with 3D diagrams and detailed floor plans of my house (yes, I admit it is a very spacious property for a confirmed bachelor such as myself). You may even have read the brief interview with my former cleaner, Mrs. Allgood, and the words extracted from her when she was doorstepped by a reporter. I will not quote her verbatim here, but I do recall one phrase she used to describe me... "You couldn't meet a nicer gentleman."

While perusing one such article, I failed to identify a figure captured in a blurry zoom lens photograph. *Who is that great, hulking, shapeless character shambling around the grounds of this place of my incarceration?* I asked myself. His appearance, his very bearing seemed to encapsulate, to be a walking definition of the word "menace." But then I noted the presence of the two uniformed escorts, never more than a few paces away in case their ward should attempt an escape, and I realised the menace was in fact me. I confess, I did not recognise myself as this man who I am told is a threat to others.

All of which brings me to the inescapable fact that tomorrow is the start date for my trial. I have refused all entreaties, ignored advice, and decided that the best course of action is to represent myself. As to the question of what plea I should enter, I fear most people have already made up their minds. The evidence, I am told, is overwhelmingly against me.

Ladies and gentlemen of my captive jury, try to set aside any preconceived notions you may harbour about me. If you so choose, follow me quietly back to the house in Plouthorp Street now and I will grant you a guided tour. We will not be disturbed, that I can promise you. The only regular visitor during my years of solitude was Mrs. Allgood, who called once a week and was under instruction to restrict her movements to the kitchen and my spartan living quarters.

You are walking beside me, with me now. I am guiding you through the oak-panelled doorway and into the sizeable ground floor level of The Temple. This part of the property has greatly changed since the first time I laid eyes on it, since I embarked on the renovation project. I find myself dwelling on how many years, how many decades have elapsed since then. Increasingly, perhaps more so since I have been held at Her Majesty's pleasure, time is an irrelevance to me. In my inner world, time is elastic. I can stretch and contract it at my will.

Take a moment now to allow your eyes to adjust to the darkness on the ground floor. The darkness is something I have grown accustomed to because of the condition I have been living with for much of my life, but for a guest to The Temple it may create a certain degree of ocular dissonance. Peer straight ahead and out of the gloom you are now beginning to discern the presence of a large white rectangular screen that appears to materialise in midair. We have found ourselves in my private screening room.

The sole item of furniture in the room is a functional double sofa. As my fingers brush against the arm of the sofa, I can feel a thin but distinct film of dust that has accumulated in the time since the house has been vacated. I gently rub my thumb against the tips of my fingers to disperse the dust, to disperse the memory of time spent in this room, on this sofa, where once my dear departed Sealyham Terrier curled up beside me.

I am now reaching out to a preordained location on the wall of the screening room. I am now flicking a light switch in an effort to throw some illumination on the contents of the room. If you look over your shoulder towards the shadowy rear of this space, there you may detect the presence of my 35mm projector. Housed

7

within a projection booth, it stands silent and inert, awaiting the touch of its owner's hands. Cast your eyes around the walls now and stationed there you will see a selection of framed vintage posters. Posters depicting characters, bearing images and titles I know intimately. *The Lodger... Blackmail... Murder!... Rebecca... Suspicion... Shadow of a Doubt... Spellbound... Notorious... Rope... Rear Window... The Wrong Man... Vertigo... Psycho... Frenzy...*

Accompany me now as I extinguish the light and I exit the screening room. We are now slowly climbing a set of stairs that lead to the upper level of The Temple. Follow the course of the staircase as it makes one right angled turn, then another, and we soon arrive at a gallery space. Together, we pause at the top of the stairs. Directly to our left, a pale green curtain begins to silently part and gradually reveals a large rectangular window of reinforced glass approximately 10 metres long by 2 metres high. *He* would refer to this window as "the cyclorama," and so I shall follow his example. It was fitted during the renovation project and offers a view towards the City of London, towards The △. Take a note, if you will, as "The △" is a scene of some import in the story I have to tell.

Before the cyclorama, two empty canvas chairs are in situ, poised and angled towards the skyline as if awaiting their occupants. The chair on the left is one I sat in countless times during moments of contemplation. The chair on the right is one of my most prized possessions, discovered during one of my many trawls through the catalogues of auction houses.

If I may direct your gaze to your right, there you will notice the presence of a white door that remains closed to us for the moment. Behind this door there are more rooms on the upper level to reveal to you. However, we cannot proceed there just yet. Something is interrupting us.

It is the sound of screaming that has disturbed our walkthrough, a sound I should have grown familiar with over the past months. After all, I have heard the same mechanical squealing many times before. It is the sound of refuse being collected at this facility. Pneumatic gears scream out as they take the strain and lift oversized bins up, then spill the contents into a lorry where the detritus is mercilessly compacted. Perhaps it is a strange metaphor I am about to embrace, but it seems the perfect sound to start today of all days with and it has newly aroused me to the task I am setting myself. And so I will take the strain. I will endeavour to empty the contents of my mind onto the pages set before me.

I look at my wristwatch. It is 8.10 a.m. From outside the walls of my cell, I can hear the sounds of other vehicles arriving and departing. I imagine the vehicles are carrying staff beginning or ending shifts or perhaps transporting food, laundry and medical supplies. I ruminate for a moment on the industrial quantities of drugs prescribed to the inmates here and have a vision of this institution as one vast mind control machine.

My standard issue breakfast of scrambled eggs, toast and tea is sitting untouched and I sense the queasy aroma of undigested eggs diffusing through the air. Briefly, I feel my temper rising as I recall the repeated occasions I have informed the orderlies on duty that I am more of a Quaker Oats man. I am almost at the point of literally seeing red and have to forcefully remind myself what I resolved on arrival at this facility – at all times, in any eventuality, I must appear like the surface of a distant gas giant when viewed through a powerful telescope. I must appear calm.

Composure now fully restored, I will attempt to describe for you my immediate surroundings. I face an unadorned white wall and am seated in a hunched position at a small wooden desk, my legs uncomfortably cramped in the space underneath. Two largish holes have been roughly gouged out of the surface of the desk. There is also a crude rendering of a swastika as well as a number of choice Anglo Saxon swear words carved thereon. I avert my eyes from the handiwork of the previous tenant(s) and instead

9

concentrate on the ream of blank white pages before me.

Directly behind where I now sit, there is a squat single bed that does not begin to adequately accommodate my frame and on which I have endured a succession of restless nights. At the foot of the bed is a utilitarian bookshelf, on which I have placed a number of objects which the powers that be have deemed permissible. These include a copy of The Bible and my signed first edition of *Hitchcock* by Truffaut. Above the bookshelf, perched high on a wall bracket, is a portable television on which a limited number of channels are available for my viewing pleasure. Today, as has been the case most other days, the television will remain switched off.

If I turn and raise my head to the right, I can see a small window with regulation bars on the outside. Once, I did attempt to peer through the window, braving the effects of the natural light, and was afforded a non-descript view of greenery being buffeted by the elements somewhere in the middle distance. This morning, however, it is snowing. Occasionally, an individual snowflake may drift against the grubby window pane, linger there amid the greyness and refuse to melt.

While I recognise that my current situation is far from ideal, I gain great solace in the certainty that this place of incarceration poses no great challenge to me. I know how to live a life of solitary confinement and I have other means of escape at my disposal. And so, to re-iterate, I will empty the contents of my mind onto the pages before me. I will aim to present you, my captive jury, a picture of life and death with the dull bits cut out.

In my inner world now, it is as if I am sitting once again in the upper gallery of The Temple, gazing out on a clear urban horizon. The scene appears peaceful and undisturbed. I am safe in the knowledge that the influence of The △ cannot reach me here. In the sky, I see an orderly procession of cumulus clouds, their edges tinged with watercolour crimson. The clouds appear unmoving, like spun glass suspended against an artificial backdrop.

Slowly, I begin to raise myself up from my seated position before the cyclorama. I am on my feet now, starting to guide you, and together we walk towards the staircase. The staircase that takes us back down into my private screening room.

We enter the darkened space and advance towards the front of the room, towards the screen. There are only two people in the screening room, you and I, and you must now listen only to my voice.

We are moving closer to the screen, ever closer, when it is suddenly and brilliantly illuminated by a shaft of light. I am asking you now to imagine the blinding whiteness of the screen filling your entire field of vision. There is nothing extraneous. There is only the whiteness of the screen.

Now, allow your mind to become quite blank. Allow your mind to feel the whiteness, to dwell on the whiteness...

You can feel it now. Your mind is becoming quite blank.

Ladies and gentlemen of my captive jury, please imagine you have never heard of my alleged deeds. Onto the screen before you I will project my memories. I must record my memories now before I change my mind, before they fade like a brittle silver nitrate print beyond any hope of restoration. I must record them today while my mind feels clear and objective.

And I feel my memories now unfurling. It is all coming back to me. Everything is coming back to me. Keep your eyes fixed on the screen and listen only to my voice. Concentrate your mind on the screen. It shall soon flicker into life.

And I focus my mind now to become the man who can recall the distance between Winnipeg and Montreal. To become the man who can recall who won the Derby in 1921. To become the man who can tell you the date Crippin was put to death. To become the man who can tell you who killed Cock Robin. I must become Mr. Memory.

I can see my life storyboarded before me now. I pause

11

momentarily to question myself if I should begin with a flashback, then turn to focus my attention on the bars outside my window. As the bars begin to dissolve amid the blinding whiteness, I feel myself a free man once again.

Ladies and gentlemen, please forgive me. I digress.

I digress as I regress to my childhood...

On the screen before us, a door materialises. Mr. Memory opens the door and we enter it together, you and I. We are entering The World of Youth...

The bars outside the window of my cell continue to be caught up in a cinematic dissolve. They dissolve and are transformed into the bars of a wrought iron fence. A date now appears in my mind. A date now appears on the screen. November 30th, 1959. I think that is where I came in. At least, that is the date I was discovered on. I was a foundling, you see, one of the many unfortunate waifs and strays of this world.

If I say I remember that night, you may think I am not in my right mind, but I am certain that I do. The first sight I recall is a tightly-framed, low angle shot of the bars of an iron fence with pointed spikes saluting the night sky. It was snowing heavily and I was cocooned inside a wicker basket, one handle of which had been hooked over a wrought iron spike to hold me in place.

The experts tell us that infants feel nothing but the most basic of emotions. Is fear such an emotion? That night I know I felt fear. I felt a deep, instinctual, dreadful fear at the realisation of my abandonment. And so I began to cry out in the darkness. I remember it all so clearly. I remember not being heard and I remember the frozen night air filling my infant lungs until I felt I could cry out no more. The shock and trauma of this incident, I remain convinced, was the cause of the delayed speech that would mark my early childhood.

Lying silently in that basket, I watched as the snow appeared to stop falling all of a sudden. And as the veil of snow dropped away, from somewhere beyond the railings I beheld a pale, still face looking down on me. It was a feminine face etched with fine features, its eyes replete with empathy and wisdom. It was a face of infinite compassion and understanding. It was a face that emanated tenderness, love and warmth. I was face to face with everything that is beautiful in humanity.

A sense of well-being settled over me and, at once, I knew I would be saved. Yes, I was soon extricated from the site of my abandonment. Only later, years later, did I realise that the face I saw that night was the face of a statue in the grounds of a church. It was the face of The Virgin Mary and it was the hand of another that unhooked the basket from the wrought iron spike of the fence and rescued me that night from my fate in the snow.

And so I was saved and taken under the protective wing of the church. Give us the first seven years and we will give you the man, the saying goes. They had me for somewhat longer than seven years, make of that what you will. Of the remainder of my infant years, I remember little. When I close my eyes and try to recall the early time spent within the children's home, what I see is a sort of haziness with nothing more than a vague pattern, an indistinct shape to it.

If I concentrate my mind, however, I can summon up some brief moments from these years and splice them together into a rough montage. It was a monochrome world of grey walls and damp bed clothes, dark wood panelling and unpalatable food. I recall the morning prayers. I recall the stern eyes of the adults who herded us. I recall the clip-clopping of shoes sounding off mosaic tiled floors. I recall chipped paint work and timeworn parquet flooring. I recall the bulging radiators that scorched your skin in the wintertime if you dared touch them. I recall the clothes that made my skin itch. I recall the crucifixes that adorned every corridor, every room. I recall the paintings of The Sacred Heart, depicting Jesus with his heart miraculously exposed. I recall that heart wrapped in thorns and crowned with a cross; a heart aflame and radiating divine light. I recall the night-time prayers.

Are the images I conjure up too bleak? Do not misunderstand me, I am eternally grateful for the care that I received. Truthfully, I do not remember being particularly unhappy in those early years of my regimented existence. In fact, I can state that the concepts of happiness or unhappiness were an unknown quantity to me. I was a placid being who was accepting of his place in life.

Perhaps this passivity was one reason why my fellow inmates at the home eyed me with suspicion and referred to me merely as "it." Or perhaps it was because my speech was delayed and they could not cajole me to join in their playground games. One abiding memory is of sitting in the corner of the communal yard. Each day, weather permitting, I would sit there silent and immovable from my spot under the branches of an oak tree. There, I looked at and observed the others a great deal. There, I would measure out in quiet wonder the slow passage of the seasons and their effect on the appearance of the great tree.

"He's an odd 'un," the resident caretaker Mr. Rose would observe repeatedly within earshot while leaning on a yard brush and smoking. "Oh, yes. We've got a picture, but there's no sound coming out."

Even then, I had a painful sense that I was different from my fellow inmates, that I was an "other." The smiling faces, the boisterous laughter in the playground, it was all part of a secret vocabulary I knew I would never be fluent in. I was already oversized for my age, I was clumsy and I was repeatedly mocked by my peers. I was also horribly oversensitive. Hearing the regular whispered asides about me caused me to become more withdrawn. And so I remained as if locked in my own inner world, helpless, trapped and unable to speak.

My situation may have been unbearable had it not been for the attention of a young novice nun. Her name was Sister Attracta and, for a time, I even entertained the irrational thought that she may have been my mother. She was graced with an innate, nurturing personality and seemed to single me out for special attention, doing her very best to draw me out of my inner world.

Once, I recall, she tried valiantly to get me involved in a game of Blindman's Buff in the playground. I remember her gentle eyes, blue with grey flecks, and her touch on my shoulder as she coaxed me into being the blindman. However, her encouraging words bore no fruit on this occasion as I stubbornly refused to co-operate when it came to having the blindfold slipped over my eyes.

"There's no helping that boy," Mr. Rose saltily observed from the sidelines, his teeth clamped onto a Woodbine cigarette. "You wound him up, put him on the floor, but he doesn't go!"

Sister Attracta was not easily discouraged, however, and it was she who introduced me to the only friend I made in the home. His name was Charlie and I recall him as a slightly scruffy fellow with sandy hair, orthopaedic shoes and National Health glasses. Charlie succeeded in engaging my attention in the game of marbles, which we played on hands and knees on a patch of bare earth at the foot of the oak tree. I liked Charlie as he chose not to berate me for being unable to speak and because he seemed to value my ability to quietly play a game of marbles with him. Occasionally, he would call me "mate" and once, after I won what turned out to be our final game, he allowed me to keep his favourite marble - a shiny blue orb that he had nicknamed Planet Earth.

How long did I have the friendship of Charlie? I don't know. One month or two at the most. Enough for the leaves on the oak tree to change from verdant green to a shade of amber. All I know is that one day he wasn't there any more. Sister Attracta noticed my state of bewilderment as I returned to sit in my spot in the corner of the yard. She lowered herself to my eye level, took my hand and informed me that Charlie had been sent away to Australia, away to the other side of Planet Earth on a boat, to what she called "a better life."

I cannot recall my exact state of mind, but later that day I stole into Sister Attracta's quarters and secreted myself in a wardrobe. I waited silently for some time and then through a crack in the door watched as she entered her room. I continued to watch as she began the ritual of removing her vestments. First, the black veil, the wimple and the white coif were carefully peeled off. Suddenly and miraculously before me, I beheld the sight of Sister Attracta's hair, that up until then had remained hidden. Even in the dim light of her room, the sight of that golden blonde hair entranced me as it unspooled before my eyes in spiralling ringlets. I felt the sensation of my heart trying to escape from my chest and in my inner world I had a searing vision of The Sacred Heart. A heart aflame and radiating divine light.

In my spellbound state, I suppose I must have stirred because she immediately discovered me. I feigned sleep so she would not think of me as a sinful peeping tom, but am unsure if I managed to wipe the beatific expression from my face. She gathered me up in her arms and whispered something to me about me missing my friend. She called me good and pure, her little lamb without a spot, and I was quietly returned to my dormitory where I slid between the clammy sheets and awaited slumber...

Attached to the children's home was the school wherein I received my early education. The content of the day-to-day lessons eludes me now, but they largely consisted of a dull and uninspiring daily menu of "the three Rs," and religious studies.

One advantage of my delayed speech was being excused such ordeals as having to learn tracts of poetry by rote and then reciting the passages aloud in class. Most vividly imprinted in my memory, however, is the ever-present threat of corporal punishment. The very tangible threat of the cane or the leather belt being used on us loomed over each day in that establishment like the Sword of Damocles. And the punishment was meted out by one man and one man only. Father Tobin.

I can picture Father Tobin's craggy, carved-out-of-granite face before me now. I can picture those electrified eyebrows, looking like they were permanently attached to the national grid. I can picture those nocturnal eyes. I can picture his somber expression as he would mispronounce "corporal punishment" as "corporeal punishment," or command us to "open your Bible to Ezekiel Chapter 6... 39 steps to the revelation of God in Christ." And I can recall an undying rumour that he applied black shoe polish to his hair to maintain its lustre.

Father Tobin was a true believer in not sparing the rod. If ever I was called on to leave a message in his office, I would look with sympathy on the unfortunate souls lined up outside, waiting for the call to enter Father Tobin's quarters and receive their penance. On more than one occasion, I was close enough to hear the same painful, predictable sequence of events being played out. There would be one or two practice swipes at the air and then the weapon of choice would be swiftly administered. After the punishment, the boy or boys in question would return to class, often sniffing to themselves and with hands clamped tightly in their armpits in an attempt to dampen down the pain. And every time I silently witnessed this order of service, I resolved that I would remain scrupulously well-behaved.

For most of the time, Father Tobin remained a stern, distant figure of authority in my childhood. Once, however, I remember a hushed but intense discussion that played out between him and Sister Attracta. The three of us were alone in the church. While Father Tobin and Sister Attracta talked near the confessional, I was seated in a pew, facing away from them and listening in. The subject under discussion was my future at the school and as the conversation progressed, I soon learned that Father Tobin wanted to send me away to a specialist institution for the deaf and dumb. Sister Attracta quietly but firmly protested.

"But he is not deaf, Father. He is mute. Please, watch."

A number of seconds passed and from somewhere behind, Sister Attracta rang a bell she had borrowed earlier from the church sacristy. Immediately, I turned my head in her direction and she smiled at me. She had proved her point.

"Very well," Father Tobin responded loftily. "If he is merely a mute and can perform tricks like the one you just stage managed, kindly see to it that he makes himself useful as an altar boy."

For a time, then, I became an altar boy and an exemplary one at that. Clad in my own vestments, I assiduously followed the order of the mass. I believed God was within me and I was here on Earth to serve Him. I was an apt pupil, never once failing to chime the bells at the appropriate point of the service. I often kept my hands pressed together in silent prayer. I often kept my eyes closed in reverent thought. Frequently, I was called on to perform my duties during baptisms, marriages and funerals. Often, I would have money pressed into my hands after the service by a grateful, smiling relative who would thank me for my efforts. Sometimes, Father Tobin would witness the transaction and demand I put any money I had received into the church donation box. Sometimes, he did not and I managed to secret it away in the hollow metal frame of my dormitory bed.

While I often found the classroom to be a dispiriting place of entrapment, something inside me responded to the interior of the church and viewed it as a scene of blessed escape. A feeling of immense calm would descend on me there as I imbibed the sense of ceremony during weekly mass. I recall the liturgy, the hymns and the sermons. I recall the altar, the tabernacle and the sacristy. And I recall Father Tobin. Here I witnessed him not as a man wielding a cane and dispensing punishment. Here I saw a celebrant who I believed had the power to summon up a heavenly presence as he cradled the chalice during the consecration of the host.

I was in thrall to this space. The sights, the sounds are still with me today. The holy water cool on my forehead. The elderly members of the congregation shuffling in. The genuflections. Creaking pews and creaking knees. The whispered prayers that sounded like air escaping from a bicycle tyre. The candles lit in prayer. The deeply felt wishes and entreaties of the parishioners, pleading for an intercession for themselves or for a loved one. The stations of the cross. The exotic smell of incense. The silence that would descend on the church as I was left behind to snuff out the lights of the candles on the altar. The solemn sense of ritual I would feel as I held the cone-shaped end of the candle extinguisher over the flames, starving the wick of oxygen.

And I recall the icons. Time and again I would pass by the church's carving of Jesus nailed to the cross. Time and again I would find myself mesmerised by the image and I would struggle with its meaning. Now I can articulate my feelings more clearly. As a child, however, troubling, half-formed thoughts were taking root.

*What sort of creature is man?* I would wonder, unable to fully understand the feelings that were stirring. There in my place of worship, every week, every feast day I would gaze up at the cross. I would gaze up at that man, that death-defying son of God. I would gaze up at that melancholy expression etched onto his face, his eyes aimed upwards to the heavens. And I accepted that there is brutishness in this life, that people can and will do that to another human being. I only had to study the face of Jesus to understand this was an incontrovertible fact of life.

If the slow, drawn out pain of crucifixion was not bad enough, I was aghast to learn that the suffering of Jesus continued on even after his death and rebirth. Not only that, this unending torture was something myself and my fellow pupils were repeatedly told we were fully complicit in. With the benefit of hindsight, I now recognise that phrase - "Every sin drives the nails in deeper," - was but another crude form of control to be used on us. Yet each time Father Tobin said those words, lowering his voice to a sonorous bass tone, lowering his eyebrows like two great hairy caterpillars, they had the desired effect on me. I was rapt, a member of a captive audience.

Nowhere was I more captive than in the cramped spartan space of the confessional, wherein absolution was sought for my sins. Stepping into the darkness of the booth and kneeling, as I waited for my eyes to adjust I remember I often allowed my hands to caress the dark varnished wood of the interior (as stipulated in my last will and testament, it is the sort of wood I want my coffin to be constructed from).

Because of my delayed speech, Father Tobin deemed that I should record my misdeeds in longhand on a sheet of paper. In preparation, I would roll the paper up like a piece of parchment and when the slat which separated me from Father Tobin was slid across, I would pass it through. Father Tobin would then unfurl the page, give it a cursory glance, secret it up the sleeve of his vestments and inform me of my penance. To this day I do not know if he disposed of the sheets of paper or if they are still lying in a dark drawer somewhere, the unabsolved transgressions of a juvenile mind.

Head bowed, hands joined in prayer, I would then exit the confessional. Adjourning to another part of the church I would kneel and begin to recite my penance. This was the moment I came to fear the most, because no matter how minor my infractions, as I closed my eyes and tried to pray, in my inner world I would be assaulted by visions. Visions of hammer blows and nails being driven in deeper… Visions of blood welling up around the wounds… Visions of blood falling amid footprints in the virgin snow.

In the overall scheme of things, the first six years of my schooling passed off unremarkably. As you may have gathered, I was not a popular child or one who made friends easily, but I believe I was tentatively beginning to feel a sense of purpose thanks to my duties as an altar boy.

In the final year of primary school, my class was appointed a new teacher. His name was Mr. Drew. Having previously been taught exclusively by members of the cloth, Mr. Drew was our first lay teacher. As I paint a mental picture of him now, I see an anonymous man in his early thirties, scarecrow-thin and normally dressed in corduroy (both jacket and trousers), with a wave of brown hair combed to the right, a neat mustache and silver wire rim spectacles.

My first impressions of Mr. Drew were wholly positive. At the end of his first day, he made a point of taking me aside and speaking to me one-on-one. His tone of voice was affable and encouraging.

"I know you have a problem with your speech," he said. "So if you have any issues about keeping up in class, let me know. I am going to make it my personal mission to improve you."

He laid a hand on my shoulder and leaned a little closer.

"I saw you up at the altar on Sunday," he continued. "I have never seen an altar boy perform his duties so diligently, so… meekly. And you know what they say about the meek inheriting the Earth, don't you?"

In the classroom, Mr. Drew proved to be an exemplary teacher with a rare gift for communicating with his pupils. Under his tutelage, I was amazed to discover that learning did not have to be a chore. My eyes were opened to the joy of the written word with his readings of passages from Dickens and Shakespeare, from Gerard Manley Hopkins and Wordsworth (there was that one phrase in particular from Wordsworth he would repeat to us like a mantra… "the child is the father of the man."). Whatever his subsequent sins, I shall remember Mr. Drew as my initial guide into The World of Make-Believe.

"Listen," he confided to me one afternoon. He had sidled up to my desk, hands jammed in his pockets, absent-mindedly jangling whatever loose change was lurking there. "I've been working my charms on Old Father Tobin, trying to persuade him to allow me to set up a little after-school activity. I told him I might need a helper and I mentioned your name. Would you be at all interested?"

I must have nodded or given my assent in some way, for he

continued in the same vein.

"Don't worry. It will be just like being an altar boy. Only you'll get to witness *real* miracles."

He told me no more and I was held in limbo until the next Friday. It was after the communal evening meal that he approached me again. Following a quick word with Sister Attracta, Mr. Drew ushered me out of the dining hall. Under his instruction, I shadowed him out of the building and towards his car, a navy Hillman Hunter that had not felt the touch of a chamois cloth for some time. As we walked, he talked in the amiable tones I was now familiar with.

"I'm going to need a hand with the equipment, carrying it inside, setting it up and so on." He gave me a quick glance from head to toe. "And as you're getting to be the biggest boy in school, I thought I'd enlist your help."

He unlocked the car and I spotted a number of sizeable cases tightly packed on the back seat.

"Just to let you know, we're going to have to be careful with the equipment. I've made an arrangement with a chap I know. He's the head of a society I'm a member of. I don't want to be any further in his debt, so I'm just warning you."

Mr. Drew continued to talk over the noise of the Hillman Hunter's creaking suspension as he removed the cases from the car.

"I'll do most of the work tonight, but if things go well I'll show you the ropes over the next few weeks and hopefully you'll get the proper feel for things. Does that sound like a plan?"

As I lugged one of the heavy metallic cases into the school, Mr. Drew directed me towards the assembly hall. And there I observed him carefully, skillfully set up the equipment.

"I can tell by the way you're looking at me, you haven't the foggiest idea what we're going to get up to this evening. Am I right?"

After a delay, I nodded. Mr. Drew was slightly out of breath and I couldn't help noticing the damp patches forming around his armpits.

"Well, I can tell you... We're going to watch a movie."

During those first weeks of Mr. Drew's after-school screenings, Father Tobin remained ever-present, hovering in the background while we screened a series of what must have been pre-approved titles. Among the films I recall seeing were *The Song of Bernadette*, *The Nun's Story* and a Leo McCarey/Bing Crosby double bill of *Going My Way* and *The Bells of St Mary's*.

"No chance of us falling foul of The Legion of Decency, I can assure you," Mr. Drew confided in me.

One evening, having helped carry the equipment back to Mr. Drew's car, I was stood at the rear of the vehicle while Mr. Drew was engaged in the business of arranging the cases across the back seat. As Mr. Drew laboured on and the suspension squealed out, I noticed the boot of the Hillman Hunter had become unlocked. With a steady creak, the lid of the boot slowly began to rise.

It took a few moments for Mr. Drew to spot what was happening. When he did, he wasted no time. He quickly squirmed his way out of the back seat, stumbled around to the boot and slammed it shut. Out of breath and pressing the palms of his hands down on the boot repeatedly, Mr. Drew let out an uneasy laugh.

"Been meaning to get this blasted lock seen to," he said.

I am sure I managed to maintain a calm exterior, but as Mr. Drew drove away in a swirling cloud of exhaust fumes, I thought of the items I had glimpsed strewn across the floor of the boot of his Hillman Hunter. The tyre iron. The pair of gloves. The knife. And the coiled lengths of rope...

... It was a matter of days after this incident, during a lunch break, that I found my eyes drawn towards the front page of a newspaper. Mr. Rose was standing in the doorway of his supply shed flicking through the newspaper in question. It bore the following headline...

## LEYTONSTONE STRANGLER CLAIMS
## VICTIM NUMBER EIGHT

Beneath the headline was a photograph of a length of rope fashioned into a noose. The caption underneath stated that the noose had been recovered from the latest crime scene. Noticing my lingering presence, Mr. Rose lowered the newspaper and pointed at the front page.

"I see there's another bleedin' lunatic at large," he pronounced. "This strangler... It's a terrifying thought, but I do hope you realise that he could be anyone."

Overhearing these words, Sister Attracta intervened and placed a reassuring hand on my shoulder.

"Mr. Rose, I must ask you to stop. He's much too young to know about such matters."

"Oh, I don't think he has anything to be worried about, Sister," Mr. Rose said. "The Leytonstone Strangler's not interested in kiddies. It's women who are his stock-in-trade. Blondes in particular... Are you by any chance a blonde, Sister?"

"Please be silent, Mr. Rose," Sister Attracta replied, managing to maintain her dignity. She promptly escorted me away, while Mr. Rose returned to his reading.

My curiosity had been aroused, however. After that day's lessons, I crept silently into Mr. Rose's supply shed. And as soon as I laid my trembling hands on the newspaper, I began to read.

I read how The Leytonstone Strangler had murdered eight women in the area of Leytonstone. I read how he strangled his victims with lengths of rope that were coiled into a noose. I read how clues to his identity were sparse, but an eyewitness had described the murderer as driving away from the location of one killing in an unidentified navy car.

When I had finished, I removed the front page from the newspaper and carefully folded it. I secreted the page inside my trouser pocket and I continued to mull over my private suspicions about the character of Mr. Drew.

That very evening, I went along to another of Mr. Drew's after-school screenings. Attendance was not compulsory and perhaps it was the prospect of another film starring Bing Crosby as a warbling priest that can explain why the audience numbers had dwindled. Finally, that evening there was just myself and Mr. Drew.

"Listen," Mr. Drew said. "I've moved heaven and earth and managed to convince Father Tobin about the benefits of a young man like yourself having a hobby. I've told him how I've seen great improvements in you. I've told him how I've seen you gaining confidence in your handling of the equipment. And so, in his infinite wisdom, he is allowing the screenings to continue." Mr. Drew moved his head a little closer. "You know, I've a secret nickname for him... Tobin The Terrible. What do you think of that?"

I probably turned a smile at the revelation that Mr. Drew harboured such secret feelings about Father Tobin.

"Anyway, we have had our grace period and that has helped put Old Father Tobin's mind at ease. So, tonight I'm going to show you something a little different. Something from my personal collection. I think you'll appreciate it." Mr. Drew could see that my interest had been piqued. He whispered into my ear. "It's silent... Just like you."

I have subsequently replayed that evening countless times to myself and am sure there was no sense of portent in the air, there was nothing to suggest that my life was about to change forever. Mr. Drew proceeded to go through the usual sequence of preparations beforehand - lights were dimmed, switches were flicked and a beam of light shot from the projector like God's breath bringing life to the screen. Then… a title appeared before my eyes.

*The Lodger – A Tale of the London Fog.*

It began with a silent scream. It began with blonde hair, backlit by a pulsing sign that read **TO-NIGHT "GOLDEN CURLS"**. It began with the face of a female murder victim, frozen in mute terror as the life was being squeezed out of her. It began with images lodged in my mind forever.

I cannot forget the tale it told, of a killer dubbed The Avenger, set amid the backstreets of my home city. I cannot forget those melancholy eyes hovering above a scarf wrapped around the title character's face. I cannot forget the lights gently swaying on the ceiling of The Lodger's abode, and watching astonished as the screen miraculously developed x-ray vision to reveal that the motion was brought on by the restless back and forth footfall of the title character overhead. I cannot forget my first glimpse of The △, the symbol used by The Avenger as his calling card. And most of all I cannot forget the climactic pursuit of The Lodger, now handcuffed, by an angry mob.

I watched as The Lodger climbed over some railings in a desperate attempt to evade the inner city mob. I watched as his handcuffs became ensnared over the spike of a railing and he was left hanging mid-air as the people descended on him. I had no idea how The Lodger could possibly escape unharmed from this predicament. I felt overwhelmed by the drama unfolding on the screen before me.

Then suddenly in the silence of that room, where the only noise to be heard was the whirring of the projector, suddenly there was sound. Suddenly -

"NO!"

The single word shot out of my mouth as I bore witness to The Lodger's plight. I stood up, and in my distracted state the folded up page of newspaper must have fallen out of my pocket.

In the darkness, neither myself or Mr. Drew noticed it.

After The Lodger's predicament had been resolved and the end titles had run their course, as usual I began to help quietly pack away the equipment. At some point, Mr. Drew discovered the folded front page lying there on the floor. He unfolded it and glanced at the contents. After a brief pause, Mr. Drew then regarded me.

"Is this yours?" he asked me.

I shook my head and watched as Mr. Drew pocketed the sheet of newsprint. He then addressed me, choosing not to break character and behaving in his normal, affable manner.

"Did you enjoy the film?" he asked nonchalantly.

I nodded.

"I didn't know you could talk," he remarked as an afterthought. "Is that the... first time you have spoken?"

I nodded again. Enunciating any further words was proving too difficult just then.

When I had finished hauling the equipment back to Mr. Drew's mud-splattered Hillman Hunter, I returned to my dormitory in silence. As I lay in my bed that night, I tried to dismiss the suspicions I was entertaining about Mr. Drew. As I lay there, I also wondered if the single declarative word I had vocalised would prove to be my one and only utterance to the world.

It turned out, however, that my second verbal outburst came soon after. It was during the final moments of the following Sunday mass, when Father Tobin was drawing the service to a close with the words "Go in peace to love and serve the Lord." While the rest of the parishioners answered in the usual solemn, slightly muted response of "Amen," I caught the eye of Mr. Drew in the congregation. He was in the front row, staring at me intently. At once, I shocked myself. I found myself uttering a loud, resounding "AMEN!" that echoed around the interior of the building.

Father Tobin glared at me from the altar, his caterpillar eyebrows arched downwards at an alarming angle. After the service, he muttered something in my direction about raised voices in the house of God. When I exited the sacristy, however, Sister Attracta was there waiting for me and she embraced me fulsomely. I believe I may have smiled.

"You can talk! My child, you can talk!" she exclaimed. "I never doubted you for a single second. I have always known you are special. I am going to make it my mission to get you some help."

Sister Attracta was true to her word. Weekly appointments with a speech therapist were arranged and I began to make notable improvements. It was faltering at first, but after a short period of time I surprised myself by being able to read aloud in class and being able to confess verbally for the first time to Father Tobin.

Meantime, the weekly screenings in the company of Mr. Drew proceeded, during which he continued to act and speak as if nothing out of the ordinary had happened.

"Seeing how you reacted to last week's movie," he said. "I'm going to show a few more films by the same chap who made *The Lodger*. Hitchcock is his name. Alfred Hitchcock. Watch out for his moniker at the beginning of the film. He's a Londoner, just like you and me. Lives in America now. That's where he's made most of his films."

Mr. Drew was true to his word. Each Friday that followed, we would view another film by Mr. Hitchcock. During that period I recall watching *Murder!*, *Shadow of a Doubt*, *I Confess*, *Rope* and *Notorious* for the first time.

The weeks passed and I believe that I had managed to bury my suspicions about Mr. Drew. Following one screening, however, while he packed away the reels of film, Mr. Drew began to talk. As he spoke, I noticed a deadened neutrality to his voice I had not heard before. And the longer Mr. Drew spoke, the more I felt my suspicions resurfacing.

"I've never told you," he began. "But I'm an orphan, just like you. In another life maybe we could have been brothers... My mother, she died in the war... I'm old enough to remember the horrors of the war, you know... A V-2 bomb got her. Flattened her house, it did, without warning... BANG! And that was the end of her... As for my father, I never knew him. I was told he met his maker parachuting into France without firing off a single shot at the Germans... I can't say I miss my parents... In fact, sometimes I despise them for leaving me alone in this damned world... I was brought up in an orphanage too, you see... I know what it's like... I know what people are like."

Mr. Drew dug into his trouser pocket and retrieved something.

"Memories... they're only memories... Have you ever thought about what happens to your memories when you die? Isn't it a funny thought?"

He began to unfold the item he had retrieved from his pocket.

"My memories seem as real to me now as bricks and mortar or the oak tree in the school yard, but when I'm gone they'll be gone... Somehow, that doesn't seem right to me."

The item he had retrieved was the folded up front page of newspaper. He held it before him.

"This Strangler fellow, maybe he has the right idea... But is this what a man has to do to be remembered in this day and age?"

Mr. Drew glanced at me and he laughed. The laughter sounded desperately hollow.

"Well, whoever he is, he'll have to do his damnedest to make sure he doesn't break the eleventh commandment... Do you know what the eleventh commandment is?"

I shook my head.

"Thou shalt not be found out."

I sensed Mr. Drew was gauging my reactions. He was testing me on the subject of how much I knew or thought I knew about him. Inwardly, I prayed that I had managed to conceal my private suspicions.

In the days that followed, I considered not attending any more of Mr. Drew's screenings. I soon realised, however, that if I failed to appear the next week, Mr. Drew would finally be alerted to my suspicions. And what then would be my fate?

One Monday, after the final bell had rang, Mr. Drew asked me to stay behind in class for a moment.

"I read something interesting in the newspaper over the weekend," he began. "Mr. Hitchcock is making a new film and you'll never guess where. Right here in London. Once a Londoner, always a Londoner, isn't that what they say? He must've heard the call of Bow Bells all the way over in sunny Hollywood. Anyway, listen. I know a chap who works in Pinewood Studios. I'll see if I can call in a favour and arrange a special field trip to spy on Mr. Hitchcock in his native habitat. Does that sound like a plan?"

At this news, I confess I felt a secret stir of excitement and I may even have managed to forget my private suspicions. I spent days thinking about such a trip and dwelling on its possibilities. I imagined what it would be like to simply escape from the home, to escape from the school for a few hours.

The following Friday, before Mr. Drew's next scheduled screening, I worked up the courage to ask him how his plans were coming along for the visit to Pinewood. Arms folded, he appeared detached, his tone of voice close to the neutral one he had deployed when he had talked about his memories.

"Oh yes, that... Sorry to get your hopes up, but you see, the thing is my acquaintance, he informs me that Mr. Hitchcock operates on a closed set and no visitors can get in. It's not open to mere mortals like you and me. My chum, he says Hitchcock is a peculiar sort of fellow with all sorts of airs and graces about him. Never mind, eh? We still have our screenings."

… And so, I had no other option but to continue to attend Mr. Drew's screenings.

As each reel spooled through the internal workings of the projector, Mr. Drew would observe the respectful silence of a practising cinephile. Once, however, over the opening titles of *I Confess*, he did speak about Mr. Hitchcock's habit of making brief appearances in his movies.

"You know, I'd like to compile a list of all the cameos he's made in his films some day." He raised a hand and pointed at the screen. "Look, there he is walking right to left at the top of those steps. It's him. It's Mr. Hitchcock! Do you see him?"

"Yes," I answered, noting the rotund figure striding against a section of sky.

On another occasion, while watching *Notorious*, he chimed in with an observation that left me unsettled.

"Do you recognise that actress?" he asked me. "She played a nun in *The Bells of St Mary's*."

"Yes," I answered.

"Remember her example. You will learn that, like many women, she can play both a saint and a whore."

Each week, there was a new title to watch. Each week, I had a growing sense that Mr. Drew knew that I knew his secret.

There, in the gloom at the back of the hall, I developed my own survival technique to shield myself from the fear that began to haunt me. I focused my entire attention on the screen and the life or death events being played out before me. I became expert at disengaging my conscious mind and allowing my unconscious mind to drift onto the screen, to become one with the screen, in order to avoid the reality of the situation I found myself in.

I kept telling myself that I was not under the spell of Mr. Drew. I kept telling myself that I was under the spell of the films he had introduced me to and their creator. I was under the spell of Mr. Hitchcock.

Week by week, however, no matter what I kept telling myself, I began to increasingly resent Mr. Drew's conduct towards me. There was one incident that proved to be a turning point.

It occurred away from the classroom, during an informal nature lesson with a number of my fellow pupils. The location was the church's bell tower, where a pair of doves had been discovered nesting. Around a dozen of us proceeded in single file up the narrow wooden staircase to the bell tower, with Mr. Drew leading the way.

"Keep as quiet as possible, boys," he instructed us. "We should be able to hear the nestlings cheeping if we remain quiet."

Mr. Drew unlocked a door and one by one we entered the bell tower. Inside, the space was dominated by the church bell which was suspended a couple of feet above our heads in the dead centre of the tower. As my classmates peered up at the rafters, they spoke among themselves...

"I don't hear no birds. All I hear is the wind."

"I can see a nest, but there's no birds. Where are the birds?"

"Look, there they are. Two of them. Higher up."

"Why aren't they guarding their nest?"

"Probably scared of us."

Meanwhile, I had wandered over to the single source of light in the tower – a small arched window that peered out onto the world beneath.

"Quite a view, isn't it?" Without warning, Mr. Drew had joined me. "Look how small the people appear below. So insignificant, scurrying around like termites... I call them the moron millions. Here, let me show you a trick." His hand came from behind, he took my left hand and began to manipulate the digits. "Look out for someone on the ground. Anyone. Get them in your eyeline. Put your thumb and forefinger together, squeeze... and they're gone." He proceeded to quote some Shakespeare. "Like flies to wanton boys are we to the gods. They kill us for their sport." He laughed nervously. "Look out for anyone you don't care for and try that trick again. Why not keep an eye out for Tobin The Terrible and try it out on him."

I'm sure I heard some further discussion between Mr. Drew and my classmates on the subject of nesting habits, but for a time I lost myself in thought looking out at the view from the tower. I don't know exactly how long I was peering out of the window before I realised I was alone there. I turned around to check where my fellow pupils and Mr. Drew were, only to be met with a scene of desertion. I quickly made my way to the door we had entered through, only to find that it would not budge.

I was pulling at the door handle when I sensed a creaking movement immediately behind me. I turned quickly, half expecting to ward off a blow from a hidden assailant, but instead I saw it was the church bell. It was gradually being levered up from its stationary position... higher... higher... And then it began its swift, silent descent before the clanging began.

*CLAANNGGGG! CLAANNGGGG!*

A deafening clanging. My hands covered my ears and I cowered in the corner of the tower as the bell continued to ring out.

*CLAANNGGGG! CLAANNGGGG!*

The whole space shook. Dust rose up from between the floorboards.

*CLAANNGGGG! CLAANNGGGG!*

I watched as the pair of doves flapped and made their exit through the narrow arched window.

*CLAANNGGGG! CLAANNGGGG!*

Dust particles danced in the air.

*CLAANNGGGG! CLAANNGGGG!*

I watched as the dove's nest was dislodged and fell from from its place in the rafters.

*CLAANNGGGG! CLAANNGGGG!*

The bell rose and fell, rose and fell, twelve times. I closed my eyes and waited for the reverberations to stop. The sound of the bell faded, yet in my head it still continued to ring out. For an instant I contemplated following the doves, fleeing the noise out through the arched window, not caring whatever waited for me out there. I just wanted to escape.

My head was still reverberating with the aftershock of the knelling of the bell when I realised I was blocking the entrance door and someone was banging on it, trying to gain entrance. Eventually, I shifted myself and the figure of Mr. Drew squeezed through. My memory is hazy, but I suppose he spent some time trying to calm me as my hearing gradually returned.

"Are you alright?" he asked me, his face a mask of concern. "There was a piece of masonry jammed in front of the door and I couldn't move it. Didn't you hear me telling everyone to get downstairs before the bell was rung for midday?"

I shook my head. Mr. Drew now looked to his left, towards where the dove's nest lay on the floor. His voice was a lifeless, unbroken monotone.

"Looks like a predator of some sort must've got in and killed the nestlings. Oh well... they're nothing but squawking, wrinkled little bags of flesh at that stage of development anyway."

He leaned closer and spoke into my ear.

"Do you see now? Do you see the damage unwanted noises can do? Just because you now have the power to speak, you must know that words can cause damage too. Do you agree?"

I nodded.

At that moment, I knew with absolute certainty that Mr. Drew had arranged for the door to be locked and he was now aware of my suspicions. My mentor had become my tormentor.

I considered informing another authority figure of my suspicions, but I soon came to the conclusion that that was all I had... suspicions. I could not bring myself to report Mr. Drew because of what others would, in all probability, deem as mere childish notions.

I resolved not to put my faith in any worldly form of justice.

Instead, each night before sleep, I silently prayed for an intercession to save me from Mr. Drew. I prayed to God to strike him down.

In response, however, there was only silence.

It was on the following Sunday, after mass, that Sister Attracta approached me. She smiled and remarked on how tall I was, how I had sprouted up and was now towering over her. She told me how proud she was of the progress I had made with the speech therapist, how I would always be her favourite, but I could tell that she was holding something back from me. And then she told me. The instant I heard her words, I knew my world was set to become a colder place to inhabit.

"I am to leave," she said. "My mother is elderly and needs care at her time of life. I need to be with her, to tend for her needs."

I suppose she may have seen my tear ducts welling up as she gently embraced me.

"I will be remembering you in my devotions every day and God will be looking over you at all times. Remember, God has a plan for you. God loves you."

I could not share her final sentiments, as I felt my prayers had remained cruelly unanswered.

Before we parted outside the church, she told me she was not leaving yet. Not yet, but within the next week.

Strange emotions, unanswered questions fluttered around my head. A part of me felt confused and angry at the revelation that she had a mother, that she had other people in her life who she had feelings for. *Why is she leaving me? Why now?* I asked myself.

That night, during the summer of 1971, it came to me what I should do. There was nothing left for me in this place. The only voice of kindness I had encountered was abandoning me. Unintentionally, she was leaving me at the mercy of Mr. Drew.

My prayers had gone unanswered.

That night, I hatched a hasty plan of escape…

△

Escaping was not a problem. I had been resident in the home long enough to have a good idea how to stage a getaway without being detected. It was around ten o'clock that I stole out of the dormitory. I lifted my satchel and whatever shillings I had managed to save from my altar boy duties, squeezed through a ground floor bathroom window, then made my way across the playground and over the railings.

The only plan in my head was to put as much distance as possible between myself and the home, between myself and Mr. Drew. As I look back on these events, however, I now realise that any talk of a plan is irrelevant, because my movements were in fact predetermined. My movements were part of an invisible design. Unseen hands were guiding me over the course of that night and into the following fateful day.

I recall that it was a temperate summer's evening and my progress was illuminated by a succession of flickering streetlights. At first I ran, but after half a mile or so I slowed my pace to a brisk walk. I walked blindly for some time, not knowing where my feet were taking me. My grasp of the geography of the surrounding streets was rudimentary at best and, for the first time, I was confronted with the fact that I knew virtually nothing of the world outside those wrought iron railings. My existence up until then had played out almost exclusively in three locations situated in very close quarters to each other - the home, the school and the church.

I felt a momentary sense of panic at being lost. It was a queasy physical sensation, a kind of seasickness that pulsed through me, brought on by the thought of finding myself hopelessly adrift in the labyrinth streets of London. I had a vague idea to check into a hotel or a bed and breakfast, but soon rejected this, unsure how much it would cost and fearful that the sight of an unaccompanied minor would arouse suspicion too easily. I needed somewhere to hide out while my panic subsided.

With no ideas forthcoming, I continued to walk. I walked through residential areas, peering in on families ensconced around glowing fires, around glowing television screens. I walked along high streets, past voluminously dark shop windows, past the murmuring hubbub of various drinking establishments.

I must have been walking an hour or so in an apparently random pattern when I turned a corner and my eyes were drawn towards a marquee sign, lit up in a glowing shade of green. It read The Bijou Cinema. Beneath the sign some words were spelled out in bold capitals. Words that were enough to draw me closer...

## ALFRED HITCHCOCK'S
## PSYCHO X

*Psycho Kiss*, I thought to myself.

I approached slowly and stepped inside the cinema. The front of house was deserted, but when I spotted a list of screening times pinned to a notice board on the window of the ticket booth, I drew closer to study it.

"Lost, are we?"

The voice I heard was directing itself at me from inside the ticket booth. Behind the glass was a woman meeting my gaze. She looked to be in her fifties, short of stature, with a brittle wave of blonde hair. Her face betrayed a certain dissatisfaction with her station in life.

"I'd like to see the film, please," I managed to say.

The lady in the ticket booth laughed.

"You're too late I'm afraid, young man. The screening started half an hour ago and I'm not allowed to let anyone in at the express wishes of the gentleman over there."

She gestured towards a life-sized promotional standee located in the foyer. It was a two-dimensional cardboard figure of a corpulent man in a black suit, pointing at his wristwatch and looking in my direction. I really should have identified him from his walk-on role in *I Confess*, but I asked the question anyway.

"Who is that?"

"It's the man whose name is up in lights... Mr. Hitchcock. He's been lying around here since the film first came out and whenever we re-run it, I take him out of storage, dust him off and put him out here to drum up some business. And believe me, it always works... But," she added with some emphasis, "if you direct your attention to the message he's holding, it says I am forbidden to allow anyone to enter the cinema after the beginning of the film."

I looked again at the figure of Mr. Hitchcock and saw, suspended from the index finger of his right hand, a sign that indeed showed that the lady in the ticket booth was speaking the truth.

"Now, you're a big boy," she continued. "But I don't think you'd pass for someone who I could let in to see an X Certificate film and still keep a clean conscience."

"... I do have money with me," I ventured.

"Can I ask if your parents know you're out at this time of the night?"

I did not answer, but instead changed the subject, gesturing towards a selection of snacks that lay behind the glass of the ticket booth.

"How much is a bag of peanuts?"

The lady in the ticket booth paused, looked at me, then reached for a bag of salted peanuts and tossed them towards me through a gap in the glass partition.

"Go on, take them. No charge. Now, clear off before I have to call the police to escort you back to wherever you came from."

I thanked the lady in the ticket booth and quickly strode away, stirred into action at her mention of the police.

Having been denied my chance to view *Psycho*, I had no option but to spend some more time wandering along miles of unfamiliar grey pavement. Whenever an adult drew close or I spotted a police car in the distance, I would make sure to take swift evasive action. The peanuts provided me with some much-needed sustenance, but I knew I could not spend the night aimlessly walking the streets.

Eventually, I found myself beside a park. I climbed the surrounding fence, located an amenable spot in an empty band stand and bedded down for the night, using my satchel as a makeshift pillow. Fortunately, I had chosen an ideal night for sleeping outdoors. The air remained balmy and sleep-inducing.

Before I slept an undisturbed sleep, for a time I looked upwards at the stars. I retreated to my inner world and I found myself reciting the same words over and over to myself...

*Psycho Kiss... Psycho Kiss... Psycho Kiss... Psycho Kiss...*

The next morning I was awoken by the sun beaming through the slats of the band stand. I vacated my resting place and went off in search of an exit, just managing to avoid being spotted by a park attendant doing his rounds. Feeling hungry, I made my way to the nearest high street café I could find and ordered a bacon sandwich.

I ate hastily and reflected on the fact that by now my absence at the home would certainly have been noted. I did not know how these situations normally played out, but I imagined the first call of action would be to notify the authorities. The police may already be on the lookout for me. I could be identified and picked up at any moment. Without warning I would feel the heavy hand of the law on my shoulder and, utterly powerless, I would be returned to the home. I would be returned to face the certain wrath of Father Tobin.

I had to stay alert. I had to keep my eyes open to any possible threat. Quickly, I wiped my greasy fingers on a napkin and left the café, wary of the serving staff there who I am sure were whispering about me while furtively aiming suspicious glances in my direction. I walked out onto the high street again and kept my head continuously angled towards the pavement.

The distant wail of an emergency service siren encouraged me to duck into the first shop I came across that was open. The sign above the door said DELTA BOOKS. The owner (an elderly gentleman whose angular face was framed by white mutton-chop whiskers) lowered a copy of *The Daily Telegraph* and regarded me over the rims of his glasses as I entered the shop and slowly began to pace around.

The interior of the shop was long and narrow, stacked from floor to ceiling with books, with two parallel aisles that stretched far back into a dimly lit vanishing point. I cannot clearly recall how long I spent wandering the dusty, confined aisles of that book shop before my eyes chanced upon his name once again…

## HITCHCOCK

On this occasion, it was printed on the dust jacket of a book and was joined by another name underneath, one I was unfamiliar with…

### François Truffaut

Taking great care, as if handling an ancient artefact, I removed the book from the shelf and opened it. I then began to flick through the pages, eyeing the black-and-white photographs laid out alongside the accompanying text. I recognised some images from films that I had already been exposed to, but many were from films I had not seen. Noting the initials **F.T.** or **A.H.**

preceding sections of the text, I realised that the book was in fact a transcription of a lengthy conversation between the two men who shared the title.

While the shop seemed to deal exclusively in used or second hand tomes, this copy of *Hitchcock* by Truffaut appeared to my untrained eye to be as good as new. After even such a brief perusal, it was clear to me that I needed to be in possession of this volume. I noticed an asking price of £1.00 written neatly in pencil on the top right corner of the title page. There were a few coins still left in my pocket, but I knew that it would not nearly be enough to purchase the book. I dwelled on the options available to me...

Then, working as quickly and as silently as possible, I undid the buckles on my school satchel, I deposited the book inside and I re-fastened the buckles. From the front of the shop, I could hear the restless rustling of newspaper pages. I raised my eyes and before me there was now an empty space in the shelf, reminding me of what I had just done and of what I was about to do.

However, my mind was set. I suppose I should have made straight for the door right there and then, but something held me back. Emerging from the depths of the aisle I had disappeared into, I picked up a random paperback sitting in an unsorted pile and presented it to the owner of the shop. He lowered his newspaper and a pair of rheumy eyes inspected my purchase.

"... Agatha Christie. Like a good whodunnit do you, hmmm?"

"... Yes."

"Slight crease on spine, visible foxing... It would be a crime to charge you more than two shillings for this."

I retrieved the money from my trouser pocket and handed it over.

"Shouldn't you be in school, hmmm?" the shop owner now asked me.

"I'm on my way there now," I lied.

"Of course you are." He deposited the two shillings in a

makeshift wooden till, then addressed me once more. "I'm something of an armchair detective myself, you know. And I can tell by the way your satchel is hanging that you appear to have gained some extra reading material since you darkened my doorway."

I found myself frozen to the spot. My first attempt at theft had been a complete failure. I had been caught red-handed. The store owner spoke again. This time his voice had a low-level air of menace to it.

"To avoid any hue and cry, why don't you open your school bag, my boy… give me what's in there and we'll forget this ever happened, hmmm?"

Quickly, I weighed up my options. The proprietor looked to be edging towards his septuagenarian years and I noticed a walking stick propped against the counter. The stick offered a clue to my chances of getting out of the shop without being collared. Without any further hesitation, I decided to take my chances and run. I dropped the Agatha Christie, dodged past the store owner and bolted for the door.

As I charged up the pavement, I could hear the words "STOP… THAT… THIEF!" echoing after me. I glanced backwards. The store owner was not giving chase, but standing in the doorway of DELTA BOOKS and gesticulating with his walking stick in my general direction. Miraculously, there was not one pedestrian in the vicinity, otherwise I am sure I would have been subjected to a citizen's arrest.

Continuing my flight from the scene of the crime, I soon spotted the entrance to an underground station. Believing the underground would be an ideal location to lose anyone who may be in pursuit, I stalked under the roundel sign and entered. Once inside, with some trepidation, I approached a ticket kiosk. Trying not to appear conspicuous, I handed over my last two shillings to a gentleman of Caribbean extraction who was seated inside the kiosk. I was about to ask how far two shillings would get me, when a ticket shot up from the dispenser. It was another minor miracle. The last of my altar boy earnings had covered the exact price of the ticket to my final destination.

I proceeded down flights of stairs, down into the underground, down onto a Central Line platform. All the time I stayed alert, surreptitiously eyeing-up the people I was sharing the platform with in case one of them was about to finger me as a common thief. A claustrophobic sense of panic began to close in on me. My breathing was becoming too shallow, my heart was threatening to escape the confines of my chest. Soon, however, I heard a rumbling, I felt a rush of subterranean air enveloping my body, a train pulled up before me and the doors juddered open.

Once on board the Central Line train, some time passed before my nerves settled and I allowed myself to entertain the thought that I had gotten away with it. I had broken a commandment and I had gotten away with it.

This thought was soon replaced, however, by a sense of guilt. I wondered if I should confess my act of theft on the next occasion I entered the confessional. Sitting on board that train, I waited for the visions to come to me... Visions of nails being driven in deeper... Visions of blood welling up around wounds. But the visions did not come.

Instead, in my inner world, I felt something compelling me to get off at the next station. Something was telling me to change trains, to change lines. And so from the Central Line I switched to the Circle Line. Once on the Circle Line, again I felt prompted to disembark at a seemingly random station.

I did as was asked of me. I followed the signs for the exit and I ascended some stairs back towards ground level. Raising my eyes to the daylight, I was caught off-balance when I suddenly beheld the edifice of Big Ben looming over me. Steadying myself, I turned right and advanced in the direction of the Thames. It was almost as if I was walking in a trance now. Pausing on Westminster Bridge, I took a moment to take in my surroundings.

Behind me stood the Houses of Parliament, while riding rampant into battle across the way was Boudica and her warrior daughters. I cast my eyes towards the South Bank and there I could see something happening at the edge of the river. A sizeable crowd was gathered in the shadow of County Hall, as if about to listen to a sermon. I started across the span of Westminster Bridge.

As if steered by a mysterious outside agency, I felt inexorably drawn towards the scene I could see being played out on the South Bank. I crossed the traffic lanes on Westminster Bridge and followed some steps down and to the left, moving ever closer towards the assembled crowd. A small number of people were walking around the edge of the congregation with a sense of purpose and seemed to be ensuring the public remained behind a crowd barrier. Soon, I found myself at the front of the barrier, amongst a group of onlookers collectively craning their necks to catch a glimpse of the proceedings.

"What's going on?" one man asked.

"I dunno. They're making a film or something," another answered.

"Who's in it?"

"Dunno."

"Is it a comedy?"

"How should I know?"

There was a brief respite in the back and forth, followed by another question.

"Here... what's that buzzing noise?"

Sure enough, I too could hear a buzzing noise. It was a constant whirring airborne sound and was approaching the South Bank from downriver. The two men who had been in discussion pointed skywards and began to talk excitably between themselves, but I could not hear what they were saying above the din. The buzzing, the whirring continued to grow louder. Right at that moment, a piece of grit flew up and lodged in my left eye, so I could not see what was happening.

I closed my eyes and could feel my hair being ruffled by the wind whipping around me. My left eye was watering uncontrollably and I became preoccupied with trying to remove the piece of detritus from it. After a few seconds, thankfully, the grit came free and my eyesight cleared. Through streaming eyes and blurred vision, I saw a sheet of newspaper and a polystyrene cup being blown up against the barrier. They were soon followed by an unidentified black object caught in the downdraught and rolling directly towards me.

It was a bowler hat. I reached down, arrested its progress and immediately heard a loud male voice shouting.

"Oi! You!"

I soon learned that the words were being aimed towards me. The buzzing sound was fading now, but perhaps the man shouting thought I couldn't hear him properly as he raised his voice once more.

"Oi! That's right, it's you I'm talking to!"

I lifted my eyes to see a gentleman wearing a blue shirt and jeans striding purposefully towards me, while gripping onto a walkie talkie. For a moment, I thought a plainclothes policeman had caught up with me.

Behind the man with the walkie talkie, I could make out another figure now, tottering along in the same direction but at a much slower and more deliberate pace. He was wearing a black suit, white shirt and tie. The suit was precariously held in place against a rotund stomach by a single button. Hands in his pocket, he resembled a portly civil servant on a morning perambulation.

"Watch out," I heard another crew member in the vicinity whisper. "Here comes The Guv'nor."

Something directed my eyes towards the lining of the bowler hat I now held, towards the initials stitched thereon.

# A.H.

The initials confirmed that by some sort of miracle I had been guided into his presence.

As he approached, he addressed the man wielding the walkie talkie. His tone remained serene and placating, his face remained placid.

"Now, Terry. No need for raised voices. What seems to be the problem?"

"Well, it's this boy Mr. Hitchcock. I just wanted to make sure he didn't run off with your -"

"He's still here, isn't he?" Mr. Hitchcock said. "Let's not make a scene. We'll save that for in front of the camera. Besides, I'm sure he's the young man I've been expecting."

"Well, whoever he is, he won't let go of your hat."

I suppose I must have been gripping onto the bowler hat I had retrieved, still unable to comprehend the situation I had found myself drawn into.

"Should I get a policeman to help?" the man with the walkie talkie now asked.

It was a suggestion that seemed to momentarily fluster Mr. Hitchcock.

"I beg your pardon?" he managed to say.

"A copper... A bobby... There's bound to be one nearby."

Mr. Hitchcock baulked at the mention of the constabulary.

"No need for the police. My goodness, no." He collected himself, then addressed the man with the walkie talkie once more. "Terry, let's take a break. I think we're all feeling a little windswept after the helicopter shot. Could you check if Mr. Taylor is satisfied with how it went? And while the next shot is set up, I'll sit things out in the Rolls so my young friend here can get what he came for."

I promptly returned the bowler hat and without further ado was ushered past the crowd barrier by the man with the walkie talkie. He then proceeded to escort myself and Mr. Hitchcock through the film set, parting a way for us through the dozens of extras present.

"Are you here unaccompanied?" Mr. Hitchcock asked me as we walked, the unhurried pace of his voice matching the unhurried pace of his steps.

I nodded in reply.

"And where are your parents?"

"I'm here all on my own," was the only response I could muster before I was forced to step out of the path of a trolley loaded with sound equipment.

"I see... Well, young man. You certainly display initiative and a sense of independence... Two excellent attributes that will serve you well in this life."

I watched as the man with the walkie talkie nodded to Mr. Hitchcock, then walked off to another part of the location. Mr. Hitchcock now gestured towards a Rolls Royce, parked amid the bustle of the film set.

"Join me in the Silver Shadow, if you please."

Mr. Hitchcock gingerly opened the rear door on the passenger side and lowered himself gently into the commodious interior of the car. He placed the bowler hat on the seat beside him, then raised his head towards me.

"Could you possibly close the door for me and let yourself in around the other side, my boy?" he asked.

I did as he requested, then walked around to the other side of the Rolls and let myself in. Once inside, the background hum of the city was all but silenced.

As soon as he was comfortably reclined, Mr. Hitchcock took a long intake of breath, then began.

"Now then... My assistant should be along with refreshments shortly and after our little meeting of minds I must continue with the ordeal of today's shoot... You may be interested to know that I myself am taking on a small part in this scene as a shocked onlooker. I have to pretend to be horrified on seeing something foul floating in the Thames, which I don't think will present the greatest of acting challenges."

It may have had something to do with all the years of having to endure the hard wooden chairs of the classroom, as well as the hard wooden pews of the church. Whatever the reason, as I sat there adjacent to Mr. Hitchcock on the leather upholstery of the Silver Shadow, it felt close to the sensation of floating on a cloud.

Just then, there was a knock on the car window beside me, instantly acknowledged by Mr. Hitchcock.

"Ah, excellent service. Please, open the door would you, young man."

I did as he commanded. A middle-aged lady wearing glasses and a kindly smile leaned halfway into the car. She asked me to lower an arm rest located in the centre of the back seat and onto it she placed a silver tray. On the tray was a silver tea pot, milk jug and sugar bowl, a pair of china cups and saucers inscribed with a delicate filigree pattern, as well as a tall glass of milk. My eyes were drawn straight away, however, to a tempting selection of biscuits and cake which I had to force myself not to reach for at once.

"Shall I pour for you, Mr. Hitchcock?" the lady with the kindly smile asked.

"No, it's quite alright Maddy."

"Will there be anything else?"

"I don't think so. Myself and my new friend will begin soon."

Head bowed, the lady with the kindly smile then exited the scene.

"I'll be mother, shall I?" Mr. Hitchcock said, lifting the silver tea pot. As he poured the tea into one of the two china cups, I noticed a slight trembling uncertainty in the movement of his hands. When he finished pouring, he spoke again.

"I do apologise. I did not ask if you wanted tea or if you would prefer the glass of milk my glamorous assistant provided.

Would you prefer the milk?"

"Yes, Sir Alfred."

Mr. Hitchcock chuckled.

"Not a Sir... *Yet*." He placed a special emphasis the word yet. "I must say... I'm enormously flattered by the title you have bestowed upon me, but I don't think I have been forgiven for moving to America just before the war. Besides, when I think of 'Sir This' and 'Sir That' I tend to think of knights jousting in Technicolor and I'm not exactly suited for that, given my age and my frame... I do enjoy a spot of verbal jousting, however."

Already I was feeling mesmerised by that voice... How his accent still bore the faint but discernible sound of his East London origins... How he spoke with such precise enunciation... How vowel sounds in particular were lovingly lingered over, like a gourmand savouring a cordon bleu meal...

"Well... Drink up, young man."

I did as he asked of me and drank the milk. My escape from the book shop and through the underground had left me parched. Soon I had drained half the glass and had scoffed a couple of the biscuits on offer, relishing the exotic taste of dark chocolate and macadamia nuts.

"Please, eat every crumb," Mr. Hitchcock continued. "Regrettably, I have been expressly forbidden to touch any such delicacies. Doctor's orders."

He sighed volubly, lowered a tray that unfolded from the back of the front passenger seat, then carefully lifted his tea onto it.

"No expense has been spared. The refreshments come straight from Fortnam and Masons, I'll have you know... I am, I confess, a devotee of the finer things in life." Mr. Hitchcock sipped his tea. "Please do not go telling the powers that be at Universal Pictures that it is part of the catering budget, or they may have me removed from my picture. Can I rely on your complicity in this matter?"

I nodded, still savouring the texture of the biscuit dissolving in my mouth.

"Excellent. Now, do you have a notebook about your person, in case you need to jot anything down?" Mr. Hitchcock asked. "Is it secreted somewhere in that bag you are clinging onto as if it were a life raft?"

I shook my head.

"So you don't believe in taking notes." There was a slight jangle as he placed the china teacup back on the china saucer. "Commit it all to memory then, my boy. Try not to misquote me too much." He pivoted his head and looked directly at me. "I have my legacy to think of, you know."

I found myself hopelessly tongue-tied, still incredulous at my sudden proximity to Mr. Hitchcock. As I listened intently I managed to accommodate half a slice of Dundee cake within the walls of my mouth.

"Do you have any specific questions or would you like me to ramble on? I have a pre-rehearsed script I can recite for occasions such as this one. However… it is only fair that I warn you I can go on forever."

Mr. Hitchcock continued to talk, making every word, every syllable sound carefully measured out. Behind his rather formal manner, I sensed a depth of feeling within him.

"Well, all I can say is that I'll be more than obliging to give you what you came here for."

Mr. Hitchcock then took another long intake of breath and entered into a monologue. He assumed the role of the well-versed raconteur, while I was the lone captive member of his audience. I sat totally still, caught up in the cadence of his voice and his meticulous turn of phrase. And I did as he asked of me. I committed it all to memory…

"One of the most humbling and gratifying things about becoming a grand old man of the cinema is the acolytes one attracts. I just wish I was able to fully understand and answer all of their questions… Especially the French."

Like the older parishioners I would see in church, I couldn't help noticing the physical signs of ageing in Mr. Hitchcock. The slight slur in his voice… The thinning hair on top… The stray nostril and eyebrow hairs… The parchment-like skin… The general stealth of his movements… And his breathing, which had a gentle wheezing quality to it. But still, unmistakably so, there was an agile mind ticking over behind those brown burrowing eyes.

"The sort of question I don't care for is where do I get my ideas from? Another one is why are my killers such objects of sympathy?" He gestured towards The Houses of Parliament. "Yes, it is true. My killers are more charming, more likeable, than any of the salaried sociopaths in that building." He paused, and I saw his eyes visibly flicker as a thought occurred to him. "You know, as I look at our mother of parliaments, the layout of it reminds me a little of The Bates Motel. The main building could be the motel rooms where all manner of sordid business is committed, while Big Ben represents the gothic pile towering over the motel, home to Norman and Mrs. Bates." He paused once more, took a laboured breath and trembling fingers were placed on his temple. "Please… Forgive my ramblings. I suffer from acrophobia… Fear of heights and national monuments."

He took a moment to compose himself, then carried on.

"Where was I? Ah, yes. Questions… The questions I am confronted with time and time again. Well, I often have to contend with questions about my very particular working methods… Some people call me fastidious. I simply call it being correct. I am a belt and braces person and prefer to leave nothing to chance. And as you can see, today I am wearing both a belt and a pair of braces. I also never leave the house without an appropriate matching tie… Otherwise known as the noose of my profession."

Mr. Hitchcock allowed himself another sip of tea, he collected his thoughts and continued.

"The issue of my retirement is another question journalists never grow weary of raising. Well, I can only say that I will continue to make my pictures until my heart's not in it any more... And even then, I'm sure my heart could be fitted with a pacemaker... Don't go writing my obituary quite yet, young man, but when I dwell on the matter of my legacy I have come to the conclusion that, most likely, I will be remembered as the man who brought murder to the masses." He sighed. "Let me preface what I am about to say by stating that these strangulations in Leytonstone are a dreadful business... But it is true, I am a connoisseur of the fine art of murder. In my films, characters have been strangled... stabbed... shot... they have plummeted from great heights... been bludgeoned... slowly poisoned... they have been blown up... asphyxiated by gas and pecked to ribbons by birds. I plead guilty to all of these deaths... I have, I admit, enough blood on my hands for one man. It is how I have earned my blood money... So what is my greatest legacy?" Mr. Hitchcock turned to face me. "Murder... Never mind that murder is just one of the ingredients I add to my motion pictures. I also like a dash of suspense... glamour... the occasional joke to lighten to mood... stylish costumes... elegant designs. All the constituent parts are in my head as I plan the picture. I mull over the details, I allow my soul to get into the subject. And all along the ingredients are there in my head, waltzing together."

He laced his fingers together across his stomach.

"I've had my imitators and I'm told that I am the subject of various homages... Occasionally, I do ponder the issue of who will continue my work after I am gone. I have too many projects to complete and age is catching up with me. Time's winged chariot and so on. Who will continue my work? Perhaps you will, young man?"

As Mr. Hitchcock turned his head to regard me once again, I sensed he was imparting some secret knowledge to me.

"Now, however," he continued. "It is time to turn my attention to the business in hand… Show business… Do you want me to sign the copy of Mr. Truffaut's book that I see peeking out of your satchel?"

"Yes… Yes please."

I extracted the book from my satchel and handed it to Mr. Hitchcock. From inside his suit he withdrew a fountain pen and removed the top. He then opened the book to an early page which was largely blank, apart from a single small photograph. The photograph captured himself and Mr. Truffaut seated at a desk against a backdrop of panelled wood.

"Now, tell me your name young man."

I duly imparted the information to him. As he wrote, I again noticed the slight tremor in his hand.

"I hope you will find this to your satisfaction. I like to give inscriptions some thought."

He offered me a conspiratorial wink as he passed the manuscript back to me. I glanced at what he had written.

**To** █████████
**My Young Disciple**
**Best Wishes,**
**Alfred Hitchcock**

Above Mr. Hitchcock's signature, I saw that with eight deft strokes of his fountain pen, he had also added a bulbous-cheeked caricature of himself.

"Thank you," I managed to say.

"Now," Mr. Hitchcock said, glancing at his wrist watch. "I fear our allotted time is almost over. Is there anything else?"

My mind returned to the words he had uttered to me before he offered to sign the book. I spoke falteringly.

"How… should I… continue… your work?"

"Oh, I'm afraid I don't do the hiring around here. Besides, you're much too young to start your working life… However, that is a question I often get asked by the young people of today and I'm glad I can leave you with some solid advice." He formed the shape of a rectangle with the thumb and forefinger of both his hands, he raised the rectangle to his right eye, then turned to look at me and framed me within the rectangle. "Buy a camera... After a lifetime, I have reached the point where I don't even need to look through a viewfinder." He lowered his hands and continued his train of thought. "If you give me the focal length of a lens, I have the ability to visualise exactly what the camera will see. I have already viewed the film in my head before it is completed in the cutting room. And so, in a strange way, I feel I have the power of foresight... Listen to me very carefully now, young man... You must train yourself to identify with the camera... To see as I see... To calmly, objectively, view the drama of life and death."

As I sat pinned to the seat of the Silver Shadow, Mr. Hitchcock slowly moved the bulk of his body around until he was facing me. He raised his right hand to his eyes. Those glistening brown eyes, appearing to me like the sun reflecting off the swirling, silty Thames. He touched his eyelids with the second and third fingers of his right hand. He touched his eyelids, then began to extend his right hand towards me. The second and third fingers of his right hand were tracing a direct line from his eyes towards mine own eyes. I noticed his hands were no longer trembling.

"Remember this advice," he told me. "And you will begin to see as I see."

The two fingers of his right hand were now hovering above my own eyes.

"See as I see," Mr. Hitchcock said again.

I closed my eyes. Mr. Hitchcock's fingers continued to hover there.

"... See as I see..."

I could feel heat emanating from Mr. Hitchcock's fingers. I

could feel the energy leaving his fingers and entering my eyes.

"… See as I see…"

I could feel the energy leaving Mr. Hitchcock's fingers and entering my very being.

"… See as I see…"

I felt as if I was receiving a mysterious sacrament, a private benediction.

"… See as I see…"

At once, I felt an immense calm descend over me, as my body continued to be imbued with this unknowable force.

"… See as I see…"

My eyes still closed, in my inner world I began to feel as if I was drifting away on a cloud… Up, away from the Silver Shadow… Away from the assembled crowds on the South Bank… Along the course of the Thames.

"… See as I see…"

Further now… Tower Bridge was raising its bridge to salute me… I was floating through the billowing smoke issuing from the stack of a tug boat… I was drifting away from my troubles at the home, at the school… Suddenly it all seemed strangely irrelevant.

"… See as I see…"

I found myself drifting higher, passing through the clouds… I looked below me and for the first time shining there I saw it… The △… Mapped out beneath me…

"… See as I see…"

… I saw its area of influence extending from Bloomsbury Street in the north, down to Battersea Park and across to Camberwell Road… And at once I knew the power of The △ was real.

"… See as I see…"

A rapping on one of the car windows abruptly broke the spell. I opened my eyes and looked to my left. Mr. Hitchcock was sitting, fingers drowsily interlaced across his midriff. His eyes were half open and his lower lip was jutting out, revealing a row of teeth crowded together at abstract angles.

The lady with the kindly smile who had served the tea now opened his door.

"Mr. Hitchcock," she said. "They need you on the set in five minutes."

Mr. Hitchcock withdrew a handkerchief from an inside pocket and dabbed his mouth.

"I do apologise, Maddy. I think I was having a little moment there, shall we say. I must have drifted off."

How long had we, Mr. Hitchcock and I, been having this "little moment"? I don't know. I do know, however, that it was truly a meeting of minds. Our two minds, one young, one old, had waltzed with each other.

I watched as Mr. Hitchcock now slowly stirred himself back into action.

"Time to return to the director's chair, I'm afraid. Did you get what you came here for, young man?"

"Yes, Sir Alfred."

Mr. Hitchcock chuckled.

"There you go again, dubbing me a knight of the realm. Perhaps you now have the power of foresight also?"

"Calling you Sir Alfred... I believe it will come true."

"Whatever will be will be, young man... Rather a fatalistic saying, don't you think? I prefer to at least try to control my own destiny and that of my characters." His eyes flickered with the onset of an idea once again. "You know, I'm sure there is a critic somewhere now writing a treatise on the theme of predestination versus free will in that popular Doris Day song... Or some such nonsense."

Suddenly, the meeting was over, I was stepping out of the Silver Shadow and in a daze I was being escorted back to the crowd barrier by Mr. Hitchcock and the lady with the kindly smile.

"I will say goodbye to you now," Mr. Hitchcock confided to

me as we walked together. "I'm sure I will see you again. Look for me... I'll be among the coming attractions."

Approaching the edge of the location, I spotted a smartly turned-out young man in a school uniform. He was perhaps a year or two older than me, carrying a shorthand notebook and talking to the man with the walkie talkie.

"Mr. Hitchcock," the man with the walkie talkie said as we drew close. "This is the schoolboy who has come to interview you."

"Oh... but I've already –," Mr. Hitchcock gestured towards me. "Oh dear... I think this falls into the category of a mistaken identity... Raised eyebrows all around." He then shrugged his shoulders. "No matter. I made my choice."

And with that, Mr. Hitchcock shuffled away to continue the day's shoot.

I felt the eyes of the smartly turned-out schoolboy glaring at me as I walked away from the film set and I am sure I heard the word "impostor" being called out in my direction. I was oblivious, however, to any sense of injustice he may have been feeling. My mind was otherwise occupied in the wake of my preordained meeting.

I was just beginning to sense the full import of what Mr. Hitchcock had said to me, of what he had bestowed unto me.

"... See as I see..."

I left the South Bank behind and walked back onto Westminster Bridge. I approached the first policeman I spotted and informed him I was a runaway. With Mr. Hitchcock's words echoing in my head, I felt ready to face up to anything that would be awaiting me back at the home...

△

... Within a matter of hours, I found myself sitting in the darkened interior of Father Tobin's office. Father Tobin himself was seated behind his desk on a swivel-chair. For a minute or more he had been drumming his fingers on a leather-bound gilt-edged copy of The Bible.

As he prepared to address me, Father Tobin stopped drumming his fingers. His eyebrows visibly bristled.

"You know why you're here, don't you?"

I nodded.

"And this is your first time in my study, is it not?"

"Yes, Father."

"Despite the fact that this is your first infraction, I am afraid I cannot allow myself to be lenient. Your guardian angel Sister Attracta has pleaded your case oh-so-very-eloquently, as she has done before on your behalf. She informs me that you are inordinately upset at her having to leave our establishment. Your sin, however, is a serious one. To steal yourself away from here, to wander off into the night away from the place that has cared for you for so many years. I need you to realise the gravity of your offence... Where did you sleep last night?"

"In a park."

Father Tobin briefly pondered my response.

"We have had runaways before, you know. Most, it has to be said, lasted longer than you. So I can only imagine the glimpse you had of the world outside these walls, of the real world, was one you did not like."

"Yes, Father."

Father Tobin lowered his eyebrows.

"The real world is cruel, boy. The real world will crush you with its indifference. The real world is hard and unforgiving, especially to a boy like you with your difficulties and disadvantages. Now, listen to me. I have watched you during our services... I have watched how you have conducted yourself when carrying out your altar boy duties... You show promise...

With some instruction, I think you could be a candidate for the priesthood. The church is always on the lookout for new disciples. Think of what we have done for you here. Think of what you may have been without our influence... I want you to keep that in mind."

"Yes, Father."

"... Now, I need you to stand up."

I did as he requested of me. Father Tobin himself stood up and came out from behind his desk. Briefly turning his back, he leaned over to his left and reached into an umbrella stand positioned in the corner of his room. When he faced me once again, he was holding a two-foot length of cane. He spoke gravely.

"... Now, I need you to hold out your right hand."

Again, I did what was asked of me. Father Tobin ensured the palm of my hand was as flat as possible, then he raised the cane. Hanging on the wood-panelled wall directly in my line of vision was a portrait of Pope Paul VI, towards which I focused all my attention. There were a couple of swipes in midair, then ten swipes landed on my hand in swift succession. The repeated impact of the cane stung, no doubt, but the pain was not as bad as I had anticipated over all those years of having witnessed the punishment being dealt out to others. Father Tobin was, I sensed, more than a little unnerved by how unmoved I was by the discipline he had meted out. Slightly out of breath from his exertions with the cane, he promptly dismissed me.

As I left Father Tobin's study, a minor jolt went through me when I saw Mr. Drew seated outside in the waiting area. He did not speak to me when I passed by, but lifted his eyes and fixed me with a watery gaze. I continued to walk further up the corridor, then cast a glance back over my shoulder. It was just in time to catch sight of the door closing behind the slightly cowed figure of Mr. Drew as he was escorted into Father Tobin's study.

A few days passed. In the classroom, Mr. Drew seemed to look through me or ignore me and his overall demeanour was more subdued than usual.

The following Friday, I made the grave mistake of bringing my copy of *Hitchcock* by Truffaut to class for a reading period. The previous day, I had removed the dust jacket and replaced it with one from another book I had borrowed from the school library, a collection of tales by Edgar Allen Poe.

Maybe the dust jacket was too ill-fitting, but somehow Mr. Drew deduced that I was not reading *Tales of Mystery and Imagination*. At the end of the day, while the other pupils filed out, he halted me.

"Who are you now, *The Man Who Collected Poe*?" He prised the book off me, opened it and looked at the interior. "This is not from the school library, is it?"

"No," I replied.

"Where did you get it?"

I answered that I had saved up for it. I answered that I had bought it with the money I had earned from my altar boy duties.

Mr. Drew flicked through the book until he came upon the page Mr. Hitchcock had signed.

"What is this signature? Where did you get this? Where did you go when you ran away? Where did you go? Where?!"

With each unanswered question, Mr. Drew's voice ratcheted up in intensity.

"It's my book," I replied firmly. "Mr. Hitchcock signed it for me. I met him on his film set. We talked together and he signed the book for me."

Perhaps Mr. Drew was surprised at the forcefulness of my own voice, for he said nothing more, handed the book back to me and I was free to exit the classroom.

He was not finished with me, however. That night, Mr. Drew stole into my dormitory while I slept. He bound my hands with cord and gagged my mouth. He lifted my copy of *Hitchcock* by Truffaut and forced me barefoot from my bed.

"I forgot to tell you," he whispered into my ear. "As part of your punishment, Tobin banned me from showing any more movies… But I think you deserve one last screening."

He took me, grabbed me by the arm and dragged me along silent corridors, then outside and towards the church. He paid no attention to my whimpered protests when he forced me to walk across the rough tarmac without shoes. Once inside the dimly-lit interior of the church, Mr. Drew pulled me in the direction of the aisle. Raising my eyes towards the front of the church, I saw that Mr. Drew had set up the projector there before the altar.

He sat me down on a chair facing the projector. Immediately it struck me that I was sitting directly in front of the projector lens, the lens that under normal circumstances would be aimed at the screen. Mr. Drew was panting heavily and his forehead was glazed with sweat. He allowed himself a little time for his breathing to come under control, then began.

He held my book aloft.

"Who… who do you think you are with your secret day trips to film sets and your book signings? Who the *hell* do you think you are? These are serious transgressions."

There was an unnerving, agitated tone to his voice.

"And what exactly did you tell Tobin? What did you tell him? Why couldn't you just stay silent? You know he's accused me of putting ideas in your head… He says he might not want me back next year. He says my job is on the line. How would I live, then?"

Mr. Drew dropped the book at his feet and then seated himself on the pew nearest to the altar. His voice changed now, assuming a chilly neutral tone.

"*How* would I live?… *Why* should I live?… Why should *anyone* live?… To be alive… It's a sort of hell, isn't it?"

Mr. Drew appeared to stare at the stain glass window above the altar, but he could just as easily have been staring into empty space at that moment.

"Do you ever wonder when all this is going to end?"

I shook my head.

"I do," he continued. "And secretly I yearn for the end of everything... The buildings, civilisation, humanity, the whole rotten façade... I've found myself dwelling on the subject quite a bit lately... The horrible flux of this life... Atoms smashing against atoms for no discernible purpose... The inevitable entropy of it all... Do you know there's a black hole at the centre of the universe and that's where we're all going to end up one day? Down the cosmic plughole... Sometimes when I go back to my flat, I light a candle, I turn out the lights, I empty my mind and imagine it is the last dying light in the universe... Then, after some time, I snuff out the candle and I let the darkness settle over me... Do you know that feeling yet? I will teach you about it."

As he continued to stare into nothingness, Mr. Drew's eyes took on the lifeless appearance of a waxworks figure.

"What kills me about the whole situation is that deep down I'm a people person... I really am... I like people... And I like women... So why don't they like me? It's not fair, really... That's why he does the things he does... The Strangler."

He directed his empty gaze towards me.

"By the way, it's time to meet him... The Strangler... Are you ready?"

I watched as Mr. Drew regarded me with his unblinking, glassy eyes... I watched and I witnessed him begin to change... I watched him take on the persona of The Strangler... I could only sit, powerless, and listen as The Strangler narrowed his eyes at me and began to speak in tones devoid of any feeling.

"I don't know why I want to confess everything to you," he said. "But I do... I suppose I just want somebody to understand what it's really like to be me... A miscreant soul... Somebody has to understand... Mr. Hitchcock, I've a feeling he would understand... If I had met him, I would've told him everything...

**65**

I would've told him how his work has inspired me... I would've told him how I like the look on their faces when the penny drops and they realise what's about to happen... Yes, they struggle and they fix you with their pleading eyes... Eyes full of anger and outrage and fear... But finally there is always a beautiful, calm surrender... I've witnessed the whole gamut of emotions play out on their faces... And I enjoy arousing the emotions of these women... These people." He paused. "People... with their insignificant little lives... As if they matter... As if any of this matters... You'll learn that it doesn't matter... I've had a bellyful of people... People like Tobin... They try to put the fear of God into you... But that is not an emotion I feel any more... Real fear is fear of the man sitting quietly behind you on the tube... Real fear is fear of the man loitering with intent in the corner of your vision... Real fear is fear of the man in front of you now... I will teach you about fear... That's why I'm here, isn't it? To teach you... You're not the first one I've taught... There have been others."

The Strangler moved closer.

"However, you are the only one to know about my identity... Which, in a strange way, makes you my accomplice... Nobody else suspects... Not one sinner... But I know my secret is safe with you... I know you'll not tell anyone... I'll make sure of it."

The Strangler then took a couple of paces towards the projector.

"I've been very methodical, you see... I've disposed of all the evidence back at my flat and in the boot of my car."

The Strangler flicked a switch on the projector. A blinding light blasted from the lens, accompanied by an airburst of heat. I immediately averted my eyes. The Strangler addressed me once more.

"Tonight's feature presentation is *The Lodger*... I want you to look directly into the light of the projector... I want you to keep your eyes directed towards the light... Do not avert your eyes from the light."

Before I knew what was happening, The Strangler had me pinned down. Even if I managed to close my eyes momentarily, the searing brightness proved impossible to escape.

"Keep your eyes open!" he commanded me.

There was no escape from The Strangler. No escape from the searching glare of the projector's light. From out of the light, the opening scenes of *The Lodger* began to play.

*It began with a silent scream.*

And then at some point, The Strangler's hands encircled my neck from behind and closed firmly around it. He was beginning to throttle me.

*It began with the face of a female murder victim, frozen in mute terror as the life was being squeezed out of her.*

I could feel my windpipe being constricted. I could feel my eyes bulging. My arms struggled against the cord binding me, my entire body struggled, but The Strangler was too powerful for me.

From out of the pulsing light, a sign…

**TO-NIGHT "GOLDEN CURLS"**

And all the time the blinding light of the projector continued to shine into my eyes. I felt the searing heat of the light. I felt the heat like I had felt the heat radiating from Mr. Hitchcock's fingers as they hovered over my eyes, imparting his advice to me.

"… See as I see…"

And momentarily the light appeared to me like one immense, coiling optic nerve… An optic nerve fashioned from countless strands of dazzling blonde hair, the light carried within the strands streaming past me streaming through me.

**TO-NIGHT "GOLDEN CURLS"**

There was a high-pitched throbbing in my head, almost like a sound produced by a theremin or Trautonium. And suddenly the light spoke to me. It whispered to me from out of the darkness and I heard its call.

I opened my eyes wider and I welcomed the blinding embrace

of the light.

The light was shining on me and I was in and of the light spilling out of the darkness, spilling out of that miraculous machine. It went into me, through me and it spoke to me. At first, the blinding light was all I could see. But then I saw them, moving through the light towards me... Mr. Hitchcock's fingers were there, hovering just above my eyes.

"... See as I see..."

And I saw it. In my inner world I saw The △.

"... See as I see..."

It was followed by a vision of a pair of feet... A pair of feet dressed in light blue socks with red toes... A pair of feet dropping... Dropping through the air, coming to an abrupt violent halt and then dangling mid-air.

"... See as I see..."

All this time, The Strangler's grip was getting tighter around my neck and I was desperately struggling for air... And then from out of the light I began to hear a voice inside my head... It was whispering the same word over and over to me.

"... strangle... strangle... strangle... strangle..."

It was Mr. Hitchcock's voice.

His voice was the last thing I remembered before I blacked out...

... I cannot be sure how long I was unconscious for. When I finally came around, the lights in the church were on and I was on the floor being cradled by Sister Attracta. She was in a night dress and the spiralling ringlets of her blonde hair were draping over me. She did not speak, but her face expressed great concern as she gently removed the gag from around my mouth, the cord from around my wrists.

Nearby, Father Tobin was standing surveying the scene with a look of incredulity on his face. I watched as he turned and then began to interrogate Mr. Drew, trying in vain to keep his voice at a low register.

"What is the meaning of this... this desecration?!"

The projector was lying on its side, spewing its light onto the figure of Mr. Drew, who was in the process of trying to get himself to his feet. I saw his face was bruised and a line of blood was trickling down from where his head had connected with something hard. He began to speak in an agitated tone, loudly gesticulating towards me.

"The boy, he... he lost control and attacked me! It was unprovoked! It's the truth! The boy... he's a monster! He needs to be restrained, locked up! He needs to be sent to a borstal!"

My head was throbbing. As I lay there on the floor of the church in Sister Attracta's arms, as she rubbed my forehead consolingly, I felt a powerful sensation come over me. There was one all-consuming thought in my head. I concentrated my mind... I held the thought... I focused my mind and aimed it towards Mr. Drew as he raised himself to his feet, as he lumbered down the aisle and exited the scene... I could feel it emanating from me, like the light from the projector.

Under the strain of the effort, I lost consciousness again...

... Sister Attracta left the home quietly on Saturday morning. While I lay in my dormitory bed recuperating, a fellow nun approached and confided that she did not take her leave without ensuring that my condition was improved.

Despite the unholy drama that had played out in the church overnight, no mention was made of the events to me that Saturday and no outside authorities were informed. It was as if nothing untoward had happened. Like silently administered sedatives, normality and routine were allowed to return to the home.

After a few more hours of being bed-ridden, I felt I had had enough recuperation. And so I got up and readied myself. I readied myself for my regular appointment with the confessional.

I was the last boy to be heard that evening. Once inside the vacant confessional booth, I knelt down. From the other side I could hear the muffled words of absolution being uttered, followed by the sound of the door of the opposite booth being opened and then closed.

Suddenly the slat in front of me was slid across, revealing the darkened figure of Father Tobin in profile, barely visible through the interstices of the grill which separated us. I began.

"Bless me Father, for I have sinned. It has been one week since my last confession."

There was a slow release of air from Father Tobin's nostrils and it was his turn to speak. I could just make out the silhouette of his mouth moving.

"… Tell me your sins."

I went through a pre-scripted catalogue of my misdemeanours… I neglected to say my night-time prayers… I had allowed my mind to wander during mass… I also made sure to acknowledge my willful act of truancy against the school. I was sure I had covered all of my deeds, but had deliberately chosen not to speak of one. Given the surfeit of iniquities I had already admitted to, I had decided not to confess the theft of the book.

Father Tobin was silent for a moment. There was another slow release of nasal air and he addressed me again.

"… Do you have anything else to tell me, child?"

I allowed myself a few seconds to think, then replied.

"No, Father."

"… Do you have anything to share with me about the occasions on which you have been alone with Mr. Drew?"

"… I do not, Father."

"… Remember, if you fail to tell me something that you should, you are committing a sin of omission. I am here for you, my child. If you feel the need to unburden yourself… I will ask you one final time if you have anything to tell me."

Behind the chilly formality there was, I believe, an attempt to reach out and to perhaps make some clumsy form of reparation over what had happened with Mr. Drew. However, I was now more certain than ever that I could not place my faith in any earthly form of justice that Father Tobin or anyone else could offer. I answered him.

"No, Father."

I heard a sigh of resignation escape from Father Tobin. He muttered some words of absolution, then prompted me to recite the requisite five Hail Marys for my penance and I was free to go.

I did not move from the confessional, however. Something was holding me back. I spoke to Father Tobin again.

"Father?"

"You can leave now, my child."

"… Father."

"Have you finally taken to being deaf? I said you could leave."

"Father… It is your turn to confess to me."

"What is it you are saying?"

"… Confess to me."

"Get out!"

It was the first time I had heard a raised voice in the confessional.

"… Confess to me."

I aimed my mind towards Father Tobin, as I had aimed my mind towards Mr. Drew. I could see him struggling on the other side of the grill. I could see his shoulders, his head shuddering. I continued to aim my mind towards him and, in time, the words came to him.

"It was I who found you that night… You could've so easily perished… I remember hearing the crying outside… I remember the trail of blood in the virgin snow leading away from the basket you were abandoned in… I remember how blue your face was and how the colour slowly started to come back to your face when your body was placed in a warm bath… I don't know who your mother was… but you were born of sin and shame, child… Whoever she was, she wasn't long for this world of that I'm sure… I have tried to help you, but I fear your ungodly origins mean you are beyond help."

I had heard enough. I left the trembling figure of Father Tobin behind, exited the confessional and knelt in the pew nearest to the altar. As I knelt there before the altar, I emptied my mind of extraneous thoughts. I gazed up at the carving of Jesus and that sorrowful expression etched permanently onto his face. I gazed at those eyes forever directed towards the firmament. As I knelt there before the altar I began to recite the words I needed to recite.

The atmosphere in the church was one of hushed serenity. A small handful of parishioners were dotted around the interior, quietly praying or lighting candles. Briefly, the silence was interrupted by the sound of Father Tobin staggering out from the confessional. His footsteps sounded unsteady on the tiled floor as he made his way towards the altar, towards the sacristy, avoiding any glimpse of me. I noticed him dabbing his forehead with a handkerchief as a trickle of black hair dye threatened to run into his eyes.

I continued to recite the words I needed to recite. I was not reciting my penance, however. Instead, I was concentrating my mind towards Mr. Drew. My mentor, my tormentor… I was aiming my words towards him…

"… strangle… strangle… strangle… strangle…"

I sensed he was close by… I sensed that he would no longer do me any harm… I would make sure of that…

"… strangle… strangle… strangle… strangle…"

I aimed my words towards him as he entered the church…

"… strangle… strangle… strangle… strangle…"

I aimed my words towards him as he slowly ascended the narrow wooden stairs to the bell tower…

"… strangle… strangle… strangle… strangle…"

I aimed my words towards him as he entered the bell tower carrying a length of rope…

"… strangle… strangle… strangle… strangle…"

I aimed my words towards him as he firmly attached one end of the rope around the horizontal yoke of the bell…

"… strangle… strangle… strangle… strangle…"

I aimed my words towards him as he removed his shoes, then placed the noose around his neck and advanced towards the small arched window in the bell tower…

"… strangle… strangle… strangle… strangle…"

Inside the nave of the church, heads turned when the bell was heard to ring out just once. Father Tobin was approaching the sacristy door when he also turned his head in the direction of the hollow sound. The ringing of the church bell was unscheduled, not part of the normal routine.

Heads turned, but my head remained facing forward, towards the altar and the carved statue of Jesus. And then, from outside, the scream of an onlooker could be heard. There was a rush to attend to the body that had been seen plummeting through the window of the bell tower. A body now hanging mid-air, its feet dressed in light blue socks with red toes.

Ladies and gentlemen of my captive jury, I had committed my first murder. I had brought the career of The Leytonstone Strangler to an end. It was the work of a talented amateur and it was to be the closest I would get to staging a killing on top of a national monument.

That night, during my last screening with Mr. Drew, that is when it happened. As I directed my mind towards Mr. Drew, I was delivering him a death sentence. I had sabotaged his mind. I had placed an idea in his head, primed and ready to go off at any moment.

Looking into the light of the projector that night, I believe something extraordinary was imparted to me. Certain gifts. Gifts I would have to summon time and again in the years that lay ahead.

As I kneeled in the church, I had but the faintest glimmering comprehension of what had been bestowed upon me that night as I looked into the light of the projector.

Now, however, I know.

I was reborn in the light of the projector.

I was reborn as The Avenger.

On the screen before us, another door materialises. Mr. Memory opens the door and we enter it together, you and I…

In the days that followed Mr. Drew's death, I would listen in on the hushed adult conversations that played out in the corridors of the home or around the church. Normally, the conversation followed a predictable pattern and the words would be accompanied by a slow, downcast shaking of heads.

"Will he have a funeral?"

"I don't know… Not at this church, anyway."

"Taking your own life, it's a mortal sin isn't it?"

"It is… And the soul of a person who dies in mortal sin descends into hell."

As the adult voices continued to whisper in subdued shock, I listened in silence and I remained the only one to know the truth. The truth that another untraceable hand was behind Mr. Drew's death. He had died at the hands of The Avenger.

Over time, however, the hushed conversations would die away and I would spare Mr. Drew little or no more thought. Instead, I found my mind ceaselessly ruminating on the unique gifts that had been bestowed upon me. At first, I was fearful of them. Very quickly, however, I came to a decision. I resolved that my gifts should be used selectively. I resolved that if ever I should have to call on them again, I could not allow my emotions to get the better of me.

With the experience gained over years of solitude and self-discipline, I have trained myself in the art of summoning my gifts. I think of this "summoning" a little like tuning into an old analogue radio station. I focus my mind, I try to make my thoughts as clear as crystal and with continued concentration I can attune my mind to the proper wavelength. Thus, when certain of my thoughts attain the proper intensity, I can call upon my gifts.

But wait… I sense you may be responding to the mention of

77

my gifts with a degree of incredulity. As I eavesdrop on your innermost thoughts, I suspect you would concur with my psychotherapist Dr. Legatore and his initial diagnosis of me as *non compos mentis*.

Believe me when I say I empathise with this point of view. Believe me also when I say that the exact source of my gifts remains an impenetrable mystery, even to me. It is a mystery I have never fully managed to solve. And so, ladies and gentlemen, may I plead your clemency? May I humbly request that you perhaps reserve a sliver a faith for the abilities of your narrator?

I, you narrator, have faith. I have faith that my meeting with Mr. Hitchcock was not a coincidence. I have faith that it was all part of some unknowable design. I was under the spell of Mr. Hitchcock when he acted as a guide to unlocking something within me. Something that had been lying dormant inside my being.

In the years that followed, I struggled with them. I tried to ignore them. I even denied their very existence. However, as I sit here alone, captive and confined, in this my darkest hour, I can finally say I have complete faith in the power of my gifts...

Meantime, unbeknownst to me, my circumstances were about to change. Since our encounter in the confessional, Father Tobin had kept his distance and continued to look at me askance. No further mention of the priesthood was made to me and soon word was sent that I was to be relieved of my altar boy duties. Behind the scenes, it turned out, Father Tobin was beginning to make strenuous efforts towards securing my departure from the home.

I recall the whole procedure rather vaguely, but I soon found myself entering the adoption system. Other people alongside Father Tobin were also involved in the process. These other people normally wore grey suits and came armed with briefcases and biros. Perhaps it was the special urgency Father Tobin placed on my case, but it took a surprisingly short time for the powers that be to locate a new home for me.

Let the record show that his name was Mr. Reginald H. Smith, resident at Ambrose Road, London N5. On our first encounter, he inspected me cautiously at a distance with his hands behind his back. Wearing a trim, bespoke suit, he rocked on the heels of his shoes and addressed me thus.

"My, my, you're a growing boy. Our grocery bill is going to go through the roof."

I noted his rodent-like face, his fruity accent and his pencil moustache.

"You're going to come and live with us," he continued with his nose cocked in the air. "We have a large garden and you can have a room of your own to do with as you please. All I ask is that you mind your p's and q's... Well, what's your answer?"

I knew I had no choice in the matter, so did not complain when Father Tobin spoke up on my behalf.

"His answer is yes."

"Well, it's all decided then," Mr. Smith announced with an air of finality.

A matter of days later, the transaction was all signed off and my time at the home was suddenly over.

It was a balmy day in late summer that Mr. Smith rolled up in his Jaguar to chauffeur me to his house. I had prepared as best I could, gathering up a few prized possessions and placing them in my satchel, before I had to leave the home behind forever.

Once I had settled in the passenger seat, Mr. Smith pulled on a pair of leather driving gloves, then told me to secure my seat belt.

"Clunk click every trip, as the funny fellow on the telly says."

During the course of the journey, Mr. Smith proceeded to inform me of his car's stand-out features.

"This is a top-of-the-range Jaguar XJ6... It has air conditioning, power-assisted steering, leather upholstery, all mod cons. Believe me, if I could fit a toilet in, I would."

"... It's a very nice car," I responded.

Mr. Smith's driving gloves tightened their grip on the steering wheel.

"It's better than nice... It's top-of-the-range."

It was a few miles further into the journey before he spoke again.

"Not much of a talker, are you? You'll get on well with my missus then. She couldn't come to see you in your, er, natural environment because she has her problems... That's what I'm hoping you'll be able to help her with. Her problems... She has her irrational moods, you see."

As if to change the subject, Mr. Smith reached over and turned a knob on the dashboard.

Just as he said "Let's see what's on the radio," a DJ began to introduce Charles Jolly singing 'The Laughing Policeman.'

"Oh, I like this one," Mr. Smith remarked as he turned the volume up and began to whistle along tunelessly.

Accompanied by the loud guffaws of 'The Laughing Policeman' and Mr. Smith's whistling, the Jaguar took a left turn. Suddenly, I found myself being propelled through a set of gates and along a gravelly driveway. At the end of the driveway was a large two-storey property with an exterior fashioned in the Mock Tudor style.

Mr. Smith brought the Jaguar to a halt in front of a metallic garage door. With the engine still idling, he applied the handbrake and then asked me to open the glove compartment.

"Do you see that big grey plastic gizmo with the button on it?"

"Yes," I answered.

"Do me a favour. Take it out of the glove compartment, point it at the garage door and press the button, would you?"

I did as Mr. Smith asked of me. I pressed the button on the big grey plastic gizmo and before my eyes, the garage door began to raise itself up.

"The bloke in the shop said I was the very first customer to purchase a garage door remote control," Mr. Smith let me know. "I've always been something of a gadget man."

Mr. Smith proceeded to drive his Jaguar XJ6 slowly into the garage. With another click of the remote control, the garage door began to slide shut. Mr. Smith then switched the engine off, removed his driving gloves and turned towards me.

"Welcome to your new home... It'll certainly beat slumming it at Father Tobin's or Nobby's Lodging House, am I right? Now, grab your stuff and I'll give you the grand tour."

I did as Mr. Smith asked of me, exited the car and had a brief chance to survey the generously proportioned interior of the garage.

"We'll start the tour here. This is the garage *slash -*" he made a precise diagonal swipe with his left hand to accompany the word "- wine cellar. Who says drinking and driving don't go together, eh? Now, try and keep up."

With barely a pause, Mr. Smith turned and walked a few paces towards an access door. He opened it and I duly followed him through. The door opened onto the spacious ground floor of the house, wherein the Mock Tudor style was in further evidence. Mr. Smith then proceeded to show me around the various downstairs rooms. His technique was, at best, cursory and basically involved him pointing at objects in each room as we breezed through.

"Well, here we are in the living room... Colour television... Axminster carpet... Three piece suite... Into the lounge... Over here we have a modern hi-fi centre and some long playing records belonging to the missus... Too many if you ask me... Here we have the dining room... Try not to scratch the mahogany dining table... Over there is the drinks cabinet, which you're much too young to know about... Keep up, keep up, not going too fast am I?... Here's the kitchen, where we have a modern refrigerator and so on... To be honest, I leave the Fanny Craddock side of things to the missus... She seems to enjoy that at least... Now, into the hall... Mind the pot plants... Always make sure to give your feet a good wipe on the mat before you come in, it's one of the house rules we have that I'm sure you'll pick up along the way... Now, onwards and upwards."

Mr. Smith then led me upstairs and onto a large first floor landing, carpeted in rich shades of red. Four doors led off from the landing, which he pointed out to me one by one.

"Here is where you will be sleeping," he said, gesturing towards the second door on the left. "There's a bathroom across the way with a hot and cold shower I just had put in last year." He cocked a thumb towards another door. "Myself and the missus sleep over there in the master bedroom and..." he lingered outside the room nearest the top of the stairs, his hand hovering for a few seconds over the door handle. "Oh... It would appear that I seem to have forgotten one of the house rules... I forgot that *this* is a locked door."

He swiftly withdrew his hand from the door handle, then ushered me into my new bedroom.

"The missus is having one of her afternoon naps, I'm afraid." Mr. Smith hovered restlessly in the doorway. "Still, why don't you make yourself at home. Dinner will be at six sharp."

With that, Mr. Smith closed the door behind him and my grand tour was over.

I spent most of the remaining afternoon in the bedroom, arranging the meagre possessions I had brought with me from the home. I should have felt a degree of relief at having escaped the home. I should have felt a degree of happiness at having a room to myself for the first time. Perhaps it was the unfamiliar surroundings or the curt behaviour of Mr. Smith, but a sense of uneasiness settled over me. Matters were not helped when, at one point, I was privy to a brief conversation conducted on the landing between Mr. and Mrs. Smith and an anxious female voice was heard to say...

"What have you brought into this house? I did not agree to

this."

Later, seated around the mahogany dining table, I was introduced to Mrs. Smith. She was a slight figure, plainly dressed, with long auburn hair shielding most of her face. I took some solace in not hearing her voice any further misgivings about my presence. In fact, she stayed largely silent while she served a roast dinner, allowing Mr. Smith ample opportunity to fill me in on the details of his professional life. He was, by his own admission, a highly successful businessman who owned a factory that manufactured bathroom furniture... baths, basins, washstands, bidets and, of course, toilets.

Mr. Smith's chosen line of business was something that provided him with no end of amusement. It was also the source of some visible annoyance to Mrs. Smith as she listened to him talk during that first dinner. It proved to be the first of many dinner table encounters where Mr. Smith would hold court as if he were addressing an AGM.

"Did you know I supplied your friend Father Tobin with new toilets for his organisation? Was after a discount he was too. I mean, can you credit it? Unbelievable, with all the money floating around those religious organisations and the baskets being passed around every Sunday." He gestured towards me with his fork in the air. "Don't get me wrong, I admire the bare-faced hypocrisy of him and his ilk in a strange sort of way, but I can assure you you won't find me hanging off any altar rails."

I soon learned that the fork was held in the air if Mr. Smith wanted to make an especially important point.

"It's a dirty business I'm in, boy," he proceeded to inform me while chewing on a medallion of beef. "But it's meat and drink to me. This house, the fortunes of this family, are built on people's evacuations. People's leavings going down the drain means money for me."

Looking back, I remember those first weeks in my new home

mostly as one long, extended monologue from Mr. Smith outlining his business philosophy. I would listen politely, even as my eyes could not avoid the remnants of food that would invariably linger around the corner of his mouth. And while Mr. Smith spoke volubly on the subject of how toilets were intimately tied up with his fortunes, Mrs. Smith's ongoing silence spoke volumes.

"Just think, my dear," he would say in the general direction of his wife. "Every time someone has to spend a penny it pays for the upkeep of this house. Every penny counts... You know, I had a chap in the office today who wanted to show me a prototype of a toilet with some kind of silent flushing mechanism. And do you know what I did? I threw him out on his ear, that's what I did. Do you want to know why? Because the sound of a toilet flushing is the most beautiful sound to me. It's music to my ears. Can't you hear it?" He cupped a hand to his ear. "It's the sound of money sloshing around the u-bend. It's the sound of money coming into this house. It's the sound of free trade." Mr. Smith held his fork aloft once more. "It's the sound of capitalism."

When in full flow, Mr. Smith proved himself to be a veritable lavatorial lexicon, peppering his scatological monologues with as many variations on toilet-related words as he could muster. He missed no opportunity to trot out the relevant words from his vocabulary and at times his whole act seemed as carefully worked out as a music hall routine. *Ablutions* was one of his favourites, but his glossary also encompassed repeated use of such words as *bog*, *crapper*, *gents*, *john*, *khazi*, *little boy's room*, *latrine*, *outhouse*, *privy*, *throne* and *W.C.*

"My mind may be in the toilet bowl," he would often say. "But my eyes are fixed upwards on the stars... There I go quoting literature again. Who was it said that, was it a homo? Sounds like something a homo would say. I hope they don't teach you that in school, boy. Speaking of which... We could well afford to send you to a private school, but we won't be doing that. The local comprehensive will keep you grounded. There's no high-flying ideas or airs and graces in my household, but if you *are* interested in joining *The Brains Trust*, we have a complete set of *Encyclopedia Britannica* gathering dust in the lounge. I've never looked at them myself. The missus, she got swindled into buying them by a door to door salesman."

Each meal time would end the same way. Mrs. Smith would tidy away the dishes, while Mr. Smith would lean back in his chair and proceed to pick his teeth with a tie pin.

"Everyone has their little rituals," he would say. "My old man, he used to take out his RAF tie pin and use it to remove his Sunday lunch from between his incisors. That was his little ritual. The missus, she has her own little rituals too… as I am sure you will learn."

In that respect, Mr. Smith was correct. For most of the time, he would either be behind his desk at the factory or away on lengthy business trips that took him up and down the country. And so it was I found myself sharing the house with Mrs. Smith for long periods.

Mrs. Smith was a quiet soul and we kept our own separate routines during those first weeks. Often, I would sit in my bedroom and listen to her shuffling about the house as she went about her endless cleaning duties. Often, I would listen as she would put on a recording from her collection of classical music. Only at mealtimes would we meet up and even then she remained monosyllabic and always avoided eye contact.

I was lying awake in bed one night, a month or more into my residence, when I heard the muffled sound of Mrs. Smith's footsteps on the landing carpet. The footsteps came to a halt near the top of the stairs and then I could hear the sound of a key being inserted into a lock. The door of the room beside mine, the locked room, was being opened and Mrs. Smith was entering inside. I heard the door being discreetly closed and then there was the sound of the key being turned once again. It would not be the last occasion Mrs. Smith would spend the night behind the doors of the locked room.

A couple of nights later, around the same time, I awoke and felt the need to pay a visit to the little boy's room. On my return across the landing, my eyes were drawn towards the door of the locked room. I could not help but notice that tonight the door was unlocked. It lay slightly ajar and a dim light was filtering through the vertical chink before me. Stealthily, I approached the door and saw Mrs. Smith's key still inserted in the UNICA lock. I peered through the gap and made sure there was nobody inside. Remaining vigilant, I stepped into the locked room.

I cast my eyes around the interior and at once realised I was entering a child's bedroom. It was a child's bedroom that had lain unoccupied and untouched for some time.

The walls were painted in a shade of pale blue, with circus scenes artfully stencilled onto border paper running all the way around the room. There was a small single bed, neatly made, with pillow plumped up and sheets tucked in. Set out on the bed was a folded pair of red pyjamas, large enough to fit a toddler. Nearby, there was a miniature bookcase, stocked with picture books and untouched volumes of Enid Blyton. Also spaced around the room at intervals were a number of toys in pristine condition – among them, a castle manned by a battalion of soldiers, a teddy bear, a Tonka truck, a wind-up robot and an array of colourful building blocks. Finally, there was a child's dresser. I opened the top drawer and discovered a dozen or so small pairs of socks carefully stowed away. And above the dresser, there was a mirror marked by a single seismic crack down the entire length of the glass.

I knew I should not linger too long in this forbidden room at the risk of being discovered. However, I began to feel myself being drawn across the carpet towards the bedroom window that overlooked the rear of the house. I peered out into the darkness and there, directly beneath me on the patio, I saw her. I saw a figure in a white night dress, her body prostrate and shaking. She was emitting a low moaning sound from somewhere deep inside. Her arms were outstretched, her fingers were arched and straining against the concrete slabs.

Instinctively, I recoiled at the sight of Mrs. Smith. I backed away from the window, feeling I was intruding on a private moment. I started to return to my own room, but when I thought of her outside, alone and exposed to the elements, I stopped in my tracks. Mr. Smith was away on one of his overnight trips, so I was the only person around who could intervene.

As I began to walk downstairs, from the lounge I could hear the sound of the record player stylus bumping and crackling repeatedly at the end of an LP. Lifting one of Mrs. Smith's coats from the stand in the hall, I made my way towards the back door of the house and stepped outside.

She was still there on the patio, only now she was rolled up in a ball, shivering and quietly sobbing to herself. A part of me wanted to leave her there and was fearful at how she would react to my intrusion. But overriding this was the feeling that I simply could not sit by and watch her in such a state of distress.

I approached her slowly, then bent down and gently draped the coat across her shoulders. She lifted her head up and I addressed her in a coaxing voice.

"Please... Come inside, Mrs. Smith."

I saw some recognition in her face, then she lowered her eyes. She nodded and her sobs dissipated somewhat. I took her left hand, helped her get to her feet and we both returned indoors.

I guided Mrs. Smith into the lounge, where she seated herself. After I had turned the record player off, I went into the kitchen and switched the kettle on. I duly returned with a cup of tea for Mrs. Smith and sat opposite her. She thanked me for the drink, took a brief sip, then began to talk falteringly...

"I sleepwalk sometimes, so I've been told... I must apologise if my state shocked you."

I told her I was not shocked.

"I suppose you know why you've been brought here by now... I mean, I'm sure my husband has filled you in?"

I told her I was not sure what she meant.

"My husband... Reginald... He thinks I could do with the company... His job takes him away from home a lot and he doesn't like the idea of me rattling around this old house with my memories."

She continued, her voice uncertain, and for the first time I noticed the brittle beauty of Mrs. Smith. I noticed how her delicate features, her turquoise eyes, lay almost hidden amid the lines on her careworn face.

"My son... Johnny... I lost him two years ago... I miss him every day... He hadn't been walking that long... He wandered outside, you see, and... and... I still can't talk about what happened... It was a Wednesday afternoon... It was my fault... I should have been at home... I was at work... We had a live-in nanny... It wasn't her fault, really... My husband had the pond concreted over..."

She looked into my eyes.

"Do you think... Do you think I could ever be forgiven for not being here for my son?"

She continued to look deep into my eyes. I did not know how to respond, so I said nothing. Eventually Mrs. Smith ended the silence.

"I'm sorry... I forgot myself... You're only a child... I don't know why I asked you that question... I think it's your eyes... I don't know why, but I think I could say anything to you and you would understand... I'm sorry... You're only a child yourself."

Following the events of that night, I developed a tentative bond with Mrs. Smith and, over time, she would confide her life story to me. Her maiden name, she told me, was Margot Terre. Much of her formative years had been spent in France, where she was educated by a religious order. She had, I learned, been sent there by her wealthy parents in the wake of their divorce.

There was some sketching out of a promising music career cut short. She also outlined to me how it was her late father who had originally owned the business Mr. Smith now ran, The Terre Toilet Company. A decade ago, her father had invited her to work in the family business and that is where she met Mr. Smith, who at the time was a senior sales executive at the firm.

"Charmed her, I did, at one of the company do's," was how Mr. Smith referred to their meeting. "When the mood hits me I can be quite the dandy."

Following her father's death, she inherited the business and the house on Ambrose Road that was her childhood home. Shortly thereafter, Ms. Terre became Mrs. Smith. Originally, she had been told that she was unable to have children, so when Johnny came along he was viewed as something of a miracle. She once showed me a photo album she kept, lined with Polaroid pictures of Johnny. He was chestnut-haired, round of face and never far from showing a smile.

In the wake of the tragedy that befell her son, and laid low by life, Mrs. Smith developed a fear of leaving the house. It was a fear that I would continue to endeavour to help her with.

Mr. Smith rarely addressed the subject of his wife's fragile mental state. One evening, however, after a couple of double Scotches, he eventually confided in me...

"God knows I've tried everything," he said. "I've bought her a new television set for the master bedroom, a new Kenwood Chef, the hi-fi centre she plays her music on. I've even tried to coax her into buying a new house, to get away from here... To get away from that blasted locked room... She likes to keep things as they are in that room... Don't ask me why... She doesn't even allow it to be aired... And that broken mirror... She broke it the day Johnny died and has forbidden me to replace it... I've given up trying to figure that woman out… She's living in another world to ours."

Life under the same roof as Mr. and Mrs. Smith would eventually settle into a routine of its own. As I concentrate my mind and try to impose some order on my recollections, in my inner world I feel the memories of those years in the Smith household unspooling. I feel the memories unspooling and the narrative beginning to take on some shape. I stretch and contract time – it is an act as natural as breathing to me – moulding it to the needs of the tale I have to tell. And at once, I am ready to continue to project my memories before you, my captive jury.

When Mr. Smith was in residence, I seem to remember that his time was largely spent in front of the television either watching sport or one of the many popular situation comedies of the era. Among his favourite comedies, I recall, were *On The Buses*, *Love Thy Neighbour* and *Bless This House*. He also enjoyed the array of imported American detective shows on offer and had a particular fondness for *Columbo*.

"I'd like to see an episode where someone gets away with the murder, just once," he regularly observed. "That's not too much to ask, is it?"

I also remember Mr. Smith's habit of loudly offering up his considered analysis of the state of the nation whenever he watched the *BBC Nine O'Clock News*…

"This country is going straight to hell in a hand cart I tell you. Rubbish piled sky high, unable to bury the dead and don't get me started on the bloody TUC… The Tories, they should get rid of that Ted Heath. He's a liability and, by the way, do you want to know what you can spell if you rearrange the letters in his name? The Death. I'm sure I heard someone say he's a distant relative of the murderer Neville Heath. Second cousin twice removed or something."

Mr. Smith's reading habits extended from red top tabloids and

*The Racing Post* to true crime magazines. When perusing these publications, he would linger over the details of the serial murders of Haigh, Christie and Neville Heath, often reading the lurid case histories aloud and demanding we listen.

"Are you *sure* he's not related to Ted Heath?" he would say.

Because of Mrs. Smith's nervous disposition and her husband's work commitments, there were never any holidays. On a good day, however, Mrs. Smith could be coaxed into leaving the house for a few hours and one rare family excursion does come to mind. The destination was Madame Tussauds and I recall Mr. Smith spending much of the time scouring The Chamber of Horrors. He was, he said, looking for John George Haigh's suit and tie. According to one of his magazines, these items of clothing had been donated to the exhibit by the murderer himself. On discovering that they were not currently on display, however, Mr. Smith grew red in the face and accused an unfortunate staff member of "blatant false advertising." While he tried unsuccessfully to secure a refund, I accompanied Mrs. Smith to a nearby café and some order of calm was restored to the day's proceedings.

Happier times awaited Mr. Smith most weekends, when he would go off to watch his beloved Arsenal F.C. in action and would regularly enjoy a flutter on the horses. If I am to be fair to him, Mr. Smith at first did make some attempts to get me involved in his pursuits. Gradually, however, when I showed little interest, Mr. Smith began to show even less interest in me.

Once every couple of months or so, he would stride through the front door, declare he had "won a packet on the gee-gees," and insist on taking us out to dinner if Mrs. Smith was feeling up to it. Perusing the menu, Mr. Smith would instruct us not to order "any of that foreign muck," and normally made a humorous observation along the lines of...

"Dover sole or chicken in a basket... what a choice. Murder most fish or murder most fowl?"

Outside of the Smith household, I continued to be a solitary, largely uncommunicative child. At the comprehensive school I was enrolled in, I failed to make any friends of note. This was due in part to my personality. Or rather, to be more exact, my lack of personality. But my friendless status was mostly attributable to one single factor - the very strangeness of my outward appearance. Already, at such a young age, my size was beginning to be remarked upon.

My physical appearance began to elicit comments from other children. Children who were older than me, children who were younger than me and even strangers in the street. Everyday cold-hearted strangers.

Among the names I would hear aimed at me were *Lurch, Lofty, Mongo, Oddbod* and *Frankenstein* (I didn't bother to stop and correct them on the all-too-common misuse of the name of the fictional scientist, when surely they were referring to his monster).

Over time and as I continued to grow, however, I found the name-calling eventually stopped and it would only take a steely glance from me to silence any of the cowardly perpetrators. Thereafter, the only name-calling I encountered would be carried out from a distance. Often, the offending words would be hurled at me from a street corner and I became expert at dodging the occasional crisp packet filled with unidentified liquid which would be thrown in my vicinity. The street corner would then be quickly ducked behind, thus giving the guilty party or parties plenty of time to make an escape.

All of this did nothing for my persecution complex and as my teenage years progressed, I became acutely aware of how profoundly different I was from my contemporaries. As a rule, I tried to avoid looking in mirrors. However, when I was unfortunate enough to lay eyes on my own face, I recoiled at the sight of the doughy, featureless visage pallidly staring back at me.

My physiognomy lacked any singular striking characteristics. It was as if it had been moulded by an absent-minded artisan who gave up on a bad job halfway through a commission.

I believe I managed to conceal my troubled state of mind from Mrs. Smith. However, I could not conceal my physical state and at some point she resolved to do something about my unchecked growth spurts. I remember one conversation between Mrs. Smith and her husband while he reposed in his favourite armchair with a cigar and a copy of the *News of the World*.

"Take him to a doctor if you're worried about him," Mr. Smith said. "But if it's anything serious, we're not going private. He can join the NHS queue like everyone else."

At the local surgery, I was given a full medical examination. The examining doctor mentioned that the anterior pituitary gland could be one reason for my abnormal size. He professed himself more alarmed, however, after he shone a light into my right eye and I briefly blacked out, only to re-awaken on the doctor's couch. Subsequently, I was diagnosed as suffering from a severe case of photophobia. I was advised to avoid bright lights as much as possible, to administer eye drops if I should experience any discomfort, and to wear tinted prescription glasses.

It was the beginning of my awareness of the painful malady that continues to afflict me to this day. Almost at once, I realised that the photophobia was one of the lasting after-effects of that night when Mr. Drew forced me to stare into the light of the projector. With each advancing year, my aversion to bright lights would only become more and more pronounced.

At least Mr. Smith was amused on first seeing me wearing my tinted prescription glasses.

"My, my. Look at you in your fancy glasses," he remarked. "You remind me of a younger version of that blind fellow off *Opportunity Knocks* who sings with the blonde. Peters & Lee, is that it? Yes, I think it is. Don't know which one of the pair he is. There's one of their songs I really like… What's it called again?"

Needless to say, I was required to wear the tinted glasses throughout the school day. This did nothing to improve my social standing and it also provided the name-callers with more vocabulary to add to their arsenal. Among the new epithets I soon encountered were *X-Ray Specks* and *Four-Eyed Frankenstein* to name but two. It took an enormous amount of will power on my behalf to refrain from summoning my gifts to silence the name-callers once and for all.

I am sure it will come as no surprise when I say I look back on my school days as nothing but one long, grinding endurance test. On reflection, these years may well have broken me, had I not already learned some skills in the art of endurance. Skills that were honed during my time in Father Tobin's establishment.

Regrettably, however, there were no O Level courses offered in Endurance and when it came to the mainstream academic subjects, I was a hopeless plodder. I merely went through the motions each day, thoroughly uninspired by the narrow curriculum imposed on me. Even during lessons, to escape whatever deadening chore I was expected to devote my attention to, I would find my mind drifting.

My mind would drift into the realm of my inner world. Once in my inner world, I would aim my thoughts elsewhere. In my inner world, I aimed my thoughts towards Mr. Hitchcock and his films...

All this time, I had not forgotten the screenings of Mr. Hitchcock's films and the effect they had on me. All this time, I had not forgotten my encounter with Mr. Hitchcock. I knew I needed to watch more of his work. I knew I needed to know more, to learn more.

During these years, I continued to delve deeper into Mr. Hitchcock's body of work. I regularly scoured the *Radio Times* for mention of any showings of his films on television. At weekends, I also made sure to check the cinema listings for any relevant screenings, which I would then eagerly seek out in the picture houses dotted around the city. I quickly became an expert on negotiating the underground as I mapped my journeys around London. Sometimes I would take in two or three screenings a day in geographically distant parts of the city.

Of course, the Truffaut book proved to be an invaluable guide to Mr. Hitchcock's career. Using the filmography at the back of the book, I began to mark off the films that I had seen. In a separate notebook, I would make a record of the occasions I saw each film, where and when, and the quality of the print being shown.

Tentatively, I began to map out the meanings behind Mr. Hitchcock's movies. I was sure that there was something within his films waiting to be revealed to me and I was determined to unveil whatever it was.

In my inner world, I would replay scenes from Mr. Hitchcock's films in a continual montage and I would experience an intensity of emotion I could not hope to feel in my everyday life. I carefully practised this technique of replaying moments and began to sense that I was blindly feeling my way towards the working out of a grand, beautiful puzzle. In my inner world, I was edging towards solving the most visually dazzling jigsaw puzzle ever created, yet the picture remained incomplete to me. And the picture, I knew, would remain incomplete until I had seen all of Mr. Hitchcock's films. The problem I was faced with was that some of the titles were difficult to track down, in particular a number of the early silent films.

I would think deeper, brooding on the mysteries of what had been partially revealed to me in the films I had managed to see. Often, I would go into very quiet moods and withdraw far into my inner world. Often, I would hide myself away in my bedroom or I would sit, remembering a sequence from a certain movie and find myself taken away from the realities of life. On more than one occasion, Mr. Smith would interrupt my silent reveries.

"Take that look off your face, boy," he would say.

"What look are you talking about, Reginald?" Mrs. Smith intervened.

"*That* look," he said, pointing at me. "That look that says he's not here, he's somewhere else. Daydreaming or off with the faeries. Stay away from those faeries. And what good does daydreaming do you anyway? I'll tell you... it achieves nothing. Do you think The Industrial Revolution was achieved by daydreamers? The people that made this country great, Isambard Kingdom Brunel and his ilk? No, it was achieved by do-ers."

At other times, Mr. Smith also expressed a strong dislike for how quiet I could be around the house. One night, as I padded my way across the landing from the toilet to my bedroom, I inadvertently surprised him and he accosted me thus...

"Stop skulking, boy. I don't like skulkers. Sneaking around the house at night like you're Lord Lucan. Make some noise, for goodness sake. Clear your throat when you enter the room. Make yourself heard if nothing else."

I do not think I am overstating things when I say that Mr. Smith began to harbour strong feelings of antipathy towards me. I also cannot deny that, from time to time, the feelings were mutual.

One such example comes to mind. It was the only occasion the three of us made a trip to the cinema together. Mr. Hitchcock's *Family Plot* had just been released. I dearly wanted to see it and had made the suggestion during dinner before we left. However, Mr. Smith had a different idea. He drove past the venue where *Family Plot* was showing, then continued on a few miles further to another cinema that was screening a comedy which he said had been recommended to him by "one of the fellows at work."

"Time for some down-to-earth British humour," he announced as he parked the car. "No sense in being suburban."

The film in question was *Carry On At Your Convenience* and

Mr. Smith, for one, appeared to enjoy it immensely. At times, his body was seized by paroxysms of laughter that I mistook for a violent fit of some sort. His guffaws echoed raucously around the auditorium as he savoured the comical hijinks and double entendres, played out against the backdrop of a factory that manufactured toilets.

"That film was something of a busman's holiday for me, boy," he remarked on the trip home. "I can't say I heard you two laughing much during the movie. What's the matter with the pair of you?"

"… It wasn't really my cup of tea," Mrs. Smith quietly spoke up.

I watched as Mr. Smith's driving gloves tightened their grip on the steering wheel.

"I think you must've left your sense of humour back in the convent, dear."

That was just one of the countless casual put-downs I witnessed the long-suffering Mrs. Smith having to put up with. She was a character already half-removed from life when I first met her and I will remain forever baffled at how she had ended up with Mr. Smith.

Burdened with terrible guilt over the death of her son, she also lived with another affliction I must mention if I am to paint a truthful picture of life in the Smith household. The affliction I refer to is alcoholism.

During my residence in the house on Ambrose Road, I witnessed Mrs. Smith's face undergo a tectonic change. For at least my first two years there, her skin managed to retain a youthful, pale and fragile appearance. But, with the passage of time, her face became increasingly gaunt and etched by her experience. The deadly mix of alcohol and personal remorse began to take its toll. Her eyes became reddened, her skin blotchy and if you looked closer you would see it threaded through with fine dark capillary veins.

Whenever dark moods threatened to envelope her, the one thing that helped alleviate them was her love of music. It was not unusual for her to spend hours at a time listening to recordings of classical music, and among the composers she returned to time and again were Beethoven, Wagner and Johann Strauss.

If Mr. Smith happened to be in close proximity, he would normally insist on the volume being turned down so he could listen to the football results, concentrate on reading *The Sun* or enjoy the sight of Reg Varney leering at a youthful female co-star. He would then follow up the request with a punchline. Two examples come to mind…

"You know, *I've* written a piece of music. Want to know what it's called? *The Bathroom Suite.* That's music to *my* ears!"

Or…

"That's enough of that chamber music. How about some chamber pot music? That's music to *my* ears!"

And so, like a stylus stuck in a groove, Mr. Smith's catchphrases would be repeated ad nauseam and ad infinitum…


Emotionally, Mrs. Smith remained fragile and her husband's apparent indifference to her situation did nothing to help. Her feelings were always close to the surface and soon I instinctively knew when her mind was returning to thoughts of her son. I also developed a habit of monitoring the contents of the drinks cabinet each day to give me some clue as to her present state of mind.

I knew that Mrs. Smith would never love me as she would her own flesh and blood. I knew I was a poor substitute. However, in her own undemonstrative way, I knew I was loved. I knew she would be the closest I would ever get to having a mother.

After a few years, her situation was slowly beginning to improve and she even made some progress on leaving the house more often. Despite a couple of setbacks, I do remember moments of quiet triumph when I accompanied her to church or to the local park on successive Sundays.

Regarding my education, she was starting to take more of an interest in my achievements and she made a great effort to boost my sense of self. Before I left for school in the morning, she would see me off at the front door and offer me some advice.

"Try not to walk with slouched shoulders," she would say gently. "Walk tall and upright."

Occasionally, Mrs. Smith would voice concerns about my solitary nature and the long pilgrimages I would take at the weekends on the underground. When I shared with her the purpose of my journeys, she decided to try to discourage me by signing me up for a course of piano lessons on Saturdays. However, I proved to be hopelessly unskilled and took a dislike to the ageing female tutor who had a habit of hitting my fingers with a ruler when I invariably struck a wrong note.

One Saturday, I decided I did not want to go to my lesson. Earlier, amid the cinema listings, I had spotted a reissue of a film by Mr. Hitchcock and the prospect of stealing out to view it proved too tempting. The film in question was *Frenzy*. According to the official advice from The British Board of Film Censors, I was not yet old enough to see it legally. As I handed over a ticket to an unquestioning usher, however, I discovered one distinct advantage of my physical appearance - I could easily pass myself off as an adult.

"Did you go to your piano lesson today?" Mrs. Smith questioned me when I arrived home.

"Yes," I lied.

"Tell the truth."

"… I went to see a film."

"What was it called?"

"… *Fingerprints*," I lied.

Mrs. Smith sighed, shortly thereafter the piano lessons were abandoned and I was once again free to explore the picture houses of London each Saturday.

Another pastime I began to explore was prompted by the advice Mr. Hitchcock had imparted to me in the back seat of his Silver Shadow.

"… Buy a camera… You must train yourself to identify with the camera…"

Buying a camera was, I knew, an impossibility. However, I remembered noticing a shelving unit filled with equipment in a neglected corner of Mr. Smith's garage/wine cellar. Mr. Smith had once caught me in the act of eyeing up his possessions and couldn't resist listing an inventory for me right there and then.

"8mm home movie camera and projector… Tripod… Audio tape recorder… Some basic dark room equipment… There's also a Nikon F2 SLR camera in there somewhere, complete with 50mm lens… Yes, I am something of a gadget man… I used to enjoy making home recordings… These days, my responsibilities towards the business don't give me a lot of time to use all this stuff… But maybe some day I'll dust off the cobwebs… Now, get out of here boy. Never touch any of this equipment, do you hear me? Much too valuable for you to be fiddling around with. In fact, forget you ever laid eyes on this stuff. Am I making myself clear?"

I replied that he had.

"Yes, I'm sure," Mr. Smith responded. "As clear as your U-bend after a bad case of the Delhi Belly, no doubt."

In my head, I was planning an excursion with the purpose of teaching myself the basics of how to use a camera. I had already purchased a roll of black-and-white film with 24 exposures and had borrowed a book from the public library for instruction on how to properly load a film. I waited for a suitable opportunity, then returned to the garage/wine cellar in search of Mr. Smith's Nikon. I discovered it on the top shelf, behind an empty box of photographic paper.

I had already settled on the location where I would take my

first steps in the art of photography. Perhaps it was my recent initial viewing of *Frenzy*, but I felt strongly compelled to revisit the scene of my encounter with Mr. Hitchcock. Once again, I sensed I was being guided back to the South Bank...

One Friday morning during the summer, I set out with the Nikon F2, having successfully loaded a roll of film into it the night before. The Nikon was inside a camera bag, which I gripped tightly throughout the journey for fear of losing Mr. Smith's property.

I boarded a Victoria Line train, travelled six stops, then switched to the Circle Line and disembarked at Westminster tube station. I blinked, emerged into the blinding daylight and noted the familiar landmarks. Big Ben... Boudica... Westminster Bridge. I proceeded across the bridge and made my way towards the South Bank, returning for the first time to the spot where I had met Mr. Hitchcock.

The scene that greeted me today was very different. There was no crowd barrier... No film crew... No extras... Nobody shouting orders... Only a mix of sightseers and families, ambling around under their own volition. Still, I was struck by a sudden image – that an invisible director had shouted "Action!" from somewhere offstage just before I appeared and everything playing out before me was being orchestrated for my benefit.

I was left feeling somewhat off-balance by this vision of an invisible director, so I banished it from my mind and decided to concentrate on the task I had set myself. I thought I would start off with a shot from the South Bank towards Westminster Bridge. I soon found I did not have to walk too far to find a suitable vantage point. As I extricated the camera from its bag, I made sure to handle it with great care. I placed the camera strap around my neck and removed the lens cap.

Feeling somewhat self-conscious, I edged myself into what I deemed was the best position to capture the span of Westminster Bridge with The Houses of Parliament sloping off in the background.

In the sky, I now noticed a striking formation of clouds slowly stirring. I raised the camera up with both hands and looked through the viewfinder. Immediately, I realised I would get a closer view of the frame if I removed my tinted glasses, and so I did. Once I carefully removed my glasses, I raised the camera once more to my eyeline and found myself pleased with the composition. In the foreground, the Thames was sweeping towards the bridge, while the surging banks of clouds dominated the scene, dwarfing even Big Ben.

My finger hesitated over the shutter release. I was waiting for a double decker bus to exit the frame before I would click.

Then, on the bridge, I saw the head and shoulders of a male figure slowly walking from left to right. It was a corpulent figure, wearing a dark suit and bowler hat. My finger continued to hover over the shutter release and I found myself wondering if it really could be who I thought it was.

With my mind in such a state of distraction, I failed to notice that the clouds were in motion. Suddenly, from behind a cloud, the sun appeared. A ray of light that had travelled ninety-three million miles beamed directly into my right eye, hit the retina and surged along my optic nerve with the force of an electric shock.

Somehow I managed to press the shutter release before I recoiled in pain as the onslaught of intensely bright light hit me. The pain surged through my eye, into my brain, and my head was filled with a high-pitched ringing. I had to sit down on some nearby steps and wait for the sensation to fade away. For some time, I could see nothing at all out of my right eye. It took hours for any semblance of vision to return. Luckily, my other eye had been shut at the time, so I was able to begin to trace my route back home.

For someone with the condition of photophobia, I had made the stupid and dangerous mistake of pointing a camera lens in the direction of the brightest object in the sky. After just one shot, with some certainty, I knew that my adventures in photography were at an end.

Amid these painful feelings of defeat and anger directed at myself, my mind returned to the unidentified figure I had seen crossing Westminster Bridge. I told myself that I may not be able to take any more photographs, but I needed to develop the roll of film in the camera to prove if my eyes had been playing tricks on me. On the final leg of my torturous return trip, I left the roll of film into a local pharmacy and was instructed to come again the following day.

Once back in the Smith household, I immediately returned the camera to the garage/wine cellar. Standing before the shelving unit, however, I was shocked to see that some of the equipment had been disturbed while I had been out. I felt certain Mr. Smith had been performing a random check to see if I had been meddling with his private property. He was sure, I thought, to have noticed the missing Nikon and so I mentally prepared myself for an interrogation from him at any time.

All that day, however, Mr. Smith did not mention it. That evening at dinner he did not mention it. I did sense some nervous tension in the air between him and Mrs. Smith, but I put that down to Mr. Smith's recent impulsive purchase of a brand new Jaguar XJS. "I decided to trade *up*, not trade *in*," Mr. Smith had explained testily when his wife had questioned why his old XJ6 was still parked in the garage. I had also noticed the contents of the drinks cabinet had become severely depleted of late, which should really have alerted me to something more serious...

The next day, I kept my appointment with the local pharmacy.

"A small package for such a big fellow," the man in the white coat said as he handed over a slim cardboard envelope. "Your negatives are in there too."

I paid and exited the shop. Once outside, I opened the envelope and examined the single photograph inside.

For my one and only photographic effort, I remain proud of it to this day. The composition is still a striking thing to behold. The sun is a blinding presence in the upper left corner of the picture, its light bouncing brilliant dappled reflections off the ribbon-like surface of the Thames in the foreground. Big Ben and The Houses of Parliament form dramatic silhouettes against the mountainous bank of clouds which almost fill the sky, while the span of Westminster Bridge runs diagonally across the composition.

And there as I studied the photograph for the first time, in the centre of the bridge, I detected the presence of a figure. The presence of this figure told me that I had not imagined it all. However, as I looked closer at the black-and-white print I held in my hand, I realised I could not make out the identity of the individual I had captured on film. At such a distance between myself and the subject it would already have been a difficult task, of course, but as I strained my eyesight all I could make out was a blurred, indistinct form.

I could not be sure who I had photographed.

Somewhat perplexed, I returned to the house to find that Mrs. Smith had prepared lunch for me. It was a bowl of alphabet soup. I was idly arranging the letters floating on the surface to spell out HITCH, when Mrs. Smith asked me a question out of the blue...

"Do you believe the dead come back to haunt you?"

She was sitting at the kitchen table with her head slightly lowered. Her hand was trembling as it stirred a cup of coffee. When she realised I wasn't going to reply to her question, she continued.

"Some nights, I believe I can hear him calling for me. Sometimes the sound appears to be coming from his bedroom. Sometimes it's coming from outside... where the patio is. Have you heard him? In the dead of night have you heard him? I know his voice. A mother knows the sound of her own son's voice."

I admitted that I had heard nothing. As she spoke again, she raised her head and I noticed her bloodshot eyes.

"I've tried rousing Reginald from his sleep, but when I do the voices stop. When he asks me why I've woken him up, I tell him I thought I heard a burglar downstairs. Then he goes and makes a fuss about checking all the doors and windows on the ground floor. He puffs and he pants and he resents the trouble I have caused him, so I don't want to talk to him about it any more... The next time I hear the voices, can I wake you up?"

I told her she should not hesitate to wake me if she should hear the voices again. As Mrs. Smith took another sip of coffee and I returned to my alphabet soup, I noticed a stray letter had floated into my word arrangement. Now, instead of the H, a B was hovering before the ITCH.

Later that evening, I went to bed with my usual night-time snack of a glass of milk and a biscuit. I recall drinking the milk while I sat in bed and took the opportunity to study my photograph of Westminster Bridge once more. Normally, I would have made it to the bathroom to brush my teeth with Minto Toothpaste before sleep would claim me. However, on this particular night, sleep came upon me without warning.

Sleep came upon me that night and I was visited by a dream...

In the dream, I was gliding through the doorways and corridors of a vast, white gallery. At first, I was puzzled as there were no works of art on display. However, up ahead I soon noticed a large monochrome picture and that is where I felt myself being pulled towards. As I drew closer, I saw it was my photograph. It had been enlarged and now filled an entire wall. I approached the photograph... Closer.... Closer... Close enough to make out each individual grain in the print.

I tried to pause and admire my handiwork, but I was not allowed to halt my progress. I drew closer still and at some point I began to feel myself crossing an invisible threshold and entering the photograph. I felt myself gliding through the interior landscape of the photograph... I was slowly gliding in three-dimensional space... Gliding out over the edge of the South Bank... Over the dark silent glinting surface of the Thames.

I was gliding directly towards the centre of Westminster Bridge... Towards the blurred, ill-defined figure I had photographed. And as I moved closer to the hazy form, gradually from out of the grain and the fog, the figure began to gain some solidity. Finally, the figure coalesced and I recognised the man who was standing there on Westminster Bridge. I recognised Mr. Hitchcock.

I came to a standstill and found myself hovering right before him. Mr. Hitchcock seemed to sense my presence and turned to face me.

Slowly, he raised both his hands towards his fleshy face... Slowly, he joined the thumbs and index fingers of each hand to form a geometric shape... Slowly, he folded his other fleshy fingers inwards and positioned the shape over his right eye... Slowly, deliberately, in a 33 ⅓ rpm drawl, he recited the words once again to me...

"... See as I see..."

And his eye stared out at me through the shape he had formed with his fleshy hands. The shape of The △.

"... See as I see..."

And suddenly in my inner world I had a vision... A vision of noxious fumes spewing from the end of a pipe... A confined space filling with a poisonous cloud... And an unidentified victim being asphyxiated within...

"... See as I see..."

And then Mr. Hitchcock's voice was inside my head again, whispering the same word over and over to me.

"... gas... gas... gas... gas-s-s-s..."

I awoke with a sudden start to the sight of Mrs. Smith's face in extreme close-up. She was shaking me by the shoulders and her face was a picture of distress.

"What are you doing in here? In this room?" She was beside herself, her hair wild and dishevelled. "You've been touching his toys. But it's *his* room! It's not your room! Never your room!"

Somehow, I had awoken to find myself in the forbidden room.

"*He* loved me. Why can't *you* love me? *Why*?!"

She stopped shaking me, started sobbing to herself and I was left speechless. Mr. Smith now entered the scene. He knelt down beside his wife and began to address me in angry tones.

"Look here, what's the meaning of this? Are you the source of the noises she's been hearing all these nights? Well, are you? Answer me!"

I found myself dumbfounded. I could not answer.

Mrs. Smith now collapsed on the floor of her son's bedroom. She was inconsolable. I looked around the room and noticed that some items had been disturbed. Books were lying on the carpet, toys were in unseemly piles and I saw white stuffing protruding from a vertical slash in the teddy bear's stomach.

My head was thrumming. While Mr. Smith coaxed his wife back to their marital bedroom, I retreated to my own space. I coiled myself in bed and covered my ears, but sleep would not come. My head was full of troubling thoughts and suppositions. Already, I suspected what must have happened for me to end up in the forbidden room.

Early the next morning, Mr. Smith called the local surgery and demanded a doctor come out to the house to see to his wife.

"I hope you're happy," he muttered through my door when the doctor had left. "She's confined to bed with nervous exhaustion. So take my advice. Leave her alone and don't go making a bad situation any worse."

Apart from a couple of furtive visits downstairs to fix my own meals, I spent most of that day in my room. This was not because of Mr. Smith's words, but because of the suspicions that were playing on my mind. As for Mrs. Smith, she remained sequestered in her bed with the television switched on to keep her company.

Around nine o'clock that evening, I happened to be downstairs again when Mr. Smith took a phone call. After hanging up, he went upstairs to check in on his wife and then announced the night-watchman had informed him that there was a problem at the factory. He was going to have to go and investigate.

"I don't know what time I'll be back, dear. You know what it's like down there."

By now, I was in the kitchen preparing my night-time snack. I had lifted a pint of milk from the fridge and was closely studying how the blue foil lid of the milk bottle appeared to have been punctured and ripped when Mr. Smith appeared beside me.

"I see the blessed birds have got to the milk bottle tops again," he said. "Excellent choice for a night cap. Stay off the hot toddies, eh son?"

His words caused me to stop in my tracks. It was the first time Mr. Smith had called me "son."

I poured the milk into a tall glass and bade Mr. Smith goodnight. I walked upstairs and when I heard Mr. Smith leaving via the front door I paced into the toilet. I poured the milk down the Terre Toilet Company lavatory, flushed and watched as the whiteness disappeared.

Returning to my bedroom, I could hear the sound of the television coming from Mr. and Mrs. Smith's master bedroom. A late night film, the soundtrack punctuated with dramatic music, muffled dialogue and gunshots, was playing. I lay awake for some time until I heard the final strains of 'God Save the Queen' and the day's transmission was at an end.

Gradually, silence settled over the Smith household and I fell asleep…

"Mummy! Mummy!"

I was awoken by the sound of these words. The sound was coming from somewhere close by on the landing.

"Mummy! Mummy!"

It sounded like the voice of an infant. An infant crying out in distress. At first, I was frozen in terror. And then I heard a rustling of bed clothes, I heard the sound of feet on carpet, I heard an anxious low level moaning.

"Johnny... is it you?"

"Mummy! Mummy!"

I could hear Mrs. Smith... She was on the landing now.

"I can see you Johnny. I can see you."

I could hear her pacing across the landing... I felt a deep sense of dread, but knew I had to get out of bed.

"Johnny. My darling Johnny, forgive me."

I had to overcome any fear I was feeling... I had to get out of bed to save Mrs. Smith from her certain fate.

"Johnny. Don't run away from mummy... Please stay!"

I lifted myself out of bed... From underneath the door I saw an ethereal light coming from the landing... I knew I couldn't waste a moment.

I opened the door in time to witness the figure of Mrs. Smith... She was rushing towards the top of the stairs where the light was... And there at the top of the stairs I saw what she was seeing... I heard what she was hearing... It wasn't in her head.

The vision of a young boy was there... A young boy, smiling and happy... It was the boy I had seen in the family photographs... It was Johnny... He was laughing and running... At first glance, he appeared to be running in the air.

As Mrs. Smith rushed towards the top of the stairs, she appeared to want to follow him.

"Johnny... Johnny..."

For more than a moment I was taken in by the vision, but something struck me as not right. And then I saw through what was happening.

"Don't – !" I began to shout out. I was about to move towards Mrs. Smith, but suddenly an unseen force slammed into me and I hit the floor.

Mrs. Smith had turned when she heard me cry out, but it was too late for her. As she lost her balance at the top of the stairs, she screamed. I saw her figure disappear over the edge and then heard the sound of her body plummeting downwards.

Lying prone on the landing, I found myself staring into the source of the blinding light, the source of the image projected onto the wall that Mrs. Smith in her distracted state had ran towards. It was an 8mm projector.

Mr. Smith now made himself heard.

"You little fiend. You should be fast asleep... I suppose I should've doubled the dose for someone of your size."

"I didn't drink it."

He placed one of his feet on my back and applied some pressure.

"Oh, you copped onto me did you?"

I told him that I had.

"You know too much then, don't you? A little knowledge can be a deadly thing."

As the heel of Mr. Smith's foot dug deeper into my back, I gazed into the light of the projector. I gazed into the light and I could feel my powers awakening once again. For the first time in years I summoned my powers.

"That bitch... that rotten bitch," Mr. Smith spoke through gritted teeth. "She deserved to die for what happened. She should've been home looking after him. And she loved to remind me that she was the one who truly owned the business... The business deserves to be mine! I've put my blood and sweat into it. Countless hours. I'm not throwing it all away for a circus freak like you. I'm an upstanding member of society. You're not going to stop me. All I wanted was a new start. To start a new family and keep the business. I deserve to keep it. The two of you... You have no idea of the responsibility I feel towards the workforce… It weighs heavily on my shoulders."

I whispered the words at first.

"… Confess, Mr. Smith."

"What did you say?"

"… Confess."

"… I don't have to explain myself to someone like you."

"… Confess."

"Why would the police bother to investigate the death of a nobody like you anyway?"

I focused intently and aimed my mind towards Mr. Smith.

"… Confess!"

At this point, Mr. Smith lifted his foot off my back. He lifted his foot off my back and his voice took on a deadened tone.

"Years in the planning, it was… Years… It was the perfect plan… The perfect plan… And you just had to be the fly in the ointment, didn't you? I'm not here, you see. I'm at the factory. You and the missus, you're here all on your own… I had it all set up… I was going to give her a few too many of the pills the doctor gave her… Then I was going to place her in the Jaguar and let the carbon monoxide get her, but a simple fall down the stairs will have to suffice… As for you, you come from a troubled background… We tried our best for you, but you drove her to this… That's right, you drove her to take her own life… No parents, no step parents could care for you. That's why you were abandoned. You're a bad seed. Nothing but a bad seed… I set up the 8mm projector, some home recordings I had made of the boy… I've always been a gadget man… It was the perfect plan, really… How could it fail? I ask you, how could it fail?"

I continued to aim my mind towards Mr. Smith.

The light spoke to me once again and I told Mr. Smith how this scene was going to end. I aimed my words towards him.

"… gas… gas… gas… gas-s-s-s…"

I aimed my words towards him as he began to slowly walk

**111**

down the stairs, just as the image of his dead son spluttered to an end and the reel of film unfurled on the spool of the projector.

"... gas... gas... gas... gas-s-s-s..."

I aimed my words towards him as he walked past the body of Mrs. Smith that now lay at the bottom of the stairs like a discarded marionette.

"... gas... gas... gas... gas-s-s-s..."

I aimed my words towards him as he calmly opened the door to the garage/wine cellar, then entered and closed the door behind him.

"... gas... gas... gas... gas-s-s-s..."

I aimed my words towards him as he opened the driver's door of his Jaguar XJ6, as he slipped on his leather driving gloves and turned the key in the ignition.

"... gas... gas... gas... gas-s-s-s..."

As soon as the engine began to turn over, the fumes were pumped through the hosepipe Mr. Smith had already attached to the exhaust... The hosepipe that coiled its way into the passenger side of the car.

"... gas... gas... gas... gas-s-s-s..."

As Mr. Smith began to cough and as the interior began to fill with the poisonous vapours, I instructed Mr. Smith to switch on the radio.

"... gas... gas... gas... gas-s-s-s..."

As the violins soared, as the heavenly choir hit the high notes, as the sound of Peters & Lee singing 'Welcome Home' rumbled out from the speakers, I instructed Mr. Smith to fasten his seat belt one last time.

"Clunk click every trip," Mr. Smith managed to splutter.

I, The Avenger, then focused my mind and ordered Mr. Smith to close his eyes. To close his eyes and let the fumes overcome him.

I was still lying on the landing floor, staring into the light of the 8mm projector and listening. Listening to the voice inside me, the voice of The Avenger, as he instructed me on how to deal with the desperate situation I now found myself plunged into.

I knew Mrs. Smith was already dead and that Mr. Smith was being asphyxiated towards his imminent demise. The Avenger had taken care of him.

A plan on how to proceed began to take shape. A plan I would begin to put into action soon.

I decided I would leave at least twenty minutes before I would phone the police. When they arrived I would inform them how I had awoken to discover the bodies. It would be essential for me to play the part of the innocent stepson to perfection.

Then, with my version of events on the record, I could only pray that I would not fall under their suspicion for the murder of Mr. Reginald H. Smith.

On the screen before us, another door materialises. Mr. Memory opens the door and we enter it together, you and I…

As I had predicted, the powers that be questioned me at length about the occurrences in the house in Ambrose Road. Assuming the role of the blameless stepson, I decided (for the most part) to tell the truth to the investigating officers. Eventually, they were satisfied with my version of events.

I told them how I had awoken and inadvertently stumbled upon Mr. Smith's plan. I told them how I believed he wanted to place his wife in the Jaguar and allow her to suffocate. I told them how I believed Mr. Smith wanted people to think that I had pushed his wife's fragile mind over the edge by mimicking the child-like voices she had been hearing in the night. Thus, the blame for Mrs. Smith's apparent suicide would have been placed on my shoulders. I provided the bare bones of the murder plot and then allowed the detectives to fill in the blanks through their examination of the evidence left in situ at the scene of the crime.

One plot hole was filled not long into the investigation, when it was discovered that the phone call made to the house on the night in question came from an unsuspecting night-watchman at the factory. During his rounds, the night-watchman had found a briefcase belonging to Mr. Smith on the premises. He recalled Mr. Smith repeatedly and explicitly giving instructions to contact him at home immediately if this briefcase was ever, by chance, forgotten and left behind at the factory.

According to the night-watchman, Mr. Smith arrived at the factory some time between nine and ten o'clock. He then informed the night-watchman that he had some books to go over in his office and that under no circumstances was he to be disturbed for a few hours. The light in Mr. Smith's office would remain on for the duration of the night-watchman's shift and he did not think to check on his employer at any time.

The investigating officers concluded that Mr. Smith had

purposefully planted the briefcase to facilitate his trip to the factory. Once inside his office, he had then exited through a ground floor window and returned to Ambrose Road. After he had despatched his wife, he had planned to let himself back into the factory to provide himself with an alibi. Needless to say, that is not how things worked out for Mr. Smith.

Another plot hole was filled in soon after, when it was discovered that Mr. Smith had been keeping a mistress in another part of the city. Under examination, the unfortunate woman in question claimed total ignorance about Mr. Smith's plot to do away with his wife, but did admit he had often said how he planned to marry her (no doubt, after a suitable period of grieving).

Their clandestine relationship, it turned out, had been going on for three years and had been easy to conceal, thanks to Mr. Smith's frequent business trips. The whole sorry affair was a minor tabloid sensation for a few weeks, but never made it beyond the columns of the inner pages. Mercifully, my status as a minor protected my name from being connected to the case. The lower echelons of the press pack lost interest when the police made it clear that Mr. Smith's mistress was not suspected of any involvement in the murder. The case was closed.

In the meantime, funeral plans for Mr. and Mrs. Smith had been taken care of by a fund already in place with the family company. While Mrs. Smith was laid to rest in the same plot as her son, discrete measures were taken to acquire a separate space in the same cemetery for her husband...

After my interrogation and the double funeral of my adoptive parents, I was not yet eighteen. Thus, I found myself thrust back into the care of the state. For a time, I resided in a sort of halfway house for troubled teenagers. I feared that this would be my life for more than the foreseeable future, until I was tracked down by the firm of solicitors acting on behalf of Mrs. Smith.

Summoned to their offices, I was informed of the contents of Mrs. Margot Smith's legacy. I was told that Mrs. Smith had, in fact, been the sole proprietor of the business. To my shock, I was then informed that she had her will amended some months previously and had named me as the sole beneficiary.

*Even if Mr. Smith's plan had worked,* I thought to myself. *He would have had to do away with me also.*

The executor of the will went on to tell me how things would proceed. On reaching the age of eighteen, I would receive a very sizeable lump sum. The day-to-day running of The Terre Toilet Company would pass to a panel of executive directors, who had already assumed control in the wake of Mr. Smith's death. I would be the owner of the company *in absentia* and would receive a yearly percentage of profits in keeping with my new position.

Suddenly, I found myself, more or less, independently well-to-do. Because I was still technically a ward of court, however, I had to remain in the care facility until I reached adulthood.

The remainder of my time at school came and went uneventfully, apart from the occasional whispered aside I was privy to. It was nothing more than I expected. After all, I was the young man who had been found at the scene of the apparent murder and suicide of his adoptive parents. I lived then, as I do now, with the finger of suspicion forever primed and ready to be cocked in my direction.

Finally, exams were entered into, scraped through and my school days were at an end. I did not apply myself sufficiently in order to gain a place in third level education. Besides, I did not care to pursue further mainstream studies. Instead, I successfully applied for an entry level civil service job as a clerk in the General Register Office. It was a lowly filing position, mainly dealing in the realm of births and deaths.

In my mind, I was trying to put the events in the Smith household behind me. In my mind, I was secretly troubled by the gifts bestowed on me. I told myself that I needed a dose of normality. And normality meant finding a source of gainful employment.

The starting date for my job roughly coincided with the advent of my eighteenth birthday, upon which I took receipt of a cheque from the estate of the late Mrs. Smith. With it, I put a down payment on a first floor apartment in Slade Walk, London SW3. The area was an upmarket mix of residential flats and offices and presented me with an easy commute to my place of work. There in the flat in Slade Walk I would live, by myself, for the next few years.

Meanwhile, I began my career in the General Register Office and I began playing the role of a normal human being. Perhaps I was trying too hard to be normal, because the initial impression I gave to my colleagues was of a quiet, insular drone worker. And once you have made an initial impression on people, I find, you are forever typecast. Despite this, I may well have been content in my job, had it not been for the behaviour of two of my co-workers. They went by the names of Harold Sheldrake and Fred Calthrop.

Sheldrake was the dominant member of their double act. He was tall, with a thin bearded face, angular nose and supercilious eyes that lurked behind square wire rim spectacles. Beneath the exterior persona he projected of affable chumminess, there lurked a ruthless careerist. Calthrop was his junior cohort, with tight dark curly hair atop a knobbly face and a gap-toothed grin, but he was a match for Sheldrake when it came to uttering glib remarks delivered in a self-consciously humorous tone.

My work day would usually begin with a running commentary from the pair of them as I entered the office. Normally, Sheldrake would say something along the lines of "Watch out, here comes the man mountain," or "Where's the stiff today?" This would then be followed up with a further exchange, all conducted within my earshot.

"Who, the walking overcoat?" Calthrop replied.

"Yes."

"For the life of me, I don't know... Maybe Mrs. Thatcher finally decided to bring back hanging and she needed a new man to operate the gallows."

"Yes, she looks like the type of woman who would re-introduce capital punishment... You know, perhaps the nation *does* need a strict head mistress. A matronly sort, dishing out punishment to her misbehaving subjects."

"Finally listened to the voice of the people has she, eh? You know, I can picture our colleague now, placing the noose around the neck of his next unfortunate victim. His great stony face like one of those Easter Island phizogs or something Egyptian out of the British Museum."

"He could be an Albert Pierrepoint for the ages."

Calthrop chuckled.

"Albert Pierrepoint. I like it. Priceless that is. Priceless."

And with that, Pierrepoint was the name they would use to refer to me from then on.

"Next time we have a strike," Sheldrake continued, "put Pierrepoint on the front of the picket line and they'll cave in to our demands right away. He'd put the fear of God into anyone."

Calthrop then turned and addressed me directly as I seated myself behind my desk.

"Don't look so glum, chum. You know it's just our little practical joke, don't you?"

Inside, I wanted to rise to my feet. I wanted to tower over them and command them never to refer to me as their "chum" ever again. But I did nothing of the sort. Such an action would have set me further apart from the other members of staff, who seemed to be so blithely accepting of Sheldrake and Calthrop's behaviour, so forgiving of their slippery smiles and their empty laughter.

I was trying to be normal, but already I sensed I was failing even at this most simple of tasks.

Too often, morbid thoughts would cloud my mind. Too often, my mind returned to the deaths of Mr. Smith and Mr. Drew and how I had precipitated them.

*Why am I not normal?* I wondered.

At the end of each day, my colleagues returned to their homes to share time with partners, spouses or extended families. I returned to an empty flat. It was on the streets of the city, however, that I began to feel my estrangement from life most acutely.

I had become inured to the fact that I was unattractive to the opposite sex. And yet, with the onset of adulthood, a sense of loneliness began to follow me like a cloud of fog around the city. I would often sit on the underground and watch them. Men and women. I would watch them as they talked to each other. I would observe the eye contact and the smiles they would exchange. I would observe the easy interchange of personalities, the effortless back and forth they engaged in like professional tennis players. And I would wonder to myself what was the secret language they were possessed by.

A depthless melancholy settled over my being. For months, I felt an emptiness that I would never be like other people, that I would never understand this secret language between men and women. I marked out the predictable rhythm of my days, my weeks. I marked them out and I saw my existence laid out before me like a grey corpse on an autopsy bench.

I began to hate London and the tang of loneliness it gave off. It was in the very air of the place. It was etched into the buildings and the pavements. In my growing sense of despair, dark misanthropic thoughts infected my mind. The voices of my fellow city dwellers began to sound to me like coarse, guttural mewling. Like sandpaper rubbing on the underside of my cranium. Like the death rattles of a doomed species. I began to regard the world and my fellow inhabitants with a certain quiet contempt. The hatred was embedded like shrapnel. My new found financial status could not fend off the darkening of my worldview. I was rich, but estranged from life.

And my view was, I felt, an entirely proper view to hold. Each time I encountered a turned back or a clipped remark aimed at me in the workplace or on the street. Each time I heard a patronising aside or whispered observation, they were like physical assaults on my very being. My shadow was my only friend.

I took refuge from the outside world in the darkened aisles of London's repertory cinemas. I took refuge and continued my exploration of Mr. Hitchcock's movies.

I explored and allowed myself to get lost in the rhythmic cutting between close-ups and long shots. I lived by the language of the fade out, the superimposition and the shot-reverse-shot. I explored and took solace in my proximity to the characters on the screen.

I lived vicariously through the romantic couplings of T.R. Devlin and Alicia Huberman, L.B. Jeffries and Lisa Fremont, John Robie and Frances Stevens, Scottie Ferguson and Madeleine Elster, Scottie Ferguson and Judy Barton, Roger O. Thornhill and Eve Kendall. As I witnessed their lingering kisses, I felt a real sense of intimacy between myself and the lovers projected before my very eyes.

I yearned to close the gulf that existed between myself and the protagonists on the screen. To feel the sensation of lips touching lips, hands brushing through hair, hands encircling another's body. Sitting there in the darkness, I would will my body to disassemble, to rise up and become particles in the beam of light, to become one with the image before me. Occasionally, I felt close to the sensation of achieving this state... But to my eternal frustration I remained bound within my physical body. I embraced nothing but the night.

Gradually, I came to the painful realisation that while the cinema screen was charged with secret meaning, my real life was a sluggish and deadening affair.

I became a creature of solitary habits. At night, I would often find myself sitting alone in the front room of my flat. The room was sparsely furnished and had a view of the street and buildings opposite. The only décor on the walls was an enlarged and framed print of my photograph of Westminster Bridge, which occupied the empty wallspace above a dormant fireplace. Normally, I would have classical music playing in the background. My choice of listening material was lifted exclusively from Mrs. Smith's extensive collection, which I had acquired from the house in Ambrose Road.

It was one evening in winter, as night descended over the city, that I first saw her... I had been listening to a recording of *Tristran Unde Isolde*, and had allowed the encroaching darkness to settle over the front room, when I felt my eyes being drawn to a first floor window directly across the way. A set of Venetian blinds were being raised up like a stage curtain. And as the blinds were raised, the sight of a slim feminine form was revealed to me. The figure opened the window slightly and then stood there, perfectly framed. And as she stood there, I found I could not move. I could only watch.

Silently, I watched her and I watched her movements. I watched as she proceeded to light up a cigarette and allowed the smoke to drift out the window. I watched as she raised her left hand and gently massaged her earlobe between her thumb and forefinger. I watched as she slowly rotated the wedding ring on her finger. For much of the time, her eyes were aimed down towards the street. But occasionally she would scan the buildings opposite and, for a brief moment, I believed her eyes locked with mine. However, I was sure I remained shielded by the shadowy interior of my front room.

That first night, I remember she was wearing a grey designer jacket, with black skirt and heels. That first night, I took in what she was wearing. I took in her face, her hair, her posture. I took in everything...

I write in the full knowledge that any description I put down now could not do her justice. If I write that her eyes appeared wistfully lost in thought. If I describe her skin as porcelain, her profile as finely, flawlessly sculpted, her neck as creamy and willowy. If I linger over the details of her blonde coiffure, swept back and away from her face in golden waves and elegantly coiled at the back of her head. If I summon up a word such as *statuesque* to describe her overall appearance, I am confronted by the paucity of my own descriptive powers.

She transcended mere words. She was a picture of mystery and perfection attained in human form. I was rapt.

How long was my first encounter with her? It could not have lasted for more than five minutes. Side One of *Tristan Unde Isolde* had come to an end. I raised myself up from my seated position and took a few steps towards the window. I remained within my cloak of darkness, observing her.

And then, all at once, she was no longer still. She had been looking at the street below, when something or someone caught her attention. Immediately, she closed the window and turned away. She paused at a desk to extinguish her cigarette in an ash tray, then lifted a coat that had been draped over a chair. A moment or two later, the lights in the room were switched off.

I moved closer towards the window, in time to witness her exit from the building opposite. She closed the front door of the property and strode purposefully onto the pavement. Then, with a smile, she opened the front passenger door of a green Citreon SM that was waiting there and stepped inside. In a matter of seconds, the car had left the scene and I was alone once again.

Midnight came and went without sleep troubling me. At some point later, I left my flat briefly to examine the building opposite.

I was sure that the room I had seen was not a living area. As I drew nearer to the property, I noticed a number of name plates adjacent to the front door. I looked closer and saw that the ground floor was occupied by the offices of a small publishing company, while the first floor was home to the practice of one DR. M. HOLLAND.


"Anyone special in your life, Pierrepoint?" Calthrop blurted these words out to me one day in the canteen, while he and Sheldrake hovered around a boiling kettle. "I mean to say, what's all this about women preferring the strong silent type?"

Before I had a chance to respond, Sheldrake went ahead and butted in.

"For pity's sake," he said. "Leave him be, Freddie." He then turned towards me. "While you're here, can I ask if you're going to get involved in the office Christmas tradition this year?"

I asked Sheldrake what he meant.

"Well, it's very simple. The name of everyone is put into a tombola and we draw lots. Then, whoever's name we pick, we buy a seasonal gift for him or her, the maximum monetary value of which will be decided on in due course. The identity of the buyer remains a secret, however."

I readily agreed to take part, if it would hasten the end of this conversation.

"Excellent... You know, *I* have someone special in my life," Sheldrake confided. "I'm not one for normally sharing trade secrets, but it's the kind of thing that helps when you apply to go up the greasy ladder in this game. And as you may or may not know, I'm applying for the next round of departmental promotions... Did you know that?"

I confessed that I did not.

"Well, you can now consider yourself officially in the know," Sheldrake informed me as the kettle whistled impatiently in the background.

When the time came to draw lots, Sheldrake's name was on the piece of paper I withdrew. I had no choice but to enter into the spirit of the season. I duly wandered into Harrods, purchased a winter set of scarf and gloves made from 100% wool and in the process exceeded the spending limit. Perhaps I thought such a gesture would improve the working atmosphere in the office.

In any event, the Christmas holidays were soon bearing down on us. On the final day of work, the staff were invited to retrieve their individual presents from underneath a skeletal green plastic tree. The tree was decked in garish tinsel and topped with a star roughly hewn from double ply cardboard. I followed everyone's example, lifting the wrapped item with my name on it and returning to my desk. When I unsheathed the festive wrapping, I found myself looking in bafflement at a bar of soap attached to a length of cord. I studied the object closer and saw that the bar of soap had been crudely carved to resemble a jowly human face. Still puzzled, I hazarded a guess that it was supposed to be a representation of my own face.

"Soap on a rope. The old dependable, eh?" Sheldrake commented later, pausing at my desk before he left the office. "Don't take it too bad, Pierrepoint. Whoever bought it, I'm sure it's not a statement on your personal hygiene... Mind you, I did alright, didn't I?" He gestured to the woollen scarf he had arranged around his neck. "Obviously bought by one of the more discerning of our colleagues. Oh, by the way, we're all going out for a drinky-drinky now if you want to join us."

I managed to thank Sheldrake for the invitation and wished him greetings for the season, but decided to skip the post-works drinks. I may have muttered a few choice words under my breath as I watched him stalk away with a Father Christmas hat on his head and the scarf I had bought around his neck. However, I knew I could not allow myself to see red at both his and Calthrop's conduct.

Besides, my mind was not on my work and not on the

behaviour of my colleagues. My mind was elsewhere…

Her full name, I discovered in due course, was Marion Holland. She was a psychiatrist who largely offered her services to well-heeled members of society.

For a time, I genuinely considered making enquiries about becoming a patient of Ms. Holland's. I wondered if she could cure me of my maladies. As my mind dwelt on the possibilities, I wondered if she would countenance any other sort of relationship with me. I wondered how I could go about telling her that she was my type of woman.

I gave much serious thought to the idea of offering myself to her as a case study. If I did, I told myself, I would open myself up to the experience and the effect could very well be therapeutic.

In my inner world, I allowed myself to imagine a doctor-patient relationship developing between Ms. Holland and I. In my inner world, I imagined lying on the couch in her office and rhyming off my myriad problems. And then I would imagine her every possible response to my malaise. At times, I imagined her demeanour as professional and forthright. At other times, I imagined her seated near to me, unmoving and merely listening. Once, I imagined her laughing outright at me as I bared my soul.

On another occasion, I imagined she dimmed the lights in the room, then loomed over me and shone a soft light in my face. I felt my mind wandering while laid out there on the couch. I felt my mind wandering and I eyed the books on Ms. Holland's shelves… Krafft-Ebing's *Psychopathia Sexualis*, *The Labyrinthe of the Guilt Complex*, *Sexual Aberrations of the Criminal Female*.

During my imaginary sessions with Ms. Holland, she dredged up painful memories from the recesses of my mind in an attempt to cure me. She regressed me to the scene of my childhood as part of her efforts to unravel my internal mysteries. I recalled the wrought iron railings and the face of The Virgin Mary. I recalled that face of infinite love and compassion. She regressed me and I saw the splashes of blood in the snow. I shared with her my late development as a talker... My sense of otherness... My photophobia.

I imagined unburdening my mind to Ms. Holland... Telling her about Mr. Drew... Telling her how he introduced me to the works of Mr. Hitchcock. And in these imaginary sessions, I managed to resist the urge to tell her how I subsequently delivered a death sentence on him.

In my inner world, Ms. Holland struggled to cure the disease of my mind. However, over time, she delivered her diagnosis and I played out every possible scenario.

Once, I imagined that she labelled me as delusional... Once, I imagined that she said I was too guarded and not open to the whole process... Once, I imagined that she told me I was spending too much time in darkened rooms, that I was inhabiting a world of make-believe and wish fulfillment... Once, I imagined that she prescribed music therapy to help drive the devils of unreason from my soul... Once, I imagined that she described me as an enigma and said she had been fazed by my blank expression. I was left with the thought that my mind would have been cured if only my emotions had been easier to read. Perhaps if I had chewed the scenery in the manner of, say, Charles Laughton at his most overtly theatrical.

"Do you have fantasies?" she once asked me, while crossing her legs and adjusting her skirt to below her knees. "Do you have a rich inner life?"

I hesitated, then answered in the affirmative.

Ms. Holland followed up my admission with these words... "Tell me your fantasies."

And so I shared with her my secret desires... In my inner world, I told her how I wanted to embrace her. I told her how I wanted my lips to touch her lips against an exotic backdrop in a Hays Code-approved three second kiss.

... *Psycho Kiss*...

In my inner world, I told her how I could make her love me if she was handcuffed to me for twenty-four hours. In my inner world, I imagined all these scenarios and more playing out between the two of us. I lost hours in this silent reverie.

Eventually, however, I came to realise that the thought of becoming Ms. Holland's patient was wholly irrational and so I extinguished it from my mind. Yet I could not extinguish Ms. Holland from my mind. Still, I wanted to feel closer to her in some tangible way. This need led me to purchase a brass refractor telescope that came equipped with a 60mm lens and 20x-60x magnification.

Each evening, I hastened myself back to my flat in the knowledge that Ms. Holland's work often called on her to stay late in her office. Once I had returned, I set up the telescope at a safe distance from the window, making sure it could not be spotted from across the way.

I cannot forget the first time I looked through the lens of the telescope at her. The shock of intimacy I felt was deep and immediate. As I looked through the lens, the distance between myself and Ms. Holland, the space that separated us, instantly evaporated and I was hovering ever-present near her.

She was seated at her desk and her back was turned to me. Looking through the lens of the telescope, I lingered over the strands of her blonde hair in extreme close-up. I lingered over the nape of her neck.

I believed if I concentrated I could make the fine hairs on her neck move, as if they were reacting to the breath of a lover at close quarters. I focused my mind, I aimed my thoughts. I did all this and I saw her skin tingle and the fine hairs on her neck perceptively rise. I watched as Ms. Holland turned her head momentarily, feeling an imaginary presence, then rubbed the back of her neck and returned to her paperwork.

*You felt my presence, didn't you?* I wanted to tell her.

Once, when I was due some annual leave from work, I took a week and spent it observing Ms. Holland. Over the course of that week, I came to know her routine and I even came to recognise a number of her patients. Most were expensively dressed middle-aged women, but I noticed at least three male patients.

During the day, if the Venetian blinds were down, the slats were often at such an angle that they still afforded me a view of the contents of her office. Ms. Holland's chair and her desk sat in the foreground, with a number of items neatly arranged along the top of the desk – an ashtray, a desk calendar, a letter opener, a telephone and a miniature bust of Sigmund Freud that acted as a paperweight. Also on the desk was a photograph in a silver art nouveau frame of a young girl riding a pony. The girl's scarlet hair billowed behind her in vivid, brilliant brush strokes.

The desk sat on an oversized Persian rug that covered much of the floor. Another comfortable chair was positioned on the rug near to the couch, whereon with careful positioning of the telescope, I could observe Ms. Holland's patients. The edge of the couch was just visible from my position, but facing it on the opposite wall was a mirror. Occasionally, if the patient sat in a particular spot, I would aim the telescope at the mirror and would be granted a view of a body part. To illustrate, I remember once having a view of a male patient's fidgety hands through a haze of cigarette smoke. His nails were bitten to the quick and his fingers were yellow with nicotine.

But my gaze would always return to Ms. Holland. I gazed at her from a distance as she listened to her patients. I gazed at her, like a visitor to an art gallery sits in silent awe of beauty.

*Who are you?* I wondered. *Why do I long for you?*

Often, lost in the moment, I would find my hand reaching out as if to touch Ms. Holland, so real was the illusion.

One Friday evening, I watched as she stood at her window once again. She was waiting, just as she had been waiting on that first night I saw her. On this occasion, however, she was not picked up in a car. She was picked up on foot, by the man who I soon learned was her husband. Impulsively, I made a decision to follow the couple. I knew Ms. Holland's routine well enough by then to have my coat, my Homburg hat and my umbrella at the ready.

At the sight of Ms. Holland in the company of her husband, I admit I felt a pang of jealousy. The pair walked and talked hand in hand for a time, while Ms. Holland clutched on to a yellow purse. I tried to gauge her mood, but I dared not approach too close to them.

Ms. Holland's husband appeared to be a young professional gentleman, at ease with himself and the world. He was tall, with neat black hair and was conventionally handsome in a way that would remind you of a certain kind of leading man. The kind of leading man who always got the girl by the final reel.

I followed the couple along a succession of streets, being careful to maintain some distance and keeping the brim of my hat angled downwards. I followed them from Slade Walk to South Kensington tube station. The journey took no more than five minutes.

I followed them down into the underground... I followed them under the glare of the fluorescent tube lighting... I followed them down escalators... I followed them onto an Eastbound Piccadilly Line train, entering through a different door in the carriage.

I occupied myself by noting the names of the stations as the train trundled onwards.

South Kensington... Knightsbridge... Hyde Park Corner... Green Park... Piccadilly Circus...

I followed them surreptitiously off the train, through the underground, up the escalators and out into the evening air. I followed them out into Piccadilly Circus, where I saw the statue of Anteros silhouetted against an array of garish electronic billboards.

I shadowed them as they continued to walk through the streets and watched as they entered a Moroccan restaurant. I held back from entering the establishment myself, however, reasoning that a man eating alone would be too conspicuous.

Instead, I purchased a copy of the *Evening Standard* and lingered on the opposite side of the street in the window seat of a café, cradling one cup of tea after another. After an hour or more of diligent surveillance, I observed the couple emerging from the restaurant. I immediately followed in their wake.

Ms. Holland and her husband walked onwards amid the Friday night crowds, then paused outside a cinema with the name Apollo emblazoned in yellow on the marquee. The pair appeared to study the posters on display, then entered the building and joined a small queue. I followed their example, allowing two other couples to file in behind Ms. Holland and her husband before I joined the line. I was close enough to hear her husband address the vendor in the ticket booth...

"Two for *Dressed To Kill*."

When my turn came, I asked for a single ticket for the same movie.

Making my way through the foyer, I paused as my eyes were drawn towards the poster for the film in question. Against a backdrop of bathroom tiles and gleaming surfaces, a pair of shapely female legs clad in high heels and stockings were pictured perched on the edge of a bath. Reaching into frame, a hand appeared to adjust one of the stockings, while in the background a shadowy male figure cloaked in hat and gloves lingered menacingly in a doorway.

After a quick visit to the gents (having imbibed rather too many cups of tea), I made my way to the auditorium that was screening *Dressed To Kill* and seated myself in the back row.

The film began. I confess, I was getting quite caught up in the plot, when I spotted movement from somewhere towards the front of the screening room. At first one familiar figure, then another, got to their feet and made their way into the aisle, past me in the darkness and then exited the auditorium.

It was Ms. Holland and her husband.

I questioned whether I should follow the couple. I noticed they were both carrying their coats and Ms. Holland had her purse with her, so I reasoned that they would not be returning. And there was something in the urgency of Ms. Holland's exit that suggested she was leaving for good. I waited perhaps half a minute, then followed with the idea that I could take a diversion to the little boy's room if they were in close proximity.

As it happened, they were already in the foyer, en route to leaving the cinema. Or rather, Ms. Holland was leaving and her husband was following. I could see that Ms. Holland was evidently upset about something. Her body language betrayed her state of mind.

Part of me resisted bearing witness to this lover's quarrel, but the urge to watch proved irresistible. I followed the couple, now no longer holding hands. I followed them to the entrance of Covent Garden tube station, where Ms. Holland's husband seemed to be trying his best to make amends to her. I stopped and pretended to study the contents of a window display in an upmarket gentleman's tailors, while I continued to observe the unhappy couple reflected in the glass. Then, with shocking suddenness, Ms. Holland removed her wedding ring and cast it aside onto the pavement...

Her husband made some mollifying gestures, but if anything Ms. Holland's attitude appeared to harden. It wasn't long before she proceeded into the ticket hall of the station, leaving her husband to retrieve the wedding ring from the ground.

At once, I turned away from the window and recommenced my shadowing of Ms. Holland, while her husband headed off into an area of Covent Garden. I followed her into the station and saw her entering the lifts that transported travellers to the subterranean platform. I tried to make it in time to enter the same lift, but as I approached, the doors closed on me. I did not want to lose track of Ms. Holland, so I was forced to make my way on foot down the 193 spiralling steps that led me deep into the underground. I moved rapidly down... down... downwards... and finally I staggered onto the platform, just in time to board the same carriage that she had boarded.

I was feeling slightly out of breath and dizzy following my exertions. I sat quite still in my seat, waiting for my heartbeat to slow and my head to stop reeling. I sat and I dwelt on the possible reasons for the argument between Ms. Holland and her husband. Already, I had surmised that there must have been another explanation for her behaviour other than a dislike for the film they had walked out of.

As I regained some sense of equilibrium, I noticed that compared to the earlier reverse journey the carriage was half-empty. Out of the corner of my eye, I became aware of Ms. Holland's presence close by and I wondered if she was looking at me. I wondered if she was looking at the oversized man in the dark glasses who was having difficulty catching his breath. I dared to steal a glance in her direction.

I stole a glance and the glance soon became a gaze. Ms. Holland appeared oblivious to the other passengers on board. She appeared oblivious to her surroundings. For a time, her head was downcast, then she lifted her eyes and stared vacantly out the window. I studied her demeanour and saw she was in pain.

As I watched her, a feeling came upon me. A feeling that I needed to give expression to the longing that was inside me.

I knew I was gazing at the object of my adoration, but I also knew with horrible certainty that any approach I would make, any attempt to make my feelings known, would be a mistake. I was gripped by the painful knowledge that even if I did manage to be alone with her, I would not have the slightest idea of what to say.

I dwelt on the scenario of carrying out a romantic gesture, something approaching what I had seen enacted on the screen. But I was hamstrung by the certainty that anything I may attempt would merely be a clumsy, amateurish charade.

In my inner world I approached Ms. Holland... I approached her and confessed my feelings for her... I confessed my feelings of desire for this impossible object... I confessed my yearning for her beauty... I confessed, even in the knowledge that I would never grasp it, never possess it, never kiss it.

... *Psycho Kiss*...

I became so utterly lost in my thoughts, I failed to notice that at some point Ms. Holland had disembarked from the train.

I returned to my shadowy abode and still the urge to act in some way remained. After some reflection, I decided it should be an act through which I could still retain my anonymity.

And so, the following day, I made a trip to a jewellers and purchased a gift for Ms. Holland. I purchased a simple, elegant pair of silver earrings in the design of a mockingbird. Each earring featured a diamond stud where the mockingbird's eye would be. That evening, I wrapped my gift and placed it in a plain envelope. I addressed the envelope to Ms. Holland and posted it through the letter box across the way. My gesture was complete.

At work the following week, a phone call was patched through to my desk from reception.

"There's someone in the conference room to see you," a surly female voice on the other end of the line informed me.

"... Who is it?"

"Don't know. It's a woman."

"... Do you have a name?"

For a moment, my heart fluttered arrhytmically. The thought was crossing my mind that perhaps Ms. Holland had tracked me down.

"I'm just passing on a message," the female voice continued

in monotone. "It says here she's been waiting a long time to see you. It says here it's... it's a lady friend."

"I-I don't -"

I failed to finish the sentence.

I placed the receiver back in its cradle and got up from my desk. I made the short journey past the communal canteen and approached the conference room.

My hand hovered momentarily over the handle of the door. I paused, then I entered. Inside, the room was gloomy. The conference room had a window, but I noticed the vertical blinds were closed, blocking out any natural light. I tried the light switches, but nothing was working. Amid the dimness, however, I could make out a figure with blonde hair and wearing a charcoal jacket seated at the conference table. The figure was sitting very still, facing away from me and towards the window. I began to approach.

I paced towards the figure cautiously and wondered how I should address her. Possible outcomes were coursing through my mind. Perhaps, I thought, Ms. Holland *had* tracked me down. And yet a part of me knew there was something unreal in this whole scenario.

Finally, as I stood close to the unidentified figure, I thought I should be the first one to break the silence. Speaking in the softest of intonations, I began to form a few words of introduction.

"Hello. I was told to come here to... to -"

Words failed me, as they have so often in my experience. Words failed me, because at the same time that I started to speak, the figure slowly began to revolve.

The figure revolved to reveal not a living, breathing person, but a skeleton. I am sure I yelled out in shock, but any sound I made was drowned out by the laughter coming from underneath the large conference table.

Sheldrake and Calthrop had some difficulty emerging from their hiding place, from where they had manoeuvred the swivelling motion of the skeleton. Sheldrake was the first to speak, in between the fits of laughter that were convulsing his body.

"If you could see your face... If you could see your face... What do you think, Fred?"

"His face? It's a picture, alright. Stand back, I think he's going to blow his top."

"I do apologise, Pierrepoint. Only a little workplace prank. Nothing personal, you understand. My younger brother, you see, is a medical student and allowed me to borrow this little beauty. And, well, we thought we'd have a bit of a laugh."

"No hard feelings, eh?" Calthrop chipped in. "As the eunuch once said to the actress."

I may have managed to display a crooked smile to my colleagues. I may have managed to conceal my secret fury. Following the incident in the conference room, however, I decided to apply for the same departmental promotion that Sheldrake had previously mentioned. As a junior member of staff, I knew I had little or no chance of success, but I was becoming more and more irritated by their games of casual cruelty. The plan was to let them know that I was no pushover.

Day-in day-out, Sheldrake and Calthrop continued with the same pattern of behaviour, a tiresome mix of jokiness and sub-Machiavellian office politics. When it was discovered that I had also applied for the promotion, however, their attitude began to take on an increasingly sinister tone.

Once, I could not prove it, but I became convinced one of them had laced a cup of tea I had left unattended with laxatives, causing me to spend the rest of the day making trips back and forth to the W.C. The sound of their muffled laughter from the far side of the office was a sure sign of their collective guilt.

Away from the increasingly unsavoury atmosphere of my workplace, I continued to observe Ms. Holland closely when time and circumstances allowed me to do so.

The Friday following her disagreement with her husband, I found myself poised behind the telescope once again.

That night, I remember I watched her as she attended to some paperwork. That night, I remember I watched her push back the chair from her desk. She stood up, then paced towards a part of her office that remained hidden from my line of vision.

Within a matter of minutes, she returned. She returned and stood before the mirror in her office, turning her head slowly to the left and then to the right. As she regarded herself, I felt a fluttering surge of emotion when I noticed what she was wearing. She was wearing the mockingbird earrings I had delivered to her.

Ms. Holland then turned, took a few steps towards the window and looked out on the world. There was something about her bearing that evening as she stood at the window that suggested a change. On this occasion, she did not linger in front of the window. Instead, she put a black raincoat on over the white polo neck sweater she was wearing, and made to exit her office.

Immediately, I made a decision to follow her again. As I picked up my umbrella, my Homburg hat, as I pulled on my coat, thoughts began to swim through my head.

*Is now the time to finally make myself known to her?* I wondered. *Would she be as taken with me as she was by the mockingbird earrings?*

I allowed myself to entertain this and other thoughts that swirled around my mind as I began to follow her. And as I walked I found I was not at all conscious of putting one foot in front of another. It was almost as if I had become disassociated from my body. As if I was a shapeless entity, floating or slowly gliding along the streets, invisible to all.

Up ahead, Ms. Holland was perhaps twenty paces in front of me, walking in black knee high boots.

Everything else, my surroundings, seemed to slip out of focus as I shadowed her. When she entered a red telephone box, I paused and managed to snap myself back to some kind of reality. I watched from a safe distance as she brought out an address book from her purse, consulted it, then placed a call. I continued to watch as she spoke into the receiver. Her head was angled away from me, so I could not accurately gauge her mood. A minute or more passed, then she ended the call and stepped once more into the night. She continued to walk in the direction of the underground station and I followed in her footsteps.

Once inside South Kensington station, she took the same route she had the previous week and proceeded towards the same Eastbound platform. I entered the same carriage as Ms. Holland and felt sure she was on her way to meet her husband once again. Perhaps, I thought, she had misinterpreted the gift as coming from him. Perhaps she thought it was an apology of sorts. I wondered if her husband would take credit for buying the earrings. Or would he concede that he had nothing to do with them? Would she then surmise that she had a mystery admirer?

Underground stations came and went... Knightsbridge... Hyde Park Corner... Green Park...

Again, I had succumbed to the habit of running a series of imaginary plot threads through my head. Again, I had to stop myself in order to keep up with Ms. Holland as she stepped off the train at Piccadilly Circus.

I followed her once more up escalators, out of the underground and I awaited the inevitable reconciliation scene between Ms. Holland and her husband. The lovers would be reunited. I would bear witness to their tender embraces and their vows never to upset one another ever again. At some point, I was sure I would have to avert my eyes from the aching predictability and clichéd romanticism of it all.

I observed Ms. Holland as she continued to follow the same route as she had before. However, a different scene was awaiting her and awaiting me. It was not her husband who raised his hand in greeting from underneath the statue of Anteros. It was not her husband who she walked towards. There was no embrace between the two of them, but there was a gentle hug instigated by the man in question.

He appeared to be in the early years of middle-age, tall and slim, with crinkly silver hair and narrow eyes. It was hard to tell if the lines on his brow were laughter lines or came from excessive furrowing. He took rapid, nervy draws on a cigarette as he engaged Ms. Holland in conversation.

I was sure I recognised this new man in Ms. Holland's life from somewhere. I scanned the contents of my mind and an image came to me. It was a mirror image of the gentleman she was meeting tonight. I had glimpsed a partial reflection of his figure through a fog of cigarette smoke in the mirror of Ms. Holland's office. The restless hands, the nicotine-stained fingers, the chewed-up fingernails. He had been lying on the couch. He was a patient.

I slunk heavily back towards the underground, away from Ms. Holland and the new man in her life. Away from the gaze of the statue of Anteros. I could not bear the idea of her being with another man. And the fact that he was a patient was an additional source of pain.

I questioned why I had persuaded myself out of asking her for professional help. A special bond may have developed between the two of us. I could have been the one she wanted to share an evening out with.

I felt the pain of unrequited desire surging within me and the pain was intense.

I slouched back to my flat. Once cloistered inside my front room, I put on side one of *Tristran Unde Isolde* and sat before my photograph of Westminster Bridge. Keeping the lights switched off, I surrendered myself to my situation and allowed a dark mood to settle over me.

At some point I drifted off...

… I drifted off and I found myself returning to Westminster Bridge…

Once again, I entered the monochrome interior landscape of my photograph… Once again, I glided over the darkly glinting surface of the Thames… I glided towards the hazy figure on the bridge… The hazy figure who once again revealed himself to be Mr. Hitchcock… And Mr. Hitchcock once more formed the shape of The △ with his fingers… And as I hovered before him, Mr. Hitchcock once more spoke the words to me…

"… See as I see…"

And suddenly, in my inner world, I had a vision… A vision of a hand holding onto an indeterminate object, clutching onto an object… The hand and the object it was clutching onto were in motion… The hand and the object were repeatedly rising and falling…

"… See as I see…"

And then Mr. Hitchcock's voice was inside my head again, whispering the same word over and over to me.

"… bludgeon… bludgeon… bludgeon…"

I was jolted awake. From outside I heard the abrupt sound of a car door slamming, which may have been what caused me to stir. It was soon followed by the rumbling of what I discerned was a taxi driving off.

I turned my head in the direction of the street, in time to see the lights coming on in Ms. Holland's office.

I watched as she entered my field of vision, as she moved towards the window and began to close the Venetian blinds. I had never witnessed this before. I wondered what the reason could be for her returning at such a late hour.

The blinds were only partially lowered when the new man in her life suddenly materialised behind Ms. Holland. She turned and appeared shocked at his presence.

The new man in her life advanced towards Ms. Holland, then put his arms around her waist. She appeared deeply uncomfortable with this physical contact. She wriggled free of his hands and moved around her desk. At the same time, I moved into position behind the eyepiece of the telescope.

The new man in her life must have accompanied Ms. Holland back in the taxi I had heard driving away. But it was clear from her reaction that she had not expected him to follow her upstairs.

Trying to fill in the gaps of the evening, I endulged in some speculation. Perhaps the evening had not went as she envisaged. Perhaps she had questioned the new man in her life if he had purchased the earrings and had been disappointed at his response. Perhaps she was having second thoughts about the inappropriate nature of this doctor-patient relationship. Perhaps Ms. Holland now realised her mistake, but it was too late and she found the new man in her life difficult to get rid of.

I looked on as Ms. Holland picked up a set of keys from her desk and then indicated that they should both move towards the door. Had she forgotten the keys and returned to her office to retrieve them?

If I had been an expert lip reader, no doubt I would have been more attuned to the finer details of the situation. In truth, however, the emotions of the two protagonists were not overly difficult to follow.

The new man in her life was holding a cigarette, which he proceeded to stub out in the ash tray. As the last remnants of smoke curled upwards, he motioned towards the couch. Ms. Holland demurred. It was not the answer the new man in her life wanted to hear. He began to move slowly towards Ms. Holland. He smiled, he extended his arms in a non-threatening gesture. Then in a rapid movement he lunged at her mouth, grabbing her with both hands and kissing her.

Ms. Holland struggled. She wrestled herself free of the new man in her life and with her right hand she slapped him across the face. A light fitting in the ceiling felt the upward impact of Ms. Holland's hand and it began to sway back and forth.

The new man in her life retained an insolent smile as his eyes remained fixed on Ms. Holland. His brow furrowed, his face twitched, but it did not register any pain.

She backed away from him, but soon found herself cornered as he continued to advance towards her. The new man in her life then grabbed Ms. Holland. I watched, horrified, as he pinned her down on the desk and forced himself on top of her.

Now, with hindsight, I realise this was the point at which I should have reached for the telephone and called the relevant authorities. However, I was very much in the moment and what I saw was Ms. Holland in imminent danger. Immediate and swift action was called for.

I watched as Ms. Holland was manhandled onto the desk and objects were sent tumbling to the floor. The ash tray, the desk calendar, the letter opener, the telephone, the photograph of the young girl on horseback, reams of paperwork.

One item remained on the desk - the bust of Sigmund Freud.

Ms. Holland was now lying prone, helpless and struggling on the desk. Each time she moved her head, the eye of the mockingbird earring caught the light from the swaying bulb overhead. It caught the light repeatedly and reflected it at me down the lens of the telescope. And the light was blindingly bright.

Looking through the telescope, I eyed the bust of Freud and I knew what I had to do.

I aimed my thoughts at Ms. Holland. I projected my feelings.

I eyed the bust of Freud on the desk.

Ms. Holland had already managed to get one of her arms free and it was flailing.

The new man in her life was on top of Ms. Holland. He was attacking her.

Through the telescope I saw shadows on the wall, bodies in motion, tussling.

Ms. Holland's arm stretched back. It stretched back and her

hand chanced upon the bust of Freud.

And Mr. Hitchcock's voice was inside my head again... I recited his words... I aimed his words...

"... bludgeon... bludgeon... bludgeon..."

Ms. Holland's hand felt for the bust, but her situation did not allow her to grab it cleanly and so it evaded her grasp.

The bust of Freud was poised on the edge of the desk. It could have so easily rolled beyond Ms. Holland's grasp.

"... bludgeon... bludgeon... bludgeon..."

Her hand knocked into the bust once again. The impact sent it spinning precariously towards the very edge of the desk.

The eye of the mockingbird caught the light repeatedly... The light so blindingly bright...

I looked directly into the light and I continued to will her on. I continued to concentrate my mind. I eyed the bust of Freud.

"... bludgeon... bludgeon... bludgeon..."

At once, Ms. Holland's hand stopped its frantic movements. Her hand reached behind her prone body and with great dexterity, in one clean movement, she picked up the bust of Freud.

"... bludgeon... bludgeon... bludgeon..."

She had it in her hand and it was a matter of a mere moment in time before she guided it in an arc and slammed it forcefully into the head of her assailant.

"... bludgeon... bludgeon... bludgeon..."

Immediately, the new man in her life reared up from his position and cried out. In turn, I moved from behind the telescope and proceeded to the window of my flat.

I stood there, watched and waited.

The new man in her life staggered to his feet, while Ms. Holland dropped the bust of Freud to the floor. She managed to raise herself up from the desk, then moved unsteadily away from her attacker and withdrew into an unseen part of her office.

The new man in her life lurched towards the window. His arms steadied himself on either side of the frame. He looked out to the street below, perhaps in an attempt to make his plight known to a passerby. But the street was empty. I watched as blood began to trickle down his face from the open wound on his head.

I moved ever closer to my own window and witnessed the desperation in his face. I witnessed his desperation as he raised his head and our eyes met. Our gazes locked and in my mind I did it.

From my position across the street, I delivered a final death sentence on him.

I concentrated my mind and I made Ms. Holland's patient recoil. I made him stagger backwards on his heels, his movements appearing to me like a string-puppet. He knocked clumsily against the desk, then he finally lost his balance and fell backwards onto the floor of the office.

Having dealt the fatal blow, I withdrew into the shadowed recesses of my flat and kept my eyes on Ms. Holland's office. I was convinced her patient would bother her no more, but I needed to be sure.

I repositioned myself behind the telescope, peered through the lens and I saw a pair of black shoes jutting out past the side of the desk. There was no sign of movement. His body remained still, laid out on the Persian rug he had fallen on.

After a few minutes, as I continued to watch, I detected some movement in the room. It was Ms. Holland, returning to the scene. Understandably, she appeared shocked and dishevelled. Her blonde hair hung in unkempt strands and I found it more than a little distressing to witness her in such a state, no longer a poised vision of beauty.

I felt at once removed from the events playing out before me and yet intimately involved in Ms. Holland's plight. She was visibly trembling as she approached the inert body of her ex-patient. She stood over the spot where he had fallen, then bent down and appeared to check his condition. However, I already knew it was too late for him.

As I watched, I used my skills in physiognomy. I interpreted Ms. Holland's movements and her facial expressions as one would interpret a silent movie actress. In her face I saw fear, trepidation and confusion at the situation she suddenly found herself in. And I felt her torture.

Eventually, Ms. Holland managed to compose herself. I watched her as she looked around the office and then retrieved the phone from where it had been knocked to the floor. Her movements were still uncertain and her hands were shaking. She was on the brink of tears as she dialled a number. She dialled a number and then held the telephone receiver to her ear, her hands continuing to tremble.

I looked through the eyepiece, through the lens of the telescope, and saw her mouth and the telephone receiver in close-up. I sensed her mood was edging towards one of hysteria. Her hand touched her face in distraction and ran through her hair. Occasionally, her eyes would nervously regard the inert body on the floor.

It was clear she was attempting to describe what had occurred to whoever was on the other end of the line. Soon, the phone conversation came to an end. The receiver was jangled back into its cradle and Ms. Holland once again withdrew out of my field of vision into an unseen part of her office.

My gaze remained fixed on Ms. Holland's office, but the scene remained as still and unmoving as the feet that were jutting out from the side of the desk. I wanted to intervene in some further way. I wanted to aid Ms. Holland in this her hour of need, but still I felt I could only watch over her from across the way.

I was wondering if it could have been the police on the other end of the phone with her, when I noticed a green Citreon pulling up in front of her premises. A figure stepped out from the car, approached the front door of the building and pressed a bell.

It was Ms. Holland's husband.

On the first floor, I watched as Ms. Holland made her way to the door. Next, I saw her at the front entrance of the building, allowing her husband to step inside furtively.

I continued to watch as the couple walked upstairs into the office and Ms. Holland's husband carefully, quietly closed the door behind them. I noted he was doing his best to placate her.

Ms. Holland's husband turned his head to survey the room and I watched in close-up as the expression on his face became grave when he spotted the body laid out on the floor. The look lasted just a moment, however. Within a beat or two, he decisively paced across the room and stood before the window. He then cast his eyes at the row of buildings opposite. Once satisfied that no one was watching, he pulled the Venetian blinds and the rest of the scene was blocked from my view.

Apart from the occasional slight undulating movement behind the blinds, a suggestion of bodies in motion, there was nothing to be seen for some time. All was quiet. However, I dared not move from my position. I pondered on the various scenarios that may be playing out behind the blinds. I had already deduced that they had decided against phoning the police. I waited and wondered what Ms. Holland and her husband could be doing…

I remained in a state of readiness and did not move from my spot in front of the window. It was 2.43 a.m. when I saw the front door of the building being opened and Ms. Holland's husband emerging from within. I watched as he moved towards his car and unlocked the trunk. Acting normally, he then returned to the building. He entered, leaving the front door open.

A minute or so later, Ms. Holland's husband returned. He was carefully reversing his way out of the entrance, bent over with his fingers dug deeply into a rolled up rug he was dragging. It was the Persian rug Ms. Holland's ex-patient had fallen on. They had decided to use it as an improvised death shroud.

While Ms. Holland's husband struggled to pull the rug

towards his parked car, on the first floor I noticed the Venetian blinds parting slightly to reveal a pair of eyes. It was Ms. Holland. She was observing how the disposal of the body was coming along.

My own eyes could not help but to linger on the sight of Ms. Holland's pale blue orbs hovering there. By the time I looked once again in the direction of the street, the deed was done and her husband had closed the trunk.

His actions came not a moment too soon, as a random police car cruised past just as he was walking away from the rear of his car.

I watched as the police car slowed down. I watched as Ms. Holland's husband glanced at the police car.

I watched as the red brake lights of the police car lit up and the vehicle came to a halt. Ms. Holland's husband continued to walk nonchalantly towards the entrance of the building. Perhaps Ms. Holland had sensed some danger from the lingering police car, as she suddenly appeared at the front door. She closed the door behind her, then she and her husband made their way to his parked car.

The red brake lights of the police car were extinguished and it slowly began to drive off. Once inside their own car, Ms. Holland and her husband had obviously decided not to remain any longer in the vicinity of Slade Walk. The engine of the green Citreon started up immediately and it moved off in the opposite direction to the police car.

The evening's events were at a close. I retired to my bed, sure in the knowledge that there was nothing else to witness that night.


I endured a restless night's sleep and rose early the following morning. Entering the front room in my dressing gown, I was beginning to turn my mind towards the subject of breakfast when I spotted Ms. Holland across the way. She was standing at her window, deep in thought, arms crossed tightly over her chest.

The light was still dim and I was sure I remained well concealed in my flat. Carefully, I moved the telescope to a suitable vantage point and I looked through the eyepiece...

I watched as Ms. Holland's husband materialised in the background, carrying a cup of tea or coffee. He set it on the desk.

I glanced at the desk and noted that everything was back in order. The ash tray, the desk calendar, the letter opener, the telephone, the bust of Freud, the assorted paperwork, the photograph of the young girl on horseback. Apart from the missing rug, there was no visible clue that a life and death struggle had recently taken place.

As I watched, I wondered how Ms. Holland and her husband had filled in their recent hours together. How did it feel to have gone through the overnight ordeal they had just experienced? Where had they gone in the car? What had become of the body sheathed within the folds of the Persian rug? What had been their plan and had it been foolproof?

I watched as Ms. Holland's husband slowly approached her. I could see that he was attempting to soothe her. I confess, I felt a stabbing pang of jealousy. I felt a welling-up of self-hatred at my own inability to come to Ms. Holland's aid after I had delivered the fatal blow to her attacker. I watched through the eyepiece as Ms. Holland's husband's arms encircled her waist and he drew closer.

However, Ms. Holland appeared to resist his entreaties. I continued to watch as her hands gently but firmly removed his hands from their position.

She uttered some words to her husband, her head bowed. I watched as her right hand moved to the back of her neck and she rubbed it. She arched her head and her shoulders and then, absent-mindedly, began to massage her right ear lobe.

She massaged it for a moment, then withdrew her hand. She looked at her thumb and forefinger, then rubbed them together. There was a scarlet residue visible there, a spot of blood.

Immediately her left hand moved to her left ear lobe and there she felt what was missing from her right ear. The mockingbird earring.

At once I felt a shockwave surge through me.

*Where was the other earring?*

I watched as Ms. Holland began to communicate her distress to her husband. I watched and I experienced the exact same emotions. Part of me could not bear to watch the drama unfolding across the way.

I watched in speechless agony, knowing with a sickening certainty how the scene would play out. I already knew the emotional highs and lows the scene would strike. But still I watched the couple experience the ebb and flow of emotions, still I witnessed their final crashing realisation of what must have happened to the missing earring.

At first, Ms. Holland and her husband spent some time examining the floor of the office in close detail. However, there was nothing to be found. Then came a lengthy dialogue between the two of them. It was a scene punctuated with florid gestures, raised voices and recriminations. As Ms. Holland paced up and down the room, she was a picture of nervous exhaustion. Tears marked her face and her hands gesticulated in a language of despair.

I watched as her husband stood with his back to the window. As he addressed his wife, he gently extended his hands with their palms downwards. He appeared to be trying to calmly talk her through what their options were. At one point, Ms. Holland removed the other mockingbird earring and placed it on the desk. Her husband at once reached over, picked it up and pocketed it. I believed his intention was to hide any incriminating evidence.

As I had predicted, the couple came to an inescapable conclusion. The earring had been removed during the violent assault and it was now somewhere inside the Persian rug along with the ex-patient, on or about his person. I wondered if they intended to try to retrieve the missing earring from the body. The husband's demeanour suggested otherwise to me, but I did not know for sure. I wondered if he was trying to convince his wife that the earrings would be impossible to trace back to her. I was not so sure, however, and began to wonder if a description of the man who had originally purchased the earrings would soon be circulating in the London newspapers. At once, I felt sick with anxiety at the whole situation.

I was at an utter loss about what to do. I hid myself away for the remainder of that day, living in silent fear of what could be awaiting both myself and Ms. Holland.

In my fevered condition, I found my mind fixating on the issue of what my next move should be. Should I finally approach Ms. Holland and inform her that I knew her secret? If I did, I told myself, I would swear my secrecy and endless devotion to her. I would offer myself as her protector.

In my private delirium, I imagined other outlandish scenarios. I imagined that, in return for my avowed silence, I could demand that Ms. Holland make herself available to me.

I told myself I would share in Ms. Holland's guilt. I knew well my part in the death of her patient. I was more than a bystander, willing her on in the act of murder. It was my hand, the hand of The Avenger, that was on the bust of Freud. It was my hand that guided it, slamming it into the head of her attacker with such unforgiving force.

I spent most of Saturday slumped in bed, sure that the heavy hand of the law was bound to come rapping on my door soon. I swore to myself that I would never offer up any knowledge of what had occurred in Ms. Holland's office across the way from me. But how could I deny the purchase of the earrings? That would be more problematic, perhaps impossible and foolhardy.

And so it was with a thud of inevitability that the Sunday newspaper arrived on my doorstep the following morning, bearing the headline I did not want to see...

## MYSTERY OF BLUDGEONED BODY
## FOUND DEAD IN PARK

... The headline was accompanied by a blurry photograph of human remains being stretchered from the scene by police.

I felt too shaken to read the entire story. I read enough, however, to learn that already at this early stage of the investigation, the victim had been identified as one Mr. Bernard Vosper.

I was positive now that it would only be a matter of time before I heard the doom-laden knock on the door. I was positive I had hours or days at the most.

The best minds in the force would already be working on locating any shop where the earrings could have been purchased. Premises would be reopened. Staff would be questioned. Records would be consulted. Brains would be wracked. Descriptions would be arrived at. Photofit IDs would be agreed upon. Statements would be issued along the lines of "police are interested in speaking to a gentleman fitting this description." Memories would be jogged. Phone lines would be jammed. Handcuffs would be deployed. A lawyer would be arranged.

My stomach lurched, my head spun. The only thing I could do was return to my bed and hide myself away.

After hours of repeatedly running through the possible outcomes, my situation looked hopeless. I was sure there was to be no escape for me. Strangely, it was at this moment, as I stared into the abyss, that I began to feel a sense of calm descend on me. Calm descended on me and I became resigned to my certain fate. I was sure my only hope now was to commit a bold and noble gesture, so I set my mind upon such a course of action. I would confess all to Ms. Holland. I would tell her of her blamelessness in the case.

I would tell her it was The Avenger who was the guilty party. It was The Avenger who had guided her hand. I will assure her that I will be her protector. I will beseech her to come into my arms. I will tell her that once in my arms, there she will find that my love will shield her completely.

My mind set, I dressed and entered the front room. Immediately, I sensed Ms. Holland's presence across the way. I allowed myself a moment to watch her at her window one final time before I would make my feelings known.

I was sure that she had already seen the newspapers. Would now really be the right time to act, to confide in her? I found myself hesitating. As I watched her, I wondered if she was trying to seek me out. I wondered if she was sensing my presence through the power of my thoughts.

I watched as Ms. Holland, in a state of suppressed anguish, turned from the window. I watched as she donned her black raincoat, then exited the office. I watched as she left the building and turned right.

I knew at once I had to follow her.

Without pausing, I put on my overcoat and my Homburg hat, then made my way onto the street. Ms. Holland had already turned the corner at the end of Slade Walk, so I increased my pace. As I did so, I spotted a police car pulling up in front of Ms. Holland's premises. Two uniformed officers then stepped out of the vehicle and walked towards her building.

I had no desire to hang around and see if the police would next turn their attention to my residence. I angled the brim of my hat down, pulled my coat collar up and set off in pursuit of Ms. Holland. I had lost track of her, so quickly decided the best course of action was to head towards South Kensington tube station. My instincts proved to be correct.

Up ahead I saw her walking, almost in a trance-like state, into the station. I followed her at a distance through the ticket barrier... I followed her down stairs and in the direction of the District and Circle Lines... I followed her onto the Eastbound platform.

*When should I approach her?* I wondered. *When should I finally make my feelings known?*

I watched her as she stood close to the edge of the platform, her face quite still. I watched the strands of her golden hair, now carelessly unfurled, as they were buffeted by the air stirred up by an approaching train.

I followed her onto that Circle Line train.

... South Kensington....

*How should I approach her?* I wondered as I sat in the carriage. *How will I extricate us from this horrific situation?*

... Sloane Square...

*There is no need to worry,* I would tell her. I would use my most reassuring tone of voice.

... Victoria...

There would, of course, be a courtroom drama to endure. And the opprobrium of the great British public, which should not be underestimated.

... St James' Park...

Already, I was steeling myself to the idea of being a star witness for the defence. I would be Ms. Holland's saviour. I would use my gifts to convince the jury of her innocence.

"... The next station is Westminster..."

Ms. Holland at once arose and stepped onto the platform. I followed her.

My train of thought continued. I was allowing my mind to drift and to imagine my testimony in court. I was the lonely peeping tom neighbour, besotted by the beauty of Ms. Holland, who had witnessed the vicious unprovoked assault on her that night. Manslaughter by reason of self-defence. That may be the most lenient sentence she could hope for, but I would deliver a faultless performance before the judge and jury.

The walls of the underground seemed to press relentlessly inwards on me. Thoughts clung to the underside of my cranium, like the hoardings that appeared to be moulded to fit the convex tiled surfaces of the walls.

Ms. Holland was now exiting Westminster tube station. She was slowly walking up the steps that tonight revealed Big Ben lit up like a Belisha Beacon against a purplish sky.

Around me, I saw familiar landmarks. I saw Boudica... I saw The Houses of Parliament... I saw red buses and black taxis... I saw Westminster Bridge.

I wondered where Ms. Holland could be heading. Did she know the deep significance of this location to me? Or had she planned a rendezvous with her husband? I decided that I should approach her before any pre-arranged meeting.

I would prove myself worthy of her. I would save Ms. Holland, whereas her husband had proved incapable of even concealing a body in the undergrowth with due diligence.

Ms. Holland crossed the road and I followed her, trying to close the distance between us. I watched as she stopped at the centre of the bridge. I watched as she stopped to look out at the view of distant lights dotted along the Thames. I watched as her hair undulated in waves, stirred by a light breeze that was blowing along the length of the river. I paused to look at her, my one and only object of desire. Already, I was closer to her than I had ever been.

For a moment I stood where I was to take in her beauty. Yes, even in such an impossible situation, she was beautiful.

I was almost there. I was almost there with Marion. I told myself I would help her. I told myself I would aid her in this, her darkest hour of need. I felt my heart ratcheting inside my rib cage. I felt my heart pumping, threatening to burst free of my chest. I was so engrossed in my thoughts, I failed to notice what Ms. Holland was doing.

Her movements were smooth, deft and decisive. As I drew

closer, she was already perched on the edge of the bridge.

With as much gentleness as I could muster, I reached out and touched her on the shoulder. My hands were trembling, my heart was pounding as I leaned in to speak my first words to her.

"… Ms. Holland, I -"

My heart was ratcheting inside my rib cage and the Thames the great pumping artery of the city was roiling beneath my feet.

I could not have foreseen the effect my presence would have on her. I had a moment to register the look on her face as she turned towards me. It was a look of outrage and terror. It was followed by a scream and then she jumped. There in the darkness, she plummeted. Her face turned to regard me as she fell. There was a look of undiluted horror on her face and then she was swallowed up into the great river.

Immediately, it was my turn to be shocked by a voice.

"Did you see anything?"

It was a male passerby.

"No… No, I assure you. She… she jumped."

A couple more people stopped.

"Somebody, get to a phone box and call 999. Get the police."

"The river police?" someone asked.

"Any kind of police!"

I made a move at the mere mention of the police.

"I have to go now."

"Listen, you should really hang around. They'll need witnesses. There'll be statements to take, y'know. You were standing near her when she went over the edge, weren't you?"

"Yes. But I really must go now."

Somehow, in the confusion of the scene, I managed to make my escape. I knew I could not afford to be found at the location of Ms. Holland's death. Yet, a part of me sensed that I was merely postponing the inevitable. A part of me suspected that the powers that be would soon be paying me a visit and The Avenger's mission would be brought to an end. As soon as a description of the original buyer of the mockingbird earrings was forthcoming, then my fate would be sealed. A life of incarceration would await me.

Heavy thoughts clouded my mind as I shuffled blindly through the streets. I was in no doubt that Ms. Holland was dead. As soon as she hit the water, I knew she was doomed. I had watched her body enter the water of the Thames and immediately be drawn under by the strength of the current. The current had magnetically sucked her body down as the river sluiced its way eastwards.

I tortured myself with unanswerable questions. Did she jump because of me? Had I startled her? Did she perhaps believe I was an officer of the law?

I walked under a miasma of despair. I walked accompanied by raw feelings of grief and anger. I now realised that The Avenger could take life, but he was incapable of saving life. I questioned my calling.

My path took me from Westminster Bridge, into the south of the city. I walked through the night. Then, as daylight loomed, I found myself wearily trudging across Tower Bridge.

I paused for a moment on the bridge. I paused, and as I stared into the silty soup of the river I contemplated joining Ms. Holland.

It was then that I resolved never to enter The △ again.

"Enter The △ and death will follow," I muttered to myself.

I was stirred from my dark reverie by a short blast on a horn and a belch of smoke issuing from a boat on the river beneath me. I walked onwards.

From Tower Bridge, I ventured into Wapping. I walked aimlessly into this area of the city I was unfamiliar with and saw cranes like praying mantis legs poised on the skyline. I tried to aim my mind at the great metal structures, to make them crumple and fold to the ground. In my mind, I saw immense columns of dust clouds in their place, but the cranes remained erect. In the sky, I saw vapour trails and they felt to me like shafts of steam venting from my head. I tried to will the Heathrow-bound aeroplanes to tumble out of the sky, but to no avail.

When I closed my eyes, I was confronted with the vision of Ms. Holland's inert body tumbling amid the silt and the mud of the great river. The lifeless body of the woman I could have protected... In my arms I would have protected her, shielded her, caressed her, kissed her, loved her. I fell to my knees, sobbing.

I was facing towards the east, towards the morning sun. The sun gave the Thames the appearance of a golden tributary flowing ever onwards. I closed my eyes, then removed my tinted glasses. I opened my eyes and stared defiantly in the direction of the sun.

That is when he appeared to me once again.

His figure towered above everything else. His figure towered above the skyline, above the cranes. His figure towered there as it floated on a cloud of spun glass tinged with red. It was the figure of Mr. Hitchcock.

He sat there calmly in his dark suit, with his fingers interlaced and his face immobile. His appearance had not changed much since I had met him in the flesh those years ago. In the background, I heard music playing and a ghostly female chorus hitting the high notes. I knew this music. It was 'Storm Clouds Cantata' by Arthur Benjamin. And there at Mr. Hitchcock's side was an unidentified blonde, cloaked in diaphanous white silk, her hair billowing softly around her head. It was impossible to make her face out, but I am sure the figure bore a resemblance to Ms. Holland.

I was unaware of any surrounding noise. There was just the sound of the female chorus. Then, from a gap in the cloud, a shaft of light appeared and hit the ground. Mr. Hitchcock seemed to shift gently in his position. He gestured towards the spot where the sunlight was directed. He cleared his throat and spoke only four words.

"... Build me a temple..."

I continued to look too long in the direction of the sun until my eyes hurt and my head throbbed. I continued to look until the vision had disappeared.

The intervening hours, between Mr. Hitchcock's intercession and my initial phone enquiry into buying the property in Plouthorp Street, are a blur to me. It was only later that day that the full import of what I had seen properly hit me. It was when I saw the headline in the evening newspaper...

### ALFRED HITCHCOCK DIES

And I knew it then. At the very moment when Mr. Hitchcock had appeared to me, he was hovering between life and death. And by some miraculous force of will, his spirit had appeared to me. His message had been delivered from on high and it had hit me full force, like an assassin's bullet, between the eyes. From that day onwards, my course was set.

That day... I cannot forget that day... How can I forget that day, that date?

April 29, 1980.

△

My decision was made. My mind was made up. I tendered my resignation the very day I arrived back in the office. I was then duly informed that I would have to see out two weeks notice, after which time I would be a free man.

It did not take long for the news that I was leaving to filter through the workplace. On hearing of my decision, there were some mild expressions of bemusement from my colleagues in the General Register Office. I offered vague explanations of pursuing studies and was met with a variety of well-meaning platitudes from my fellow workers, most of who offered their best wishes for my future endeavours.

Perhaps I should have exercised more caution in abandoning such a secure employment opportunity. However, I had two reasons to believe I was doing the right thing. Firstly, because of the endowment left to me in Mrs. Smith's legacy I was already in the fortunate position of not having to work. Secondly, and more importantly, there was the fact that I now had a higher calling.

As I started off on my way home that evening, I found myself being ambushed in the street by a pair of colleagues who, rather conspicuously, had made a point of not approaching me all day.

"Pierrepoint!" Sheldrake bellowed too close to my ear. "So sorry to hear you're leaving, chum. I hope our little office japes have played no part in your departure?"

I assured him that they had not.

"Listen, I know this is not standard practise. But myself and Freddie are having a post-work drinky-drinky to celebrate some other momentous news. Have you heard about it?"

I informed Sheldrake I had not heard anything, prompting a response from him of mock incredulity.

"You mean to say you haven't heard about my promotion?"

I told him I had not, but made sure to congratulate him on his career advancement. Not wanting to linger, I made an attempt to continue on my way, but in a swiftly executed pincher movement Sheldrake moved to one side of me and Calthrop moved to the other. They both put an arm around my back and began to escort me along the pavement as Sheldrake continued to speak.

"And what with your leaving, I thought we could make it a double celebration. Well, when I say celebration... That didn't really come out the way I intended it to, did it? As the actress said to the er..." His words trailed off. "Anyway, I insist you come in and join us for a libation. Just to show there's no bad blood between us."

And so I was effectively press-ganged into accompanying them to a drinking establishment that went by the charming moniker of Guts By Gaslight. The pub, I soon learned, was named thus in an attempt to capitalise on the enduring popularity of the Jack The Ripper murders.

Perhaps I should have been more forceful in extricating myself from the company of Sheldrake and Calthrop. Somewhere in the back of my mind, however, I was thinking about the mockingbird earrings. I was still somewhat apprehensive about the police and what might await me should I return to my flat. To sit things out for a couple of hours, I reasoned, no matter how unsavoury my companions, could provide a distraction from these worries.

Once inside, I was guided towards a circular beer-stained wooden table beside a jukebox. Looking around, I saw only a handful of early evening patrons who had decided to sample the wares of this tavern. Sheldrake, in the meantime, had strode in the direction of the bar from where he then addressed me.

"What's it to be, then? A pint of premium bitter? Pale ale? A whiskey and soda? A large pink gin?"

I chose the first option. While I waited, I took a moment to study the interior of the pub. The walls were painted in darkest vermilion and decorated with framed facsimiles of Victorian London newspapers covering The Ripper's reign of terror. When the pint glass was set in front of me I found myself gulping down most of the contents in one go. I suppose I needed a drink after everything I had been through of late.

"Whoa, slow down there Pierrepoint," Calthrop remarked. "What's your rush?"

I explained that I was thirsty.

"Well," Sheldrake began after his first mouthful of pale ale. "Now that we're out here in a relaxed social situation, away from the filing systems and all the office paraphernalia, we can talk honestly as soon-to-be ex-colleagues, can't we? Would you agree,

Pierrepoint?"

"I suppose so," I answered guardedly.

"Well, all I wanted to say was I hope you didn't take everything to heart that we said and did in our workaday world."

I assured him that this was not the case. I was lying, of course, but I wanted this encounter to pass off without incident.

"I'm glad to hear so. Very glad. Let's face it - and please do not take this as a criticism - but you perhaps did not have the requisite skills for the cutthroat world of the public service."

I took another gulp of premium bitter and asked him what he meant.

"Skills... You know, people skills... I mean, we've enjoyed having you about the office and all. But you're also not the most... How can I put this? What the devil is the word I'm looking for? It's a word to describe someone who isn't very good with words. They're not very..."

"Articulate?" I offered.

"Yes. That's the word I was looking for.... At least I think so."

When the time came for a second round of drinks, Calthrop placed the order. I had another premium bitter, while Sheldrake had another pale ale and Calthrop had another stout. When Calthrop returned to the table, he unfolded a copy of the *Evening Standard* he had about his person and began to peruse it. Promptly, he alighted on the first story that grabbed his attention.

"I see that Alfred Hitch-hock is dead."

"... It's pronounced Hitch-COCK," I corrected him.

"No need to get saucy with me, ducky," he replied in the archly self-conscious style of a pantomime dame. "It says here he liked to be called Hitch. Hitch *without* the cock. Fancy that, eh?"

"You know, I'm not sure I liked his films overly," Sheldrake offered. I gripped the pint glass in front of me and had to forcibly quell the urge to smash it into deadly shards.

"Me neither," the other one now joined in. "I'm more of a

**163**

*Tales of The Unexpected* man, myself." With a gaze into the middle distance and a slow sweep of his hand, he proceeded to paint a domestic scene for us. "I put my feet up on a Sunday evening with a glass of G&T, admire the lovely lady dancing in front of the flames and I try to guess the ending."

Brief monologue delivered, Calthrop returned to the contents of the newspaper. It wasn't too long before he was addressing us once again.

"Hmmm... There's another story in here Mr. Hitch-COCK might have appreciated. The headline says it all... Mysterious Suicide of Shrink Linked To Body In Park."

"Sounds juicy," Sheldrake observed. "Do go on."

"Well, let me see... It seems like a shocking business, really... A female psychiatrist suspected of the murder of one of her patients threw herself off Westminster Bridge... It also says that a six foot plus non-descript man in a trench-coat and a Homburg hat was spotted leaving the scene and is wanted as a material witness."

"... Sounds a little like our friend Pierrepoint."

"Highly unlikely, I'd have thought."

"Yes," Sheldrake chuckled. "Only joking, chum. I don't think you'd hurt a fly, let alone hurl a murderess off a landmark bridge to her certain death, would you now?"

I may have managed to force out a mirthless half-laugh as I spluttered over my drink and Calthrop continued to recite the facts in the case.

"... And they haven't found the body of the woman in question either. They've found Sweet Fanny Adams, as the saying goes. If you ask me, the guilt is written all over her blonde hairdo."

I excused myself, with the intention of ordering another round of drinks. As I got to my feet, I immediately sensed my head beginning to tilt on an invisible axis. I was momentarily perturbed, but the dizziness soon passed and I made it to the bar. I had another premium bitter, while Sheldrake had another pale ale and Calthrop had another stout.

At this juncture, I suppose it would be helpful if I placed the events of that evening in some sort of context. This was, I confess, the first occasion on which I had imbibed such a quantity of alcohol in such a concentrated space of time. But wait… I must be more precise in my recollections. This was, in fact, the first occasion I had ever drank alcohol.

My head felt slightly woozy, but I noted that overall the alcohol was having a relaxing effect on me. Goodness knows I needed to be relaxed when I returned to the table and had no choice but to listen to Sheldrake and Calthrop as they continued to discuss the suicide on Westminster Bridge.

"It says here her name was Marion Holland," Calthrop commented. "You know, I can't really say I'd go for a lady with the surname of Holland."

"Why's that then?"

"Well, for all I know she could be as flat as Holland."

Sheldrake chuckled.

"Yes. Or with a name like Holland it might mean she isn't interested in the company of men."

"Really?"

"What I mean to say is she may be full of dykes."

The pair shared another laugh at that. Again, I suppressed an urge to say something and instead polished off my third drink. I thought this would be an excellent opportunity to excuse myself and visit the toilet facilities. As I stalked the length of the bar, I noticed the invisible axis in my head was proving slightly more difficult to keep level. However, I found that by keeping my eye fixed firmly on the door of the gents I managed to maintain a more-or-less straight course towards my final destination.

When I returned, Sheldrake was at the bar ordering another round of drinks. As I sat down, Calthrop asked me if I was a smoker. I duly replied in the negative, prompting Calthrop to call up to his friend.

"Buy two of the best cigars in the establishment while you're up there, will you?"

"The best? Not the biggest?"

"Alright then, go for the biggest *and* the best."

"Trying to overcompensate for something are we?" Sheldrake quipped.

"No. Sometimes a cigar is just a cigar."

Again, that grating, self-consciously amusing voice was put on for all to hear.

"Yes, but occasionally it could symbolise a huge male appendage, my dear boy."

Calthrop gestured towards me in an overtly theatrical manner.

"Oh my, is it overheated in here or have we made Pierrepoint blush?"

I noticed a double measure of whiskey on the table in front of me. I downed it in one and within seconds felt a liberating warmth spread through my innards, like a blood stain spreading out on a Persian rug.

All of a sudden, the interior of the pub appeared to undulate and the invisible axis in my head shifted further off kilter.

It was too late to regret coming here. It was too late to regret the amount of alcohol I was ingesting.

A feeling was upon me. A horrible, queasy sensation that was unfamiliar to me. A feeling that demanded to be fired up, stoked and fuelled and the fuel was alcohol. I managed to take a deep breath and the invisible axis realigned itself, just as the pair of them started talking to me again.

"You know," Sheldrake said, pointing at me with the tip of his cigar. "Maybe you're doing the right thing. You're still a young fellow, still in the prime of your life. What sort of job were you thinking about anyhow?"

"… I don't know…"

"How about funeral parlour attendant?" Calthrop grinned.

"… You're very funny," I murmured, starting on another pint. "Both of you… Very funny… Like a low-rent Charter and Caldicott."

"What's he on about now?" Calthrop asked his partner in crime.

"Something about chartered accountants I think," Sheldrake ventured. "Is that the area of work you're moving into, old sport? Been doing night classes on the quiet, have you? Crafty devil."

He drank his double shot of whiskey and addressed me once again.

"Listen, I'm sensing some bad blood here and we can't have you leaving without clearing the air, can we?"

"Yes," Calthrop offered. "I mean, *someone* had to go up a pay grade…"

"I don't care about -" I tried to say.

"… and that's just the law of the jungle. Survival of the fittest and all that."

"Survival of the shittiest, more like," I muttered through gritted teeth as I lurched uncertainly towards the bar. Once there, I steadied myself, then ordered three double shots of anything along with a premium bitter, a pale ale and a stout. Rather unwisely, I imbibed the unidentified green spirit I was served as I stood at the bar. I then began to stagger towards the toilets, increasingly disturbed by the lack of control I could exert over my limbs and the fact that the door of the gents now appeared to be tilted at an impossible 45° angle.

I forced my flailing body inside, entered a cubicle that appeared to have the dimensions of an upended coffin and bolted the door behind me. Panting for breath and perspiring, I removed my tinted glasses to wipe the sweat from my face. I raised my eyes, only to be momentarily dazzled by an overhead light bulb. Averting my gaze downwards, I was then greeted by the sight of some familiar lettering printed on the toilet bowl. The lettering read The Terre Toilet Company.

My head was spinning now in the manner of an out-of-control gyroscope, but somehow I managed to unzip and take aim. I took aim and I allowed my bladder to empty itself, not paying particular heed if the occasional stream hit The Terre Toilet Company lettering point blank.

After I was finished and I had flushed, I peered down. I peered down, but instead of the toilet bowl I was greeted with the sight of something else entirely. I saw the churning surface of the Thames there beneath me. I was astonished to find myself standing on Westminster Bridge.

I raised my head, then looked to my left and there alongside me was Mr. Hitchcock. Slowly, he lifted his hands in front of his face and he made the shape of The △.

Mr. Hitchcock once more spoke the words to me.

"… See as I see…"

And then Mr. Hitchcock's voice was inside my head again, whispering the same words over and over to me…

"…tick… tock… tick… tock…"

My head was tilting. My stomach was lurching.

"…tick… tock… tick… tock…"

I closed my eyes…

"…tick… tock… tick… tock…"

… and when I re-opened them I was back inside the cubicle.

"…tick… tock… tick… tock…"

I unbolted the door and escaped from the gents, only to return to the table where Sheldrake and Calthrop were speaking at the top of their voices in their best faux comic tones.

The bar had filled up with customers and in the background on the jukebox a raucous song that made repeated use of the word "gertcha!" was in full swing.

"Want to hear a knock-knock joke?" Sheldrake began.

"Alright then, in your own time."

"Knock-knock."

"Who's there?"

"Ivor."

"Ivor who? Ivor Biggun? Ivor Novello?"

"No. Ivor got to know Pierrepoint's secret."

They shared a laugh at that, then Calthrop got to his feet and retrieved a bottle of champagne from the bar. Still giggling, he poured the golden liquid into a trio of glasses, allowed it to overflow each time and then beckoned to me.

"C'mon... Celebrate with us. We may not have this opportunity ever again."

Before I could reply, Sheldrake posed a question to me point blank.

"So exactly why *are* you leaving then, Pierrepoint?"

"I know!" Calthrop exclaimed. "He's an undercover government agent, reporting on time and motion or working directives or some such thing. It's a top secret mission personally sanctioned by the PM herself."

At this point, I was utterly exasperated by their prattling on and on. Perhaps, yes, this was the reason I had agreed so readily to have a drink with them. To finally tell them the truth. To finally tell them face to face what I thought of them. I felt my tongue loosening.

"You really want to know why I'm leaving?"

They both recoiled slightly at the forcefulness of my voice, but Sheldrake spoke up.

"Go on then, Pierrepoint."

"Here's why I'm leaving... I'm sick of your empty chattering in the office... It creates a horrible atmosphere in the place and I fear if I had to spend much longer there I might snap and would not like to be held responsible for what may occur."

There was a second or two of silence, then Sheldrake looked me in the face.

"You *are* jealous about my promotion. There, I told you, Freddie."

Calthrop wore an expression of mock outrage.

"We had a bet on that that was the reason you were leaving, so thank you very much Pierrepoint. You've just cost me the princely sum of five pounds."

"I don't care about the promotion," I continued. "In fact, you can stuff your rotten promotion right up your jacksy."

"*In vino veritas*!" Calthrop declared. "*In vino veritas*! As my old Latin teacher used to say when he came in with a hangover. Looks like I get to hold onto my fiver. Thanks for that, Pierrepoint!"

"Well, I'm a little shocked at your tone I have to say," Sheldrake spoke up. "You know, you really are a queer bugger, Pierrepoint. I've often thought there was something not right about you. Something not normal."

"Norm… Norman… normal." I was having an increasingly difficult time forming my words properly. "Who cares about what's normal? The normal are normally cold-hearted."

"What is he on about now?" Sheldrake asked his colleague.

"*In vino veritas*!" Calthrop kept chanting. "*In vino veritas*!"

In the background on the jukebox, another track started to play. It was a mid-tempo pop song, wherein the lead singer repeatedly queried his lover about the details of who she was with in the moonlight.

I took another drink and the feeling came upon me with renewed force. My tongue was loosening and all of a sudden I found myself veering the conversation into dangerous territory. It was as if I was drunk and behind the wheel of a car careering down a steep hillside with hidden curves and bends that I was incapable of negotiating.

"And you know what?" I stated boldly. "I was there on Westminster Bridge. I was the man in the Homburg hat."

"What is he talking about now?" Sheldrake wondered aloud.

"Is it that suicide?" Calthrop hazarded. "Is that what he's talking about?"

"Yes. I do believe it is."

"You're pulling our leg."

"I do believe you're having us on, Pierrepoint."

"No I am not." The feeling was upon me and I banged my fist on the table. "Myself and Ms. Holland, we were having a love affair... It was a pure love. A meeting of minds. Something I don't expect either of you will ever stand a chance of understanding or come close to experiencing..." My words were slurring. My head was spinning. The invisible axis was ominously tilted. "I was her accomplice in the manslaughter. It was a *folie a deux*. I helped her kill the man who attacked her in her office... I aided her, but to my eternal regret I could not stop her from taking her own life when the powers that be started to close in. And that is something I shall have to live with until my dying day."

The final melodramatic turn of phrase was perhaps not my style, but the sentiment was genuine.

To fill the silence around the table, I drained my last pint of the evening. There was a long continuous pause from the pair of them and then Sheldrake finally spoke up.

"You... you're serious about this aren't you?"

"*In vino veritas!*" Calthrop recited. "You don't need a lie detector or sodium pentothal when alcohol is involved."

They both sat there, staring at me, until Sheldrake broke the impasse with a fulsome laugh.

"You really are barking mad aren't you, Pierrepoint? All this time we've been sharing an office with a raving lunatic. What are the chances, eh?"

He was attempting to laugh off my confession, but through the fog of alcohol and cigar smoke I knew I had said too much.

"Yes, you're properly sozzled!" Sheldrake continued. "I think perhaps all this alcohol has been playing havoc with your grey matter."

"Best not to drink the champagne in your glass," Calthrop gestured louchely. "You've been nursing it so long, it's almost gone flat anyway."

In the background on the jukebox, another track started to play. As the male vocalist nasally sang about how accidents can happen, I decided to ignore Calthrop's advice and necked the champagne. The feeling came upon me once more as Sheldrake looked at his wristwatch.

"Well, would you credit it? It's gone past ten. I suppose we should call an end to proceedings."

"Yes," Calthrop added. "If I'm quick I can just catch the last train for Cockfosters."

I couldn't help but notice that Sheldrake was still trying to make light of my confession. Yes, I had said too much. And in the haze of drunkenness I had a blinding moment of clarity. Like a camera lens shifting sharply into focus, I realised what I needed to do.

Cigars were stubbed out and glasses were drained. On the surface of the table, a revolting cocktail of the different alcohol that had been consumed that evening was swirling around in a stomach-churning chemical reaction. I lurched towards the exit to avoid any further sight of it, then stepped outside the Guts By Gaslight pub and into a heavy downpour. The rain had an immediate sobering effect on me. Sheldrake was in the process of pulling on an overcoat when he turned and addressed me.

"Well, I'm very glad we had this chance to clear the air. It's certainly been an enlightening evening, Pierrepoint."

He took a step onto the pavement, then extended an umbrella. I watched as a gust of wind caused the tip of the umbrella to swivel dangerously in Calthrop's direction.

"Watch it!" Calthrop admonished him. "You could've had my eye out!"

I started to accompany the pair up the street, mulling over what I needed to do. I was sure I was beginning to sense something, when they both stopped dead in their tracks. We had reached a stretch of wasteland, cordoned off in a half-hearted way by a sagging wire fence and a lopsided NO ENTRY sign. Across the way there was an embankment, at the top of which stood a row of derelict houses that looked due for demolition.

Yes, I was sensing an opportunity. A presence.

Beyond the row of crumbling houses and the embankment, I could make out the glow of a POLICE sign. It was hard to say for sure how far away it was. 200 or 300 yards at most. I had already noticed Sheldrake casting his eyes in its direction.

"Well, I think we could take a short cut to the station this way. Couldn't we, Freddie?"

I discerned some trepidation in Sheldrake's voice.

"The police station?"

"No! The tube station."

"What about the No Entry sign?"

"Oh, it will be perfectly safe. A short excursion along the embankment and Bob's your uncle."

I remained silent. I was trying to focus on the presence I was feeling. It was a presence that had laid buried for years.

"…tick… tock… tick… tock…"

Sheldrake spoke to me one last time, but while he did so his eyes were turned towards the blue and white sign lit up in the distance.

"Well, Pierrepoint. All being well, we will see you back in the office tomorrow."

I stood aside as the duo clambered awkwardly over the wire fencing and up onto the embankment. I continued to keep watch as they talked together, as Sheldrake no doubt outlined to Calthrop his plan for what they would say to the authorities when they arrived at the police station.

Already, Sheldrake would be anticipating the feeling of self-importance that would descend upon him. Already, he would be relishing the idea of being lauded as a hero in apprehending a dangerous criminal like myself. Already, he would be planning the stories he would tell for years to come over his lukewarm glasses of pale ale.

I continued to keep watch and I sensed where I had to make it happen.

I stood there unmoving while great rivulets of rain poured off the brim of my Homburg hat. I watched as, in unison, Sheldrake and Calthrop looked back over their shoulders at me. I watched as they quickened their pace when they saw me still standing in the same spot.

And the presence I was sensing, it was finally revealing itself to me. The demolition work and the heavy rain had played their parts in unearthing it.

And Mr. Hitchcock's voice was inside my head again... I recited his words... I aimed his words...

"...tick... tock... tick... tock..."

It had been lying in situ there... Buried for so long... Waiting for its moment... And now the moment had arrived.

Sheldrake and Calthrop staggered onwards along the embankment, the umbrella now a hindrance to them.

The gelid rain continued to fall. The wind continued to blow. A rapturous peal of thunder sounded out directly above me. I removed my tinted glasses and my eyes were blasted by a brilliant flash of lightning.

Yes, it had been buried there for so long... I continued to focus my mind... I continued to aim his words...

"... tick tock... tick tock... tick tock... tick tock..."

In my mind I could see it clearly now, but my victims were blindly unaware of its presence.

And in my inner world I was granted a vision of how it had arrived here to serve its purpose. I saw its journey from a German munitions factory to a bomber plane on a night-time raid. I saw how it had lain here dormant in the soft earth ever since, as if it had been carefully placed there by an omniscient hand.

"... ticktock... ticktock... ticktock... ticktock..."

And the sequence of events happened so quickly. It all

happened in the blink of an eye.

Sheldrake and Calthrop had drawn close to the gable wall of a two-storey house. The interior of the house was open and exposed to the elements. I saw flock wallpaper being flayed from plaster by the beating rain. I saw a staircase leading to nowhere but into the night sky. And then a powerful surge of wind blew.

I watched as the gable wall bulged outwards. I watched as it swayed... I urged it onwards until gravity took control and the brick edifice began to topple.

Beneath, Sheldrake and Calthrop had already spotted the imminent collapse.

"...ticktockticktockticktockticktock..."

They had no other choice but to career pell-mell down the embankment and directly towards the -

"... **BANG!**..."

I turned away as the muffled explosion reverberated, as the sound of the falling rubble merged with another thunderclap skywards, as Sheldrake's umbrella carouselled off in the direction of the police station. I angled the brim of my Homburg hat downwards and set off on foot for my flat in Slade Walk. There was no need to linger at the scene of the crime. I was certain that if the UXB had not sealed their fate, then the falling masonry had.


The remains of Sheldrake and Calthrop were discovered the following day. One newspaper reported the grisly fact that when workmen arrived on the site, they had to repeatedly scatter flocks of seagulls and carrion crows that were congregating on the bodies. The report did not go into any further details, but I did not have to try very hard to imagine what acts the birds had been performing on my former colleagues.

Ladies and gentlemen of my captive jury, I assure you I did not take any sense of satisfaction from the ending the pair had met. I admit I had let my emotions get the better of me. I admit the double murder of Sheldrake and Calthrop was committed when my creative juices were not fully flowing. It was a run for cover killing and, yes, a killing of necessity. However, it was not The Avenger's proudest moment and caused me once again to question my calling. A part of me felt guilty at the events that had occurred in the vicinity of the Guts By Gaslight bar. A part of me sensed that following my failure to save Ms. Holland, following the artless and haphazard method I had deployed in despatching Sheldrake and Calthrop, it was time for The Avenger to be retired.

Increasingly fearful of my gifts, I once again silently pledged to myself that if I should ever need to call on them in the future, I should use them sparingly and responsibly.

When the deaths were learned of in the General Register Office, a hushed shockwave passed through the place. And because I was in the company of Sheldrake and Calthrop on that fateful night, I naturally faced a barrage of questions from my co-workers.

*What the hell were they doing walking there?* Was one question I was asked repeatedly.

*Did you see what happened*? Was another.

I pleaded ignorance on the first and I lied about the second.

Another consequence of these two sudden and unexpected deaths was a request for me to reconsider my resignation. Reconsider, I was told, and you could be offered the promotion Sheldrake had successfully applied for. I took a few moments to consider, then politely refused the offer.

I was tired of being an employee. I was tired of trying and failing to be normal. And I could not forget the message Mr. Hitchcock had imparted to me. A message that was still reverberating through my head.

"… Build me a temple…"

In my inner world, time is elastic. In my inner world, I now stand poised like a conductor in The Royal Albert Hall. I focus my mind and I begin to orchestrate the opening bars of a cinematic collapse of time. Take my hand now and I will guide you as together we move through a space that spans over thirty years.

These are the years I resided in The Temple…

Within a matter of days, I had placed an offer on the house in Plouthorp Street and it was accepted. The youthful, rotund estate agent I dealt with queried whether I wanted to view the property before coming to a final decision. I replied that it would not be necessary.

"Going to tear the old place down, then?" he commented obsequiously. "Very far-sighted, sir. Very far-sighted. It's an up-and-coming area you've decided to invest in. You stand to make a killing."

I replied that I did not need somewhere to invest in, but rather somewhere to live in. The estate agent appeared momentarily baffled, but continued nonetheless.

"And do you want to know why it's the only building standing in that street, sir?"

I humoured him and asked him why.

"You see, the rest of the houses were obliterated during a single night of bombing in The Blitz… I suppose one thing war is good for is urban regeneration." He forced out of couple of hollow laughs. "All joking aside, your property has had something of a charmed history already, I think it's fair to say, and I'm sure it will continue under your ownership."

On the very day I collected the keys, I took an exploratory journey to Plouthorp Street. As previously described, the property was situated in an anonymous cul-de-sac that lay in close proximity to the Thames. The three-storey end terrace dwelling was attached to an adjunct and sat on a patch of land delineated with spiked wrought iron railings.

As soon as I unlocked the front door and stepped inside the

end terrace section of the house, I was confronted with the scale of my challenge. It was a house that harboured a catalogue of abandonment issues. Downstairs, there was a dilapidated kitchen and spartan living quarters. Damp stains blossomed everywhere. On the first floor were two large rooms gutted of any features. One room, I thought, could be large enough for a study, but I had to use my powers of imagination to see beyond the broken floorboards, the cracked plaster and the hopelessly faded and frayed carpets.

On that first visit, however, it was the adjoining premises that I was drawn to explore more fully. The space was accessed via a connecting gunmetal iron doorway on the ground floor of the house. Beyond the door, there was only darkness.

Fortunately, I had thought to bring a torch with me. I switched the torch on, took a step inside the adjunct and slowly the decrepit interior began to reveal itself to me.

I was within a large hall or nave with bare brick walls and a stone floor that gave the place the appearance of a courtyard. I aimed the beam of the torch upwards, towards a makeshift corrugated pitched tin roof that was doing an effective job of blocking out any daylight.

To my right, there was a stage. What looked like a narrow wooden altar or lectern was lying on its side nearby, while off in the corner, shrouded in dust and cobwebs, was an organ.

As I examined the space closer, I tried to imagine what kind of use it had been put to in the past. Was it a meeting house or some sort of place of worship?

Located behind the stage was a shuttered window, partially concealed by an ancient, wilting curtain. Beneath the window lay scattered shards of glass and a dust-sheathed mural, decorated with indecipherable daubings. I peered closer and saw one panel of the mural featured the image of an indistinct globe with a flash of light emanating from it.

Casting my eyes around, I saw stains of unknown origin on

the floor and the strewn remains of broken wooden chairs. All that was missing was a sign reading This Property Is Condemned. Despite all this and more, I saw great possibilities.

While I continued to linger around the area of the stage, I heard some light scuttling movements coming from inside the organ. I directed the torch light at the instrument and ventured a guess that some rats had made a home out of it. Rather than explore any further, I quickly decided to make my exit from the adjunct.

I retreated through the metal door, then left via the main entrance of the property. Once outside, I paused to regard the front section of the adjunct. The exterior wall of the place was alive with a bristling exoskeleton of ivy. Three weather-beaten steps led to a double panelled oak door, the key to which the estate agent had informed me was missing. A pair of ionic columns fashioned from Portland Stone stood either side of the door, supporting a carved entablature and triangular pediment. The pediment bore the faintest hint of a design and some lettering, but it was impossible to clearly decode. I could just make out the vague form of a semi-circular shape rising up from the base section of the pediment and lines radiating out from it, but it was no more than a shadowy imprint on stone.

Overcome by the arcane air of mystery about the place, I locked the property and made my return to Slade Walk. I now had a project worthy of dedicating myself to.

The flat in Slade Walk would remain my base and from there I began to tentatively map out my plans for the restoration project. It was a lengthy process, around thirteen months from start to finish. But, as the saying goes, the mills of God grind slowly...

During those months, I focused intently on the restoration process. I began by teaching myself the basics of building regulation and became intimately aware of the different stages involved in renovating a property. The first task was to have a thorough building survey carried out, which brought up a number of issues that needed to be addressed – in particular, some minor subsidence and a touch of dry rot that was present in the house.

The memory of that time is now a blur, but it is a pleasurable blur of a mind fully occupied. I found great solace in the planning and the previsualisation of the project. I had to mobilise every brain cell to realise my plans, allowing for as little compromise as possible. When confronted with the many technical challenges which arose, I found it particularly satisfying to sit down and methodically work out how to overcome them.

After I had hired an architectural firm to draw up the plans for my conversion, the next stage was to select and employ a construction company. I found one by the name of Shamley Construction who proved themselves to be consistently hard-working and reliable. Often, after hours, I would visit the site to inspect how the work was progressing. It took so long, and demanded so much toil, to achieve the simplicity of style I had in mind. The construction firm oversaw the damp proofing, the necessary repairs to the roof, the replastering, the rewiring, the insulation, the painting and the decorating. When it came to the installation of a new bathroom suite, I could have saved on the cost thanks to my continued absentee ownership of The Terre Toilet Company, but instead I opted for another brand. The prospect of having to look at the company lettering each and every day was simply too much to contemplate.

Concerning the adjunct, the major structural change was my decision to build an upper level, creating space for a number of adjoining rooms. There was also one additional feature to the façade, directly above the pediment. I requested that a panoramic window be installed and specified that the glass should be slightly tinted to shield my photophobic eyes. The view faced west. It faced towards The △.

It was in the dying days of the summer of 1981 that I finally moved in to the property on Plouthorp Street. For three decades and more it was to be my safe haven.

Years passed and I began to notice changes to the part of the city I lived in. Many of the derelict warehouses in the area surrounding Plouthorp Street were being converted into luxury flats. I found myself having to fend off repeated advances from property developers, wishing to purchase my small plot of land. Each time their spiel sounded the same.

"Change is on the horizon," they would say. "There are killings to be made."

Years passed. Years that I spent in splendid solitude. The Avenger was no more.

For long stretches during those years, it felt almost as if I was floating in a state of suspension, blissfully unaware of the passage of time. Often, I admit, I would find myself clueless as to the exact date or even the exact month it may be. I had no more than a sense of the rhythmic movement of the seasons... The long summer evenings that were followed by the creeping advent of the darker autumnal gloamings. With the onset of the new millennium, I learned to mark the beginning of each new year by the annual fireworks display staged in The △, the lights from which pulsed explosively on the low horizon while I remained seated before the panoramic window.

In my inner world, I would often find myself magically unbound from my physical body. In such states, I was allowed to fly unhindered out through the glass of the panoramic window and from there I would glide over the expanse of the city. In my inner world, I would allow myself to enter The △. I would allow myself to land on Westminster Bridge and, each time, I would attempt to catch Ms. Holland before she fell. Each time, however, I failed to save her. Even the act of re-entering The △ in my imagination proved too much of a struggle for me. The memory of what had happened still tormented me. And, too often, I sensed some unspecified danger was lurking within The △. With great foreboding, I sensed it there. Waiting for me.

Years passed and as my photophobia advanced with age, it became increasingly difficult for me to leave Plouthorp Street. Eventually, I found I could only venture out at night or on the most severely overcast of days. In the rare moments of self-pity I experienced, I told myself I did not choose isolation. Society had pushed me adrift. I admit that my contact with other people was minimal. The only person I would see on a regular basis was my redoubtable cleaner Mrs. Allgood, who never once questioned my lifestyle and who I suspect had me classified as an eccentric but harmless shut-in.

For the most part, however, I was content with the life I had chosen. It was a cloistered life, with myself as the sole disciple of an enclosed monotheistic order. It was a life of routine, religiously adhered to, in which order was prized above all.

To save time in the procurement of foodstuffs, for example, I arranged for a delivery of groceries each Friday. And each week I would plan the next seven days, detailing the timing of my meals and what I would eat. With unerring regularity, I would dine on veal and ham pie, steak and kidney pie and beef wellington on specific days. I also developed a taste for fine wine and endeavoured to have at least a couple of bottles of Muscadet or Montrachet in storage at any time. Occasionally, Mrs. Allgood would arrive with offerings, normally a plate of food left over from her family's Sunday dinner, all of which was gratefully received.

You may think I had a lot of time to kill, but my mind never once stopped working. These months, these years were spent in complete devotion to the work of Mr. Hitchcock.

I screened Mr. Hitchcock's films for myself. I studied books. I collected memorabilia to place inside the house in Plouthorp

Street. I had listened and understood his instruction. I was building him a temple.

I knew that I needed to populate his temple with relics of genuine significance. And so I set myself a personal quest. My quest was to collect a 35mm print of each of Mr. Hitchcock's films. During the renovation, I had already set aside a special room in which to store the prints. Situated on the first floor of the main section of the house, the room was fitted with heavy duty shelving, as well as a temperature and relative humidity monitor.

In the early days and weeks of my quest, I managed to pick up a number of prints through specialist magazines. And it was through an advertisement in one such publication that I made a valuable contact in the USA. For the sake of discretion, I shall refer to him as Myron.

Following a couple of trans-Atlantic calls, I made Myron aware that Mr. Hitchcock was my specific area of interest and assured him that I was able and willing to pay above the market value for any prints he could source.

Myron was, understandably, suspicious at first. But when our initial deal for a print of *To Catch A Thief* went through smoothly, we began to build up a fruitful working relationship. Once he was sure of the dependability of my business, Myron became a valued collaborator in my quest. I was never under any illusion about the nature of our partnership. Put purely and simply, money was at the root of it, but I could never place a high enough value on his efficiency and his American know-how. Often he would phone at inconvenient hours and I would unwaveringly accept his reverse charge calls. Not once did I question the methods he hinted at in our lengthy dialogues about how he managed to gain access to the studio vaults or other personal collections. I was willing to overlook everything in pursuit of the quest.

Having provided Myron with a hit list, he began to work on it with steady results. Most of Mr. Hitchcock's movies dating from the 1940s and thereafter were relatively easy to track down. A quartet of films had been taken out of circulation altogether by the director himself, but somehow Myron was able to deploy his own unique skills of acquisition to locate even these missing prints.

Over the ensuing months and years, I would become an expert at dealing with the financial aspect of the quest – whether it was authorising wire payments to U.S. bank accounts or writing cheques to cover the import duty on cans of film. With each delivery, after careful examination I was never less than satisfied with the quality of the prints Myron had managed to source. Before five years had elapsed, he had provided me with a print of every title on his hit list.

While my American contact focused on Mr. Hitchcock's Hollywood back catalogue, I concentrated on the British years of 1927 to 1939. As I had suspected, the earlier films did prove more problematic to locate. However, occasionally a lot would come up at a specialist auction in London and I soon became adept in the art of phone bidding. I even managed to lay my hands on two extremely rare and sought after prints – the silent version of *Blackmail* and the alternate German language release of *Murder!* entitled *Mary* which Mr. Hitchcock had shot.

With that pair of elusive titles now in my possession, I owned a print of every film Mr. Hitchcock had directed. Every film, that is, apart from one…

I purchased a sturdy and reliable projector which I had installed at the rear of the screening room, in a space that had been partitioned off during the renovation. The repeated reel changes were performed by me and me alone. Goodness knows, I needed some physical activity. There were no full-length mirrors in the house in Plouthorp Street, but I suspected the rather sedentary lifestyle I was leading (as well as the rich food Mrs. Allgood provided me with) was attributing to my increasingly portly appearance.

I cherished the rituals that went into the running of the projector – the regular cleaning and maintenance of the different parts of the machine, the touch inspection of the prints, the loading and threading of each reel. Everything was performed with careful, self-taught diligence. I always made sure to handle the prints with great care and due reverence. In turn, I feel the celluloid responded to my touch. With some pride I can say that throughout these years I never once damaged any of the prints.

There is something miraculous about the ceremony of viewing a motion picture in the way it was originally intended to be viewed. Something miraculous happens and it takes place in a secret realm located somewhere between photo-chemistry and magic. Base matter is passed through a bulky machine and through this industrial process, visions are produced that are luminously alive. I sense something mysterious and other worldly in the beam that emanates from the arc lamp. I sense it on screen in the shivering, glistening richness of the greys and silvers, the velvety blacks and ivory whites. I sense it in every grain of film as the celluloid spools and slides its way through the internal workings of the projector…

Years passed. Each year was measured out in celluloid and was landmarked by my repeated viewings of Mr. Hitchcock's work. Each year I remained the lone member of the audience. And with each repeated viewing, I gleaned new meanings. Watching his films over and again became as natural to me as breathing. It became the meaning, the rhythm of my life.

Occasionally, rather than going through the routine of loading the projector, I confess that I did succumb to the convenience of television. Mr. Hitchcock's work was becoming a rather regular feature on the channels available to me and I often made use of a VCR to record any screenings, which I could then re-watch at my leisure. Later, with the arrival of the laserdisc and DVD formats, other viewing opportunities were presented to me. These

187

alternative options made sense in order to prevent the prints I now possessed from the possible wear and tear of repeatedly loading and reloading them. Each day, however, I made sure to project one of the prints for myself in my private screening room.

Often I would re-watch a certain film in its entirety with the sole purpose of viewing a cherished scene or witnessing a bravura camera movement, of reacquainting myself with a particular line of dialogue or experiencing once more an emotion Mr. Hitchcock had stirred within me. With each viewing, I had the sensation of being intimately involved.

I watched and re-watched until I knew the scripts and camera shots by heart. Time after time, I would get caught up in the artful rhythm of those shots. Time after time, I would go to my bed with the scenes I had witnessed - the love and death, the sex and murder, the fear and desire - waltzing together in my head. With each viewing I felt that, yes, I was inching closer to solving that grand, beautiful puzzle. Closer to unveiling the secret meaning behind Mr. Hitchcock's films.

And yet, from time to time, I found myself tested. I found myself struggling with the messages within Mr. Hitchcock's films. I recall, for example, dwelling for a prolonged period on the meaning of *Rear Window*. In particular, I recall being unsure of who I was meant to identify with.

On my initial viewings, I identified very closely with the protagonist of the photographer L.B. Jeffries, as I suspect most people do. However, on a subsequent screening, I found myself empathising with Jeffries' neighbour and villain of the piece, Lars Thorwald. As I watched the drama unfold, I found myself imagining the years of marital trauma Mr. Thorwald had endured to finally, irrefutably, arrive at the inescapable conclusion that he had no other option but to murder his wife. All Mr. Thorwald desired was to escape. To escape from the apartment wherein he was imprisoned with the bed-ridden wife who was his gaoler. Thorwald's only crime was to see a way out from his predicament. In desperation he grasped it and Jeffries had the audacity to deny him his freedom.

I spent one whole week watching nothing else but *Rear Window* and repeatedly found myself on the side of Mr. Thorwald. I even imagined an alternate version, where Thorwald successfully seduced Jeffries' elegant fiancée Lisa Fremont. In my imaginary cut of the film, Mr. Thorwald convinced Ms. Fremont to elope with him and together they lived the high life, surviving on residuals from re-runs of *Perry Mason* and *Ironside*.

However, it was with shame that I then recalled my own personal experience at the hands of Mr. Smith. I considered the real life consequences of what he had done to his wife, of what he had planned to do to me.

*Why can't I think of Thorwald as the villain of the piece?* I wondered.


One desolate December evening, during the thirteenth year of my residency in Plouthorp Street, I was making a rare excursion into the outside world when I found myself walking past a pet shop. The sign above the door said Davidson's Pet Shop and through the window I could see a selection of cats and dogs on display, housed in tiers of single occupancy battery-like cages. Some of the animals were asleep, while others were grooming themselves or scratching habitually. There was something about the baleful expression on one canine face in particular that made me pause there. I then did something and in the process I managed to surprise myself. I pushed open the door of the shop, I entered and approached the owner.

"Good evening," I started off. "The Yorkshire Terrier... Is he for sale?"

The owner, a short man of pensionable age with a jowly face and glinting eyes, was in the process of cleaning up some cat litter that was strewn across the linoleum floor.

"Everything's for sale, my friend. But he's not a Yorkshire

Terrier, he's a Sealyham Terrier."

"… Oh, I see."

"Are you still interested?"

"… Yes."

The owner carefully made his way over to the display, each step accompanied by the gravelly crunch of cat litter underfoot. He then opened one of the doors and retrieved the dog from inside. Straight away, I noticed the cowed expression and nervy trembling enveloping the little animal's body. I asked the shop owner what was wrong with the dog.

"Well my friend, this particular dog comes with a warning of sorts. You see, his previous owner abandoned him. He was left outside the shop door overnight in a cardboard box and I discovered him myself. He was in a bad way… Weak, undernourished and, truth be told, he came very close to being put down."

I spotted a collar and name tag around the dog's neck. I read the name.

"Nietzsche."

"Quite a mouthful, isn't it? See the way he's looking at us? He doesn't trust people and who could blame him? I'm not going to lie to you. He could be hard work, this dog. He may not be the sort of companion you're looking for."

I took note of the shop owner's advice, but I simply could not allow this most vulnerable of creatures to be returned to the cage he had just been released from.

And so I gained myself a companion. At first, Nietzsche was indeed distrustful of me. He spent much of his first days cowering under the kitchen table and averting his eyes from me. By the third day, however, he was allowing me to stroke his white coat and pat him on the head while he ate. By the seventh day, my spirits lifted to see him padding into the screening room and settling down on the floor while I was watching a film. Suddenly, I realised I had someone to share my quest with. Someone whose loyalty and delightful temperament would prove to be a source of great happiness for me in the years ahead.

Mrs. Allgood fussed over my new housemate on her weekly visits, even if at first she complained about the dog hairs and muddy paw prints she had to contend with. She also suggested changing his name to "a nice normal dog's name like Spot or Fido or Rin Tin Tin." It was a proposal I entertained for a day or two before deciding to stay with his original moniker.

Into my daily routine I now incorporated lengthy walks in the company of Nietzsche, usually conducted at dusk in the surrounding streets. Our routes would take in St. George's-in-the-East, Dead Man's Stairs and occasionally we would stray as far north as Poole Street. More than once, I even dared to skirt the edges of The △.

Years passed. Years during which countless reels were changed. Years during which the house in Plouthorp Street became furnished with an enviable collection of Hitchcockian relics.

Years passed and at some point I began to mark my advancing age by the gradual lengthening of time it would take me to walk up the stairs to my bedroom each night. Often, I would find myself having to pause to catch my breath. Entering my third decade sequestered in the house, I noticed a gentle wheezing developing somewhere deep within the cavity of my chest. One night I stopped and finally realised my frame was almost filling up the space in the stairway. I pictured myself as an overfed baby stuck in a birth canal.

As I dwell on the memories of my life in Plouthorp Street, I feel a powerful urge to walk through my inner sanctum once again. Within the confines of my current living quarters, before I close my eyes each night, I often imagine I am back there. Back within the walls of my house...

My house... My Manderlay... My Sweetland House... My Number Seventeen... My Minyago Yugilla... My Bates Motel.

And as I write these words, I find myself returning there once again. I am returning to the adjunct... to The Temple... to my private screening room.

From there, I begin to move upstairs and I imagine a camera following the course of my ascension in a vertiginous crane shot. There, on the first floor, facing west... facing towards The △... I behold my cyclorama. And before the cyclorama, two canvas chairs are sitting aimed towards the view. They are a pair of director's chairs. I acquired the one on the right at an auction and it remains perhaps my most treasured artefact. I remember the thrill of the phone bidding. I remember the surge of excitement I felt when it was delivered. On the rear of the chair, a name is stencilled. The name reads **A. HITCHCOCK**.

When I would sit before the cyclorama, I would often lose track of time watching the sky as clouds skimmed lazily across the horizon and as Technicolor sunsets played out before me. On occasion, I would gaze for hours and imagine I was looking out at nothing but an exact miniature reproduction of the London skyline, lighted by incandescent bulbs.

I turn my attention away from the cyclorama now, however, and in a point-of-view shot I pan right, towards the space immediately behind the director's chairs. I turn and I regard the door there. Beyond that door, there are three further doors that lead onto a series of adjoining rooms. My original purpose in constructing these rooms was to create extra storage space, but they have remained locked and vacant ever since the completion of the building renovation.

I mention these rooms, because it was only recently that I began to hear the footsteps around my fragile fortress. Slow, methodical footsteps, as if a ghost was giving itself a guided tour of the place.

One evening, as I screened a print of *Spellbound* for myself and Nietzsche, I heard the footsteps directly above me in the locked rooms. Nietzsche stirred, his ears pricked up and his jet black eyes lifted towards the ceiling. The footsteps were tracing a path unhindered from room to room, as if each adjoining door had been left open.

Somehow, I managed to discount the sounds and retired to my bed. The following morning, however, when I walked to the first floor of the adjunct, I noticed that the first door was slightly ajar.

It was now an incontrovertible fact.

I was not alone in the house.

You and I are now leaving behind the rooms where my distant memories are stored. Instead, I am beginning to recall the recent events in my life. The events that would lead to my present circumstances.

Instead of entering a room through a door, this act of remembering feels more akin to climbing a long, twisting staircase. Occasionally, I may pause during our ascent or I may even retrace my steps. It will only be a pause, however, before the recollection of the past weeks draws us both upwards...

The first mistake I made that day was my decision to leave the house.

My interest, however, had been piqued by an upcoming public auction. The auction, I learned, was to feature items of movie memorabilia ranging from the early years of British cinema up to the 1960s. Following a cursory glance at the auction catalogue, I noted at least a couple of lots I had a strong urge to acquire. Firstly, there was a listing for a rare poster, dating from 1930, for the film *Elstree Calling*. Mr. Hitchcock had directed a number of sequences for this revue-style production. As a completist, I felt it belonged in my collection.

Of particular interest to me, however, was the inclusion of a life-sized standee of Mr. Hitchcock, used in the promotion of *Psycho*. As I studied the catalogue picture of the item in question, I found my mind teetering on the edge of a recollection. I found myself wondering if it could possibly be the same standee that I had seen during my escape from the home all those years ago.

Normally, I would have conducted my bidding over the phone, but when I contacted the auction house on this occasion I was informed that I had left the arrangements rather too late. There was considerable interest in the auction, I was told, including enquiries from overseas bidders, so if I wanted a chance to win the items I coveted, I would have to show up in person.

I am sure I would have been better prepared and more focused under other circumstances, but unfortunately I had become distracted by a tragic domestic situation that had arisen.

It was Nietzsche. For a few weeks, he had been extremely lethargic and simply not his old self. When I started to see the contents of his food bowl repeatedly remaining untouched, I finally became convinced that something was seriously wrong.

It was against my better judgement, then, that I went ahead and left Plouthorp Street. Carefully, I plotted my route to the auction house, I skirted the perimeter of The △, and arrived in time for the event.

Once I had entered through the building's elegant façade, I followed directions and joined an orderly line that was forming in the hallway outside the auction room. Standing directly in front of me in the queue, there was an imposingly tall man wearing mirrored sunglasses and dressed in a long black overcoat. I couldn't help but notice that he was watching a scene from a film on a handheld computer screen. I knew the scene that was playing. It was a musical number from *Elstree Calling*, featuring Little Teddy Brown and His Band. Dressed in a bulging dinner jacket, band leader Teddy was a sight to behold – a roly-poly fellow who also happened to be a virtuoso xylophone player. The man in the mirrored sunglasses laughed audibly at the sight of Little Teddy Brown and his surprising dexterity on the xylophone. He continued to laugh as he was handed a paddle for use during the auction and as he strode through the doors into the room beyond.

In turn, I was provided with a paddle with the number 40 stamped on it. Little Teddy Brown's xylophone music was echoing through my head as I entered the auction room and took a seat at the rear of the brightly lit space. People continued to file in and soon there was a crowd of around one hundred. Through the lenses of my tinted glasses, I began to study the other people in the room.

Ten minutes or more passed before the auctioneer appeared at the rostrum to begin his preamble. On the sidelines, other members of staff were standing by to man the phones. There was some time before the specific lots I was interested in would go under the hammer, so I allowed myself to relax…

… I relaxed… I focused my mind and I found myself summoning one of my dormant gifts.

It is not a gift I have called on frequently, but I have always known it was there. I closed my eyes and I focused. I aimed my mind towards the auctioneer and I allowed myself to assume his point of view. I allowed myself into his eyes. I continued to focus and was granted a view from the rostrum. A view of the room and my rival bidders. As I observed the room and the bidding process, I gained a new appreciation of the gimlet-eyed skills of perception required to be an auctioneer.

Watching remotely from my position at the back, I began to notice that there was one patron who was bidding repeatedly on specific lots related to Mr. Hitchcock. He was a good deal taller than most of the other people in the room and his head was crowned with a growth of dark hair, styled and swept back from his brow. He was wearing mirrored sunglasses and the number 39 was stamped on his paddle. It was the man I had witnessed viewing the Little Teddy Brown clip.

Before the lots I was interested in were due to come up, I decided to enter the bidding for an item in order to give myself some practice. The item in question was an original one sheet poster for *Sabotage*. I already had one in my possession, so I was not unduly concerned when the price went over the estimate and the mystery bidder had no problem making it his own. In the background, Little Teddy Brown's xylophonic melody continued to carousel around my head.

Then, it came to the *Elstree Calling* poster, which I originally had my eyes on. With the bidding standing at £1000, the mystery bidder flummoxed me by suddenly doubling the price with an uncouth yell of "Two thousand pounds!"

I was disappointed to have lost out, but I still had my hopes pinned on acquiring the standee of Mr. Hitchcock.

At first, my guard was let down when I saw the mystery bidder stand up from his seat and appear to leave the auction room. Initially, the bidding was left to me and a few other stalking horse candidates. However, I had allowed myself to become complacent. Without warning, the mystery bidder reappeared at a spot near to my shoulder and once again yelled out an extortionate bid...

"Ten thousand English pounds!"

There was a collective sharp intake of breath from the assembled crowd. I found the mystery bidder's behaviour completely untoward, but I was determined not to let this piece go.

"... Going once..." I heard the auctioneer say.

Frustratingly, at that very instant, I lost my composure. In my haste to raise the paddle, I caught the leg of my glasses.

"... Going twice..."

My tinted glasses fell onto the floor and the light inside the auction room proved too much to bear. I closed my eyes, lowered my head and blindly tried to retrieve my eyewear.

"... Sold! Once again to the gentleman at the back of the room."

The auctioneer had failed to notice my aborted bid. The standee now belonged to the mystery bidder.

Once my glasses were back in place, I turned around with half an idea to confront the mystery bidder. However, he was already nowhere to be seen.

One final lot remained and I listened as the auctioneer introduced it...

"Now, onto our next lot and the last item for this evening. Not the most glamorous item on the list, perhaps, but still a little piece of cinematic history. This is a chest originally from the British International Pictures studio which was once used, we think, to store props. But, who knows, perhaps once Jessie Mathews, Lilian Hall-Davies or Gracie Fields sat on it during their lunch break."

Interest was waning in the room at this late stage of proceedings, so I managed to pick the chest up for a final bid of £525. It was a price I could easily afford, considering how I had not managed to win either one of the lots I had originally came here for.

After the auction, Little Teddy Brown's xylophone music was still going around my head as I left payment and arranged for the delivery of the chest. It was still lodged there as I exited the auction house. The melody was whirling around now, affecting my perceptions. So much so that, when I stood there on the pavement, at first I believed I saw Mr. Hitchcock standing some twenty feet away at a street corner.

The rhythmic, bone-rattling tune of Little Teddy Brown's xylophone continued to play in my head. And then I saw Mr. Hitchcock move. His entire body was in motion, but his movements appeared disconcertingly jerky and unnatural. It took me a few more seconds to realise that Mr. Hitchcock was being carried. Or rather, it was the standee of Mr. Hitchcock that was being carried away by the mystery bidder.

And that is the point at which I made my second mistake. I decided to follow the mystery bidder.

I made sure to maintain some distance and kept my eye forever on the figure of Mr. Hitchcock. Little Teddy Brown's xylophone music was still there, playing helter skelter in my head. It was now an inner soundtrack, accompanying my pursuit of the cardboard standee.

The mystery bidder's pace was somewhat quicker than mine and soon I began to feel my breath shortening as I struggled to keep up. I could feel sweat forming on my brow, sweat pooling on the surface of my shirt.

Why was I following the mystery bidder? Perhaps secretly I

wanted to confront him. Perhaps I wanted to persuade him to hand over the goods to me at a reasonable price, to try to persuade him to stop over-inflating the market. Briefly, I considered stealing back to the auction house to borrow the auctioneer's gavel in case he might need extra persuasion.

Little Teddy Brown's xylophone was stuck in an infernal up-tempo loop as I continued to shadow the mystery bidder, as I continued to eye the immobile face of Mr. Hitchcock... His inscrutable face, continually staring out into the nocturnal streets.

Soon, I found myself walking past a number of drinking establishments and had to quell the urge to step inside. I walked past The Globe. I walked past The Nell of Old Drury. Along the way I spotted a street sign. The sign said Henrietta Street, WC2.

I then realised my grave error. I had allowed myself to get caught up in the chase and, purely by accident, I had entered The △.

A sense of unreal panic descended on me... Up ahead, I watched as the mystery bidder turned a corner.

I had to stop, catch my breath and plot my next move. I wondered whether I should retrace my steps and exit The △ without delay. Or should I keep on the trail of the mystery bidder and follow him deeper into the territory of The △?

I had started to cross the thoroughfare in pursuit when, without warning, a black taxi veered around the corner from where the mystery bidder had disappeared. The taxi's horn blared at me. I reeled back, and saw the darkened profile of the mystery bidder... I saw the inert face of Mr. Hitchcock, lopsided and staring out from the rear window of the taxi. For a moment, my eyes met with Mr. Hitchcock's... His brown eyes, swirling like the surface of the Thames.

Already off-balance, I staggered backwards and caught my heel on the edge of the pavement.

Suddenly, I was falling back in mid-air and my feet were glancing against a succession of stone steps. Little Teddy

Brown's xylophone music was still criss-crossing through the pathways in my head.

To my left, my eyes registered the presence of a handrail. I made a frantic attempt to reach for it, but without success. I was an unstoppable force now. Gravity had taken hold and only terra firma could arrest my progress. I continued my rapid descent into darkness, not knowing if I was falling into a cellar or catacombs of some description. My hands continued to flail around in search of something to try to grab onto. To a casual viewer or passer-by, I'm sure I would have presented a comical sight.

And then I felt my head clanging against something. It was an overhanging sign giving off a green glow. Instinctively, my hands shot upwards and I managed to grab the sign in an attempt to slow my descent. Of course, it could not hold my considerable weight and at once it came away from its fixings. The wiring was ripped loose and began to give off a spectacular shower of sparks like a roman candle.

Finally, with a crashing thud, I barrelled through a set of swinging doors and came to rest on a tiled floor, still holding the broken sign. The neon was now lifeless but it spelled out the name of the establishment I found myself inside...

As a face approached and then loomed over my horizontal figure, all I could hear myself saying was "I sincerely apologise... I can pay for everything... I can afford to pay."

I suppose I was a pathetic sight, but somehow I got to my feet unaided. Thankfully, I had not broken any bones. I merely felt winded and there was a dull thrumming at the back of my head. One positive side effect of the fall, I noticed with some relief, was that I could no longer hear Little Teddy Brown's xylophone.

Rather gingerly, I began to head in the direction of a nearby barstool. As I did, I took in my surroundings. The interior was dark, almost monochromatically dark, but individual spots of illumination allowed me to make out a bar and the row of stools before it, all unoccupied apart from the one furthest away from me. Sitting on that was a man in silhouette with one elbow on the bar and his head tilted in my direction.

I collapsed onto the stool and then noticed the male figure who had hovered over me moments earlier now standing behind the bar. He regarded me for a few heartbeats and then spoke. The acoustics of the place gave his voice an echoey quality.

"I bet you could murder a drink."

He was wearing a pale blue shirt and his face had a vaguely walrus-like character to it, complete with wavy hair, crease lines on his forehead and an arch of a mustache. I watched as he retrieved a bottle and proceeded to pour me a double shot of brandy.

"I'll do the introductions," he continued. "I'm the landlord… Forsythe's the name."

When the brandy was set before me, I promptly drank up, an action which the landlord marked by uttering the words "chin-chin."

As I sat at the bar, I took a further glance around the place. To my left across the way I counted nine booths, each one of them illuminated by a triangular lamp. The interior of the bar was decked out in wood panelling and embossed wallpaper that looked as if it pre-dated the world war (although which world war I couldn't quite say). I saw a silent, inactive juke box set against a far wall and an obsolete television set staring blankly at me from above the bar. Apart from myself and the silhouette sat several stools away, there appeared to be no other customers, although it was difficult to be absolutely sure in the dim light.

Then, I heard another echoey voice…

"Each man has their exits and their entrances. And, let me say, your entrance was the most dramatic I've seen in a long time."

It was the man sitting at the end of the bar in silhouette. I noted a certain Irish brogue to his voice as he continued.

"It's like in the pictures, isn't it?"

Perhaps because I did not reply immediately, he spoke once again.

"I said, it's like in the pictures, isn't it?"

"Never mind him," the landlord instructed me. "He's just one of our regular characters."

The silhouette at the end of the bar ploughed on nonetheless.

"Oh yes, it's a real murder picture in here sometimes. They should change the name of this place to The Torture Garden… You don't have to do anything in this here public house. You just stay still and things happen."

The landlord turned and directed his next remark to the silhouette.

"Any more out of you and you'll be barred."

"For how long?" the silhouette remonstrated. "For life? Forever? Don't make promises you can't follow through on."

"Just try me and see, sunshine," the landlord snarled. "Now, are you going to allow me to speak to our newest patron or what?"

The silhouette made a mock courteous gesture.

"You may proceed by all means. Let the interrogation begin."

The landlord cleared his throat, then leaned conspiratorially across the bar towards me.

"So… What brings you around these parts? Was someone after you?"

"… I was following someone," I replied guardedly.

"Really? Who?"

"… Someone. I don't know his exact identity."

"Keep it down over there!" the loquacious silhouette piped up. "Some of us can't hear ourselves drink!"

"Have you got cloth ears? I said give it a rest!" Another warning delivered, the landlord returned his attention to me. "And this… individual. Why were you following him?"

"… I don't know… I suppose you could say he has done me a disservice."

"A disservice? This sounds like a grave situation… What sort of disservice are we talking about?"

"… He took something from me. Something that is rightfully mine."

"He stole from you?"

"Tsk… tsk... tsk…" The disapproving noises I heard were coming from the silhouette at the end of the bar.

"Hmmm…," the landlord continued. "And do you know of this individual's whereabouts?"

I confessed that I did not.

"Well, if what you are saying is true… If you *have* been done a disservice by this individual… Then surely you deserve some form of restitution."

Perhaps I was unnerved by his line of questioning, but all of a sudden, a feeling came over me. A feeling that I had to return to Plouthorp Street immediately. I had a sense of dread that I would live to regret my accidental incursion into The △. At once, I informed the landlord of my decision. His face dropped.

"Oh… Well, do return any time if you are ever in need of a sympathetic ear. Our door will remain forever open for you."

"Wait," I said, now realising something. "I need to pay for the damage I have done."

"That can wait," the landlord assured me. "You've had a hell of an evening. Come back any time and we'll come to some sort of an arrangement."

"But I –"

"Didn't you hear the man?" the silhouette spoke up. "He said payment can wait."

"… How do you know I will return?" I asked.

"Oh, you'll return!" the silhouette at the end of the bar declared. "We need to know what happens next. Please don't keep us in suspense." He raised an unsteady right hand and pointed in the general direction of the landlord. "Forsythe! Start a tab for that man!"

Once again I found myself apologising profusely. I then retreated through the doors of The Pleasure Garden… I walked past the spot where the sparks were still flying… I climbed the steps back onto the nocturnal streets… I retraced my journey and returned to Plouthorp Street… I returned home to a darkened house.

At once, I noticed Nietzsche was not there to greet me on my arrival. He was also not to be seen in his preferred spots under the kitchen table or on the sofa in the screening room. From the screening room, I walked up the stairs of the adjunct and it was on the first floor, before the cyclorama, that I found him.

Immediately, I knew the situation was grave. Nietzsche's breathing was shallow and laboured. His eyes merely moved mechanically up to regard me as I approached. I knelt down and gently stroked his back, which at least seemed to offer him a little comfort.

Inwardly, I cursed myself for my foolish behaviour. My decision to attend the auction… My shadowing of the mystery bidder from the auction house… My blundering into The △.

If not for that chain of events, I could have returned to be with Nietzsche. I could have accompanied him to the local veterinarian for treatment. I knew his health had been failing for some weeks. So why had I delayed booking an appointment for him? With a heavy certainty, I knew the sort of treatment that he would have been offered.

In my inner world, I had played out the scene many times and it was a scene I wanted to avoid playing any part in. There would be a brief examination, followed by kind words about domesticated pets and the health complications that come with old age. A sedative would be administered to Nietzsche and then my friend would be spread out and etherised on a metallic table. The attentive veterinarian would shave off a portion of fur on one of his legs and then another injection would be administered. And this time my companion would be no more... There would only remain a lifeless, soulless carcass to be clinically disposed of.

As I replayed the scenario in my head, I seated myself in one of the canvas chairs looking out of the cyclorama, looking out towards The △. Tenderly, I lifted Nietzsche onto my lap. I sat there with my hand on his stomach, feeling the barely perceptible rise and fall of his lungs. I sat there and registered the faint beating of his canine heart.

I wondered had Nietzsche expended the last of his energy climbing the stairs and gazing out of the cyclorama, gazing out towards The △. From here, had he sensed that I had stumbled into that zone, knowing as I do the truth about The △?

... *Enter The △ and death will follow...*

I continued to sit there, gently supporting Nietzsche, sensing the life-force slowly ebbing from his delicate frame.

At some point, sleep claimed me...

... When I awoke, I was cradling a corpse.

I spent much of the following morning preparing a final resting place for Nietzsche. I selected a spot at the side of the property, a favourite patch of his territory which he made his own on sunny days in particular. Often I had tossed a ball towards him and watched him play from the shade of the adjunct, never daring to enter the direct sunlight because of my condition.

After digging a hole approximately two-foot-deep, I placed his inert body into the grave and began to refill the void with clay-heavy soil. With this grim task completed, something about the moment made me think I should say a few words. I managed to get as far as the opening sentence of the burial rite – "I am the resurrection and the life, saith the Lord," - before I collapsed to my knees.

Eventually, I composed myself. I returned to the house and poured myself a stiff drink. I retired to the screening room and it was then that I heard the sound of footsteps once again coming from the first floor of the adjunct.

The footsteps had a slow, deliberate pace to them. Like a heartbeat in repose.

I listened as the footsteps halted directly above my head. I waited, then I began to walk slowly and stealthily upstairs, fully prepared to confront an intruder. The sudden bereavement I had experienced had left me strangely inured to any sense of fear about whatever may be awaiting me.

When I arrived on the first floor, however, I found nobody there. The only detail out of place was the door that led into the first room. Once again, it was lying ajar.

Just then, I heard a loud rapping coming from downstairs. I returned to the ground floor with no time to dwell on the mystery of the self-opening door or the origin of the footsteps.

I composed myself as best I could and answered the front door to two men dressed in navy blue boiler suits. In the background, I could see a truck idling on the roadway.

"Sign for a delivery?" one of the men asked. He looked to be older than his partner by a couple of decades.

A handheld device the size of a mobile phone was presented to me, along with a pointed stylus attached to the device by a coiled cable. Perhaps the gentleman sensed my confusion, as once I was holding the stylus between my finger and thumb, he pointed at the screen.

"Just sign, squiggle or scrawl in the box, please."

I followed his instructions, still unsure what the men were

doing here.

"Where do you want it, then?" the younger of the pair now questioned me.

"… Where do I want it?" I repeated cluelessly.

"Yes. We're from the auction house."

"Oh!"

I apologised at once. They were, of course, delivering the chest I had managed to win. I requested that the item be taken up to the first floor of the adjunct, having decided to finally avail of the extra storage in the empty rooms there. I then directed the two men through the screening room and up the stairs.

"I think I may have strained my deltoids lugging that thing all the way up here," the younger of them complained, panting like a failed contestant in a weightlifting tournament. "What's in it anyway… a batch of Uranium 235? A dead body?"

"Stop making a meal of things," the other said as they reached the first floor.

I placed my hand on the door that led into the first room. I pushed the door open, hit a light switch and then instructed the men to carry the chest inside. The light revealed an empty space with varnished wooden floorboards and walls painted in brilliant white. It was a space that I had not been in for many years. As the pair were preparing to lower the chest, the younger man suddenly lost his grip and it slammed down awkwardly on one side onto the floorboards. The older gentleman was not amused, but after a quick check it was soon ascertained that the chest had not been damaged.

"Here… Something fell out of it," the younger of them said as he retrieved an item from the floor. "It must've slid through the gap between the lid when it was upended."

It was a slim red notebook of some description. He placed it on top of the chest. Despite the accident that had occurred, I gave the men a £20 tip and thanked them for their efforts. The more senior member of the team accepted the money genially, then lowered his brow and nodded in the direction of the chest.

"Going by the amount of rust on that padlock," he said. "I'd hazard a guess that whatever's inside there hasn't seen the light of day for over a lifetime, so good luck with opening it."

Having listened to these parting words of advice, I escorted the two delivery men to the door, then immediately returned to the first floor of the adjunct. I returned to examine the chest more closely.

I was sure that I had seen the chest somewhere before now. It was a rather non-descript, functional piece of furniture, but I was sure of it. The fact that it had been reclaimed from the British International Pictures studios was a clue. Yes… I had seen it many times before, lurking behind that door, beside that wooden chair with the floral cushion cover. I knew now that it came from the residence of the Boyle family in *Juno and the Paycock*.

The exact contents of the chest remained unknown to me, but that was something I resolved to deal with later when I had figured out how to negotiate the monstrous padlock made immovable with rust.

In the meantime, I idly picked up the notebook that had escaped from the chest. It was pocket-sized and bound in faded red cloth. On the front cover were three words handwritten in ink.

### "THE CANONICAL MURDERS"

I was about to open the notebook when I began to hear the footsteps again… The sound of footsteps on wooden floorboards… I was standing in the doorway on the threshold of the first room… The first room, standing empty and unfurnished, its walls painted brilliant white… The footsteps continued to approach me… They drew closer… All these rooms locked and vacant… I felt a presence passing through the exact space where I stood… I felt a presence and the footsteps proceeded onwards, towards the canvas chairs in front of the cyclorama… Then, the sound of the footsteps stopped… I continued to stand in the doorway… I was shaken… Finally, I heard a voice in close proximity… It was coming from one of the chairs.

"… *In pace requiescat…*"

He was sitting quite still in the canvas chair that bore his name. At first, his figure seemed to flicker as he continued to talk.

"*Media vita in morte sumus…* In the midst of life, as the poet says… Latin is to the English language what silent movies are to the talkies… So clean, so precise. Like a window pane… Would you agree?"

He was wearing a black Marinari suit, a white linen shirt and a black Italian tie. While his overall appearance took on corporeal form, his skin still retained a translucent quality. He gestured towards the other canvas chair.

"Please… Sit with me… We have much to discuss."

Mr. Hitchcock laced his hands together. He proceeded to slowly rotate his thumbs one way and then the other, as if winding and then unravelling an invisible yarn.

"Remember what I told you all those years ago? Yes, our meeting may have been a case of mistaken identity. But, it has proved to be a fortuitous one for me. Because, you see, I need someone working on my behalf. I need someone looking after my legacy."

He then lifted both hands before his face and formed a rectangle with the thumb and forefinger of each hand. Holding the rectangle before his right eye, Mr. Hitchcock closed his other eye and then proceeded to slowly pan across the view presented by the cyclorama.

"The things that spell London to me have all but disappeared. Perhaps one day, however, you will make the lights go out across this great city in memory of me… You know, what you have realised within these walls has such power… You have shut yourself up here and your thoughts have been so keenly focused they have spread through the walls and out into the world." Mr.

Hitchcock lowered his hands. "Yes, your idea is spreading... It has travelled through psychic ley lines and has dropped down into other minds. Soon, others will follow in your footsteps. Imitators. Inferior fellows. But you remain my first and truest disciple."

He turned to regard me.

"Listen carefully to my words... I want you to think of the city as one immense film set. I want you to think of me as your director... Tonight, you must travel in a westerly direction. I'm rather embarrassed to say there is yet another season of my work screening on the South Bank. I sense that is where you must go. Do not, however, play the method actor and ask me what your motivation is yet. Simply remember this... At all times, you must remain watchful."

I looked on in silence as Mr. Hitchcock slowly began to fade and flicker out of sight...

"... But before I leave you, there is one more thing... You have, may I say, a peerless collector's eye... The notebook you hold in your hands. You may be interested to learn that it once belonged to me. If you care to look inside, you may well be surprised. I think you will find it a fascinating design. Take some time to study it... Forever, if you so wish."

And with those parting words, the canvas chair was left vacant once again...

That evening, I followed Mr. Hitchcock's instructions. I followed his instructions and undertook a tube journey to the South Bank. I knew that the route would once again return me to The △. Perhaps I was becoming bolder under Mr. Hitchcock's direction, but somehow I managed to convince myself that The △ no longer held power over me.

Sitting on the train, I decided to use this time to study the notebook that had been hidden inside the chest. I withdrew the notebook from the depths of my overcoat pocket and began to read.

On the first page, the title **"THE CANONICAL MURDERS"** was penned in ink and in the bottom right corner I saw the initials **A.H.**

I turned the page…

On the next page I saw a rendering in ink of a pair of hands advancing towards the neck of an unsuspecting victim. Beneath the picture was a caption… **I STRANGLE**.

I turned the page…

On the next page I saw a rendering in ink of a hand grasping a kitchen knife, the blade on a downwards trajectory. Beneath the picture was a caption… **I STAB**.

I turned the page…

On the next page I saw a rendering in ink of a hand cradling a circular object with a lighted length of fuse wire emanating from the top. Beneath the picture was a caption… **BANG!**

I turned the page…

On the next page I saw a rendering in ink of a hand holding a revolver, hammer cocked and trigger ready. Beneath the picture was a caption… **I SHOOT**.

I turned the page…

On the next page I saw a rendering in ink of a pair of hands, palms facing outwards, and between the palms there was a body falling away, arms and legs splayed and helpless. Beneath the picture was a caption… **YOU PLUMMET**.

I turned the page…

On the next page I saw a rendering in ink of a seagull angling its beak in the direction of a terrified female face. Beneath the picture was a caption… **PECK!**

I turned the page…

On the next page I saw a rendering in ink of a disembodied hand gripping onto a poker, the poker held upright and poised to strike. Beneath the picture was a caption… **I BLUDGEON**.

I turned the page…

On the next page I saw a rendering in ink of a bottle labelled XXX and a drop of the contents being carefully decanted into a teacup. Beneath the picture was a caption… **I POISON**.

I turned the page…

On the next page I saw a rendering in ink of an unidentified body lying face down inside a domestic oven. Beneath the picture was a caption… **GAS-S-S-S**.

I turned the page…

On the next page I saw a rendering in ink of a triangle and atop it an eye. Beneath the picture was a caption… **I AVENGE**.

It was the final page in the notebook.

"… The next station is Waterloo…"

The voice of the female announcer alerted me to the fact that I had arrived at my destination. I pocketed the notebook and moved to disembark from the train.

**I AVENGE**.

It was time to concentrate on the task assigned to me by Mr. Hitchcock. I set off on foot towards the location he had mentioned.

Soon, I was in the vicinity of the South Bank and standing before the building in question. The exterior was a monolithic construction of glass and metal. For a moment, I was unsure if I was about to enter a cinema or an industrial warehouse of some kind.

I stepped inside the building and into the midst of a sizeable crowd of people. Taking a minute to study the posters on display, I saw that there was indeed a season dedicated to Mr. Hitchcock currently running. Unsure about exactly what Mr. Hitchcock had sent me here for, I decided to join a queue for the ticket desk. Once I had reached the front, I approached the desk and I asked for a ticket for the next screening.

"Are you here for the book launch?" The young lady posing the question was a brunette with an alarming display of piercings in her nose, ears and lips.

Still unsure of my purpose here, I went ahead and answered in the affirmative. Having paid for a ticket, I then followed the signs for the relevant screen. I entered, then seated myself at the back of the auditorium. For a minute or so, I found myself alone. It was not too long, however, before the room began to fill up.

At once, I was hit with the realisation that I had not been in a cinema with other people for a considerable length of time. I questioned myself what I was doing here. I experienced a mild sense of panic and almost got up to leave.

Matters were not helped by remarks I overheard from some of the patrons sitting nearby. One youthful male, sporting a beard that he may have been inspired to cultivate after viewing a Mathew Brady daguerreotype from the American Civil War, flicked through the programme for the Hitchcock season and wondered aloud to his female companion...

"Why would I want to go to the cinema to see this ancient stuff?"

Elsewhere I spotted other patrons talking loudly among themselves, talking into phones or gazing intently at phones. All grave offences, in my opinion, against the experience of attending the cinema.

I tried to ignore my fellow audience members and turned my attention towards the stage, where I noted the presence of two chairs. Placed between the chairs was a coffee table, two bottles of water and two glasses, while at stage right there stood a lectern. At some point, a caption appeared on the cinema screen...

### BOOK LAUNCH
### 'Dial M For Misogyny'
### by Alice Elvey

I looked at my ticket. The event was due to start at 8.00.

At the allotted time, a pale woman with raven hair came onto the stage. It soon became clear that she was to be the emcee for the evening. She welcomed the audience, then proceeded to explain the format of the event. There would be a reading from the author of the book, accompanied by some clips from Mr. Hitchcock's films. The reading would then be followed by a question and answer session, after which the author would be glad to sign copies of her works.

She went on to describe *Dial M For Misogyny* as "part novelistic enquiry, part critical study into the misogynist urge in Hitchcock's work. A worthy follow up to Elvey's earlier book *The Love Song of Alfred J. Hitchcock*." Without further delay, she then introduced the author, whose entrance was accompanied by fulsome applause.

Absent-mindedly at first, I watched the slim feminine form striding confidently out onto the stage. She was dressed in a green satin blouse, black skirt and heels. Part of me thought that I was seated at too far a distance to be sure. Then, with the jolting power of a jump cut, I saw it. Her hair was a different style and a different colour, but I saw that she had returned to me. She had red medium length hair, fashioned into a bob cut. Otherwise, her facial features appeared identical. Suddenly, it felt as if no time had passed. The intervening years and decades appeared to evaporate. My feelings for her had not aged. She had not aged. Time could not touch her. She had returned to me. Once again, I was beholding that face. Her face.

It was Marion Holland's face.

Of course, ladies and gentlemen, it was simply impossible that the creature before me was Marion Holland. The rational side of my mind was telling me that too much time had elapsed for it to be her. In no way am I expert at gauging people's ages, but I estimated her to be in her mid to late thirties. Either that or ageless, as if she had emerged from the water fully formed. As she began to speak, my gaze remained focused on her.

Ms. Elvey thanked the audience for attending, then proceeded to give some context to the passage she was about to read. As my heart ratcheted, I listened...

"In my new book, I delve deep into the minds of the people who remain mostly forgotten when we think about Alfred Hitchcock's films. I'm talking about the victims, and specifically the female victims. The opening scene of *Frenzy*, shot not far from where we are now, features the naked body of a nameless female murder victim floating face down in the Thames. Rewatching the film, I found myself wondering what her story was. And so it is *her* voice that guides the reader through the serial crimes committed against women by Hitchcock's camera."

Ms. Elvey proceeded to read from the opening chapter of her book. Her sing-song voice and her sinuous use of language drew me in. I found myself lost in the act of watching her and listening to her for the duration.

A few contextualising clips were screened from Mr. Hitchcock's body of work. There was another spoken excerpt from the book. Then, before I knew it, the audience was applauding and Ms. Elvey was moving from the lectern and seating herself opposite the emcee. The question and answer section of the evening was beginning.

Among the questions I remember being posed were...

"The image of the first victim in *Frenzy* is so repulsive. Do you think Hitchcock deliberately staged it to look like a discarded tampon floating in a septic tank?"

"Would you agree that the character of Miss Torso from *Rear Window* is the ultimate de-personalised sex object in Hitchcock's films?"

"Can I ask why, compared with your first book, you seem to have become more disenchanted with Hitchcock?"

"I was seduced by Hitchcock's technique," Ms. Elvey confessed to that question. "However, when I looked beyond the technique, when I tore the front off so to speak, what I discovered was not as beautiful as his understanding of the vocabulary of the cinema. It was a little… off-putting."

There was one final question from the chap with the outlandish beard in front of me.

"Do you think that male readers will struggle with the meaning of your book?"

"I'd like them to struggle." I discerned a touch of humour in Ms. Elvey's reply. "My father, funnily enough, is a man. He's read it and I'm glad to say he didn't think it was a load of old rot."

At this point, the emcee intervened.

"I think we're out of time, but let me remind you all that Alice will now be signing copies of her book."

I had already decided to buy a copy of Ms. Elvey's book in order to see her at closer quarters. There was an aspect to her appearance that I needed to be sure about. It was not just the extreme likeness she bore to Ms. Holland. There was also something about the way the light in the auditorium caught an object on or about her features.

I waited for one final round of applause to subside, then slowly levered myself out of my seat and made my way into the aisle. Some members of the audience were already in the process of leaving the auditorium, but there was a queue leading towards the stage which I joined. At the bottom of the stage, I could see an ad hoc book stall had been set up. Ms. Elvey was seated beside it and was already going about the business of signing copies of her book.

The queue shuffled its way forward, as if we were lining up to receive holy communion. As I approached the ad hoc book stall, I reached for a copy of *Dial M For Misogyny* and began to flick through it.

"Sorry, sir," a male attendant with yet another sprouting beard gently instructed me. "Can I ask you not to squeeze the goods till they're yours?"

I suppose I may have been bending the spine of the book a little, but I informed the attendant that I intended to buy both it and *The Love Song of Alfred J. Hitchcock*. I promptly handed over my payment in cash and as I struggled to pocket my change, I turned and suddenly found myself directly in front of the author.

In close proximity to Ms. Elvey, I could plainly see what I had suspected.

"Thanks for coming," she addressed me, smiling. "Would you like me to sign your book?"

I snapped out of my state of suspended animation and handed her the books. As her eyes lingered over them, I studied Ms. Elvey's fine features.

"Oh… Do you want me to sign this also?"

I looked down and in shock saw that somehow I had managed to give her the notebook I had brought with me. Ms. Elvey recited the title.

"*The Canonical Murders*."

"Forgive me… my mistake." I reclaimed the notebook and held onto it.

"And who should I make these out to?"

I duly informed Ms. Elvey and, moments later, she was handing both her works back to me.

"Are you also an author?" she asked.

I answered that I was not.

"Oh," she paused. "Perhaps I've been too deep in my research, but I think I recognise the penmanship on that notebook. Do you mind if I ask where you found it?"

"I'm a collector," I said. "I found it by chance at an auction."

"Well, if it belonged to who I think it may have belonged to, it could be worth a penny or two."

"… I'm afraid I'm not interested in selling, Ms. Elvey."

"I completely understand…" After the briefest of interludes she continued. "You know, if you're not selling, I'm sure my father would still be interested in studying it."

"Your father?"

"Yes. He's curating this season." She gestured towards a gentleman near the exit with his back turned to us who was deeply engaged in a two-way conversation.

"Well, I'll certainly keep that in mind Ms. Elvey."

"You know," Ms. Elvey now said, leaning forward slightly and looking at me rather intently. "You remind me of someone."

"… I do?"

"Yes… I hope you don't mind me saying so, but have you ever seen *The Lodger*?"

"… I have."

"Not the Hitchcock version. It may be sacrilegious to say this, but I prefer the 1940s Hollywood version. You remind me a little of the star."

"… Really?"

"Yes, you do."

I was beginning to feel a little uncomfortable about how closely Ms. Elvey was regarding me, so I thanked her for signing her books, then excused myself and turned to leave the auditorium. I was surprised that I had managed to retain some composure before Ms. Elvey, before this vision who bore such an uncanny resemblance to Ms. Holland. As I studied her hypnotic beauty I had found my mind teetering on the edge of a precipice. From that precipice, it would have been so easy to allow myself to plummet… To plummet and fall and surrender myself to the sweeping embrace of my memories. My mind teetered further, sent reeling by the sight of the small detail about her appearance which I had suspected. Up close, I had confirmed it…

Ms. Elvey had been wearing a pair of mockingbird earrings, the eyes studded with a small diamond that brilliantly caught the reflection of the light.

Dazzled, I continued on my way out of the auditorium. And as I did so, I could not resist the chance to look at the man she had pointed out as her father.

The man in question had aged, but despite a slightly less pronounced jaw line, he was ageing with undeniable style. I recognised him almost immediately. Beneath the distinguished silver streaks of hair, behind the fashionable bifocals he now sported, I recognised him. It was Ms. Holland's husband from all those years ago.

As I staggered in a heightened state of shock from the auditorium, a member of staff handed me a leaflet. Unthinkingly, I took it and placed it in my pocket.

In my inner world, I saw the eye of the mockingbird glinting at me.

I walked blindly and questions flew around my head.

Why had Mr. Hitchcock directed me here?

How had I ended up in the presence of Ms. Holland's husband after this time?

How had I ended up in *her* presence?

I walked blindly through the streets, my feet taking me in a northerly direction.

My mind teetered and I recalled an image I had first seen through the lens of the telescope from my flat in Slade Walk... It was an object that had sat on Ms. Holland's desk... I recalled a silver art nouveau frame... I recalled the photograph framed within of a young girl with rampant red hair astride a pony.

I realised now that she had a daughter. Ms. Holland had a daughter.

In my inner world, I continued to see the eye of the mockingbird glinting at me.

I thought of the undying beauty of Ms. Holland. I thought of Ms. Holland's husband and Ms. Elvey and I felt as if I had been ushered into the presence of ghosts from my distant past.

In my inner world, I saw Ms. Holland plummeting into the water of the Thames.

... *Enter The △ and death will follow*...

**I AVENGE.**

I was unaware of how long I had been walking when I had to pause to catch my breath. My head was swirling and I now sensed the presence of a pulsing green light in the extreme bottom left of my field of vision. I turned, looked down a set of stairs and saw that somehow I had arrived back at the entrance to The Pleasure Garden.

I needed somewhere to sit and take stock of my situation, so I did not hesitate. I descended the steps. I entered through the doors, I approached the bar and with a creak perched myself on the same bar stool. Inside, it appeared as if nothing had changed since my last visit. The interior was lit in the same low-key chiaroscuro style and the same lone customer was slumped in silhouette at the distant end of the bar.

A voice then came from somewhere amid the shadows.

"We meet again... How's your head?"

The landlord, Forsythe, stepped forward. He had a tea towel slung over his shoulder and was drying a pint glass.

"My head?" I replied.

"Yes. Your head... Or did that fall give you a touch of amniocentesis?"

I knew that the landlord had used the wrong medical term, but decided it was probably best not to correct him.

"My head is fine, thank you... I see that you fixed the sign."

"Oh? It was nothing more than a simple do-it-yourself job."

I placed the books I had just purchased on the bar and began to search for my wallet.

"Please. Allow me to pay for the damage I caused."

The landlord made a dismissive gesture with his hands.

"I won't accept a penny from you, sir. Becoming a regular would be payment enough."

"I'd take him up on that offer if I were you." It was my garrulous fellow customer, his voice echoing in the gloom. "An uncommonly generous offer, that is. Uncommonly generous."

Without my asking, the landlord then poured me a double brandy and set it before me.

"Now," he declared. "Where were we? Oh yes... Well, have there been any further developments?"

"... I'm sorry?"

"Developments... You know, in the case of the pilfered thingamabob. I know you didn't have any firm leads, but I was just wondering if anything had happened in the meantime."

"No... No," I confessed. "I'd sort of forgotten about it to be honest."

"Well, whoever did it, they deserve to end up in chokey."

I nodded silently in agreement and drank the brandy while the landlord withdrew to occupy himself with some business behind the bar. In the meantime, the silhouetted resident barfly was prising himself from his seat and starting to walk in my direction. The silhouette had already placed himself two stools away from me before he thought to say the words "Mind if I join you?"

"... No, please do."

He may have drawn closer, but his features remained obscured in shadow. I suppose my tinted glasses did nothing to aid my skills of perception, but I could just discern a fleshy, stubbly mound of a face which now leaned over the bar to regard the books I had set there.

"To be frank," he pronounced "... This may not be the best place to catch up on your reading." His head then swayed upright and he turned to face me. "Sorry to get all existential on you, but why the hell are you here?"

"... I don't follow you."

"Escaping from the missus are you? The trouble and strife?"

"... I'm afraid I'm not married."

"A confirmed bachelor are you, then? No man is an island, you know," he informed me wistfully. "Mind you, on the other hand, eagles fly alone and sparrows fly in flocks."

"... I beg your pardon?"

"And where is your island?"

After a hesitation, I informed him.

"You're a regular Prospero, my friend... But there must be something that brought you back here tonight... Is there something on your mind?"

"... As a matter of fact, there is... I've just seen someone I haven't seen for many years."

"Ah... Someone has finally washed up on your private island, eh?"

With those words, the silhouette's head dipped and he became silent. For all I knew, he may well have fallen asleep.

As I sat there, my eyes wandered momentarily to *The Canonical Murders* and to Ms. Elvey's books stacked on the bar. Lurking underneath them, I now spotted the leaflet that had been handed to me earlier in the auditorium.

I could see the word **Hitchcock** clearly printed in the body of some text, so I removed the leaflet from its hiding place and began to read...

---

**XTC Presents**
**'THE HOUSE OF MR. HITCHCOCK'**

**An immersive walkthrough installation**
**recreating the work of**
**Alfred Hitchcock.**
**Dare you enter?**

**"In The House of Mr. Hitchcock,**
**I have created an artwork that**
**equals anything achieved by**
**Hitchcock." – director Xavier T. Cutts**
**(*Jeffrey Dahmer Is Unwell*).**

**Opening in Leytonstone August 13th**
**Closing Date December 11th**
**Advance Booking Essential!**

---

All of a sudden, my perusal of the leaflet was interrupted by an enormous belch of steam emanating from behind the bar. It rose in a cloud and settled around me.

"Sorry, gents," the landlord managed to say from somewhere out of the vaporous fog. "Haven't quite got used to the modern technology of dishwashers."

Nearby, the silhouette appeared to have awoken from his doze.

"Talk about a pea souper," he commented while making extravagant waving gestures and coughing sounds. He then gestured towards the books. "Careful of your reading material, my friend."

At once, I could see that the covers of Ms. Elvey's books had curled up slightly. I was more concerned, however, about the effect the deluge of steam may have had on *The Canonical Murders*. As I grasped the notebook, I feared the worst when the endpapers immediately became unglued before my eyes. I then caught a glimpse of something falling out between the unglued page and the back cover. Something that had been concealed within the lining of the book.

A small key pinged onto the surface of the bar.

"What's that the key to?" the barfly piped up. "A chastity belt? The Bank of England vaults? Pandora's Box?"

I allowed the steam to disperse, then picked up the key. As I regarded it, I knew I had to return at once to Plouthorp Street.

I left hurriedly, without explanation, with the barfly's parting words echoing in my wake.

"I will see you in the not too distant future... You're a regular now. Like me!"

Again, I retraced my journey and returned to Plouthorp Street.

Once inside, I retrieved a spray can of lubricant from under the kitchen sink, then proceeded to the first floor of the adjunct. I stepped through the door that led into the first room, then knelt before the chest. I liberally sprayed the lubricant onto the padlock, then tried the key that had been hidden inside the lining of *The Canonical Murders*. The key fitted. As the decades of accumulated rust mingled with the lubricant, the resulting mixture began to resemble iron-rich blood. It took some persuading, but eventually the mechanism shifted and the padlock opened. I removed the padlock and set it aside.

I then applied more lubricant to the hinges of the chest and attempted to raise the lid. My muscles tensed, the hinges squealed out, and with some effort I managed to lever the lid of the chest back. Peering inside, I saw a collection of old magazines. To be precise, it was a collection of *Kinematograph and Lantern Weekly*. I lifted a number of the magazines out and carefully examined their brittle pages. At first, I believed the chest was filled with them. Underneath a couple of layered inches of the magazines, however, I discovered other items. I discovered a Gladstone bag and an unopened box containing a Universal Film Splicer, an archaic implement for splicing strips of celluloid together.

I removed both items from the chest and set them to one side. It made me hopeful that there would be other relics hidden within. But when I reached the bottom of the chest, there was nothing remaining there but the musty odour of forgotten magazines.

As I stood up and regarded the interior of the chest, however, I felt that something was not quite right.

I had excavated all the contents, but I was sure that the bottom of the chest did not line up with the exterior of the base. And when I tilted the chest at one side, I indeed gauged that there was some extra weight inside.

I tilted the chest further and suddenly a false floor in the interior of the chest was revealed. From within the hidden compartment, a large perfectly round metallic object fell onto the floor of the room. I dropped the chest in shock and backed away as the round object rolled towards me and started to whirl around on the floor.

Its metallic surface caught the light as it spun, glinting like the eye of the mockingbird earring. It appeared to me as bright as the light from a projector. It appeared as bright as sunlight... As bright as lightning... It shone its light on me and in the whiteness of that room I suffered a blackout...

... When I finally awoke, I was unsure how much time had passed. I looked at my watch. The time and date were telling me that twenty-four hours had elapsed since my attack of photophobia.

*Could I have been unconscious all that time?* I asked myself.

The lights were still burning brightly in the room, still reflecting off the brilliant white walls. As for the metallic object, the sight of which had precipitated my photophobia, it was now lying flat on the floor. I recognised it as a film reel.

With some difficulty, I managed to get to my feet. Feeling achy and unsteady, I decided that I needed to sit down before I did anything else. As I staggered over to seat myself before the cyclorama, I couldn't help noticing the orderly stacks I had left of *Kinematograph and Lantern Weekly* were now strewn around the floor. On the landing near the canvas chairs, the two books signed by Ms. Elvey were also lying on the floor. I picked the books up and set them on the coffee table between the two chairs. Finally, I collapsed into my chair in front of the cyclorama.

It was then that Mr. Hitchcock appeared to me once again... It was then that he spoke to me again...

"Personally, I prefer a clear horizon," he stated. He was seated in his chair, staring out at the view. "Only things that are creative and not destructive... Your horizon, however, is not clear... There are storm clouds on your cyclorama."

He turned to face me.

"I am sorry to be the bearer of bad news, but you are missing three items."

"… I am?"

"To be precise, you are missing the Universal Film Splicer and the Gladstone bag, as well as my own short pictorial work *The Canonical Murders*."

"… Who took them?"

"I imagine it was some sort of thief in the night." Mr. Hitchcock sighed, then interlaced his fingers across the equator of his stomach and continued. "I shall address the matter of how to deal with these thefts in due course. In the meantime, may I ask if you studied my book?"

"Yes, Sir Alfred."

"A crude series of tableaux perhaps, but ocularly interesting nonetheless… It is almost as if I had a blinding moment of foresight and saw my career laid out before me… And if you don't mind me saying so, much more compelling reading material than the other books you picked up on your trip to the South Bank."

He gestured dismissively towards the books I had placed on the table.

"… Really?"

"I'm afraid so. I find myself rather unamused at Ms. Elvey's musings… Feminism is the cause that will not shut its pretty little mouth, would you agree? The author seems to be of the opinion that I am a monstrous misogynist. I'm sure the words myopic, murderous and malodorous are also used throughout her rather slim volume… The M section of her dictionary must be well thumbed, what?"

"… I haven't read it."

"It is so easy to defame the dead, would you say so? And in a book that is so frugal and mean… And as for this so-called art installation which I have become aware of… I find myself most displeased… Speaking for myself, I am of the opinion that most modern art should be exhibited in the torture chambers of the world and then consigned to the chamber pot of history… Does that qualify as gallows humour or toilet humour? I suspect it's hanging somewhere in mid-air between the gallows and the toilet."

Mr. Hitchcock carefully levered himself up from his canvas chair. He then stood before the cyclorama, his gaze fixed in the direction of The △.

"I apologise for my digressions… Do not fear… The main feature is about to start and you have a vital part to play."

"… I do?"

"A leading role. Your idea, you see, has already spread… I can sense something building up, like the sense of expectation that grows in an audience before the crash of cymbals. Every good mystery needs a detective and I want you to keep your eyes open. Find the stolen notebook and you will solve the mystery."

"… Find the stolen notebook?"

"Precisely. I need a collaborator who knows how to share credit… Are you that sort of collaborator?"

"… Yes," I answered.

"Be the detective, then. My senses are clouded, but I feel this mystery pulling me towards Leytonstone."

"… That is where the installation is."

"Most interesting… I sense the culprit, the thief, will make a personal appearance there. And *The Canonical Murders* may be a source of inspiration for him, or indeed her. An inspiration for whatever it is they have planned."

"… I see."

Mr. Hitchcock turned to face me.

"I will leave you now to do my bidding. Remember, as you go out sleuthing, I want you to do your best to protect my legacy. To punish the plagiarists. To smite the Philistines."

"… Yes, Mr. Hitchcock."

"One final thing… I know you are also preoccupied with the question of Ms. Elvey's father and the role he has played in your past."

"… Ms. Holland's husband?"

I watched as Mr. Hitchcock returned to the director's chair and began to lower his body into it.

"Perhaps you have forgotten the newspaper reports from around the time of Ms. Holland's suicide, but her husband's name was and remains Elvey… Using her female prerogative, Ms. Holland decided to retain her maiden name throughout their marriage… In any event, Mr. Elvey may prove useful in solving the mystery. Might I suggest you look at the contents of the reels you discovered in the chest? I believe they will pique his interest…"

His instructions delivered, the figure of Mr. Hitchcock then began to fade away… Soon, his form became quite transparent… Moments later, he wasn't there anymore.

I allowed his words to sink in, then got up from my seated position. I made my way through the open door and into the first room. As I walked past the chest, I saw more canisters hidden there within the base.

I stooped over and picked up the canister that was lying on the wooden floor. As I examined the canister, I felt my eyes, I felt my mind, struggling to interpret the reality of what I saw before me.

It was a reality I never really believed I would come face to face with. The reality that my quest was, at last, complete.

The following day, I decided to pay Mr. Elvey an unannounced visit. I knew I had many questions to ask him, but what was uppermost in my mind was *The House of Mr. Hitchcock* and my recent, momentous discovery.

I retraced the trip I had made to the South Bank. I boarded a train, I got off at Waterloo, then walked on foot until I stood before the ominous modern edifice of glass and metal…

I entered and approached the ticket desk. The same young brunette with the multiple facial piercings was on duty.

"Are you here for the screening of *The Criminal Life of*

*Archibaldo De La Cruz*?" she asked me.

I replied that I was here to see Mr. Elvey.

"Oh… Do you have an appointment?"

"No, but you could tell him it's in regards to a notebook his daughter saw a couple of nights ago."

"A notebook his daughter saw?"

"Yes."

"And your name is?"

I duly informed the young lady, whose piercings suddenly reminded me of the hooks on a shower curtain rail. I watched as she lifted a phone, then punched in a couple of numbers and spoke into the receiver. I watched as she explained the situation to Mr. Elvey. I watched as she then hung up and addressed me once again.

"Alright, he'll be with you shortly if you'd like to wait."

I thanked the young lady for her help. I then quietly withdrew from the area of the ticket desk to hover around the gaping lobby of the building. I did not have to wait too long before Mr. Elvey appeared. He approached the ticket desk and consulted with the young lady. She pointed towards me, then Mr. Elvey pivoted and strode in my direction. He extended his right hand and I shook it. He was the very embodiment of affability.

"Hello," he said. "Thank you for seeing me."

Following our handshake, Mr. Elvey asked that I accompanied him to his office. We approached a door, he punched a secret code into a console, then we climbed a set of stairs. Soon, we were seated in a room with a view of the Thames roiling past. Mr. Elvey assumed his position behind a walnut desk. On the rear wall were shelves lined with dozens of books on the subject of Mr. Hitchcock. Among the titles that I recognised were *Hitchcock's Adventures In Morbidity* by Art Melnick, *Hitchcock – The Glorious Mysteries* by Primo Ransohoff, as well as the two titles penned by his daughter which were prominently on display.

"Care for a tea or coffee?" Mr. Elvey began by asking.

"No, thank you."

"Very well... very well." He leaned back in his swivel chair. "So, you're the gentleman Alice was talking to on the night of her book launch, am I right?"

"That's correct," I replied.

"Alice tells me you may have something. A notebook. She's got a faultless eye for these things, you know. Now, if we can establish some sort of provenance I'm sure -"

"The notebook has been stolen," I interrupted matter-of-factly.

"Stolen? Really?"

"I'm afraid so."

I tried to interpret if the apparent shock Mr. Elvey displayed at the news of the theft was genuine.

"When?"

"Yesterday. From my home."

"Well, if what Alice told me about it is true, this is terrible news."

"I am following certain leads regarding the notebook," I informed him sternly. "However, that is not the reason I am calling on you today."

"Really? Well... How else can I help you?"

On hearing about the loss of the notebook, I believe Mr. Elvey's tone became somewhat more disinterested. Nevertheless, I continued.

"I am in possession of something that may be of interest to you... A film."

"Oh, really?"

Now, his voice took on a distinctly patronising quality.

"It's in relation to the season you are running at the moment. The season dedicated to Mr. Hitchcock. The title of the film in question is *The Mountain Eagle*."

"... *The Mountain Eagle*?"

"Yes."

"… The silent film? But it's lost."

"It once was lost, but now it is found."

Immediately, the disinterested tone was replaced by one that was more excitable.

"You have a print of *The Mountain Eagle*?"

"Yes."

"Do… do you realise what you've got?"

"Yes. Yes I do."

"It's been on our most wanted list for years. Absolute years. It's the missing Hitchcock."

"I know."

"The powers that be will be most interested. Wherever did you get it, Mr. –?"

"I'm a private collector. I did not find it, however. It found me."

"Well, this is incredible. Simply incredible. It's too late to include your print in this season, but I know the public interest in it will be huge. Have you watched it yet?"

"No I haven't, but I've performed a touch inspection and I can assure you it is in remarkably good condition… There's little or no deterioration to the print."

"I'm so glad you came to me with this. So glad. What I think the next thing to happen should be is –"

I raised my right hand and gently but forcibly cut Mr. Elvey off in midflow.

"I believe you mentioned that you are in my debt."

"I did?"

"Yes."

"Well, I'm not sure if I actually -"

"I want you to cancel the art installation I have read about. From what I know, I feel it must surely cheapen the memory of Mr. Hitchcock's work."

"Art installation? Are you talking about *The House of Mr. Hitchcock*?"

"Yes."

"I'm afraid that has nothing to do with me. I do know there have been dozens of people working for weeks and months on it and it would be impossible to cancel it. Not to mention grossly unfair to the thousands of people who have pre-booked tickets."

I purposefully struck an imperious tone with Mr. Elvey now.

"In that case, if you cannot meet my request, I feel I cannot grant access to my print of *The Mountain Eagle*."

Mr. Elvey shifted uncomfortably in his chair.

"Please, hear me out... Let's not be unreasonable... Let's find some common ground and work together on this... A print such as this should belong to everyone, would you agree?"

Inwardly, I disagreed. Inwardly, I wondered if this was the kind of language Mr. Elvey had used to persuade his wife to go along with his plan to dispose of the body. I did not give voice to these thoughts, however. I merely listened as he continued.

"It should belong to the nation... It should belong to the world... If what you're saying is true, you've discovered an immensely valuable cultural artefact... I'm sure if I can contact the relevant authorities, a figure could be arrived at so the print could be stored in proper conditions and thorough restoration work could begin on it."

"I'm not interested in money. I'm interested in legacy."

"Legacy? Oh, you mean you want to bequeath it to us in a will?"

"No, Mr. Hitchcock's legacy. I fear it is being cheapened by this so-called art installation."

Mr. Elvey pondered my words for a moment.

"You know, I think I could arrange for you to visit *The House of Mr. Hitchcock*. Is that something you would be interested in? I can guarantee you would be impressed by what you see there. The whole thing has been done with complete reverence to Hitchcock and I believe any true Hitchcock disciple would relish it."

I paused to consider this turn of events.

"You should also really meet Xavier," Mr. Elvey added.

"Who?"

"Xavier T. Cutts, or XTC to his legions of fans. He really has one of the most brilliant creative minds I've ever encountered. I've been privileged to see him on set and, believe me, it's like watching Jackson Pollack paint."

"… I'm more of a Walter Sickert man, myself."

"Sickert, eh? Didn't I read somewhere that Hitchcock owned an original painting or two by him?" Mr. Elvey adjusted his bifocals and leaned in ever so slightly. "You know, I met him once."

"… Walter Sickert?"

"No. Hitchcock… At least, I was supposed to meet him. It's a funny story, I suppose. I won a competition to interview him for the school newspaper, you see. I had my questions prepared, everything was ready, but when I got there he wouldn't meet with me." I feigned ignorance, but felt my mind teetering. "Another child, a big scruffy-looking fellow, got there before me. And the old man did the interview with this imposter instead of me. Can you believe it?"

While Mr. Elvey shook his head and allowed himself to laugh in disbelief at the memory of this injustice, I felt my mind teetering further, then plummeting. My mind plummeted and finally surrendered to the past… I felt myself swept back in an instant to another time on the South Bank… Back to the day Mr. Hitchcock imparted his gifts to me.

"I suppose," Mr. Elvey continued "I should have paid heed to the old saying about how you should never meet your heroes."

"… Imagine that…" was all I managed to say in response.

In time, Mr. Elvey's mind returned to the present, as did mine.

I sat a little longer in his office, while a number of phone calls were placed to help arrange for me to visit *The House of Mr. Hitchcock*. A taxi was booked to pick me up at Plouthorp Street the next day and drop me off outside the location in Leytonstone. In return, I promised I would give serious consideration to Mr. Elvey's request for access to my print of *The Mountain Eagle*.

Following my encounter with Mr. Elvey, I meandered my way back to the house in Plouthorp Street. I lost track of time and place and at some point, I found myself alone in the darkness. I found myself standing beside a gibbet erected on the Thames foreshore, close to the Prospect of Whitby public house.

I stood there on the foreshore and questioned how worthwhile the proposed trip to Leytonstone would prove to be. Then, however, I recalled the words Mr. Hitchcock had directed towards me from his chair in front of the cyclorama...

"I feel this mystery pulling me towards Leytonstone... Be the detective... Find the stolen notebook and you will solve the mystery."

I stood there in the darkness and my gaze was drawn across the river towards Canary Wharf, where hundreds of office lights were still burning. In particular, my gaze was drawn towards the tallest of the buildings there. For the first time, I noticed that atop the building was the structure of a huge black obelisk. For the first time, I noticed a light at the very apex of the obelisk. The light was blinking at me, like an eye preparing to awaken itself from a lengthy slumber...

I stood there for some time, quietly mesmerised by the sight that had been set before me, then I returned home to Plouthorp Street.

△

The following evening, as planned, I was chauffeured by taxi to Leytonstone. The driver was a personable fellow who attempted

237

to engage me in conversation about the pressing issues of the day. My mind, however, was elsewhere and the replies I gave were muted and monosyllabic. After a few sets of traffic lights, the driver understandably gave up and he left me in silence.

I continued to brood anxiously in the back seat, unsure about what I had allowed myself to get involved in. I believe I was on the verge of asking the driver to return to Plouthorp Street when the taxi came to a halt.

"… Where am I?" I asked, in a vain attempt to get my bearings.

"Leytonstone… I was told to drop you off at this very address." The driver peered out his windscreen at the stand-alone building he had pulled up in front of. "Is this the right place?"

I replied that I was sure that it was.

The taxi was idling before a looming, expansive exterior wall that had been painted white. On one half of the wall, I saw the words **THE HOUSE OF MR. HITCHCOCK** spelled out in bold stylised black lettering and stacked vertiginously. On the other half, the final touches were being made to an impressive two-storey high rendering of Mr. Hitchcock's signature profile.

I stepped out of the car and allowed myself another moment to survey the scene before me. As the taxi trundled off into an adjoining street, I approached a trio of artists who were focusing their attention on the cheek section of Mr. Hitchcock's profile and asked them where the entrance to the installation was. One of them withdrew the cigarette he was smoking from his mouth, performed a lazy right turn motion with his hand and told me to go around the side of the building.

I followed his advice, dimly aware of him sharing an inaudible joke with his co-workers as I walked around the corner into an area that was steeped in darkness. Once I allowed my eyes to adjust, I managed to detect the presence of a few steps that led to a double door. Taking care, I negotiated my way up the steps and I entered…

I found myself in a foyer area that was in the process of being fitted out for the installation's opening. Looking around, I saw Mr. Hitchcock's trademark caricature rendered in pulsing red neon. Also, displayed in chronological order around the walls, there was an impressive array of international posters and lobby cards for Mr. Hitchcock's films.

I was studying a poster for the Polish release of *The Birds* - the poster featured the image of a human skull with wings sprouting from its temples - when a figure approached me from a side door. He was twenty-something, carrying a clipboard and wearing a T-shirt imprinted with the image of Charles Manson's face.

"Hi, I'm Gary Graveley," he announced from beneath an unkempt fringe. "You're here to check out the experience, right?"

"Yes," I answered guardedly. "Are you... Mr. Cutts?"

"I'm afraid not. I'm Gary Graveley." It was almost as if he had to restate his name to reassure himself of his own identity. "I'm a mere cog in a wheel in a corner of Xavier's brain. He should be along soon, but he told me to make sure you got a private view of the whole experience."

"... What am I expected to see exactly?"

"I'm sorry, I'm under penalty of death not to give any spoilers away."

"... Oh."

"Don't look so serious. I was only joking about being under penalty of death."

He then turned the clipboard around to face me and handed me a pen.

"Before anything, could I ask you to sign this form? It's just some health and safety bullshit they make us abide by."

I gave the form a cursory glimpse, then signed, while Mr. Cutt's factotum continued to fill me in.

"And just to let you know, there are some hidden cameras inside. It's purely a security thing, you understand."

I returned the clipboard to him.

"The first door is straight ahead and they're ready whenever you are... You look a bit apprehensive, but don't worry. I promise you, it's not a case of *Abandon all hope, ye who enter here.*"

With that, he began to retreat towards the door he had appeared from.

"Just a minute," I called after him. "What am I supposed to do now?"

"It's simple. Just follow Mr. Hitchcock's directions."

His eyes moved towards a bowler-hatted silhouette on the wall some twenty yards directly ahead of me... It was a silhouette of Mr. Hitchcock... His silhouette was pointing towards a white door.

Alone now, I followed Mr. Hitchcock's directions and walked cautiously towards the white door... I was about to reach for the handle, when the door swung open automatically... I walked forward... I entered and found myself in an antechamber...

Once inside the antechamber, once the door had closed behind me, I heard the words "Good evening" being spoken... I stood for a few seconds in silence, then heard the words "Good evening" again... It was, I realised, a recording of Mr. Hitchcock's sonorous voice and the words were being played on a loop.

While Mr. Hitchcock's salutations echoed and re-echoed, I glanced around the antechamber... I looked up and directly above me saw a square section in the centre of the ceiling constructed from glass... Hanging from the glass ceiling was a three light chandelier of antique vintage.

Three of the walls in the antechamber were white and featureless... The fourth wall to my left, however, was decorated with a plethora of illustrations... Daubed in red paint, they presented stylised renderings of various implements and methods of murder... They may have been executed in a somewhat different style, but I felt a nagging suspicion that a small number of the pictures closely resembled the ink drawings from *The Canonical Murders*.

On the wall I saw coiled lengths of rope... I saw knives... I saw revolvers... I saw bodies falling from great heights... I saw a variety of blunt instruments... I saw a bottle with a skull symbol... I saw a bomb with a fizzing fuse wire... I saw sharpened avian beaks and claws... I saw plumes of deadly exhaust fumes emitting from a car... I saw the victim spread out nearby.

The illustrations were artfully arranged around a life-sized painting of Mr. Hitchcock and hovering above his figure were these words...

## SEE THE WORLD THROUGH
## MR. HITCHCOCK'S EYES

An arrow jutted down from the slogan towards Mr. Hitchcock's head... I looked closer and saw two peepholes in the place of Mr. Hitchcock's eyes.

I stood for a moment, not sure what to do, then approached the figure of Mr. Hitchcock... The chandelier was giving off a soft flickering light... Cautiously, I removed my tinted glasses in order to get a closer look through the peepholes.

I peered through into the darkened space beyond the eyes... As I peered through, the space became illuminated and I saw an oversized prop revolver held by an oversized prop hand... At first, the gun was pointed away from me... Then, moving mechanically, the gun swivelled... It swivelled 180° until the sleek shiny barrel was aimed in my direction... It swivelled until I could see the bullets in the chamber and the black hole of the muzzle... I heard a loud **BANG!** and there was an intense flash of red that left me dazed.

I backed away from the peepholes... Away from the life-sized painting of Mr. Hitchcock... Away from the methods of murder before my eyes... My hands were shaking as I replaced my tinted glasses.

"Good evening," Mr. Hitchcock continued to say.

When I eventually managed to compose myself, I noticed another white door ahead of me... I walked towards the door... As I reached for the handle, the door swung open automatically... I walked forward... I entered and found myself in another room... I knew this room.

In the background, I heard music playing... I knew this music... It was a piece by Miklós Rózsa.

Before me, I saw a large hanging veil with around a dozen eyes painted on it... Swirling interconnecting strokes of paint seemed to suspend the eyeballs perilously against a darkened backdrop flecked with stars... I watched on as a figure entered the scene, wielding a pair of oversized scissors... He then proceeded to attack an eyeball in the centre of the veil, tearing through it in a zig zag pattern... The figure wielding the scissors was a tall man wearing a black dinner jacket and bow tie... I watched as the tall man completed his task, then turned to reveal a face that was blank, white and featureless... I knew the man in the mask... I knew this character.

"... Are you The Proprietor?" I asked him.

The Proprietor nodded silently, set the scissors to one side and ushered me forward... Behind the torn veil of eyes there was another white door... As I approached, the door swung open automatically... I walked forward... I entered and found myself in another room... I knew this room.

I saw ripped curtains... I saw strewn possessions... I saw fittings turned topsy turvy... I saw feathers... I saw a body slumped in the corner of a ruined bedroom... I saw bare feet, bloody legs and shredded pyjamas... I saw bloody voids for eye sockets... It was a scene of private carnage I had intruded into and it was horribly realistic.

The Proprietor moved to close a window... As he did so, a

seagull I previously thought was dead suddenly re-animated... Its head darted through a jagged hole in the glass, its beak making daggering motions... And with that, I heard the growing cacophony of the birds... I heard the caws and the screeching and the squealing intensity... The noise grew deafening... I covered my ears, closed my eyes and was sure I felt a wing brush past my face.

The Proprietor retreated from the window, then quickly ushered me towards another white door... As I approached, the door swung open automatically... I walked forward... I entered and found myself in another room... I knew this room.

I was inside the office of The Blaney Bureau... In the background I heard the shrieks of the birds begin to fade... They faded and were replaced by orchestral music... I knew this music... It was a piece by Ron Goodwin.

I saw the body of the blonde victim lying slumped in her leather chair... Also present was Chief Inspector Oxford... He turned in my direction, eyed me suspiciously and asked if I had witnessed anything... As I stood there, I could not bring myself to provide him with the name of the guilty party... The name of Bob Rusk.

Oxford then handed me a necktie... His mustache twitched as he spoke... "Make yourself useful and look after this evidence, would you?" he asked... I accepted the necktie and pocketed it.

While the inspector continued to survey the crime scene, The Proprietor ushered me forward once again... He ushered me past the inanimate body of Mrs. Blaney and I glimpsed the ligature marks on her neck... He ushered me towards another white door... As I approached, the door swung open automatically... I walked forward... I entered and found myself at the bottom of a set of gently curving stairs.

Nearby, to my immediate left, I saw a nightstand... On top of the nightstand, there was a silver tray which held a tall glass of milk... The contents of the glass were glowing phosphorescently... The glow added to the dramatic scheme of shadows laid out before me... I felt trapped momentarily within the shadows.

The Proprietor lifted the tray, then ushered me up the stairs while he carried it... On the next floor there was a landing... The Proprietor invited me to pause there before a large window... It was a window divided with three horizontal blinds... I stood there and watched as each blind in turn was raised up by invisible means... The blinds opened to reveal a view.

I looked out and, across the way, I saw a building... Most of the windows in the building were in darkness or had their curtains drawn... One window on the first floor, however, was illuminated... It was the window to the right of the fire escape.

Then, as if he had been prompted, a man entered the square of light across the way and began to go about his work... I did not need a telephoto lens to clearly make out what he was doing... He was inspecting a saw, ensuring it was up to the job of dismembering the body of his wife... I paused before the window and continued to watch as Lars Thorwald inspected first the saw and then an enormous knife.

Suddenly, the opening bars of a familiar piece of music erupted... The music was loud enough to draw Lars Thorwald to his window... He adjusted his glasses, squinted and for a second or two he locked eyes with me... Then, his eyes aimed up and towards the roof of the building I was standing in.

A theatrical scream pierced the air.

I knew this music now... It was a composition by Bernard Herrmann.

The screaming continued and in the upper field of my vision I registered the presence of something... It was a body... The body of a woman, elegantly dressed, her face masked by rippling waves of blonde hair... The woman was screaming as she was falling... Falling past the window I was positioned before... Her fall had been slowed to a glacial pace and it perfectly matched the rhythm of the Bernard Herrman music... It was the Prelude from *Vertigo*.

Around me, I was aware of dramatic flashes of green and red... I was aware of spiralling patterns projected on the walls... I continued to regard the female body gracefully descending through the air before me... A part of me knew it was all an elaborately stage-managed illusion... I clearly saw the wire that was anchoring the performer... A part of me knew there was a wind machine positioned somewhere that was causing her hair and her clothes to billow around in the night air... I sensed the unreality of it all, yet I found it impossible to move.

And then the falling woman turned her head towards me and I saw her face for an instant... In that instant, I believed she had the face of Marion Holland.

The falling woman turned her head away once more... Her blonde hair swirled in the air, and she continued her downward trajectory until she fell out of view... Across the way, Lars Thorwald continued to stare blankly at me.

Meanwhile, The Proprietor had materialised at my side again... He allowed me a moment to recover, then he ushered me forward... He ushered me towards another white door... As I approached, the door swung open automatically... I walked forward... I entered and found myself in another room... I knew this room.

I was inside a smartly furnished urban apartment... In the background, I heard music playing... I knew this music... It was 'Mouvement Perpetual No.1' by Francis Poulenc.

Before me I saw two figures standing behind a large chest fashioned from mahogany... They were dapper young gentlemen wearing dark suits and leather gloves... I knew these two characters... The one called Brandon beckoned me.

"We need your help," he said. "It's a storage problem."

I advanced towards the pair... The body of their victim lay limply over the chest and the rope was still twisted around his neck... The other one, Philip, now addressed me.

"If you could deal with the head," he said. "We'll deal with the legs."

The Proprietor stood by while I took part in the scene.

I did not think my participation in the act was absolutely necessary... The victim was a man of medium build, so I suspect it could have been a two man job... However, I did what was asked of me and I confess a part of me savoured the role.

I grabbed the body of the victim around his rib cage, then helped lift him into the chest... As the lid was closed, I looked down at the face of the victim... I looked down and, for a split second, I believed I saw the face of Mr. Drew... I recoiled, but the deed was done.

The Proprietor appeared at my side once again... He allowed me a moment... Then, as Brandon lit up a cigarette and savoured the first lungful, The Proprietor ushered me forward... He ushered me towards another white door... As I approached, the door swung open automatically... I walked forward... I entered and found myself in another room... I knew this room.

I was inside a bucolic farmhouse kitchen... Before me, I saw the farmer's wife, her hair tied back and dressed in muted floral colours... I stood to one side for a short time and watched the drama begin to unfold... I watched as the woman of the house became distressed at the appearance of the government agent... The agent chewed gum sardonically and was clad in a dark leather coat, the collar upturned like black wings.

I watched as he threatened the farmer's wife... And, as he prepared to alert the authorities by telephone, I watched as she hurled a pot of rice at his head... At that point, I was beckoned forward by the woman to assist her... I knew the part I had to play and I took on the role willingly.

First, I strode towards the government man... When I saw him draw a gun, I knocked it forcefully out of his hands and immediately set upon strangling him... As expected, he put up a fight and proved fiendishly hard to dispatch... The woman of the house then advanced towards us, kitchen knife in hand... While I restrained the agent, she stabbed him near his left collar bone... The blade of the knife snapped, leaving the point embedded in the victim... I ruminated for a moment on the inferior quality of kitchen implements in the Eastern Bloc, then my mind returned to the present and once again I was fully caught up in the scene.

I watched as the farmer's wife disappeared then reappeared wielding a spade... She slammed the spade into the agent's ankle four times... With each impact, for a split second, I believed I saw the face of Mr. Vosper.

There was life in the agent of the state yet, as I felt him forcefully dragging me to the floor to engage me in an obligatory tussle... I went along with everything... And then I saw the woman of the house expertly hitting her marks... I saw her over by the gas oven, turning on the tap... I knew how this scene ended... I knew what was being asked of me... I knew the part I had to play inside and out.

I dragged the body of the nefarious agent forward... He was still resisting the inevitable... I dragged him closer until I could place his head in the oven... The gas appeared odourless, but I averted my head and let the life drain slowly out of him... His hands twitched... They twitched and then eventually they were still... I looked down at him and for a split second I believed I saw the face of Mr. Smith... Kneeling over the body of the agent, I felt dizzyingly short of breath... I also felt exhilarated.

As my breathing and my heart rate returned to something like normality, I stood to my feet... I looked around for The Proprietor, but he was nowhere to be seen... The woman of the house uttered some words in German and pointed to another white door, urging me to make my escape from the scene of the crime... I followed her instruction.

As I approached, the door swung open automatically... I walked forward... I entered and found myself in another room...

I did not know this room.

The walls were painted brilliantly white... On the floor there was an arrow directing me towards three words...

## ENTER
## THE
## AVENGER

Beyond that was a square of reinforced glass... I recognised it as the section of glass ceiling I had already viewed from downstairs in the antechamber... I followed the arrow, I paced forward and stood on the square of glass... It held my weight and, as I looked down, I saw the chandelier underneath begin to gently sway back and forth.

I stood on the glass ceiling and looked to my left... I looked towards a set of floating shelves where a number of objects were on display... I saw a hangman's noose... I saw a poker... I saw a pair of gleaming scissors... I saw a revolver... I saw a set of handcuffs... I saw a cut-throat razor... I saw the tall glass of luminous milk on the silver tray... I saw a raven perched rigidly in a cage... I saw a Gladstone bag.

However, it was the figure directly in front of me that dominated the room... It was the figure of Mr. Hitchcock... This figure was not a silhouette or a painting... It was the cardboard standee I had bid on at the auction... The cardboard standee I had failed to win.

At once, I spotted that the standee of Mr. Hitchcock had been altered... I saw that something had been attached to his right hand... A kitchen knife.

Mr. Hitchcock's figure stood to one side of another white door... From the layout of the house, I knew that I was facing the final door of the installation... I do not recall how long I was standing there before I heard the voice... I could not be sure if it was coming from the figure of Mr. Hitchcock or if the source was elsewhere.

"Choose," the voice said. "Before you enter the final room, you must select your weapon of choice."

My eyes moved across the items on display... The noose... The poker... The scissors... The handcuffs... The revolver... The razor... The glass of milk... The raven... The Gladstone bag... The knife... The knife in Mr. Hitchcock's hand.

"Choose your weapon of choice," the voice repeated.

I found myself frozen to the spot.

"Choose," the voice said.

And in my head, there were other voices now.

"... Strangle..." I heard the voice of Mr. Drew say.

"... Gas-s-s-s..." the voice of Mr. Smith said. "Gas every time, my boy... Silent but deadly."

"... Bludgeon..." the voice of Mr. Vosper said.

"... BANG!!!" the voices of Sheldrake and Calthrop cried out in unison.

"Why ever is there no bomb?" I then heard the voice of Sheldrake wondering. "Seems like something of an oversight if you ask me!"

"Yes," Calthrop concurred. "It's all rather disrespectful to our memory and how you had us blown to kingdom come, old chum."

"Oh well... A lot of water has passed under the bridge since then."

"Yes indeed... Water and drowned, bloated bodies."

The voices of my victims crowded in on me... As they crowded in, I picked up the Gladstone bag and deposited a couple of items inside... I needed to be prepared for any eventuality, I told myself.

I was so lost in my thoughts, a jolt shuddered through me when the raven, which I had believed was stuffed, emitted a loud "CAW!" and began hopping around its cage in agitation.

My heart ratcheting, I returned and stood before the final

door... I stood before the figure of Mr. Hitchcock... From the gap underneath the door, a green glow was visible... I chose once more, then remained still... My hand was outstretched, hovering over the handle of the final door.

And as I stood there, I felt the hand of another descend on my shoulder... I pivoted around, not knowing who or what would greet me... I turned and I saw that it was The Proprietor... The Proprietor addressed me... He spoke through the white material that was covering his face.

"Why didn't you enter the final room? All you had to do was choose one weapon and enter the final room."

I cannot recall if I responded... I may just have continued to stand there speechless... In my head, I had finally worked out why I had been asked here... Before I could give voice to my thoughts, however, The Proprietor spoke again.

"Well, no matter. I think I've seen enough."

"...You have?"

The Proprietor proceeded to remove his mask... He removed his mask and revealed a face I already knew... It was the face of the mystery bidder... He then withdrew a pair of mirrored sunglasses from a breast pocket, put them on and smiled broadly at me.

"Hi. Thanks for coming. I'm XTC."

"... I know."

"A-ha... But are you aware of the origin of my name?"

I found myself lost for words, so Mr. Cutts took it upon himself to answer his own question for my benefit.

"I call myself XTC because that's what anyone who views my films experiences... Did you see my last movie? It was called *Jeffrey Dahmer Is Unwell.*"

"... No... No I didn't."

"It was about a bunch of attractive teens who get menaced in a wax museum dedicated to the great serial killers of recent times. Some critics called it derivative, but what the hell do they know?

It's grossed $150 million and counting. Do you want to hear about my next movie?"

"I -"

"It's about a bunch of attractive teens who get locked overnight in an art installation dedicated to Alfred Hitchcock. And here's the twist... You're standing in the set."

"... This is a film set?"

"Sure it is." Mr. Cutts was looking at me closely. He was studying me. "Y'know, you remind me of an actor I've seen in something... I think he's dead. Who am I thinking of?"

"... Someone once said I resembled Laird Cregar."

"Who?"

"Laird -"

"Never heard of him. What did you think of the walkthrough experience anyway? You're our very first customer."

"... It was very -"

"I want each person to experience it on their own. Just like death is experienced on your own. Know what I mean?"

"I -"

"I was trying to create something authentic. I also believe in doing things to excess. After all, the road of excess leads to the palace of wisdom, right? Actually, my original idea was to call this place *Hitchcock's Palace Of Wisdom*, but wiser, saner heads prevailed. Don't you just hate the wiser, saner heads sometimes?"

"... Yes."

Mr. Cutts drew closer and spoke with a quiet intensity.

"Y'know... I've been watching you. And now I've seen how you've performed here, I've made up my mind. You recognised my persona from *Spellbound* straight away and you really got into the interactive aspect of the installation... Especially in the *Torn Curtain* room. The actor said you were very physical. He might have a couple of bruises, but don't concern yourself, he'll be fine... I've been on the lookout, you see. I'm in the early stages of casting my new movie and I want you to be the main character in it."

"... The main character?"

"That's right."

"... In a movie?"

"Yeah. I was watching you very closely as you moved from room to room. I've been looking for an unknown, a total nobody, a zero and I'm sure now. I'm sure you can be the killer."

"... The killer?"

"Uh-huh. I want you to be my Norman Bates. My Bob Rusk. My Uncle Charlie. My Avenger."

"... The killer?"

"Yeah. The killer. I was auditioning you. I picked you out of a line-up. You're just who I'm looking for. What do you say, are you interested?"

I began to back away from the final door, back over the reinforced glass ceiling... I turned and opened the door that led into the *Torn Curtain* room and retreated through it... Meanwhile, Mr. Cutts started to pursue me... He followed me through the *Torn Curtain* room, now deserted, and then back through the *Rope* room... He called after me.

"Hey, hold on!"

He pursued me back onto the landing and stood at the top of the stairs, blocking my exit... Suddenly, I could not control my thoughts, my words any longer... I turned towards Mr. Cutts and confronted him.

"You're a thief in the night!" I told him. "You stole the standee of Mr. Hitchcock from me at the auction! And you stole this Gladstone bag from me, didn't you? You stole my notebook! Where is it?"

"I haven't stolen anything. What are you talking about? What notebook?"

"*The Canonical Murders*. Return it to me."

"I don't know anything about any notebook."

"You thief in the night!"

"Okay, so I take it you don't want to be in my movie?"

Standing there before the window, I turned momentarily to my left... I turned and I saw Lars Thorwald was still there, staring blankly at me... At that moment, a feeling came upon me... A feeling came upon me and I saw red... Swiftly and decisively, I pronounced my judgement on the plagiarist before me.

"I am The Avenger, Mr. Cutts. I am The Avenger and *I* live in the palace of wisdom!"

I reached inside the Gladstone bag and retrieved an item... I retrieved my weapon of choice... Mr. Cutts was standing at the top of the staircase when I raised the revolver and fired at him... He cried out once and fell backwards down the flight of stairs.

Immediately, I realised I had to get away from this place... I had to escape... I proceeded with haste down the staircase, past Mr. Cutt's body now lying motionless at the bottom... I did not linger.

I hurried to free myself from this torture chamber that seemed to have been specifically designed for me and me alone... It had all been an elaborate performance piece... A charade expertly staged for my benefit... All that work put in by all those people... All that time and effort spent on torturing me, on entrapping me... Entrapping The Avenger.

Eyes darting, chest heaving, hands clenching, I retraced my route back through the rooms on the ground floor... Back through The Blaney Bureau... Back through the bedroom that had been laid siege to by the birds... Back through the veil of eyes... Out through the antechamber where the implements of murder were painted red on white like blood on snow and where I heard Mr. Hitchcock say the words "Good evening" one final time... Out through the foyer... I dropped the revolver at some point and blundered past a number of cowering assistants, among them the young man wearing the Charles Manson T-shirt.

"You monster!" someone yelled in my wake as I lurched

through the exterior doors and into an unrelenting rainstorm.

And then I ran... I ran to get as far away from the scene of the crime as possible, turning my head now and then to ensure I was not being followed.

*I'm a real murderer now*, I thought... *They'll catch me for this one for sure... What I did back there was not The Avenger's style... He would disown that murder...*

I ran until I found myself outside Leytonstone Tube Station... I fought my way through a sea of bobbing black umbrellas and entered.

Inside the station, I passed by a series of mosaics on the walls... Mosaics that artfully replicated scenes from Mr. Hitchcock's movies... Desperately short of breath, I lingered before a mosaic depicting Roger O. Thornhill running for his life from the airborne terror of the crop-duster... Using the sleeve of my overcoat, I wiped away the raindrops from the lenses of my glasses and, before my eyes, the colours of the mosaic smeared... Before my eyes, the tiles distorted themselves further... They began to resemble oversized film grains, crystallised and tessellated into a pattern of geometric shapes... The shapes then fractured and splintered in front of me and soon they all took on the shape of The △... I lowered the brim of my Homburg hat, gripped onto the Gladstone bag and staggered onwards.

I purchased a ticket and I entered a world of delirium.

I followed the signs for the citybound Central Line trains, then stood on the overground platform and waited... As I waited, I saw him at the very extremity of my field of vision... He was so perfectly still, at first I believed the standee from the installation had somehow been transported here... However, as I heard the growling approach of a citybound train, I saw the bowler-hatted figure of Mr. Hitchcock move to board the same train as me... I followed Mr. Hitchcock's example... I boarded the same carriage and took a seat at the opposite end from him.

The train departed from Leytonstone and, from my seat, I watched the outside world pass by... I saw a car park... I saw an overhead pedestrian walkway... I saw the lights of terraced houses in the middle distance following my progress.

I cast my eyes to the rear of the carriage and saw Mr. Hitchcock sitting there quite still.

Once more turning my attention to the outside world, I saw a procession of streetlights... I saw a road running parallel to the tracks I was being propelled along and felt sure all the vehicles were speeding along in pursuit of me...

*I'm a real murderer now... They'll catch me for this one for sure...*

Jolted by the rapid blur and the clatter of another train rocketing past on the opposite track, I struggled to compose myself... I struggled to plan my next move, to plan my escape.

"Solve the mystery," Mr. Hitchcock had said to me... But I was failing to recall what mystery I had been asked to solve... The Sorrowful Mysteries? The Joyful Mysteries?

"... The next station is –"

*Jesus is condemned to death.*

"... The next station is Leyton..."

At the next stop, I watched from my seat as the train came to a halt on the platform... I watched as another Mr. Hitchcock came into view and then boarded the train... This Mr. Hitchcock was carrying a double bass.

The train continued onwards... I cast my eyes to the rear of the carriage and saw two Mr. Hitchcocks were now sitting there quite still.

Suddenly, the overground world disappeared and the train was swallowed up... I was going down, down into the underworld... I sensed the proximity of the past... I sensed the proximity of London's plague pits... The smell of wet earth... The smell of layered stratums of buried corpses surrounded me... I thought of my dear departed Nietzsche and tears welled up at the memory of our years of companionship... As rapidly as it had descended, the train then resurfaced overground and a prolonged squeal of brakes filled my head.

"... The next station is Stratford..."

At the next stop, I watched as another Mr. Hitchcock came into view on the platform... He was wearing a cowboy hat and standing underneath an advertisement for **Reduco OBESITY SLAYER**... This Mr. Hitchcock entered the same carriage as me and took a seat... I cast my eyes to the rear of the carriage and saw three Mr. Hitchcocks were now sitting there quite still.

The train continued onwards... Down it descended into the tunnelling darkness once again... I tightened my grip on the Gladstone bag and I began to repeat the words of a prayer I hadn't recited for years...

*I Confess to Almighty God*

"... The next station is Mile End..."

*And to you my brothers and sisters*

At the next stop, I watched as another Mr. Hitchcock came into view on the platform... He was being pushed in a wheelchair by an attentive nurse... This Mr. Hitchcock was wheeled towards the train, then he got up and walked unaided into the same carriage as me... I cast my eyes to the rear of the carriage and saw four Mr. Hitchcocks were now sitting there quite still.

I took a moment to regard my fellow passengers to try to ascertain if they were witness to the growing number of Mr. Hitchcocks in our midst... Each and every one of them appeared either untroubled by or unaware of the presence of the interlopers.

"... The next station is Bethnal Green..."

*That I have sinned through my own fault*

At the next stop, I watched as another Mr. Hitchcock came into view on the platform... He was walking a pair of terriers from right to left... This Mr. Hitchcock entered the same carriage as me... I cast my eyes to the rear of the carriage and saw five Mr. Hitchcocks were now sitting there quite still.

I peered out the window as the train picked up speed from the platform... I peered out and I saw pillars... stairs... people... hoardings... I saw darkness... I saw lights outside in the tunnels... I saw great cables feeding the city feeding the underground.

The train continued onwards... Inside the carriage the lights flickered... I cast my eyes to the rear of the carriage and alongside the incarnations of Mr. Hitchcock, I now saw the figures of my victims... Mr. Drew... Mr. Smith... Mr. Vosper... Sheldrake and Calthrop... All of them standing at the rear of the carriage, eyeing me impassively.

"... The next station is Liverpool Street..."

*In my thoughts and in my words*

At the next stop, I watched as another Mr. Hitchcock came into view on the platform... He was dressed incongruously in period garb – top hat, waistcoat and jacket - and standing underneath an advertisement that posed the question **Are You Satisfied With Your Circumstances?** This Mr. Hitchcock entered the same carriage as me... I cast my eyes to the rear of the carriage and saw six Mr. Hitchcocks were now sitting there quite still.

With an inhuman yawping growl the doors opened and closed... Closed and opened... Throughout the journey passengers got up and got off the train occasionally... But the various manifestations of Mr. Hitchcock remained.

"... The next station is Bank..."

*In what I have done and in what I have failed to do*

The train continued onwards and in the window opposite me I saw a reflection of a youthful Mr. Hitchcock... The reflection suggested that this Mr. Hitchcock was sitting beside me reading a book... I looked on as a young boy leant over from an adjacent seat and pulled Mr. Hitchcock's hat down over his face, intensely annoying him in the process.

"Excuse me," a female voice interrupted. "Do you know

which of these stops is closest to the Old Bailey?"

I cowered, speechless... I found myself incapable of formulating a reply... Incapable of raising my eyes from the sight of the flowing black hem of her nun's habit and the high heels visible underneath... I closed my eyes and waited for the vision to disappear.

"... The next station is St Paul's..."

*And I ask Blessed Mary Ever Virgin*

I opened my eyes and the vision was no more... When I cast my eyes to the rear of the carriage, however, the six Mr. Hitchcocks were still there, alongside my victims... My victims continued to stare blankly in my direction... Unsettled, I decided to move further down the carriage away from them.

"... The next station is Chancery Lane..."

*All the angels and saints*

As I got up, I passed another previously unnoticed Mr. Hitchcock... This Mr. Hitchcock was playing cards and was in possession of a complete suit of spades... I left him to his phantom game.

"... The next station is Holborn..."

*And you my brothers and sisters*

At some point, I sensed I had entered The △ and began to notice the space between the stations shortening... With each stop more people crowded into the carriage... But none of the new passengers chose to sit on the seats occupied by any of the Mr. Hitchcocks.

"... The next station is Tottenham Court Road..."

I regarded my fellow passengers... Some were sitting with their eyes shut, their arms crossed and their legs unassailably straight... Others were reading newspapers... I saw leads dangling from ear sockets... I saw fingers hovering over screens... I saw eyes hovering over everything... Were these people even human, I wondered, or addendums to the machines they carried?

My fellow passengers appeared oblivious to my crimes... They appeared oblivious to what I had done and what I had failed to do... Oblivious to the presence of the myriad Mr. Hitchcocks they were sharing their journey with... The myriad Mr. Hitchcocks that were arising from their seats now and preparing to exit the train.

"... The next station is Oxford Circus..."

*To pray for me to the Lord our God*

"... Change here for Bakerloo Line..."

*Amen*

At Oxford Circus, I watched as the various Mr. Hitchcocks departed en masse... I followed their exodus.

"Please mind the gap between the train and the platform," a smooth, reassuring female voice instructed me over the train's low mechanical humming.

I stepped out of the carriage and onto the bustling platform... I looked around for signs... I looked around for one of the Mr. Hitchcocks, but I had lost track of them in the crowd.

I began to walk... I passed a garish painting of a corpulent jester, laughing accusingly at me from a poster... I passed a sign for Bakerloo Line and decided to follow it... I followed the sign for Bakerloo Line and was in such a state of distraction I almost tripped over some loose change that was strewn like shrapnel on a red cloth... The cloth was spread in front of a musician who was playing a theremin... The theremin warbled like a canary in an underground cage and I recognised the piece of music it was playing... Inside my head, I screamed the words of the song... 'Que Sera Sera.'

I managed to regain my footing and, up ahead, I believed I spotted the Mr. Hitchcock who was carrying the double bass... I lurched onwards, towards the Southbound Bakerloo Line platform... Once on the platform, I saw Mr. Hitchcock and his double bass... He was standing close to the edge of the platform with his back turned to me... I approached Mr. Hitchcock... As I felt the subterranean air shifting around me, as I heard the approach of a train, I moved closer... Mr. Hitchcock then turned towards me and he spoke...

"Sorry old bean," he informed me. "You are following the wrong man."

Mr. Hitchcock cupped his face in his hands and formed a gaping hole with his mouth... The scream he emitted became the scream of the train's breaks... The scene morphed into a tortured, swirling Edward Munch landscape... I watched on as Mr. Hitchcock then jumped in front of the train pulling into the platform.

I staggered backwards, half expecting someone else on the platform to cry out in horror at what had just occurred... But the scene before me was one of complete normality... People were departing from and boarding onto the train... Among the dozens of people boarding, I caught a glimpse of a familiar bowler hat bobbing up, down and into one of the red white and blue carriages... I followed the bowler hat and just managed to make it through the doors before they closed.

"... Please mind the gap between the train and the platform..."

As I had suspected, the bowler hat belonged to Mr. Hitchcock... It was the same Mr. Hitchcock who had boarded the train with me eleven stops back in Leytonstone.

"... The next station is Piccadilly Circus..."

The train continued onwards... I said goodbye to Piccadilly and found myself pitched betwixt Heaven and...

"... The next station is Charing Cross..."

For the duration of my short journey on the Bakerloo Line, I kept my eyes forever fixed on the bowler hat that was part of the crowd... I kept my eyes fixed on it until...

"... The next station is Waterloo..."

... the train pulled in.

The bowler hat bobbed up and down, part of the crowd, and

exited through the carriage door... Trying to keep the bowler hat in my line of sight, I stepped off and I minded the gap... Despite my best efforts, however, once on the platform, I lost sight of Mr. Hitchcock again.

I stood on the curved platform at Waterloo Station until the throng had dispersed... Unsure what to do, I blindly began to follow the directions towards the way out... I took the escalator to the underground concourse... As I ascended, I happened to look up and I saw him there at the top of the escalators... He was walking screen right to left.

I followed the figure of Mr. Hitchcock... I followed him to the main concourse... I followed a sign for the South Bank... I exited into the night air and continued on foot.

I could see him now walking ahead of me... The bowler-hatted Mr. Hitchcock was smoking a cigar and was dressed in a Saville Row suit of the darkest navy... I followed and I realised that this was how I had mostly seen him... Walking screen left to right... Walking screen right to left... Walking towards the camera... Walking away from the camera... Walking towards me... Walking alongside me... Marking every inch of the screen as his natural territory.

I had witnessed his restless perambulations in the streets of other cities... New York... Quebec... San Francisco... And now I was walking in his footsteps.

I continued walking, but no matter how much I increased my pace, no matter that Mr. Hitchcock was moving along in a slow, dawdling shuffle, I could not seem to close the distance between myself and him... I kept my gaze focused on the figure of Mr. Hitchcock... His flickering figure that seemed to be gliding along on a cloud of smoke billowing from his cigar.

*Where is he leading me?* I wondered. *Where is he directing me?*

I walked from York Road towards Riverside Walk in pursuit of Mr. Hitchcock... I passed the blazing orb known as The

London Eye hanging there in the night sky... I passed the spot where I had first met Mr. Hitchcock... At one point, I glanced over my shoulder and, behind me, I saw the figures of my victims shuffling in my wake... I saw Mr. Drew... Mr. Smith... Mr. Vosper... Sheldrake and Calthrop... I grasped onto the handle of the Gladstone bag, quickened my pace and cut a path through the crowds on the South Bank.

Up ahead, I saw Mr. Hitchcock was already crossing Westminster Bridge... I watched as he paused at the centre of the bridge and wielded his cigar... I watched as he took one final puff and then tossed the smoking carcass of it into the Thames... I watched as the cigar hit the water and an incense-like fog began to roll in.

I welcomed the fog... I could escape into this London particular... I could escape my victims... I could escape any mob before they caught up with me and dispensed their own form of justice.

I strode up the steps to Westminster Bridge amid the rising fog... I passed a police van that was parked there and I kept a wide berth... Once I had arrived at the centre of Westminster Bridge, I followed Mr. Hitchcock's example and paused... I paused and for a time considered throwing myself into the water of the Thames... I wondered how it would feel for my body to be drawn down into the murk and the depths, to be pulled along in the stew, in the silty soup of the river... There I could be reunited with Ms. Holland... There I would embrace her bloated and silt-sodden body.

This dark mood lifted when I glanced to my right and saw my victims now on the bridge... I saw the five of them slouching past the stationary police van in my direction... I banished thoughts of surrendering myself to the forces of the Thames and I walked on through the fog... I walked past Boudica and Big Ben... I walked past The Palace of Westminster and Westminster Abbey.

The fog mingled with fumes from black taxis and red double

deckers... I lurked deep within the choking, satanic smoke... In the fog, I began to feel uncertain of my geography... In the fog, I began to catch momentary sightings of Mr. Hitchcock in different incarnations... I saw him dawdling at a post box... I saw him carelessly discarding a cigarette packet outside a Music Hall... I saw him pacing in the environs of a railway station... I saw him reading a newspaper at a newsstand and was relieved when I spotted no mention of my crimes on the front pages.

I then saw the Mr. Hitchcock I was supposed to be following... I saw him in close proximity, stepping onto a London omnibus... I rushed forward, boarded the bus and paid the fare... As the bus prepared to pull away, I saw another Mr. Hitchcock trotting towards the doors and looking crestfallen when they were shut in his face.

Meanwhile, on board, I soon spotted Mr. Hitchcock again... He was at the rear of the vehicle, sitting quite immobile, in close proximity to a man with matinee idol looks and some chirruping caged birds... I was preparing to settle in for a lengthy excursion, but my journey came to an abrupt end when Mr. Hitchcock's figure drifted down the aisle and alighted at the very next stop... I followed his example.

On exiting from the bus, Mr. Hitchcock turned left and he passed a pair of uniformed police officers - one male, one female - on the beat... I watched as he gave them a deadpan over-the-shoulder look... I felt sure it was a reaction shot staged for my benefit... He then glided off into the fog.

I took off in pursuit of him, but after a few steps I heard a voice call in my direction... I turned to see the two police officers regarding me... I was fully prepared to make a run for it, but the female officer was holding something aloft and she was saying I had dropped it... It was the Gladstone bag... I reclaimed the bag and muttered a few words of gratitude... I lowered the brim of my Homburg hat and then walked into the same patch of fog Mr. Hitchcock had disappeared into... When I found my route had taken me uncomfortably close to New Scotland Yard, I knew I had lost track of him again.

Outside New Scotland Yard, I saw another Mr. Hitchcock... He was loitering with intent, brandishing a Brownie camera and taking a snap of me, the guilty party... I walked on... I walked until, off to my left through a plaza, I saw The Cathedral of the Most Precious Blood.

I approached the Cathedral... Light shone on and around the building... I craned my neck to savour the spectacle of the tower, constructed from Neo-Byzantine brick and stone in layered hues of red and white.

*... How lovely is your dwelling place, Lord God of Hosts...*

I seated myself on the steps of the Cathedral... From within, I believed I could hear a requiem mass for the dead being conducted... As I sat, head in hands, I recited the words...

*Eternal rest grant unto him O Lord*
*Let perpetual light shine upon him*

Mr. Hitchcock was nowhere to be seen and I knew I needed to locate his whereabouts... My situation was perilous and so I summoned one of my dormant gifts... Nearby, I spotted a crow that had just touched down on the lid of a bin... I summoned one of my gifts, I focused my mind, and I allowed myself to enter the eyes of the carrion crow... I was able to project myself and suddenly I felt my wings spread and my body in flight... I felt my body rising through the air, then ascending to the top of the Cathedral's tower... I was travelling as the carrion crow flies... I was climbing up 273 ft. in search of Mr. Hitchcock.

From atop The Cathedral of the Most Precious Blood, I viewed the unreal city beneath my feet... Laid out below me, I saw the cloud-capped towers, the gorgeous palaces, the Solemn temples, the great globe itself.

And as I surveyed the city in search of Mr. Hitchcock, the dizzying reality of my situation hit me... I found myself pondering impossible questions... What should I do? Where should I go?

I briefly considered Madame Tussauds as a possible place of concealment for me... I considered lurking unseen among the waxen faces of the statues there... Perhaps in years to come, I would even become immortalised... Perhaps people would take their grandchildren to the Chamber of Horrors and point out my fearsome visage.

However, I knew there was no real hiding place in such a modern metropolis... I considered surrendering to my situation and returning to the house in Plouthorp Street... There, I would sit calmly in front of the cyclorama... There, I would observe the morning sky for one final time and wait for the cold, heavy hand of the law to descend upon my shoulder.

I allowed my mind to wander and I considered my limited options for escape.

I considered changing my name... My mind ran through the various aliases I could assume... Beechcroft Manningtree... Beechtree Manningcroft... Huntley Haverstock... H.H. Hughson... Chubby Banister.

I wondered if I should take on the guise of Spring-heeled Jack to evade capture... I wondered if I should assume the persona of another famous Jack... If that was the deadly course of action I had set my mind on, I would need to summon my gifts like never before... I would need to conjure my darkest thoughts... I would need to execute the darkest deeds of my imaginings... I would need to litter the streets with my victims.

... *Behold I, even I, shall bring a sword upon you and I will devastate your high places...*

I allowed my mind to wander... And as the carrion crow took flight, as an aerial view of the capital played out before me, I dwelt further on my situation.

Following the shooting of Mr. Cutts, I knew the police would be closing in on me... I knew the net would be tightening... "We've got to find him before his appetite is whetted again," they would be saying as they drew up their plans... I imagined the police in their situation room as they outlined the shape of The △ on a street map in an attempt to triangulate my attacks... The Avenger's attacks... In my febrile state, I imagined it would only be a matter of time before they connected the dots between the incident in Leytonstone and the previous murders... Sheldrake and Calthrop... Mr. Vosper... Mr. Smith... Mr. Drew... And so my fate would be sealed.

I have never cared for policemen and their prying ways, their I-know-best tone when they speak to you... Soon, I was sure, I would see those knowing, superior faces of the law looming before me... Soon, before I knew it, I would hear the dread sound of a metal door closing behind me and the chill finality of a key being turned in a lock... Soon, I would be caught up in the wheels of the British justice system... The inevitability of it all was too harrowing to contemplate.

As the carrion crow soared higher above the fog, I allowed my mind to wander further... I allowed my mind to wander and I pondered my slim chances of escape... Should I stop following Mr. Hitchcock, I wondered, and somehow stage a disappearing act?

I considered the possibilities... I considered fleeing on the next express train to the channel or to the Scottish Highlands... I imagined the thrill of being an innocent man on the run on a train scything through the landscape... The carrion crow soared higher and a vague sense of motion sickness overcame me... I had never once been outside the city of my birth... Nevertheless, I contemplated fleeing to Dover and then onto Calais... At Dover, I would pause at the white cliffs to push some innocent bystander over the edge and into the briny surf below... *Bon Voyage*, I might say.

The French would love me, in the same way that they love Dr. Petiot... Bluebeard... Landru... Pierre-Francois Lacenaire... Gilles de Rais... Joseph Vacher... Monsieur Hire... I would amass my own coterie of French worshippers... During my sojourn, I could take the opportunity to visit The Musée de la Cinémathèque at Cinémathèque française... Eventually, perhaps the Chevalier de la Legion d'Honneur would be bestowed upon me and, in time, I would be referred to in hushed whispers as "Le chevalier de la mort"... In my acceptance speech, I would adopt a tone of suitable deference to my hosts...

*Renew the Arts on Britains Shore*
*And France shall fall down and adore...*

Yes, I would say in all humility, like Monsieur Hitchcock I made it my life's work to renew the fine art of murder.

The carrion crow continued to fly in a northerly direction... It then began to descend, down through the fog... It returned to street level and, with uncanny homing instincts, it led me directly towards Mr. Hitchcock once more... Through the eyes of the carrion crow, I watched as Mr. Hitchcock entered an establishment I was familiar with.

I focused my mind once more... I uncoupled myself from the carrion crow and returned to The Cathedral of the Most Precious Blood... I knew Mr. Hitchcock's location now and so I set off on foot after him.

I had not gone very far, however, before a powerful sense of fatigue overcame me... The events of this evening, everything I had experienced since I stepped out of the taxi in Leytonstone, had taken a greater toll on me than I had imagined... In particular, the sheer concentrated effort it took to maintain my link to the carrion crow had left me physically and mentally drained... I told myself I needed to rest if I wanted to make it through the night.

The sign above the entrance said The McKittrick Hotel... I stepped inside and paid for a room with half a notion to lie low until things blew over... When I proceeded upstairs to locate my room, however, one of the Mr. Hitchcocks was already there... I saw him as he surreptitiously exited from another door and he shared a furtive glance with me… He was not the Mr. Hitchcock I was looking for.

I returned to the ground floor and spotted another Mr. Hitchcock in the hotel lobby… He was nursing an incontinent infant on his lap… I spotted him again, this time coming out of the hotel's elevator, flagrantly smoking in violation of health and safety rules… Neither of them were the Mr. Hitchcocks I was looking for.

I turned, entered the hotel bar and ordered a double shot of brandy to steady my nerves… In the background, I heard music… I knew this music… It was 'Funeral March of a Marionette'… As I stood there, I found my eyes drawn to a faded photograph above the bar… In the photograph, men in dinner jackets were sitting around a table at a function of some description… And there was Mr. Hitchcock among them… He was part of the coterie of the great and the good, smoking one of the biggest cigars in the business.

I drank the double measure in one fell swoop, felt the warmth spread through my innards, and allowed my mind to wander… I allowed my mind to wander and suddenly I was sure I knew who was orchestrating this army of Mr. Hitchcocks who had been crowding around me… It was another Mr. Hitchcock… It was the first Mr. Hitchcock who had appeared on screen… His first incarnation… In my inner world, I replayed the moment…

An untrained eye may not have spotted him… He was on screen for merely six seconds or so… He had his back to the camera and was sitting at a desk… But it was unmistakably him… This incarnation of Mr. Hitchcock was on the phone and it was clear to me now that he was giving directions to the other Mr. Hitchcocks to do his bidding.

With this revelation, a further thought occurred to me… There could be another Mr. Hitchcock also behind tonight's proceedings… It could be a case of two Mr. Hitchcocks plotting the movements of the other Mr. Hitchcocks… I was thinking of the last Mr. Hitchcock… His final incarnation… A shadowy face behind frosted office glass… The words on the glass reading **REGISTRAR OF BIRTHS & DEATHS**… This Mr. Hitchcock was passing on his final orders to the Mr. Hitchcock on the phone who in turn was relaying the messages to the Mr. Hitchcocks who were now surrounding me… The Mr. Hitchcocks who were directing me… Directing me towards my next destination… Towards The Pleasure Garden.

Fortified by the brandy, I footed it into the London fog again… I walked with a renewed purpose through the streets… I followed the northerly route mapped out for me by the carrion crow… Before long, I was descending the steps, I was passing underneath the glowing sign and I was walking through the doors of The Pleasure Garden.

Once inside, the first thing I noticed was the presence of around a dozen or so new patrons… They were seated in the booths and in the dim light their faces appeared to me grey, blurred and out of focus… I had the vague impression of heads and mouths moving, but I strained to hear any discernible words… One thing I was sure of was that Mr. Hitchcock was not amongst them.

In the background, I heard music emanating from the bar's jukebox… I knew this music… It was 'The Band Played On'.

I perched on my usual stool, fully prepared to abandon hope of ever catching up with Mr. Hitchcock… A silent feeling of desperation hovered over me as the landlord, Forsythe, stepped forward out of the shadows with his arms crossed.

"Glad you could make it squire," he said. "The smog is something shocking out there, isn't it?"

I nodded in agreement.

"Well," he continued. "Have you finally taken care of things?"

"… I'm sorry?"

"Don't you remember? The person who did you the

disservice."

"… Oh… Yes. Yes, I have taken care of that."

The landlord shifted closer and adopted the tone of a trusted confidante.

"Need somewhere to hide, do you? Need somewhere to lay low?"

"I don't under –"

The drunken silhouette at the end of the bar had gone unnoticed until now… He chose this moment to make himself heard.

"You've been careless, haven't you?" he slurred.

"… I beg your pardon?"

"You've been careless… You've been making your own cameo appearances on the CCTVs stationed around the capital, haven't you?" He raised his voice and pointed upwards. "Because they see you, y'know. The cameras. In the sky. On the lampposts. Everywhere. They're watching our every move. There's no escaping from them… They're takin' bleedin' liberties! *Our* bleedin' liberties!" He tilted his frame in my direction. "Are you in possession of The Knowledge? Because a creative kind of geography has to be employed to avoid the cameras… Just where have you been tonight?"

I struggled to recall the itinerary of my night's journey.

"Ah… Leytonstone… Westminster Bridge… The Cathedral of the Most Precious Blood."

"Most precious blood," the silhouette muttered to himself… He then started into what sounded like an inebriated incantation. "Precious blood… Blood… Lud… Lud…" His head nodded and then dipped… I believed he had drifted off into an alcohol induced stupor… As did the landlord, who took the opportunity to prop an elbow on the bar and continue his dialogue.

"Now, where was I? Oh yes, tonight is a very special –"

But just then, the silhouette sprang to his feet without warning and enunciated at the top of his lungs.

"Save us, oh almighty state, from our very basest natures! I offer praise and thanks to the powers that be for watching over us! We used to believe that God was watching over us, but who needs God when you have CCTV? Yes… It's enough to make a man barmy! We are such stuff -"

"That's enough!" Forsythe finally intervened.

"Well… I'm sure my friend can fill in the blanks."

Lines delivered, the silhouette slumped back onto his bar stool… He remained silent for the duration while Forsythe picked up where he had left off.

"As I was saying, it's a rather special night tonight… You've taken care of your personal business, which in itself is a cause for celebration. And then there's the fact that a certain someone has graced us with his presence tonight." The landlord appeared slightly exasperated that I did not jump in at this point. "Well, don't you want to know who I'm talking about?"

"… Who are you talking about?" I finally replied, trying hard not to convey the level of bewilderment I was feeling.

"I'm talking about The Guv'nor."

"… The Guv'nor?"

"That's right… The Guv'nor."

The landlord reached underneath the bar and flicked a switch… On the back wall, above the jukebox, a flashing sign came to life and three familiar words were illuminated…

### TO-NIGHT
### "GOLDEN CURLS"

Forsythe nodded in the direction of the sign.

"And here he comes right on cue."

I turned and watched as Mr. Hitchcock entered the bar from stage right… I watched as he lingered under the sign… I watched as he extended an arm and was then joined from stage left by a slim, elegant female form… She was dressed in a luminous green gown and her face was hidden from view behind a mask fashioned from multicoloured feathers... Mr. Hitchcock linked arms with this exquisite vision and they began to walk in my direction... My eyes remained fixed on the figure of the woman who was walking arm in arm with Mr. Hitchcock.

As they drew closer, Mr. Hitchcock gently uncoupled himself from the woman in green... He allowed her form to linger in the background as he approached me and then spoke.

"I am afraid our night is not yet at an end," he said. "We still have some ground to cover... However, I do believe we have a little time at our disposal... We have a little time for pleasure... After all, that is what you came here for... Am I correct?"

He removed his bowler hat and placed it on top of the bar.

"Tell me, what is your idea of the ideal woman? Is it a delicate, pouting beauty with cupid lips? Is it a socialite who knows her way around an outboard motor? Or... Is it her?"

He gestured towards the lady adorned in green.

"She is here to please... You have just enough time for one dance, so I'm afraid I cannot allow you to escort her back to The McKittrick Hotel where, goodness knows, you could get up to all sorts... You could buy off her unhappiness or even try to examine her uccipital capillary... No, no, we simply do not have the time... My advice? Try to charm her... Try to be the cat thief of her heart."

Mr. Hitchcock then turned 180° and shuffled towards the rear wall... He shuffled towards the jukebox... The masked woman in green remained standing in the middle of the floor of The Pleasure Garden as Mr. Hitchcock made his selection.

"I believe a waltz would suit the occasion," he said. "Something by Strauss? Or perhaps... A-ha!"

Mr. Hitchcock raised a finger, then prodded at a button on the jukebox... There was a pause and then music filled the room... I knew this music... It was the 'Merry Widow Waltz' by Franz Lehar.

The woman in green was standing poised in the centre of the floor... She was awaiting me... I removed my overcoat and my Homburg hat and I advanced towards her... I took her hands in mine and we began to dance... We waltzed together... We waltzed and as we did the room swirled gracefully around us.

As I span, I saw light pulsing from the sign on the rear wall... I saw light shining on the figures in the booths... As I span, I saw my victims seated there... I saw Mr. Drew... Mr. Smith... Mr. Vosper... Sheldrake... Calthrop.

As I span, I saw other figures illuminated in the booths... I saw Uncle Charlie... I saw Bruno Antony... I saw Lars Thorwald... I saw Norman Bates... I saw Bob Rusk... I saw The Avenger.

As I span, I saw Mr. Hitchcock... He had returned to the bar and was in the process of downing a glass of champagne.

And as I span, I saw the woman in radiant green... I saw her blonde hair spiralling before my eyes... As I span, I looked closer... I knew that face... I knew those eyes... I knew those lips... I knew whose visage lay behind the mask... I yearned to speak to her... I yearned to offer my depthless regret that I had failed to save her... I yearned to embrace her... I yearned to kiss her...

... *Psycho Kiss*...

Time seemed to contract and, before I knew it, the waltz was at an end... My eyes met with hers and we stood there on the floor of The Pleasure Garden hand in hand... My heart ratcheting my mind teetering... And I felt closer to her than I had ever been.

"Miss Holland," I began.

But at that moment, she withdrew her hands from mine... She withdrew her hands and rushed towards the doors of The Pleasure Garden, where Mr. Hitchcock was already waiting... Mr. Hitchcock held the doors open for her, then replaced the bowler hat on his head and staged his own exit.

I hurried in a daze towards the bar and began to lever my arms

273

into the sleeves of my overcoat... I was about to leave when I felt a hand reaching into one of my coat pockets and retrieving something... I pivoted around and saw the figure of Bob Rusk beside me... He was already fixing his tie back on and grinning raffishly at me.

"Thanks for saving my neck back there in Leytonstone," he said. "I just know you're the sort of bloke The Guv'nor can depend on."

"I really should -" I gibbered uselessly... However, I did not have to wait long for Mr. Rusk to complete my thought for me.

"Follow The Guv'nor, I know."

The landlord then materialised nearby, holding my Homburg Hat and the Gladstone bag... He handed them to me.

"You look like a man in need of some Dutch courage," he said. "Are you sure I can't tempt you with one more drink for the road?"

"No... I really should –"

As I fled towards the exit, I heard him call after me...

"Never forget! You belong here... We all belong here!"

... And as I stalked through the doors, a switch was flicked and The Pleasure Garden was plunged into immediate darkness.

I did not look back... Instead, I set off on the trail of Mr. Hitchcock... Keeping his figure forever in my sight, I walked past Victoria Station... I walked through tree-lined streets... And as I walked, I felt pursued by phantom footsteps... I sensed shadows chasing me as I edged past lampposts... I looked over my shoulder, fearing vengeful victims still on my trail... But there was no-one there... As for the shadows, they were only the slanted and gaunt shadows cast by the lampposts I had left in my path.

I continued my trek and, as I was led into the area of SW3, I realised I was leaving The △... Up ahead, I saw Mr. Hitchcock veer right... I followed his example.

And as I followed him I recognised the street I was walking

along... I recognised Slade Walk... The street was silent and deserted, apart from the figure of Mr. Hitchcock... He was standing in the middle of the thoroughfare now... His figure was dramatically backlit and the shadow cast before him was at least twice his length... Mr. Hitchcock waited for his cue to step forward... His face was still in darkness as he addressed me.

"It has been a long, dark night for the soles of your feet... Have you enjoyed your night walk?"

"... Where is Ms. Holland?" I chose to ask.

Mr. Hitchcock's reply was gentle but insistent.

"Please... Be patient."

He then gestured towards a location I was already familiar with.

"You never divested yourself of your previous abode... Very wise to have a second retreat... Shall we proceed? Please, after you."

I walked ahead of Mr. Hitchcock... I gained access to my flat in Slade Walk... I stepped inside and allowed Mr. Hitchcock to follow me.

The place had changed somewhat since I last remembered being here... I found myself standing in a largely unfurnished room... My framed photograph of Westminster Bridge remained the only item of décor on the walls... In the centre of the room, there was a functional table with a number of items arranged across the surface... While I reacquainted myself with my surroundings, Mr. Hitchcock positioned himself by the front window.

"I must say, it's as dusty as an old family crypt in here." I watched as he ran a finger along the window sill, then fussily crumbled the collected dust particles between his thumb and fingers. "Good housekeeping is obviously not your forte... I suggest that you refer to Mrs. Beaton's tome for further guidance... That is not the reason why I have brought you here, however... May I ask you to cast your eyes towards the table?"

I did as Mr. Hitchcock asked and directed my attention towards the table positioned in the centre of the room... On the table, I saw all the proof that I needed to see... I saw the Universal Splicer and the Gladstone Bag that had disappeared from Plouthorp Street... I saw *The Canonical Murders*...

"... *Find the stolen notebook and you will solve the mystery*..."

*The Canonical Murders* had been placed atop a film canister... I lifted the canister, opened it and examined the reel within... I examined it and saw lengths of 35mm expertly spliced together like a jigsaw... The methodical cuts had been done with the aid of The Universal Splicer.

"I-I don't remember any of this," I managed to say.

"Quite understandable," Mr. Hitchcock calmly observed. "Your mind was otherwise occupied... All the work happened when you experienced your unfortunate blackout... One of your dormant personalities took over and carried out everything... You were extremely industrious... Firstly in arranging transport for your collection of prints and then in your skilled use of the Universal Splicer."

"... My prints? Where are they? What's happened to them?"

"No need for a scene," Mr. Hitchcock reassured me. "I watched over you as you worked diligently... Reel by reel... Print by print... Night and day on our joint creation... I watched you as you carefully stacked each reel, each print in the adjoining room."

I looked behind me into the area that used to be my kitchen... I looked and saw my collection of 35mm prints arranged there, taking up the entire floor space.

The evidence was damning and it was there in front of my eyes... I was the guilty party... The thief in the night was me... It was I who had left the notebook here... It was I The Avenger who had done it all.

All this time, I was my own double... My own

doppelganger... Bruno Antony to my own Guy Chambers... Roger O. Thornhill to my own George Kaplan... Lars Thorwald to my own Benzedrine-fuelled David O. Selznick.

While my mind teetered, Mr. Hitchcock plodded towards a clock that had been left sitting on the mantelpiece following my move to Plouthorp Street... Left to the forces of entropy the clock had run completely down in the intervening decades... I watched as Mr. Hitchcock tutted disapprovingly, then opened the clock face and proceeded to wind it.

"Time... It is of the essence... Isn't that what they say?"

As the second hand sprang to life again, Mr. Hitchcock offered me his direction.

"Yes... Time is of the essence... Our collaboration has reached an important juncture... Take the reel of film and any possessions you can carry... It is now time to return to The Temple... You know the way... Step into the street and hail a taxi... Then, instruct the driver to aim his car exactly towards the Ratcliffe Highway and press down on the accelerator."

On the screen before us, another door materialises. Mr. Memory opens the door and we enter it together, you and I...

... Half an hour after departing from my flat in Slade Walk, I was stepping out of a taxi and approaching the door of the house in Plouthorp Street. Carrying the film canister and one of the Gladstone bags, I entered and walked without hesitation into the screening room... I stepped inside and saw Mr. Hitchcock already there in the darkness waiting for me... He was standing near the door of the projection booth with his arms behind his back... He drew breath, then spoke to me.

"There is something sacred about stepping into a cinema... But so often what is offered up to us on the screen is profane, would you agree?"

As Mr. Hitchcock continued, he retreated further inside the projection booth... I followed his lead.

"I wish to apologise for deploying a certain degree of misdirection in the lead up to tonight's events... But I assure you it was all for the greater good... Do you think I would entrust my life's work to anyone?"

"... No."

"Precisely... I must say, you have proved yourself a very apt pupil... Through your deeds, my memory will continue to live on... You are my purest disciple... You are a living, breathing repository of my work... I live in you and through you."

Mr. Hitchcock turned and faced me.

"However, your vision is not quite complete. It is missing something... A final act."

He was standing beside the projector.

"You know, I have followed your progress with great interest... I know of the death of your mentor, your tormentor Mr. Drew... I know of the manner in which Mr. Reginald Smith met his demise... I am also fully aware of how you heroically directed Ms. Holland in her act of self-defence... And then there is the double murder of your former work colleagues, blown to kingdom come and pecked to ribbons by our feathered friends... To this can be added Mr. Cutts. That represents another murder in the bag, am I correct?"

I nodded.

"... Yes."

"Very well... Mr. Cutts was victim number six. As you already know, *The Canonical Murders* posited nine methods of murder... Three more victims and all will be revealed."

Mr. Hitchcock fixed me in his gaze.

"Now, I must ask you to listen attentively to my words... I need you to follow my instructions step by step... First, you must carefully load the reel of film you are holding into the projector... Then, all you simply have to do is remove yourself from the booth, assume your normal position in front of the screen and take in this morning's entertainment... Following that, we will move on to the next stage of proceedings."

I did what Mr. Hitchcock asked of me... I carefully loaded the reel of film... I fed the leader tape through the feed sprocket... I fed it through the intermittent sprocket... I fed it through the take up sprocket... I attached it to the take up reel... I then exited the projection booth and sat before the screen... As I perched on the edge of the double sofa, Mr. Hitchcock's voice came to me.

"There is so much more to my body of work than the simple act of murder. However, that is what people seem to remember me for... It excites the blood... And so we will give them what they want... Let us... You and I... Give the public something to lap up... Could I now ask you to remove your darkened glasses?"

I did what Mr. Hitchcock asked of me.

"Excellent... Now, keep your eyes on the screen... Forever on the screen... I believe you will enjoy the fruits of our collaboration."

I heard the familiar whirring noise of the projector as it sprang to life... I saw the beam of light as it shot through the atmosphere

of the screening room... The screen was white... Blindingly
white... But I did what Mr. Hitchcock asked of me... I kept my
eyes fixed on the screen... On the screen, the words **PICTURE
START** materialised for an instant and then vanished...

And amid the blinding brightness I saw a countdown.

**8**...

I began to watch the fruits of our collaboration...

**7**...

And as I write these words, it is as if I am watching it unspool
before me in the here and now...

**6**...

I remember every scene...

**5**...

I remember every shot...

**4**...

I remember every victim...

**3**...

I remember every splice...

**2**...

I hear a beep and the screen goes black until...


... On the screen before me, I see Mark Rutland... He is wearing
a dressing gown and is seated in Marnie's bedroom... I know this
scene... He is attempting to heal his bride with a spot of DIY
psychoanalysis... Rutland appears collected... He appears primed
and ready to fire... I know the game he is about to play... It is a
free association word game... At first his tone is relaxed.

Mark Rutland speaks... Mark Rutland says the word "...
Water..."

**SPLICE!** I see a silent death in the South Seas I see a hand
placed on a native girl's head forcing her underwater I see her
body flailing I see her hands flailing **SPLICE!** I see a corpse like
flotsam washed up on a beach and the raincoat belt like jetsam
that choked the life out of her I see a slo-mo insert of screaming

seagulls **SPLICE!**

Mark Rutland speaks once again.

Mark Rutland says the word "… Air…"

**SPLICE!** I see Tracy the blackmailer stumble and then dive through the dome of The British Museum **SPLICE!** I see Beaky plummeting to an imagined death I see his tie flapping comically around his face **SPLICE!** I see Handel Fane on the trapeze committing career suicide I see him committing actual suicide **SPLICE!** I see Uncle Charlie plunging to his death into the path of an oncoming train **SPLICE!** I see Bruno Antony bursting a child's balloon with the tip of his cigarette **SPLICE!** I see the squire throwing himself off the rigging with a final cry of "Make way for Pengallon!" **SPLICE!**

Mark Rutland speaks once again.

Mark Rutland says the word "… Sex…" and his lips curl suggestively around the sound of it.

**SPLICE!** Constance Petersen and John Ballantyne kiss and I see the first door opening **SPLICE!** I see bodies tussling behind a curtain in an artist's studio **SPLICE!** I see the second door opening **SPLICE!** I see one of the Riviera's most fascinating sights I see a Technicolor spectrum of fireworks exploding in the night sky **SPLICE!** I see the third door opening **SPLICE!** I see a train gliding sleekly into a tunnel **SPLICE!** I see the fourth door opening **SPLICE!** I see Bob Rusk gnarling out the word "Lovely!" between gritted teeth **SPLICE!**

Mark Rutland speaks once again.

Mark Rutland says the word "… Death…"

**SPLICE!** I see a woman's shoulders heaving I see her turning to face the camera I see her scream mutating into the scream of a train **SPLICE!** I see Mrs. Danvers trapped in her hellish inferno I see the rafters come tumbling down **SPLICE!** I see a grotesque shrunken head placed between the folds of a bedsheet **SPLICE!** I see the sudden drop of the iron safety curtain and the demise of Jonathan Cooper **SPLICE!** I see Arnie Rogers armed with a ray gun regarding the body of his father Harry **SPLICE!** I see an inanimate corpse on the top floor of the house I see the body lit up by the blare of a passing train **SPLICE!** I see a door mysteriously opening of its own accord to reveal... **SPLICE!**... Harry's feet protruding over the rim of a bathtub **SPLICE!** I see Marnie blasting her injured horse out of its misery **SPLICE!** I see a gravestone with the name Eddie Shoebridge inscribed thereon **SPLICE!** I see the unreal figure of a burning man utterly and instantaneously consumed by a warehouse blaze **SPLICE!** I see Ballantyne as a young boy sliding down an exterior stone balustrade I see him accidentally pushing his brother I see the brother fall I see the brother impaled on the railings below **SPLICE!**

Mark Rutland speaks once again.

Mark Rutland says the word "... Needles..."

**SPLICE!** I see Bob Rusk remove his bejewelled tie pin **SPLICE!** I see Shoebridge in disguise jab a needle into the bishop's arm I see the face of the bishop jerk upwards I see his eyes close I see his face drop **SPLICE!**

Mark Rutland speaks once again.

Mark Rutland says the word "... Black..."

**SPLICE!** I see a black sea of umbrellas on the steps in the rain **SPLICE!** I see a shot of the black coffee appropriately laced and served to Alicia Huberman **SPLICE!** I see a reflection of Manny Balestero in a broken mirror **SPLICE!** I bear witness to Juno's daughter Mary Boyle and her wailing out the words "There isn't a God!" **SPLICE!**

Framed in close-up, Mark Rutland sternly raises his hand and points screen left... Mark Rutland speaks once again.

Mark Rutland says the word "... RED!"

**SPLICE!** I see the blood on the floor of Marnie's childhood home **SPLICE!** I see the blinding crimson flash from the muzzle of Murchison's gun **SPLICE!**

I see a silhouette of Mr. Hitchcock standing on a deserted

sound stage… "This is Alfred Hitchcock speaking," he intones **SPLICE!** I see Mr. Hitchcock floating in a murky body of water… "I daresay you are wondering why I am floating around London like this," he says. "I am on the famous Thames River investigating a murder."

**SPLICE!**

And I can see the pace of the montage becoming more frenzied now… **SPLICE!** I see the violence of each cut inflicted on Mr. Hitchcock's prints… **SPLICE!** My prints… **SPLICE!** I see the lurching succession of images before me… **SPLICE!** And I feel the pain of each splice…

**SPLICE!**

I see Bob Rusk's necktie tightening around Bab the barmaid's windpipe **SPLICE!** I see Herman Gromek grappling with the hands of the blue-eyed American clamped around his neck

*… strangle strangle…*

**SPLICE!**

I see a dagger in Lester Townsend's back I see discord in the United Nations Headquarters **SPLICE!** I see the kitchen knife snapping on impact with Herman Gromek

*… stab stab…*

**SPLICE!**

I bear witness to a gunshot in a Cuban villa I see the upward gaze of the beautiful victim I see her dress elegantly spilling across the tiled floor **SPLICE!** I witness another gunshot I see Eric Todhunter falling and dying in a state of bewilderment at the side of the rails

*… shoot shoot…*

**SPLICE!**

I see a white scarf for the murderer I see the latch key killer pulling it tighter around her tapered neck I see her rearing back I see her struggling against him **SPLICE!** I see the hands of a murderer glide into frame **SPLICE!** and around the windpipe of the Alpine singer I see his warbling in code cut short by the throttling

*… strangle strangle…*

**SPLICE!**

I see the victim reaching back for something anything I see the gleaming scissors I witness the swift plunge into her attacker's back and I see it lodged in his spine **SPLICE!** I see Ms. White hurling the cutlery across the room in shock at the mere mention of the word "KNIFE!"

*… stab stab…*

**SPLICE!**

I see a gun emerging from behind the red drapes I see the cool assassin with the reptilian face aiming at his quarry and awaiting the clash of cymbals **SPLICE!** I witness a gunshot in a music hall and soon the mind of Mr. Memory will be lost to the world

*… shoot shoot…*

**SPLICE!**

I see Scottie Ferguson frozen in fear I see him watching powerless as a uniformed colleague falls to his death from a twilight rooftop **SPLICE!** I see Philip Vandamm's henchman plunging from the face of Mount Rushmore I see death by national monument

*… plummet plummet…*

**SPLICE!**

I see Herman Gromek sustaining a blow from the flat edge of a spade **SPLICE!** I see Dick Blaney wielding a tyre iron and thumping a bed-ridden corpse

*… bludgeon bludgeon…*

**SPLICE!**

I see Mitch Brenner caress Annie Hayworth's lifeless face as he covers the bloody slash marks **SPLICE!** I bear witness to the fluttering the chattering the flapping the squawking the cacophony of wings I see Melanie Daniels desperately trying to fend off the beaks the claws

*… peck! peck!…*

**SPLICE!**

I see the long-suffering Herman Gromek's head in the oven I see his hands spasm in an ecstasy of fumbling and then go limp

... *gas-s-s-s*...

**SPLICE!**

I see the crop-duster ploughing into the tanker and Roger O. Thornhill stumbling as he makes his escape

... *BANG!*...

**SPLICE!**

I see the victim's demise reflected in the lens of her own glasses I see her last desperate gasping moments at the end of her one-way trip to MAGIC ISLE

... *strangle*...

**SPLICE!**

I see a street scene in Morocco I see the hooded pursuer plunging a knife into Louis Bernard's back

... *stab*...

**SPLICE!**

I see the guilty man withdrawing a pistol from his pocket outside the courthouse I see his wife pointing a finger and accusing him I see him silencing her with a single bullet

... *shoot*...

**SPLICE!**

I witness the saboteur falling from The Statue of Liberty and from the projection booth I hear Mr. Hitchcock offer these words "... Bring me your huddled mass murderers..."

... *plummet*...

**SPLICE!**

I see an arrow pointing screen right with the word **DIRECTION** emblazoned on it I see the camera dolly through an open window I see an inert body and the murder weapon nearby

... *bludgeon*...

**SPLICE!**

I see a brilliantly white glass of milk balanced on a tray I see it enmeshed in a web of shadows

*… poison…*

**SPLICE!**

I see a dropped match and a gas station inferno I see the flames spread I see Bodega Bay erupt in chaos amid the conflagration

*… BANG!…*

**SPLICE!**

I see Mr. Drummer Man confessing how he twisted the belt 'round his wife's neck and choked the life out of her

*… strangle…*

**SPLICE!**

I witness the garbled words the outstretched hand the genteel cough the clutch of the chest the last gasp of life the theatrical dive onto Hannay's bed I see the knife in her back

*… stab…*

**SPLICE!**

I see a photo opportunity for an assassin on the steps in the rain I see a camera flash and a gunshot

*… shoot…*

**SPLICE!**

I see the avuncular would-be assassin performing a plunge from the tower of Westminster Cathedral

*… plummet…*

**SPLICE!**

I see five of the survivors one armed with a plank pummel the übermensch into submission and throw him overboard into the Atlantic swell

*… bludgeon…*

**SPLICE!**

I see Alicia, her treachery measured out coffee cup by coffee cup, collapsing at the foot of the stairs

*… poison…*

**SPLICE!**

I see the body of Dan Fawcett I see blood pooling where his eyes should be

*... peck!...*

**SPLICE!**

I see Brandon and Philip in the immediate aftermath I see the rope still tightly coiled around David Kentley's neck

*... strangle...*

**SPLICE!**

I see a killing over a roast dinner I see her hands hovering over the implements of death I see her sudden swift movement I see her planting the carving knife in his torso I see a main course to savour

*... stab...*

**SPLICE!**

I see Murchison's gun execute a smooth dreamy movement I see it pivot, pause, then aim directly at my point of view

*... shoot...*

**SPLICE!**

I see death viewed through a telescopic lens I see The Hairless Mexican pushing the wrong man over an Alpine precipice

*... plummet...*

**SPLICE!**

I see blood on the hem of her dress I see blood on the Axminster Carpet I see blood on the poker that points towards the lifeless victim

*... bludgeon...*

**SPLICE!**

I see Henrietta Flusky encouraged to imbibe the sleeping draft in one fell swoop

*... poison...*

**SPLICE!**

I see Charlie struggling for breath as the fumes cloud around her in the family garage

*... gas-s-s-s...*

**SPLICE!**

I witness the silent scream of the girl with the golden curls

… *strangle…*

**SPLICE!**

I see a hand reaching out from behind the billowing curtains and chancing upon a knife

… *stab…*

**SPLICE!**

I see the bullet hitting its intended target on the dance floor I see a deadly blossom of blood ruining the victim's crisp white shirt

… *shoot…*

**SPLICE!**

I see the slashed face of Detective Arbogast I see his shocked expression as he falls backwards I see arms thrashing I hear feet clattering I hear violins shrieking

… *plummet…*

**SPLICE!**

I see another inanimate victim laid out on the Axminster I see another poker murder amongst theatrical folk

… *bludgeon…*

**SPLICE!**

I see Johnnie Aysgarth placing the glass of milk on Lina's bedside table

… *poison…*

**SPLICE!**

I see the countdown to a bomb on a London bus I see the ruddy-cheeked schoolboy in his peaked cap I see a puppy dog and more blown to smithereens

… *BANG!…*

**SPLICE!**

I see an intertitle for a silent film that reads "Shoot! There's nothing left to kill." **SPLICE!** I hear three bursts of gunfire and in the Boyle household I see the light in the candle beneath the statue of Mary and Jesus extinguished **SPLICE!**

I see the whiteness now **SPLICE!** I see the whiteness of the rooms **SPLICE!** Amid the whiteness I see blood spiralling down the plughole **SPLICE!** Amid the whiteness I see blood on the snow **SPLICE!** I see a fork drawn across the surface of a white tablecloth **SPLICE!** I see the striation marks left behind **SPLICE!** I see the face of The Virgin Mary and everything so blindingly white **SPLICE!** See as I see **SPLICE!** I see the flash of L.B. Jeffries' camera **SPLICE!** I see Lars Thorwald momentarily blinded **SPLICE!** I see the projector shining directly into my eyes now **SPLICE!** I see another flash from L.B. Jeffries' camera **SPLICE!** I see the sun blinding me **SPLICE!** I see Mr. Smith's projector shining into my eyes **SPLICE!** I see another flash from L.B. Jeffries' camera **SPLICE!** I see the eyes of the mockingbird earring **SPLICE!** Build me a temple **SPLICE!** I see another flash from L.B. Jeffries' camera **SPLICE!** I see bursts of sheet lightning overhead **SPLICE!** See as I see.

And I could feel it... I could feel the sensation of lips touching lips... Hands brushing through hair... Hands encircling necks... Knives entering torsos.

I raised myself to my feet... I turned and I saw Mr. Hitchcock... He had exited the projection booth and was standing at the foot of the staircase.

"Despite your recent tortured moods, you exercised much good technique in your cutting of the montage," he said. "You have, if I may say so, a mortician's eye for spectacle... Now, however, we reach the climax of this chamber piece... Your virtuoso solo... Please, take the Gladstone bag and accompany me upstairs."

I did what Mr. Hitchcock asked of me and began to follow him... As I passed the projection booth, from within I caught a glimpse of the end of the reel of film... It was spinning like a

Catherine wheel and slapping furiously against the take up reel.

And as I continued to follow Mr. Hitchcock, a feeling came upon me...

*strangle stab shoot*
*plummet bludgeon poison*
*gas-s-s-s...*

I followed Mr. Hitchcock up the stairs - one right turn, then another - and onto the first floor of The Temple...

*strangle stab shoot*
*plummet bludgeon poison*
*peck!*

Mr. Hitchcock positioned himself outside the door of the first room...

*strangle stab shoot*
*plummet bludgeon poison*
*BANG!*

Mr. Hitchcock regarded me...

*The Powers That Be*
*Bestowed Unto Me*
*See As I See*

Mr. Hitchcock spoke...

"We share so much, you and I," he began. "You also prefer to work in the studio and not on location. It is so much easier to control the variables."

Mr. Hitchcock gestured towards the first door.

"An empty room, without a victim, is just dead air and empty space. You will populate these rooms with screams and this house will live once again. You will make a national monument of this place... Aim for nothing less than the apotheosis of your art, my dear boy... Take a little time to survey your work... Our work... You have cast your final victims well... It is time to meet your captive audience... They are awaiting your hands... Are you getting quite worked up to it?"

Mr. Hitchcock ushered me towards the first door... I was

about to reach for the handle, when the door swung open automatically... I walked forward and entered the first room of The Temple.

"I do like a house with well-oiled hinges," Mr. Hitchcock commented. "No unnecessary creaking."

Inside the first room, I saw the chest I had won in the auction... Stacked on top of the chest, I saw the reels containing my print of *The Mountain Eagle*.

Mr. Hitchcock did not linger... He ushered me forward... He ushered me towards the second door... As I approached, the door swung open automatically... I walked forward... I entered and found myself in the second room of The Temple.

Inside the second room, I saw white walls and a wooden floor... I saw a figure seated in an ornate gilt wing chair... He was sitting quite still with his eyes closed... I recognised this person... I recognised Mr. Elvey.

As I stood before the figure of Mr. Elvey, Mr. Hitchcock spoke.

"Here we have victim number seven... Of course, you are already acquainted with Mr. Elvey... Consider the evidence, if you will... Here is a man who wants to remove *The Mountain Eagle* from your possession and to give it to the fickle, brainless idiots of the world... And then there is his questionable behaviour regarding Ms. Marion Holland... What is his fate to be? Reach into the Gladstone bag and all will be revealed."

I did what Mr. Hitchcock asked of me... I reached into the Gladstone bag... I felt my hand close around an object and I withdrew it... It was a bottle, finely filmed with dust and labelled with a skull and crossbones... The bottle contained an unidentified liquid, partially crystallised through age... Mr. Hitchcock gestured towards a side table and a cup and saucer sitting there.

"We can decide later on a suitable dosage, depending on the efficacy of the solution... Now, shall we proceed?"

I placed the bottle with the poison symbol on the side table and Mr. Hitchcock ushered me forward... He ushered me towards the third door... As I approached, the door swung open automatically... I walked forward... I entered and found myself in the third room of The Temple.

Inside the third room, I saw white walls and a wooden floor... I saw white tiles... I saw a bathtub... I saw the overhanging shower head... I saw a shower curtain... The whiteness of the room was quite overwhelming... Inside the third room, I saw a figure... A figure lying supine in the bathtub... She was lying quite still with her eyes closed... She was dressed in a white bathrobe... The words BATES MOTEL were stitched into the fabric of the bathrobe... She was wearing the mockingbird earrings... I recognised this person... I recognised Alice Elvey.

As I stood before the figure of Ms. Elvey, Mr. Hitchcock spoke.

"Before us now is victim number eight... Ms. Alice Elvey... Like her father, she is in a sort of trance... I suppose to some, this place can be quite overpowering... I am, as you know, most displeased with her musings... Is her pen mightier than the sword? Reach into the Gladstone bag and we shall see her fate."

I did what Mr. Hitchcock asked of me... I reached into the Gladstone bag... I felt my hand close around an object and I withdrew it... It was a kitchen knife.

"She is sitting pretty, is she not?" Mr. Hitchcock observed. "Most photogenic... What's beautiful is indeed worth men's lives... Yes... Her fine, soft flesh certainly brings my pulse up a beat or two... Some words by Mr. Edgar Allen Poe come to mind... 'The death... of a beautiful woman is, unquestionably, the most poetical topic in the world.'"

"... I have never -"

"Every good murder story needs a detective and a murderer. You have played both these roles to perfection. I am calling on you now, once again, to be my Uncle Charlie... My Lars

Thorwald... My Bob Rusk... My Norman Bates... I am calling on you to become The Avenger."

As he addressed me, Mr. Hitchcock moved and positioned himself beside the fourth door... I looked towards the door... I looked towards it as Mr. Hitchcock opened it a crack... I saw a subtle green glow emanating from within... I began to move towards the fourth door of The Temple... However, Mr. Hitchcock firmly closed it as I approached.

"I'm sorry to stand on ceremony," he said. "But before you enter the final room, you must deal with victims seven and eight."

"... Oh," I said.

I paused, then returned to the figure of Ms. Elvey.

I set the Gladstone bag and the knife on the floor... I reached over towards the recumbent figure of Ms. Elvey... I reached over and gently removed the mockingbird earrings from her lobes.

"Hmmm... Very wise not to allow her to enter the shower wearing those," Mr. Hitchcock commented.

I cradled the mockingbird earrings in my hand and spoke up.

"Before proceeding, I think I need some answers."

Mr. Hitchcock sighed.

"Are you not quite finished your role as detective?" he drawled. "Very well... I will do my best to provide you with the relevant backstory."

I picked up the Gladstone bag and began to retrace my route back through the rooms of The Temple... I walked back through the second room where Mr. Elvey was seated... I walked back through the first room... I returned to the canvas chairs positioned before the cyclorama... I seated myself in my usual chair, as did Mr. Hitchcock.

I then set the Gladstone bag on the adjacent table... I withdrew the contents of the bag, placed them on the table and regarded them... I regarded the kitchen knife... I regarded *The Canonical Murders*... I cupped the mockingbird earrings in my hand and regarded them also.

From his director's chair, Mr. Hitchcock proceeded to speak...

"Yes... Your life has been mysteriously entangled with Mr. Elvey... Rather like a pair of snakes entwined on an ornate bracelet... Can you believe he was in possession of the earrings all this time? I am afraid I know his motivation all too well... He saw his wife flaunting these gifts from her mystery admirer... Following the death of her patient, he hid them from her... A part of him wanted to torture her... A part of him wanted her to suffer, to feel guilt, to –"

"Die?"

"That is for you to decide... As a couple, they were going through certain marital difficulties, shall we say... A distressingly familiar story... Perhaps he was not paying enough attention to her... Perhaps he was jealous because of the earrings... For her part, Ms. Holland was intrigued by the gifts and became sure they came from one of her patients... She felt she was about to experience a genuine meeting of minds... She sensed someone reaching out to her... Someone who needed her... And so she entered into her catastrophic and short-lived liaison with Mr. Vosper... It was a momentary lapse of judgement... Then, on that fateful night, she phoned Mr. Elvey and he performed his husbandly duty by agreeing to dispose of the body... It was, as you know, a hopelessly botched job... Perhaps subconsciously he wanted the body to be discovered, for his wife to be found out and to be punished... As a final act of contrition, before she took her own life, Ms. Holland left a note behind exonerating her husband from any involvement in the killing."

Mr. Hitchcock turned his head in my direction.

"Now, may I suggest you return your mind to the present and prise your thoughts from the past... Remember why we are here... The father and daughter in the rooms behind us are guilty... One seeks your print of *The Mountain Eagle*... The other writes a study of me that brands me a woman-hater... They

297

are every bit as guilty as Mr. Drew... Mr. Smith... Mr. Vosper... Mr. Sheldrake... Mr. Calthrop and Mr. Cutts... Your previous work was committed using the power of your mind... Now, it is time to roll up your sleeves and allow your hands to get dirty."

"Remember *The Canonical Murders*," Mr. Hitchcock went on. "Remember how I chose you over Mr. Elvey all those years ago... Once you deal with him and his daughter you may enter the final room... And once you enter the final room, there you will be reunited with Ms. Holland... Do you sense her reaching out to you?... There, in the final room, you will embrace her... There, you will kiss her."

*... Psycho Kiss... Psycho Kiss...*

As I sat there in front of the cyclorama, I began to interrogate myself...

"*You could so easily do it*," The Avenger whispered from within. "*You could kill them as Mr. Hitchcock instructed... You could kill them and be with Ms. Holland.*"

"How can I be sure Ms. Holland is in the final room?" I countered. "She is dead... I was there... I witnessed her death scene."

"*Amid the green glow she will return to you*," The Avenger answered.

As my mind teetered, I continued the interrogation.

"*The Canonical Murders* spoke of nine methods of murder... Who is to be victim number nine?"

"*Everything awaits you within the final room*," The Avenger rasped impatiently.

My mind teetered... Outside, I saw an ochre tincture begin to seep then spread across the morning horizon like embalming fluid... I regarded the items laid out on the table... The kitchen knife... *The Canonical Murders*... And The Avenger sensed my growing doubts.

"*I AVENGE! I AVENGE!*"

"… Marion's daughter…"

"*I AVENGE!*"

"… Ms. Elvey…"

"*I AVENGE!*"

"… She is alive…"

"… *I avenge*…"

"… It is not too late…"

"… *avenge*…"

"… I could protect her…"

"…"

"… I could love her…"

My mind teetered and I felt the presence of The Avenger begin to recede.

I stood up from my chair and began to walk… Mr. Hitchcock was nowhere to be seen… I walked through the first room… I walked through the second room… I entered the third room of The Temple… I then walked towards the bathtub… I bent over and gathered Ms. Elvey into my arms… I returned to the canvas chairs in front of the cyclorama… I placed Ms. Elvey in Mr. Hitchcock's chair… I could see that she was already stirring.

"Alice, wake up," I whispered.

I would have gone on, but at that moment I heard the footsteps downstairs… I heard the footsteps entering my house… Footsteps finding their way… Footsteps in the screening room… Footsteps frantically ascending the stairs… I turned my head and I saw Mr. Cutts standing there, out of breath.

"The police are on their way," he declared theatrically.

"… Victim number six… You're not really here," I calmly informed him. "You're in my head… I already killed you."

"What, back at the installation? That wouldn't be very sporting, using a real gun would it?"

I raised myself to my feet.

*I strangle I stab I shoot*

As I did, Mr. Cutts took a couple of paces forward and saw

the figure of Ms. Elvey.

*You plummet I bludgeon I poison*

He then peered through the open doors and into the rooms beyond.

*gas-s-s-s… peck! BANG!*

"Whoa… What sort of a freak are you exactly?"

"I strangle I stab I shoot."

"What?"

"You plummet I bludgeon I poison."

"I told you the cops are on their way, right?"

"I do not fear the powers that be."

I stooped to retrieve my weapon of choice from the table.

"Hey, put down the knife!" Mr. Cutts cried out as he retreated into the first room of The Temple.

I advanced towards Mr. Cutts… I was quite lost now.

"I'm afraid I can't allow you to be here," I said.

The feeling was coming upon me with a renewed force… I began to surrender myself to it… I was becoming The Avenger.

"I stab."

I raised the knife and aimed to strike at Mr. Cutts… The Avenger was fully in control.

"I stab."

But I had underestimated Mr. Cutt's reflexes… He managed to grab on to one of *The Mountain Eagle* canisters and held it in front of him… I saw the knife slamming into metal and a part of me was horrified at the idea of inflicting any damage on the print.

I retreated back to the space in front of the cyclorama… I retreated and I witnessed Ms. Elvey opening her eyes… I saw a look of terror on her face… I saw her try to lift herself out of the chair… To escape from the situation she had found herself caught up in… I moved closer… I wanted to reassure her that she was not in any danger… Meanwhile, Mr. Cutts saw his chance… I turned just in time to see him lifting the heavy table above his head and propelling it in my direction… I took evasive action and just managed to avoid the oncoming slab of furniture... It impacted with a heavy thud against the window and I saw a crack appear in the glass... Ms. Elvey let out a scream... I wanted to move to her aid, but Mr. Cutts was taking advantage of my momentary lapse... Mr. Cutts now rushed towards me at full force... He roughly tackled me and sent both of us flying in the direction of the cyclorama.

Somehow, Mr. Cutts managed to pull away from me at the last second... Everything else happened so quickly... I felt my body slam into the window... I heard the sound of glass shattering and I saw Mr. Cutts look on in triumph.

"I STAB!"

I was still grasping hold of the knife as I fell backwards out of the cyclorama.

*I stab I stab I stab*

Then, for a prolonged moment, I was in free fall... I was falling amid a shower of glass shards... Falling into the morning light... I looked up and I saw curtains billowing... I saw Mr. Cutts peering down at me in astonishment... I saw he had already gathered Ms. Elvey into his arms and he was shielding her... He was comforting her...

*I plummet*

And I saw Mr. Hitchcock standing there at the cyclorama... I saw him standing screen left.

*I plummet*

I read the look of disappointment on his face.

*I plummet*

I had failed him.

*I plummet I plummet I plummet*

All that was left for me to do was to close my eyes from the sight... I closed my eyes and awaited the finality of impact... I closed my eyes and awaited the onrush of darkness that would swallow me soon after.

Consciousness was fleeting in those first few days... I remember awakening in hospital, where I was informed that I had sustained two broken legs... I remember glimpsing the figure of a policeman stationed outside the room I was sequestered in... I remember being read my rights.

After a couple of weeks, I was deemed fit enough to be transported to my current place of incarceration. I voiced concerns that I did not belong among the ranks of the criminally insane. My protestations, however, fell on deaf ears. Yes... It takes a truly civilized society to devise a punishment like the one meted out to me.

Still, I sit hunched over the desk in my cell, pen in perpetual motion. The day is almost over and I find the task that I set myself is nearing completion. From time to time, I have heard the guards approaching the door. I have been aware of their eyes observing me through the peephole and, no doubt, wondering what exactly it is I am up to.

During the course of the day, I have paused occasionally to watch the movement of the searching, relentless winter sun as it shone its light through the prison bars. Occasionally, I paused to watch the refracted square of light cast by the sun. I watched it climb low and slow on the wall of my cell.

Once, I swore I saw the shadow of the gallows hanging on the wall and an empty noose dangling there. But it was merely a trick of the eye... It was the faintest imprint of some graffiti scrawled there by a previous inmate... A game of hangman I already knew the answer to... A six letter word, the first two letters **P** and **S**... It reads **P S** _ _ _ _ , like postscript.

The act of writing this epistle has provided me with a welcome distraction to the rather pressing matter of my impending trial. It is time now, however, to return my mind to present realities and the ossified courtroom drama that lies ahead.

During the planning of my defence, with access to police interviews, I have learned more about my chances in court and I feel cautiously optimistic. In their statements, Ms. Elvey and her father remember calling on me to conduct an initial inspection of *The Mountain Eagle* print. They remember being shown the screening room and then being guided upstairs. However, once they entered the rooms, their minds became quite blank. The toxicology reports I have seen found traces of a powerful sedative in both father and daughter. No matter what official explanation is given, however, I know that ultimately they were under my control. They were under the control of The Avenger.

It was just yesterday afternoon, in an attempt to relieve a lingering sense of monotony, that I happened to switch on the television in my cell. Scheduled between racing from Chepstow and an antiques programme, by chance I stumbled across a showing of Mr. Hitchcock's *The Wrong Man*. It was a fortuitous screening. As I watched its story unfold once again - from Manny Balestero's wrongful imprisonment, through his personal struggles, to an eventual deliverance – I was left with a feeling of great solace.

And so I will channel the spirit of *The Wrong Man*. I will channel the spirit of Manny Balestero during the trial. I will remain stoical in the face of any injustice handed down to me by the court. And I am sure that if I do, there will be an intercession.

As I present the case for the defence, I will also channel the spirit of Manny's honourable lawyer Frank O'Connor. I will assure the court that I can be cured. Throughout my stay here, I have been careful to project the image of a model prisoner. With a good psychiatric report, I believe I could get out in six years. I will confess that I was not in my right mind on the night in question. I will mention legally diminished responsibility. I will mention Dissociative Identity Disorder and how it can result in memory impairment. It will all be part of the rich tapestry I will spin in defending myself against the kaleidoscope of motives and misdeeds attributed to me.

I realise, however, that it may turn out to be an open and shut case. I do not underestimate the severity of the crimes that The Avenger committed, or the expert witnesses ranged against me by the prosecuting side.

Keeping my own counsel has proved to be a lonely business. For my sins, I have experienced moments of doubt and despair within these walls. I have heard the laughter. I have seen the tears and the cruel eyes of my fellow inmates close up. I have been subjected to the ongoing interrogations of Dr. Legatore (a poor substitute for a confessor), who I am sure has my case filed under M for Monomania. I have wondered if this place is destined to be my own final private trap. Am I to be clamped in here for the rest of my days, never to get out, never to budge an inch? Never to view my print of *The Mountain Eagle*?

I have felt despair in the knowledge that I failed Mr. Hitchcock. I have felt despair in the fact that he has not reappeared to me since that morning I plunged through the cyclorama.

Amid the storm of negative emotions that have clouded my mind, I have found my sense of purpose wavering. *Why not surrender to the system?* I have asked myself. *Why not simply plead guilty and throw myself on the mercy of the state?*

Perhaps that is the course I would have pursued, had I not read an interview with Mr. Cutts. It was a transcript of an interview he gave to an American entertainment website. I would have been completely unaware of its existence, had someone not taken the trouble to print off a copy and slide it under my door. I do not know who the culprit was, but I suspect it was one of the prison guards trying to goad me in some way.

In the interview, Mr. Cutts branded me a failed serial killer. He also talked about how he saw the comic potential in such a premise and how it made him rethink the script of his film, which he is currently in the midst of rewriting. With interest, I noted that he had also decided to change the title of his film to *The Canonical Murders*.

It was obvious that Mr. Cutts was savouring this new-found aspect to his fame. He was now the hero who had rescued a father and daughter from the clutches of a maniac. However, there was one final detail in the profile of Mr. Cutts that made me see red... He and Ms. Elvey are now engaged to be married.

Mr. Xavier Cutts... The man who stole the standee of Mr. Hitchcock from me... The man who stole *The Canonical Murders* from me... The man who has stolen Ms. Elvey from me.

Ms. Alice Elvey... She could have been Beauty to my Beast... Linda Darnell to my Laird Cregar... Lisa Fremont to my Lars Thorwald... But I should have known better... I should have realised that The Beast normally ends up destroyed, incarcerated or subject to an unbreakable magic spell.


Yes... I am incarcerated for now... But they remain unaware of the true extent of my powers... The powers of The Avenger... A sense of serenity descends on me when I dwell on the heinous crimes that I got away with... The deaths of Mr. Drew, Mr. Smith, Mr. Vosper, Sheldrake and Calthrop... I The Avenger remain unpunished for those deeds and I can, if I choose, get away with more.

During the trial, I will appear like the surface of a distant gas giant... Calm viewed from millions of miles away... But look closer and you will be confronted by a seething mass of boiling matter exerting a powerful gravitational pull... The true extent of The Avenger's powers remain untested... If I really wanted to, I could break out of this facility at the drop of a bowler hat... All I would have to do is focus my mind... Focus it to the desired frequency and I would escape... Guards would crumple at my feet and doors would be opened on my demand... Minds would be changed, innocent pleas would be entered and accepted.

Meanwhile, I bide my time... Like time served on a studio contract... The Avenger's powers have not deserted me... They are merely lying dormant in a region of my mind... I must be patient... I must await the judgement of the court.

Whatever the outcome, I am no man's prisoner... I have my own means of escape... When I lay down on the bed in my cell, when I close my eyes, I break through the confines of these walls with ease... Each one of Mr. Hitchcock's films is forever imprinted on my mind... As I replay them, I feel myself lifted through the prison bars... I feel myself drifting away... I feel myself passing through the clouds... I feel myself floating above London... Floating above The △.

I remain optimistic about my chances... And the thought occurs to me that this epistle may come to be viewed as a prelude of sorts.

It was last night that I was awoken by a faint whisper carried in the air... I asked him if he had abandoned me... And he replied...

"Nonsense, dear boy. There is still much work to do."

He then gently reminded me that while he had never made a sequel, he did direct one remake of note... He reassured me that he would be with me tomorrow on my journey to Criminal Court Number One.

Tomorrow, as I approach the sweet Thames running softly... As I approach The △... The Avenger will return.

Mr. Hitchcock will direct me.

This is the voice inside your head... This is your narrator speaking... I am addressing you directly in the hope that you will now indulge me a little further and allow me to offer you a brief epilogue to my tale...

Some years have now passed since I wrote the final words of my epistle. If you followed the reports in the media, chances are you already know how I managed to emerge from the horrors of my trial relatively unscathed and how I duly served the sentence handed down to me. Everything turned out, more or less, as I had predicted.

Months later, armed with a working knowledge of the Data Protection Act, I was successful in having my manuscript returned to me. With it, I also obtained the introductory note authored by my gaoler/therapist Dr. Legatore, which I believe effectively conveys the gravity of the situation that I faced as an inmate here.

During my consultations with Dr. Legatore, I would project the most benign version of myself I could conjure up. Not once did I break character and my performance evidently had the desired effect. Over time, Dr. Legatore would come to change the opinions he held about me until finally he classified me as nothing more than a harmless fantasist. After a couple of years of submitting to the good doctor's treatment, I can report that **(i)** my status as a Category A prisoner was downgraded, **(ii)** the investigations into my past proved nothing and were abandoned, and **(iii)** apparently I was cured.

There are a number of strict conditions I must abide by (including the matter of the restraining orders taken out against me). However, tomorrow I am be be released. Tomorrow, dear reader, I return to Plouthorp Street...

△

Ladies and gentlemen of my captive jury, I fear I have detained you too long. I have welcomed you, guided you through my house, through my inner world. If you have made it thus far, the truth is that I have perhaps unwittingly led you rather too deep inside my realm.

During your guided tour, may I ask if you found yourself doubting the existence of my powers?

I know your answer with some certainty, but be under no illusions - this is *my* inner world and I believe I can sense your presence with me here now.

We are quite alone, you and I.

I confess, it may prove difficult for you to retrace your footsteps through my inner world... Can you summon your own Mr. Memory?

Do not succumb to any rising sense of dread or fear. I make you this promise... I will guide you out of my inner world if you remain in my company a little longer.

You see, I could do with some help around the troublesome issue of the restraining orders... It would be most unwise for me to be spotted anywhere in the vicinity of Ms. Elvey's marital home or Mr. Cutts' production offices as he finally gears up to shoot his oft-delayed work of plagiarism, *The Canonical Murders*... However, if you are amenable, I believe you could be of assistance to me.

I am asking you now to imagine that I am standing before you... And as I stand before you, I must ask you to listen only to my voice... I fix you in my gaze and I direct the following words at you...

"Soon I will be free to follow Mr. Hitchcock's instructions again... To complete the only version of *The Canonical Murders* that matters... Watch for me... I may be the man sitting quietly behind you on the tube... I may be the man loitering with intent in the corner of your vision."

I am asking you now to look straight ahead... I am asking you to look in my direction... As I remove my tinted glasses, I begin to summon one of my gifts... Please, do not be alarmed... And if you hear the sound of the door shutting behind us, do not be overly concerned.

Can you hear the music now? Can you hear the violins soaring? Can you hear the heavenly choir hitting the high notes? Peters & Lee are singing 'Welcome Home'... The doors are closing now... All the doors are swinging shut, one after another.

And as the green glow of my inner world envelopes us, I touch my eyelids with the second and third fingers of my right hand... I extend my right hand towards you... I extend it and the second and third fingers are tracing a direct line from my eyes to yours.

Soon, my fingers are hovering above your eyes... And I begin to recite these words to you...

They are his words...

Mr. Hitchcock's words...

I recite the words to you, my willing accomplice...

"... See as I see..."

# Bibliography

While Alfred Hitchcock's movies were the primary source of inspiration for *The Man Who Knew Too Much Hitchcock*, many books were also consulted during the writing process. The following is a list of works that deserve special mention...

*Hitchcock's Secret Notebooks*, Dan Auiler
*Vertigo: The Making of a Classic*, Dan Auiler
*English Hitchcock*, Charles Barr
*Vertigo*, Charles Barr
*The Hitchcock Murders*, Peter Conrad
*Alfred Hitchcock's London*, Gary Giblin
*Hitchcock on Hitchcock*, edited by Sidney Gottlieb
*Me and Hitch*, Evan Hunter
*The Wrong House: The Architecture of Alfred Hitchcock*, Steven Jacobs
*Alfred Hitchcock: A Life in Darkness and Light*, Patrick McGilligan
*The Birds*, Camille Paglia
*Alfred Hitchcock and the Making of Psycho*, Stephen Rebello
*Hitch: The Life and Times of Alfred Hitchcock*, John Russell Taylor
*The Dark Side of Genius: The Life of Alfred Hitchcock*, Donald Spoto
*Hitchcock's Music*, Jack Sullivan
*The Moment of Psycho*, David Thomson
*Hitchcock*, Francois Truffaut

Made in the USA
Columbia, SC
11 December 2017